S0-AAI-800

"ABSORBING"
—PUBLISHERS' WEEKLY

"When stodgy university trustees invited alumnus Emory Monck to use his youthful wheeling-dealing to bail them out of a decade of financial disasters, they had no idea he and his oil-rich colleagues would steal their thousands of students and their faculty . . .

"The villain of the trustees, rightist General Fenton, rigged his power company so Emory had no electricity. Emory's answer—incorporate as a municipality! And so Emory survives student strikes, a rigged bedroom plot and even the perils of love . . ."

—LIBRARY JOURNAL

THE
MAN
WHO
STOLE
A
UNIVERSITY

by Phoebe and Todhunter Ballard

CURTIS
BOOKS

MODERN LITERARY EDITIONS PUBLISHING COMPANY
NEW YORK, N.Y.

1

☐ He was a bear of a man with a shagginess that reminded people of Wendell Willkie, big, friendly, rumpled. His hair was a soft yellow mop graying into sand color and the wide face had a Swedish cast, the light blue eyes an intense penetration. He was Martin Luther Strindberg, dean of the Physics Department, senior faculty member of Wellington University, holder of the Nobel Prize for his work in nuclear fission. He was tired, and angry.

At the core of his anger was Major General Jerome Fenton, retired, with whom he had never shared a kindred thought.

At sixty-five the stamp of the Service was on Fenton. Erect and soldierly as he had been at the age of fifty when he led the assault on Pork Chop Hill during the Korean War, he was unbending as a Grenadier and as unimaginative as a tank. He was a product of the community. His father had been superintendent of one of Amos Wellington's mills. He owed his appointment to West Point to Wellington. He had never forgotten it, and in the cliché-studded hodgepodge which he considered to be his personal code, "he always paid his just debts." Paying his debt had brought him back to Riverdale, had prompted him to accept a place on the board of university trustees charged with governing the corporation, and his military record had assured his election as chairman. He was opinionated, dogmatic, dictatorial, and this was not the first time that he and Strindberg had been at odds.

He walked with a clean parade stride in comic contrast to Strindberg's shambling gait, but he tailored his steps now to accommodate Wellington's short legs.

Amos Wellington, Junior, was a small, round man as his father had been, but there all resemblance ceased. Amos, Senior, had been a fighter, a tiger who had clawed his way up through the early battles of the steel business to establish his sheet and tube company as one of the most efficient plants in the Ohio Valley. Not until he had amassed his fortune did his interest turn to education. Then, feeling the need of a monument, he had offered the struggling Riverdale College his farm estate and an endowment of ten million dollars if the school would assume his name and enlarge to university status.

That had been sixty years before, and in the interim the world, education, and the school had greatly changed. Where once pure-bred cattle had grazed across the four hundred rolling acres that surrounded the hilltop Wellington home, now ten thousand students crisscrossed the campus in antlike trains from one classroom, one laboratory to another.

The plant was built around a long quadrangle on a flat knoll that overlooked the still largely wooded, steep hillsides of the river gorge. It stood in the middle of an exceedingly beautiful campus, enclosed by an ancient iron fence, its walls of yellow brick blessedly mantled by the kind of five-leaf ivy that turns to scarlet in the autumn. Rows of dormitories and Greek letter houses of succeeding architectural fashion bordered the southern line. An expanding faculty row, no longer a single street, pushed out on the west. A stadium, so new that lime was still extruding from the bare cement, rose in monolithic offense from a large asphalt parking area.

Wellington University was a potent academic community, dedicated to the higher learning and to God. And it was in trouble.

Amos Wellington, Junior, had not been born until three years after his father had endowed the school. He had grown up on the campus and spent his life in the old farmhouse which by its ugliness still dominated the residential section. In the deed of gift the father had stipulated that the place remain at the service of himself and his family for as long as any of them chose to live there. The son's only foray into the external world had been the three years he had spent at the Sorbonne.

He had proved to be a natural-born scholar of Latin, and had come back to Wellington to teach. His elevation to the presidency of the university, six years ago, had not been of his choosing. General Fenton had made the decision. General Fenton had insisted that propriety demanded the benefactor's son sit in the august chair.

Amos had submitted with reluctance, and it was a submission he bitterly regretted now as the three of them left the administration building and walked the lane beneath the thick maples toward the faculty houses.

Traffic was heavy. No motor vehicles were permitted within the inner campus and in retaliation the stampede of bicycles was terrifying. The sun was heavy above the rough brakes on the western hills. Couples strolled in casual embrace through the deep grass on short cuts toward the commons, groups wheeled around them like gulls, separating in fluid grace and melting together again beyond. The constant, high-pitched hiss of katydids, the pulse of cricket orchestration carried through and over the laughter of the girls, the shouts and halloos of the boys. It was summer semester.

A normal campus evening. That was Strindberg's mocking reaction as he dropped back a step to present a narrower target for an onrushing flight of cycles. He loved it, loved the undertow of excitement, the exuberance of youth that electrified the air.

But how much longer would it last? How much longer could it continue?

The trustees' meeting, just adjourned, had been long, heated, and barren. No miraculous solutions to the impasse had been advanced. Again the dull burning anger flooded his thick body. He had no authority in the meeting, was present only as the faculty representative, but he had spoken out freely as he always did, cutting the opposition down to size, beating down the hysteric, frantic, ridiculous proposals. Yet it was an empty victory. He had no solution of his own. That was his major frustration. That was the real source of his anger, not Fenton. If he had an answer he could whip Fenton.

Now, beyond the melee, down the quiet, shaded streets, as they passed the faculty houses, he saw the families rocking on the verandas, for this was veranda country. He saw the toys and tricycles abandoned in disarray around the steps, saw the children, like grasshoppers, playing in the sun-mottled yards.

Strindberg knew that every adult eye on every porch followed their passing, trying to guess from their manner what the action of the board had been. It was an open secret among them that Wellington University was in financial straits. Few might realize the extent of the difficulty, but all were vitally interested, and the interest poured down the hill to the town, five miles away, cramped against the bank of the mother river. After the mills, the university was Riverdale's largest remaining pay-roll. If it closed a multitude would be affected.

To the faculty Wellington was not only a livelihood, it was a way of life. They had raised their families there. Many were too old to make a happy or comfortable change. Of the students, many were local, working part time, their jobs necessary to their existence. They would not be free to transfer to other institutions, their opportunity for education would be lost in an age when every trained man was desperately needed by society.

For Riverdale the loss would be much more than simply business revenue. The school had stood as a beacon to the drab mill community, a promise that in the future there should be a better world for their children. Their forebears had been uneducated laborers. The school was their pride. They gloried in its accomplishments, its intellectual stature, its local services, the clinic it maintained. They had adopted the athletic teams as their own, teams which, in winning, brought a sense of success and unity where none had ever existed before.

Yes, Wellington had served in many ways, and if it died a great deal that was of both tangible and intangible importance would die with it. It was worth a battle.

At the Wellington home they turned up the short walk, climbed the three steps, and, crossing the wide front porch, entered the shadowed hall. It was small, square, and rose open above them; a stairway, once elegant, led upward against the left-hand parlor wall to the second-floor hall, turning like a balcony around two sides of the well.

The rooms were not large enough for today and there were too many of them for the needs of Amos and his daughter, but they possessed a dignity and charm unknown in modern ranch-type houses. The ceilings were very high, the paneled doors wide enough to admit the passage of hoop-expanded skirts. The rugs that old Amos had brought from Europe over eighty years before were still fresh, bright, warm with Persian dyes, and the furniture, while ponderous, glowed with satisfaction in its authenticity.

Alice Wellington came into the little parlor from the screened side veranda. "We're out here," she said. "It's so very warm."

It was warm. Strindberg had been so engrossed with the problem that he had not noticed, but at the mention of it he shucked off his jacket and tossed it carelessly into a chair.

"What I need's a drink, Alice."

"There's a pitcher of martinis chilling."

He made a face and the girl came forward to pinch his cheeks together in strong fingers, waggling his head back and forth. She was taller than her father, with fair hair and a slightly narrow, determined face that Strindberg had watched develop, recognizing in it some of the tough fiber which had motivated her grandfather.

"I remembered. There's a bottle of bourbon. I got it especially this afternoon."

"One." He held up a finger. "Then I'll have to go on or Helen will think the trustees ran me out of town."

Fenton did not smile and Amos' laugh was pale. Alice waved a hand toward the porch.

"She's here. We were both too nervous to sit alone. We saw you coming and she went to start the barbecue. Go sit down and relax while I get the drinks."

The porch was ample; the armchairs were caned, high-backed and inviting. Strindberg ambled to the swing at the far end and lowered himself onto it, balancing his thick body on the edge, too keyed up to give himself over to its depths, and the three of them waited, held in silent suspense by the unresolved nature of the moment.

Helen Strindberg appeared around the corner of the house from the rear yard, another tall woman, quick moving, with a thin, almost masculine figure, a straight-nosed face, and level, direct eyes. There was a charcoal smudge like war paint across one cheek and her lipstick was not quite straight. She came toward her husband, dusting her hands, waving him back as he stood up, bending for his kiss and searching out the telltale tightness around his eyes and mouth.

He nuzzled rather than kissed her. "We eating here?"

"Alice is marinating a steak. How'd it go?"

He waited to lift the glass from Alice's tray and swallow half its contents before he answered. "It didn't. We might as well have gone fishing."

An awkward silence fell over them. Amos Wellington accepted his cocktail, muttered something and vanished

9

into the house; General Fenton concentrated on finding for himself exactly the right seat on the porch rail. It was obvious that both men were more than willing to let Strindberg relay the news, or the lack of it. The physicist drained his glass and extended it to his wife who said with schoolmarmish decision, "One's enough for a while."

"Ah, hell," said Strindberg. "Be a sport. It's been a rough day for an old man."

She reached for the glass, her fingers closing over his with quick, bolstering pressure as she took it from him; then she carried it into the house. Strindberg winked up at Alice.

"When you get married, chick, don't try to reform your man. It's a waste of time. Pick a good one and then leave him be."

She flushed, a sore point having been touched, and defended herself with a try at flippancy. "Maybe you'd better pick one for me."

He moved his head in a canted nod. "Tell you what, next time I hire an assistant I'll specify that he's got to be handsome, unmarried, and good in bed."

General Fenton made a protesting noise. Alice laughed. Helen Strindberg came back with a full glass and Strindberg examined it critically.

"You sure you put any whiskey in this?"

Helen sniffed at him, looking at Alice's heightened color. "What's he been doing now?"

"Suggesting that I'm too virtuous to get a husband, I think."

"He's got a point." Helen raised her brows as though she were reflecting, and Alice laughed again. She was twenty-five years old; she had been out of Smith for three years and she was uncomfortably conscious of her single state.

"He's going to hand-pick his next assistant for me."

"If there is another one."

Helen Strindberg was in her middle fifties, holding a Ph.D. in education; since before her marriage she had been in the avant-garde, seeking better avenues for the learning process. She was a practical woman to whom the mincing of words was the long way around.

"Is the school going to close, Martin?"

He moved his shoulders.

"Weren't there any possible suggestions?"

"Possible, maybe. Good, or sufficient, no." Strindberg sipped his second drink. It was mostly water and he showed his distaste. "They kicked around ideas like cutting back on expenses. What the hell could they cut that would do any good? Then they talked about raising the tuition."

"Oh, no," said Helen. "That would put us out of reach of too many of our people."

" 'S what I told them. It comes under the law of diminishing returns, and besides it wouldn't cover anything like what we need."

The silence gathered around them again and the women turned reluctantly into the house, wheeling back a tea cart with a load of table settings. It was too early, but it was something to do. Things were no happier when they returned to the porch. Fenton had gotten restlessly to his feet.

"I still think," he said, "that the only logical way is to go to the legislature, to get the state to take us over."

Strindberg thought sourly that the general's solution to nearly everything hinged on getting money from the government, but there was nothing to be gained by showing temper and he checked his rising spleen with the forbearance of a man who has worked hard over a long time to master his explosive personality.

"I didn't argue with you at the meeting, but it's not the right answer for Wellington. I've got nothing against state universities, they're great and we need them. There are, though, important differences between them and us. They're under the state Department of Education and we would have to make too many concessions to conform. For one thing, we would be required to admit any high school graduate with a C average. That would immediately pull down our pace and what's worse, our quality. Everything would have to be geared down to a mean level. It would be a hell of a loss to our top students.

"Even if we knuckled under to all that, there's the matter of timing. Did you ever know a government agency to move fast? We need help now, not next year or the year after." He paused to finish his drink.

"We probably wouldn't get it anyhow. There's not enough political muscle at this end of the state. If there

11

were any talk of adding a new school to the system every representative and senator would start howling to grab the appropriation for his own district."

"In God's name!" General Fenton exploded. "Have you got any better idea?"

Strindberg rolled the empty glass between his palms, rueful because he had nothing feasible to offer. "Sure. Raise some loot. The spread between our income and expenses is about ten million a year. Just find someone like old Amos who will shell out the deficit." He lifted his eyes to the other, glum and sardonic. "I don't know anybody like that, do you?"

The general glared, disapproving of the acid humor. Amos Wellington had come into the doorway and stood listening.

"What we ought to do"—Strindberg twisted deeper the knife of impossible hope—"is to hire a professional money raiser. Of course he wouldn't have much time, we've got to have action before the fall term begins . . . and we couldn't pay him anything until he bailed us out, the tuition and endowment income won't carry us more than half a year as it is. . . . Do you know of a hotshot who'd take on the job for love?"

General Fenton turned his head away, lifting his chin, looking out through the screen, across the yard and the yard next door, obliquely down the street, the longest view possible from where he stood, as though removing himself from a harassing presence. He made a gesture with his hand, in which Strindberg could see the uniformed officer slapping a booted calf with a stiff crop, and he exhaled deeply through dilated nostrils, by all these signs declaring himself above such derisive comment.

Helen Strindberg gnawed unconsciously at a corner of her lips, and Amos Wellington searched once more through the literature of the history of the Roman Empire for some sonorous quotation that would give them the clue to the course toward salvation.

Alice Wellington was miserable. A campus baby, the debacle when it came would be the crashing of her home about her ears. Yet even with that to look forward to her uppermost concern was for these people. They were in effect her family, and they were troubled to a depth that she had never before witnessed. Her heart ached for each

12

of them and instinct told her that her usual tactics for glossing down ruffled feathers, restoring the placid surface of her father's faculty teas were inadequate now. She needed help. She needed the hand of someone strong and sure. She needed a white knight. And out of her childhood, out of her worshipful watching as another campus brat skated blithely through the academic jungle through which she had had to plod, as he manipulated people and events instead of being manipulated by them, out of her following from afar, after he had gone, his continuing magical rise, there came a name.

"Do you suppose?" her voice was low, barely to be heard, uncertain and wistful as that of a little girl being laughed at for believing in fairy stories. "Could Emory Monck maybe do something?"

General Fenton was the one who laughed. "I guess he's making money, all right, but I doubt that he's got as much as we need."

"I wasn't thinking about his giving us any." Now that she had brought up the subject she wanted it to be understood. "I meant that since he's doing so well, perhaps if he knew the problem he could figure out what we should do. After all, he is our most illustrious alumnus."

Her father said, "I'm afraid that simple loyalty would not tempt Emory to give anything to anybody. He was the boy who got things, not gave them."

Strindberg muttered under his breath to the effect that Amos Wellington had never been able to see farther than what was written on a blackboard.

"I thought of Emory in the meeting, honey, but I don't see what he can do. It isn't a matter of advice. The best advice in the world can't help us if we haven't anyone who can act on it, and neither I nor your father, nor General Fenton nor anyone else here is mentally equipped to be a money raiser. If we could hire Emory, sure, he might be able to do it, but you can't ask a boy who's only twenty-nine and already making a hundred thousand dollars a year to throw up his career and come down here where even if we were solvent we couldn't pay him more than twenty-five. We'd have to have something equal to or better than he has to offer him. You see that, don't you?"

"Yes . . . well . . . he is working for a group of very wealthy men. Could he ask them to help us?"

"From what I've read about that group they never put a nickel into anything that won't bring them a whopping profit. In business I don't believe that anyone gets something for nothing."

"Emory Monck . . ." Helen Strindberg had a twisting smile at the corner of her mouth. It was a momentary relief to think back to a happier time. "Life was interesting at least with him around. The organization boy . . . the campus politician . . . we certainly could use one of his wild schemes now. Do you remember when he . . ."

Strindberg did not hear what his wife's particular reminiscence was. One of his own had just leaped up, released from the file of memory by Helen's phrase, the campus politician; a day when Emory had confided to him his intention of eventually entering the political arena. The boy had been only seventeen then and Strindberg had discounted it, forgotten it, largely he would have to admit, because he had other plans for this young man.

But now he needed Monck. He had not really considered it before because he had automatically assumed that he had nothing to trade with, yet Monck was so obviously the answer. If he were still inclined toward politics, there was the lever, there was the trading tool.

Strindberg had maneuvered Emory Monck throughout his youth. With a rising excitement he wondered if he still could, if he could again sell Emory an idea and make him believe it was his own.

There was another trade to make before he would try. He waited for a break in the talk that had sprung up around the old campus escapades and then stood up to draw attention.

"Just supposing I could bring Monck down here." He addressed the two university officials. "Would you agree to making him chancellor?"

The idea took a minute to register. Their first reaction, plain on their faces, read that it was a grotesque joke; then Amos raised his hands from his sides and placed them together in front of him, unaware that the gesture appeared prayerful.

"I'd give the presidency to the man who could pull us out of this. Yes, I'd vote for him for chancellor."

Fenton would have argued on principle except that

he still did not accept the proposal as serious. "Sure," he shrugged.

Strindberg did not wait for their second thoughts. "What time is it?" he asked his wife.

Helen consulted her watch. "Nearly eight."

"Five o'clock in California. I just might catch him at his office." He was already on his way into the house.

From the porch they heard him lift the phone and heard his voice asking for a person-to-person call to Emory Monck at Alcon Electronics in Ventura, California. The wait was not long; then they heard the voice again, stronger this time:

"Emory? Martin. I'm coming to the coast tomorrow. I want to see that plant of yours and do some talking."

2

☐ For a young man who had recently committed himself to raise one hundred million dollars in cash, Emory Monck appeared to be carrying his burden lightly. He walked with an easy, swinging step as though he wore springs in the soles of his shoes, as though he could not wait to grapple with the problem he had undertaken.

Somewhat above medium height, slender but not thin, tailored with an eye toward comfort, neither overdressed nor too casual, he was the very picture of the young executive on his pre-programmed way to the top.

The dark waves of his hair shone with health. His face was too long for handsomeness, but a steady, noticeable good humor quickened the curve of his generous mouth with felicity and charm. Emory Monck's personality drew even strangers into his affection and won their immediate confidence.

How much of this was natural and how much was calculated Monck himself could not say. It was an asset that he had discovered in his early youth and continued to cultivate. He knew that he was something of an actor, that all men are actors to a degree, but the role had so absorbed the man that the two were inseparable.

Whistling, his large hands shoved into his trousers pockets, he came out of the executive building of Alcon Electronics' Ventura plant into the oven of the early August noon, bounced down the three wide steps and crossed the soft asphalt of the parking lot toward his Continental.

As he approached the car he dredged up his keys, jingling them just for the pleasure of their little music, swung around the rear deck and reached for the door handle. He stopped in mid-reach. A man was sitting in the driver's seat. For an instant he thought that he had mistaken the car, but then he recognized Harry Hertz, the president of Jennifer Air.

"Well, hello, for Pete's sake." He smiled at the upturned, cherubic face. "What are you doing way out here?"

"Waiting for you. Gimme the keys." Hertz put his hand out through the window quickly, avoiding the blistering hot ledge.

If the order and the gesture were intended to surprise Monck into reacting without argument, they succeeded. Emory dropped the keys into the extended palm and the fingers closed around them. Hertz smiled then, mildly, tenuously, and beckoned with his head toward the empty right-hand seat.

"Come on. Get in."

Monck went back around the car amiably, dropped his briefcase into the rear seat and climbed in at Hertz's side. Hertz already had the engine running, and his pulling away from the parking space gave impetus to Monck's closing of the door, to his settling against the back rest.

"What's your rush?" Monck's protest was academic, unsuspecting, joshing. "Where we going?"

"Don't ask so many questions."

Harry Hertz was always sparing of words; perhaps he wanted to get what he had to say said before he could be interrupted. This manner did not carry an affront, but it did encourage anyone trying to hold a conversation with him to edit his own sentences. Monck had thought before that among the idiosyncrasies into which people generally let themselves descend, Hertz's peculiarity was not a bad one.

He sat relaxed, enjoying the blast from the air-conditioner, waiting for the explanation that he felt would come in Hertz's own time, until they passed the main gate without turning through it. Hertz swung the car on toward the back lot and the private air strip at the north end of the company's property.

16

Monck looked at the driver but had no return glance, and a suspicion now began to form, a wholly unexpected possibility that gathered credence when he saw Hertz's personal Humming Bird blocked but not tied at the edge of the runway.

"Look, Harry . . ." he straightened in the seat. "I haven't got time today . . ."

"You've got time," said Harry Hertz, and pulled the car up beside the plane. "We'll take a little ride."

Emory Monck had two simultaneous reactions, the first of which was a spontaneous laugh; the words themselves, the man waiting in the car and his uncommunicativeness, taken all together reminded him of the old black sedan underworld *rides* to liquidation. His second reaction was to the tone in the voice which suggested something of importance and immediacy that concerned Monck and would carry more weight than whatever appointments he would miss in the next hour or so.

His decision was not hard to make. He was curious, and further, it was a pleasure in itself to fly with Hertz.

At twenty-two Harry Hertz had been one of the youngest Army Air Corps colonels in the Second World War. At forty-four he was president and production head of the giant Jennifer Air Corporation, a chunky, roly-poly man with a face that retained an incongruous baby innocence. Behind the china-doll eyes an energetic, well-balanced mind considered its problems each in turn, without panic, and solved them with a minimum of floundering. His flying was a perceivable example of his thinking. He handled the eight-place plane as if it were a part of himself, as if it would answer his commands directly, without needing his freckled hands on the controls.

Monck rode the co-pilot's seat appreciatively. He had held a private license for eight years and had logged over three thousand hours. In the business climate which he inhabited a plane was as essential as an automobile. But he knew that he would never match Hertz's mastery of the sky. Hertz had been born to the air. It was hard to visualize him in any other element.

The plane followed the coast south until the pattern on the ground which was the Los Angeles complex formed into ordered squares beyond the hills. For a few minutes Monck supposed that they were bound for International,

17

but then the Humming Bird veered east and headed toward the mountains on the rim of the southern desert. He had a premonition.

"What the hell, Harry? Am I being kidnaped?"

"Something like that," Hertz said conversationally. "You shouldn't have done it, kid. You shouldn't have resigned without talking to Sam Jordan."

3

☐ Oh. Yes, that was a blooper. Monck did not say it aloud, and the snapping of his fingers as the implications of this neglect overtook him was a mere reflex of his thumb and third finger muscles, stayed before it became apparent.

He wanted money from Jordan, a lot of money. In the plan of his campaign Sam Jordan's name led the list of potential contributors. Sam, although he did not yet know it, was supposed to give Monck his first million dollars, to be the bell sheep who would toll another ninety-nine corporation heads into a like generosity.

And in the excitement of the last few days as the magnitude of the possibility implicit in the new project unfolded to him he had, like a neophyte, leaped for the ultimate end and stumbled over the first step. Martin Strindberg's plea for help had come out of the blue. Emory Monck had believed that the course of his life, the highway to his goal was clearly defined and realistically paced and he had laughed at the first suggestion that he change direction so drastically, so apparently uneconomically. But as Strindberg talked, spinning out his web, the visions were born, the new field looked much the richer for the plow, the new road seemed straighter, faster, more sure and unassailably logical. The old scene had faded, and with it some important points that he should have remembered.

Now he had only a couple of hours to recover his fumble. Harry Hertz's silver ship was winging him swiftly through the pale sky. On the ground almost directly below, its shadow slid smoothly across the jagged roofs of the metropolitan sprawl, soon would race over the wide yellow desert from which the heat sent shimmering waves of the illusion of liquid turbulently upward.

Up the western slope of the divide, through the gathering junipers, then the dense pines, dark green and soft-looking from this altitude, dipping with a dizzying drop into the deep, castellated red wound, the gorge of the Oak Creek canyon, instantly climbing the shocking vermillion turrets and minarets and spires and battlements of the opposite wall, the shadow would hurry to the hidden emerald spa on the crest of the south running ridge . . . Sam Jordan's Geronimo's Spring . . . and a confrontation.

Emory Monck sat back in his seat to concentrate on that confrontation.

No one in his right mind ignored Sam Jordan. Sam owned half the cattle in the United States. Starting with cows he had leap-frogged into oil. Within half a century he had connived and bartered, traded, muscled, dealt his way into control of General Consolidated Oil, of Ridgeway Oil and Gas, of the Caldeon oil pool in east Texas, and of the enormous lake of oil that underlay the Kyruit Neutral Zone in southern Arabia. Sam was a major power among the wheeler-dealers who had sprung up like dragons' teeth after the Second War, the financial pirates, the spoilers, the exploiters who could smell out a growth situation unrecognized by the traditional, staid industrialists, and with a legerdemain that made inhibiting tax patterns work for them rather than against them, move in and perform sleight-of-hand feats that vaporized governmental restrictions. One of a group of confusingly inter-allied men who played the game with a bewildering tangle of enterprises, Sam was chairman of the board of the related companies, General Consolidated and Arabian Southern Oil. He was on the board of directors of Jennifer Air Corporation and on the board of Jennifer's subsidiary Alcon Electronics.

In these capacities Sam Jordan had been the man at the top of the only two organizations for which Emory Monck had worked since he left school. With a background of electronics, physics, and mathematics, Monck had taken a master's in business administration. After earning his Ph.D., he had spent four years with Arabian Southern Oil and then been loaned to Alcon Electronics.

Now, after another four years as president of Alcon, he was moving out without a by-your-leave or, thus far, even an explanation. He could picture what Sam Jordan must suppose, could visualize Sam's wrath, and he had found an explanation for Sam's reaching down out of the sky and plucking him off of Alcon's parking lot. Sam wanted him out of circulation. Sam thought that he had been recruited.

Indeed, in a fashion he had been, but he felt a welling of laughter, which he suppressed, at the thought of trying to make Jordan comprehend how a physics professor had conned him out of a job that paid him a basic hundred thousand a year and into one offering twenty-five, if and when.

Sam's understanding of a recruiter was a member of one of the hundred and fifty firms which earned between twelve and fifteen million every year by luring high-placed executives out of one organization and into that of the firm's client. It was a new occupation spawned by the explosion of American business and the acute shortage of trained managerial talent, and was itself boldly expanding year by year.

The old custom of a man leaving school, beginning with a corporation and slowly working his way up the rungs of the ladder was obsolete. Corporate management had become a game of musical chairs; salary increases, stock bonuses and promises of quick advancement were dangled to entice a desirable candidate to jump from one position to another.

Sam Jordan himself had a long history of raiding personnel from others, but he was never happy when a tool he had used successfully was turned upon him. He hated the recruiters. Scavengers, he called them, headhunters. He had threatened in fiery earnest to shoot any one of them caught on any of his properties or talking to any of his employees—anywhere.

During the past four years five of these advocates had jeopardized their lives to proselytize Monck with promises of dazzling rewards if he would leave Alcon. He had resisted partly because of the freedom he had there and partly because of the stimulation he found in his association with Jordan, Hertz, Larry Donovan, Gordon Randall and the rest of the group. He did not know whether Sam had learned of those advances, but surely the office spies would have sent him word that in the week since Emory

20

Monck had tendered notice there had been a flurry among the body snatchers, trying to contact him.

Not only Sam, but the whole group must be imagining the worst, that Monck had gone over to the enemy, carrying the secrets of the Jordan empire into a competitor's camp. Hindsight told him that if he were in their position he too would worry. Every industrial complex guarded its secrets as jealously as the State Department guarded the country's foreign policy, and with reason, for present-day industrial spying puts the James Bonds to shame. It was no fiction that only recently one of the major cosmetic companies, on deciding to expand into pharmaceuticals, had recruited the entire staff of chemists of a rival laboratory.

Yes, Sam would have the galloping jitters, and Emory needed Sam on his side. He would have to do some very convincing explaining to prove that he was not selling out. He would have to explain . . .

He caught himself up. Explanation was not the answer. Among other useful things that Sam Jordan had taught him was the art of playing poker, not only with cards, but in every facet of business. He wanted money from Sam and the sure way not to get it was to go to the oil king with his hat in his hand, with explanations, apologies or appeals to altruism. Sam Jordan did not know the meaning of that word. The only way to handle Sam was by swinging a club. You had to be in a trading position.

Emory Monck knew suddenly that he had his club, that the club was his own self. With Sam afraid of what he might do, he had a worthy weapon.

He sat back, feeling the tension that had gathered within him relaxing, and like a tourist looked out of the window, down on the mountains, to enjoy the remainder of the flight.

4

☐ At seventy-two Sam Jordan did not look very different than he had at fifty. Beneath the worn denims and khaki shirt the body was still erect, showing none of the humbling of age. There was no fat on him. He was as stringy as he had been in the days when he rode a cow pony from one end of Montana to the other. He sat hunched in an aluminum chair beside the swimming pool on the shaded patio of his Geronimo's Spring ranch.

The white stucco, red tile roofed buildings clustered beyond the patio walls simmered under the hot afternoon sun, but a breeze helped. It was pulled down from the cool heights of the mountains, across the five men around the glass-topped table, drawn into the descending canyon and out across the desert floor to replace the rising heated air.

Jordan put down his glass and pinched up the cards that had just been dealt him, palming them secretively. Poker was a way of life to Sam, and although he was one of the wealthiest of men the mound of chips in the center of the table was very meaningful to him. The accumulation of money had been his lifelong hobby, one of joyful greed, of unflagging appetite.

The three kings that peeked at him one-eyed as he fanned the hand looked like collateral. He bet them with deceptive carelessness, shoving a hundred-dollar stack into the pot, which already tempted him, for the deal had been around twice without openers.

"Here we go. Let's shake out the amateurs."

Sitting beside him, Gordon Randall bore the marks of an upbringing in the aristocratic tradition in spite of the tropic brilliance of his sport shirt and matching Bermuda shorts. A member of two of New York's oldest families, a keen attorney, he was a director in three insurance companies, was head of the financial committee of Jordan's Arabian Southern Oil, and chief executive officer of Jennifer Air. His narrow face was smooth, scored by only a few crow's-foot lines at the corners of his handsome eyes, arrogant. His hair was dark except for touches of gray at his temples. His smile was mocking as he saw Sam's bet and raised it.

"Sure you know what you're doing?"

Jordan snorted. "You'll find out. Come on, you mavericks, donate."

"Thank you," Joe Thomas told him, his pointed nose twitching in disgust as he tossed his useless cards aside. Thomas was head of the three insurance companies in which Randall participated. "It would be a donation for me to come in, and I'm against charity."

Price Davis, small and precise as if he were seen through a reducing glass, an auditor, was chairman of the financial committee of Jennifer Air. His chuckle was as dry as the rustle of newly printed bills.

"I agree. What with Sam's tax position, it's a waste to give him money that he only has to shove along to Washington. Pass."

Larry Donovan stayed for the raise. The youngest of the five, Donovan was big and blond. His face had never lost the leathery texture burned into it by the Arabian sun twenty years before and maintained in fields around the globe, for he spent little time behind his New York desk. He had literally grown up in the oil business, a roustabout with his wildcatting father at twelve, a tool dresser at sixteen, at eighteen, with Sam Jordan's help, drilling his first well.

Among the oil companies a preponderance of the top men have come up from the black mud. The fierce, cutthroat competition and the constant reckless gamble of risking millions in the search for new reserves demand toughness and steady dedication, qualities best developed through the hope and disappointment and hard labor of those who survive the drilling platforms.

From the swamps of the Gulf Coast of America to the Neutral Zone in Arabia, Donovan and Jordan had clawed their way, merging, buying, stealing until one motorist in ten filled his car at their green and white pumps, and the reserves they controlled were considered to be as vast as their foremost competitor's.

Larry watched as Sam caught his fourth king and won the pot, watched with a restless, growing lack of grace. He did not like to lose. He growled at Sam's gleeful crowing.

None of these men enjoyed losing so much as a poker hand. They had the habit of winning, the hunger that is only whetted as power increases. To them business was the greatest game. Money, in and of itself, was meaningless, for long ago they had all acquired more than they could ever use.

They formed a predatory, close-knit society in which each protected his own position and kept a watchful eye on every action of his fellows, and together they represented a power with tentacles throughout the business community, frightening in its reach.

Larry Donovan gathered the cards and shuffled them with a deftness not to be expected of his big-knuckled, work-sculptured hands. He bunched them, hesitated, and then as his impatience broke through the veneer of control, he flung the deck toward the pool, the cards fluttering onto the blue surface like parti-colored leaves.

"Hell with it. What are we doing, all rushing out here to sit and sweat because a twenty-nine-year-old jerk kid decides to jump the traces? We got along before we ever saw Emory Monck and we'll get along without him."

Sam Jordan's eyes, intent as those of a hawk, watched his younger partner from beneath drooping brows. His head moved forward on his long neck in a challenge.

"You want him in the hay with Standard? Or Gulf? Or Shell?"

Donovan did not want that. No one had to recall to him the danger involved, for, aside from himself and Jordan, Monck knew the intricacies of their operation better than any other individual. He had been present when they worked out their private treaty with the three Arabian sheikdoms. He knew about the shipment of arms to central Africa. He knew the negotiations for the Chilean copper concession. He knew too much about everything.

"What do we do, kill him?"

At the moment Sam Jordan was hungrily contemplating that very solution. Emory Monck was his mistake. The boy had hypnotized him from their first meeting. As Sam's administrative assistant Emory had proved that he could field the thousand and one questions that came to Jordan every day. Opportunities open themselves to everyone, but only a very few people have the capability of recognizing them and making instant decisions. That was the important thing, to act. If a man was right only sixty percent of the time he was invaluable to any organization so long as he could say yes or no at once. Jordan had never believed in the committee system; it was slow and it watered down judgment. His man was the one who could make an instantaneous choice and would then stand responsible. Emory Monck had been his pride.

He looked up at the western sky, hoping to see the expected plane.

"The key is," he said, as much to himself as to the group, "to find out what the kid wants. It can't be money.

24

After you hit the thirty thousand level, salary doesn't mean much, what with the tax bite, and he knows we can do as well as anybody pension-wise and with stock options. Christ, in less than five years with us he could be batting a million."

They were silent in agreement.

"So it's got to be something else, maybe a job he wants to get his teeth into. Maybe the fact that Larry is only forty-four is the reason he's jumping. Maybe he figures Larry's in his way and that it will be twenty years before Larry moves out."

Donovan lifted and dropped his shoulders in frustration. Sam did not look at him, but went on, thinking aloud.

"So maybe we'd better give him Larry's job. I'll step out as board chairman; Larry can move up, still stay chief executive officer, but Monck will be president."

Donovan exploded. Always volatile, he never managed to subdue his Irish temper.

"Why in hell do we have to bribe him? You gave him every break a kid ever had. You'd think he'd feel a little loyalty."

If they had not been so deeply concerned they would all have laughed at him. Jordan's snort was derisive.

"You know somebody who's loyal? It's every dog for himself, and if Emory didn't feel the same I'd have damn little use for him. We're going to have to give him something because we can't help ourselves. We can't have him running around loose, blabbing all he knows. The mistake I made was ever loaning him to Gordon for Alcon. If I'd kept him with me this wouldn't have happened."

Randall stirred in his chair in protest. "It was your idea."

"Sure it was." Sam sounded accusing. "That bunch you had running Alcon couldn't find their way out of a subway. Look at the job he did in four years . . . took a hatful of little outfits that we'd thrown together and whipped them into a straight-line organization. They're showing near a ten million profit this season." His tone of voice changed. "I was only going to leave him there another six months and then bring him home."

"He's still too young to run General Consolidated." Larry was stubborn. "I'll admit he's as much a genius type as I'm apt to know, but he needs more experience."

"You were drilling wells at eighteen."

"And if you remember I made a lot of mistakes that you had to bail us out of." They glared at each other.

Price Davis broke up the tug-o'-war by saying, "You can't measure maturity by calendar age, Larry. Emory was an adult the day he was born. Don't forget that he took an EE at seventeen and had his master's at eighteen, his doctor's before he was twenty-one." As he talked he turned to Thomas. "What do you think, Joe?"

The insurance man rubbed the side of his head as though awed by the thought of the boy. "I'd hire him in a minute. I'd let him pick his own spot."

5

☐ Emory Monck sat docile in his seat until Harry Hertz touched the wheels of the plane to the runway, a contact that he sensed rather than felt; then he snapped open the safety belt across his lap, stood up, put a congratulatory hand briefly on Hertz's shoulder and went back to open the rear door. When Harry had braked and turned and parked the ship in the tie-down area Monck dropped the panel of steps and descended them with his usual small boy run.

He was happy to be there on two counts: he was eager for the meeting now that he had his battle plan penciled in, and further, he had always enjoyed his visits to Geronimo's Spring.

On his first visit there he had been overwhelmed by the extent of what Sam called his hideout. He had expected it to be a working ranch because, during the time when it was being built, Sam used to say that he had to go down and see how his cows were doing. The cows, Emory learned, were women, and the community was designed as a health resort. Fat rich ladies found an extensive gymnasium and a solicitous masseuse to help them work off their excess flesh; alcoholic rich ladies found a sauna and a course of therapy to give them a respite from their demon, if not a cure; and bored rich ladies found a crew of companionable, sweet-smelling cowboys ready to escort them up and down the labyrinth of pine-sheltered equestrian trails.

There was a main building with a dining hall and a big communal room decorated to deceive the guest into believing she was living the Western life, a room in which any ranchman or cowhand would be too uncomfortable to sit down. There was an Olympic-size, temperature-controlled pool in the flagstone patio and a series of lake-pools, graduated in size and depth to tempt the less and less courageous. There was a village of a hundred individual cottages and beyond them, hidden among the trees and distant enough for olfactory and auditory discretion was a compound of stables, machine sheds, and maintenance buildings.

It was a costly establishment, all predicated on the management of one unusually able woman, one of the few people who had successfully got away from Sam Jordan. She had married Larry Donovan.

Sam had then thrown out the ladies and the pastel-shirted cowboys and moved in. He used it as a gathering place for his associates where they could play poker and drink and spin their business deals safe from the curious eyes of outsiders. He loved it, loved the bleak, remote austerity of the red canyon and the soft, secret majesty of the mountain forests, and to Emory Monck he looked at home here, while he seemed out of place in the glass hi-rise spire above Park Avenue that was headquarters for General Consolidated Oil.

Monck breathed deeply of the clean, spiced air and watched the jeep skitter toward him down the bark chip road. He heard his captor come up behind him and turned, grinning.

"Am I going back, or are you going to bury me here?"

Hertz walked forward to set the chocks and clip on the ropes, saying over his shoulder, "Ask Sam. It's his party."

It was usually Sam's party, Monck thought, and felt a quick tug of regret, a pre-knowledge of loss. He was going to miss the easy, free-for-all association that he had enjoyed for the past eight years.

Before the jeep pulled in beside him he saw with pleasure that it was driven by Sam's wife. Eli Jordan might be in her early sixties, but she was Monck's favorite woman. She owned an important racing stable, was a noted rider herself and was built like a jockey, with a creased and weathered face that she described as a walnut. She wore a man's wide-brimmed hat over her graying hair, a man's checked shirt, or more likely a boy's, and slim Levi's that many launderings had softened to a comfortable fit.

"Get in." Her smile was wide, without any hint of strain. "Harry, you can walk. You need the exercise."

Hertz flapped a hand to acknowledge that he had heard, and Eli barely waited until Monck was aboard before she spun the jeep backward into a Y turn and headed it toward the big parking lot outside the patio wall.

"Hello, young'un." She had adopted Monck as her own on that first of his visits and she looked him over now, possessively and with an eye to making sure that he was still in good repair. She did not bother to watch the road. Presumably the jeep, like a good horse, was expected to know the way. "You feeling all right these days?"

"Good as new. Better." He looped an arm over her shoulder and hugged her lightly. "Are you behaving yourself while I'm not watching?"

"You ought to behave as well." She shook her head in a friendly warning. "Sam's mad at you. Watch what you say. Sam is very, very mad."

"Believe me I'll watch." Emory Monck said it fervently, and sat rehearsing just what he would say to the oil king, until she dropped him in front of the gate.

He waited until she had driven away before he turned, and then he saw through the iron grille that there were five men instead of one ranked around the table. He hesitated, making some hasty changes in his plan of attack, opened the gate slowly and walked into the patio.

6

☐ Sam Jordan said, "Get him a drink."

It was the only greeting Monck got. He looked from one to the other, advancing with a lax, free walk, crowding down the amusement that their faces stirred in him. These men were angry, each in his own way, but Larry Donovan was the one who did not conceal his feeling. He grunted, rose and brought a whiskey and soda from the portable bar. Monck almost expected him to fling the drink into his face.

Price Davis kicked out a chair for him and Emory sat down, tasting the scotch. The afternoon sun was hot on his back and he still had on his coat. He stood up and peeled it off.

"Nice of you to ask me over."

"Why'd you do it?" Sam Jordan shoved forward, his thin body rigid, his hands clawing the table edge. "Come on, give. Who got to you? What kind of a deal did they make?"

Monck took another swallow of the cold drink. "Gimme a chance to catch my breath. I haven't been kidnaped for a long time."

"All right," said Sam, and there was an approving beam in his eyes. "Play it cozy, don't show your hand until you hear what I have to say. How would you like to be president of General Consolidated?"

Monck had thought that he was on balance, proof against surprise, but in spite of himself he choked on the liquid in his throat and Davis reached across to pound him none too gently on the back. He had expected them to offer him some bait to stay with Alcon, maybe a vice-presidency, perhaps even executive vice-president in charge of General's station operations, or head of the new distribution company they were setting up in England. But the presidency of the parent company? That was too much.

His resolution faltered. Maybe he was making a mistake. Maybe . . .

Sam pounced on his hesitancy. "I'm stepping out," he said airily. "I'm getting a little old . . ."

That statement steadied Monck's wavering decision and brought reality back into focus. The notion that Sam would ever consider himself too old for anything was plainly ridiculous. It was a ploy. It was playing games with titles without any shift in the balance of power. No matter who held what job Sam Jordan would continue to run the company as a personal fief, and, with that understood, the fiction that he would relinquish his power only betrayed the importance he attached to Emory Monck. It was a knowledge that Monck was glad to be certain of.

"The place is yours if you want it." Jordan's tone implied he knew very well Monck would want it, that any man would jump at the chance. "We'll work out a stock deal so you won't have to worry."

"I'm not worried." Monck took the time to drain his glass, to rise and meander to the bar and refill it. He needed a second drink as he never had before. He had his work cut out for him. He must now strike exactly the right balance in what he said. He had to lead them into bringing their fears out in the open, to admitting that they would go to almost any length to keep him from working for one of their competitors. He wandered idly back to the table.

"I've never been less worried in my life. I've finally found out exactly what I want to do."

He watched Jordan wince, and again stifled his laughter. He was having real trouble in keeping a poker face. This was the kind of game he loved, that Sam Jordan had taught him to love, the challenging game of the trader approaching a deal.

You must go at it by indirection. You must never let the other man know what you really want until the deal is made. If Jordan realized that he did not intend to work for another oil company, or for any other type of company that was represented within the group, his advantage would instantly be lost. He had to pry from them some verbal commitment before he told them what he was going to do, while he still held their insecurity as his club. The others were lying back quietly, letting Jordan handle the play.

"What is it?" Jordan roared at him. "What the hell can somebody else offer you that we can't?"

Emory looked away, over the wall, off into space as if he saw a vision shining there. He put no emphasis on his words, letting them sound deliberately underplayed.

"I found a real challenge."

"What's that supposed to mean? Where are you going to find a challenge bigger than running General Consolidated?"

Emory smiled at him.

Sam was sweating, and it was wonderful to watch.

"Look, kid, I won't pull any punches with you. We can't have you going to Shell, you know that. We're getting ready to move into the European market and . . ."

"Sure I know."

"So you are going with Shell?"

"I didn't say that."

"Damnit. Quit it. What will it take to get your promise that you won't work for another oil company for fifteen years?"

The fish was nosing the hook. Monck sounded as though he were commenting on the weather. "A million dollars." Now he held his breath.

All five of them sat staring at him with no attempt at dissembling. They were intimate with astronomical figures, old hands at stepping in without a dollar's investment and taking over corporations on credit. Each of them had, more than once, brazenly stolen many times the figure he had named by proxy fights, cunning stratagems and financial abracadabra; but hearing a twenty-nine-year-old whom they had raised and trained and groomed stand before them and demand one million dollars tribute to not join the opposition . . . this approached blackmail.

"You're crazy." Larry Donovan let the words out in a long exhalation. "Sam, let me throw him off the ranch. Let's take the bastard's shoes and make him hike to Phoenix."

"Hold onto your hat, Larry." Sam was watching Monck with half-closed eyes. "You're up to some mischief, boy. You're trying to sucker old Sam."

Emory shoved his hands into his pockets and kicked at the flagstones. "Did I come over here of my own free will or did you kidnap me? You asked me a question and I answered it. You don't want me working for another oil company. I'll be honest. I've been offered places with three of them, very attractive offers I might add. Now, you start talking."

"Why the million?" Sam's suspicion made his voice a whisper.

"For a very good reason, which I will tell you the minute I have your word on the deal."

The million would not come out of Sam's pocket, of course. Sam's pocket was a one-way affair. Yet Sam was hesitating longer than Monck liked.

"Tax money," he said.

"Okay. You're on. I'll gamble. But if you've buggered me you'd better watch yourself."

Monck knew that the threat was not an idle one. Sam had taught rough lessons to a lot of people who had been brash enough to try to sucker him.

"I won't hurt you in any way. My promise."

"How do you want your million?"

"A hundred thousand today, a hundred thousand a year for nine years."

"You've got it. Now for Christ sake tell us what you're up to."

7

☐ Emory Monck had not expected to find all of these men at the ranch. He had planned to talk to Sam Jordan alone, and then to Gordon Randall and Joe Thomas one at a time. He wanted a second million from Jennifer Air and a third from Thomas' insurance companies, money that would cost them nothing, for most of it would be tax deductible. He needed a little time to decide how he should make this forced presentation.

"Let's wait until Harry comes up," he said. "I hate to tell a story twice."

Jordan shrugged. "Boy, with all this build-up it had better be good. Larry, get us a fresh deck, we might as well use the time."

They played poker for half an hour, but Monck's mind was not fully on the game. He sat debating how much he should tell them, how much of his own position he should make clear. He would not, he decided, tell them the whole truth at this time.

That final point toward which he was aiming had been resolving itself gradually over a number of years, vaguely at first but in the last three years it had become definite, yet the way by which he would get there had seemed a long haul, until three weeks ago. Three weeks ago it had not entered his head that he would ever return to Wellington University.

Fresh out of school he had joined Arabian Southern Oil in an eight-thousand-dollar-a-year job, bent on advancing himself as rapidly as possible into the realm of big money. He had never doubted his ability to get there. He was a late baby and precocious. He was born to a fifty-three-year-old father who had already spent two decades teaching philosophy at Wellington and a forty-one-year-old mother well known in her own right as a concert musician. The campus had been his home.

Education by osmosis through this long and close association had been one advantage he had enjoyed, and his relationship with his parents had been another. They had given up hope of producing a family and were a little nonplused when he arrived, unable to raise him as a young couple would, with the shadow of their own childhood still upon them, and not wanting to make a toy of him. They accepted him as simply another person in the house, included him in their adult discussions and assumed that he would make his own decisions. They would not insult him by dictating to him.

He was also lucky in attending what was called the faculty school. This was a gathering of the thirty to forty children who lived on or near the campus. They used one of the older houses on faculty row and seven or eight teachers came and went according to how the school fitted into their schedules. Sometimes full professors had a go at seeing how much of their specialties the very young could absorb. Sometimes there were staff assistants and sometimes university students working toward teaching careers. All of them, though, had to pass muster with Helen Strindberg, whose energy and dedication kept the project thriving. It was not an orthodox school and was periodically at odds with the town, where groups of the tradition-minded sometimes lifted their concentration from their own affairs and raised the hue and cry that the university was using the children as experimental animals. There were no classes as such. Each child pursued whatever subjects interested him at his own pace. There was no grading until the time came to check up on a candidate's readiness for college.

Emory passed the university's entrance examination when he was thirteen and matriculated without moving farther than across a wide, tree-shaded lawn.

He was one of a generation of college men that had no worries about job opportunities. Corporation scouts interviewed all of the seniors and sometimes dug into the junior class when they caught the scent of talent. The graduates walked into salaries that were often as high as those that had been earned by their fathers at their peak performance. One man with the soul of a cheer leader had made up a chart, framed it and hung it as a shrine, or a goad, on the study hall wall. It read:

THE SCORE BOARD

Starting salary at:

Twenty-two ————	$ 7,000.00	
Twenty-eight ————	12,000.00	
Thirty-three ————	16,000.00	
Thirty-eight ————	25,000.00	Plus Bonus
Forty-three ————	50,000.00	Plus Bonus
Forty-eight ————	60,000.00	to
	70,000.00	
Fifty years and above—	100,000.00	Up and Up and Up

Its baleful implication was that unless an executive arrived at the proper stage at each age level he was falling behind the average and would probably be passed over and never achieve the pinnacle.

Emory Monck had never yet had to face that worry. His starting salary was a thousand dollars above the norm, he was two years younger than the usual graduate and he had his doctorate before the other had his bachelor's.

His rise in Arabian Southern had been spectacular. The company's geophysical division shipped him to Kyruit, where he tinkered with and perfected a "doodlebug." Fitted with transistors and painted circuits, it weighed only a fraction of what the equipment in use did, and was an instant success. Then he revamped the port facilities so that the tanker turnaround time was cut by more than half. His report caught Sam Jordan's acquisitive eye and within a year he was back in the home office as Jordan's administrative assistant, drawing twenty thousand. He was drawing seventy thousand three years later, when he was loaned to Alcon, which gave him a hundred thousand and bonuses, which hardly seemed like a raise.

He was in the big league and he was playing well. His early training in mathematics plus his long awareness of the low level of faculty salaries had given him a careful approach to money. Every year after the first one he had saved half of his post-tax salary and all of his bonuses. It was all invested in mutual funds, and the growth market had so appreciated that he was now nearing a capital worth of a quarter of a million.

And he was sitting in a game with five enormously wealthy men who thought he showed promise of working up into their class. It was going to be difficult to make them understand why before his thirtieth birthday he was tired of making money.

They themselves would never tire of piling up dollars. It was not the money itself that kept them restless and searching. It was the power that money generated, and there is never a limit to the power that can be reached for. They gambled after ever more of it; the gambling was their life.

Monck too was now gambling for power, but power in a different guise; and his road led a different way than theirs. If he told them that, they would understand, but telling them at this stage was too dangerous to risk. He could wind up saddled with them and unable to extricate himself.

He heard the gate behind him open and looked up as Harry Hertz came through, going directly toward the bar. With a full glass he came over to stand in back of Monck, kibitzing while the hand was solemnly played out.

Not until the pot was raked in did Sam Jordan acknowledge the new presence, then he said, "Sit down, Harry. Emory just hit me for a million bucks, and he wouldn't tell us why until you got here. . . . Okay, boy. Shoot."

Emory Monck shoved his chair away from the table and sat back in it, crossing one leg over his knee, his smile as beguiling, as disarming as he knew how to make it, and his voice held a laughter directed at himself.

"You're going to think I've lost my mind. I'm getting out of industry."

Their reaction told him that his guess was right. A look of shock passed across Jordan's face, then the face puckered up tightly in suspicious concern.

"Are you sick, kid?"

Emory knew that this was not an idiom for abnormal psychology, that the old man had jumped to the conclusion that some physical ailment, perhaps a faltering heart, was forcing his retirement, and he said quickly:

"Nothing like that, Sam." More slowly he added, "I have accepted the post of Chancellor of Wellington University."

The silence of embarrassment held the group. Hertz

chewed rhythmically on a piece of gum. Price Davis worked at removing a fleck of something from beneath a white, manicured thumbnail. Thomas and Randall studied the cloudless sky until their eyes were drawn to each other. Sam played with the cards in the manner of an old-fashioned gambler splitting the deck and slicing it back together in sharp little tosses that integrated a few cards at a time.

"What's it pay you?"

Monck said with no hint at all that he knew how ludicrous it sounded, "Twenty-five thousand a year. No bonus."

Sam could only grunt. None of them deigned to comment. They sat waiting for whatever he would tell them next, since the salary figure patently was not the reason for his move.

"The school is broke."

Instinctively their interest picked up. Whenever any organization was broke or in financial difficulty it was a signal for these men to begin investigating with a view to taking it over, incorporating it into one of their operations, using its tax loss, dismembering it for any other assets they could find in it. But a university . . . what possible profit could they take out of that? Their minds probed into the idea for any potential and discarded it at once.

Sam shook his head that his protege could be so taken in. "It's a sour deal, kid. There's nothing there for you."

Monck grinned at him. "I don't intend to milk it, Sam. I mean to run it."

Sam tried to make what he was hearing sound like sense, but the puzzlement in his eyes told Emory that he was not succeeding. "I don't get it, kid. The ivory towers are no place for you . . . you belong in the oil business, where you can move."

"You're right, if you mean that I'm not an educator, but that isn't what they need, they've got some of the top men in that field. What they don't have is a financial operator, and they're in such straits that they can't hope to pull out by ordinary means. When Martin Strindberg approached me he put it this way: I'm quoting, 'I want a wheeler-dealer who isn't inhibited by old-line financial practices. I want somebody who's legally honest, with a broad streak of larceny in his soul.'"

Sam Jordan reared back and laughed as Monck intended he should. It would take some of the curse off of Sam's image of the scholars.

"Well, he's alive anyway, and he's got you pegged down. Who is he?"

"Dr. Martin Strindberg, head of the Physics Department, a Nobel Prize winner. In my book he's the best teacher of physics there is, and I've known him all my life. He's the keystone that has made Wellington a much better than average school."

Monck knew that an argument based on the value of the school would have no meaning to either Jordan or Larry Donovan, but he already had Sam's promise of a donation and Sam would not go back on his given word. It was Thomas and Randall he now wanted to approach, but he chose to do it obliquely, apparently still talking to Sam.

"Let me tell you about the school," he said, and realized in surprise that his voice had taken on a warmth that was in no way an affectation. "It's back in Riverdale, Ohio, a typical river town, dirty, rat-infested, narrow, crooked cobblestone streets that run up and down a hillside that's almost steep enough to call a bluff, a hundred and fifty thousand population. The Wellington Sheet and Tube Steel plant . . . they call it The Mill . . . supports the bulk of the people and the rest scrabble some kind of a living out of the strip coal mines. When it rains the water comes down like ink, full of soot. It's an old town, and its luck is running out. They had a Navy installation, but that was canceled out and it put a dent in the economy, and now the university . . ."

Price Davis interrupted with a discovery. "Isn't that where you came from?"

"Yes. I was raised on the campus. My father was on the faculty."

"So you're going home."

The way Davis said it gave him an idea. The tone was kindly, even helpful, and it was help from an unexpected quarter, for Monck had never felt that the auditor was quite human. Saying that he was a calculating machine came closer to describing him. But the suggestion might not be a bad angle to play upon.

"That's part of it, yes, but it isn't a hearts and flowers

37

matter. The area isn't where you would look for a good university, and Wellington has been just that. It was started in the last year of the Civil War as a small denominational college, one building, ninety-four kids and an underpaid faculty of six. It struggled along barely one jump ahead of the sheriff until nineteen-o-three, and then old Amos Wellington, the steel man, gave it his estate for a campus and a ten-million-dollar endowment. That was fine then. They recruited a good faculty and their ratio of honor graduates can compete with any institution in the country."

"Not much of an endowment today." Harry Hertz's words did not match with his wink, signaling to Monck that whatever the others thought, he himself felt that a man was privileged to do what he wanted, even to make a damn fool of himself.

Monck winked back in gratitude. It was nice to know that Hertz was friendly. It would make it easier to get the money from Jennifer, even if Gordon Randall had given no indication as to how the proposition was affecting him.

"You're so right," he told Hertz. "And the school has grown a lot. With the night classes and extension departments the enrollment is up over ten thousand, which multiplies expenses. The payroll alone is over four million, nearer five."

"You're making me cry," Sam Jordan said. "If you ask me you couldn't have found a worse spot for yourself if you'd hunted from hell to breakfast. Don't do it, kid, it's a dead-end street."

They all laughed at Monck. It was instinctive with them to laugh at anyone stupid enough to put himself behind an eight ball. But Monck laughed too.

"Seems to me, Sam, that if the stories are true, you and Larry weren't exactly rolling in clover when you decided to buck the major oil companies."

"All right, all right. But we wanted something. When you want it bad enough you'll go hungry to get it. You, though, you're no bright-eyed altruist to jump in there and break your neck for the old school and love. I'll give them the money because I said I would, but you come on back where you belong and forget this crap."

"I can't, Sam. I've given my word."

"Nuts. You haven't given me one reason why."

Emory Monck felt that this was the time when he must

bear down, bore in on Randall, lay out an explicit argument. He had a suspicion that Randall was playing a game with him, remaining aloof and apparently obtuse simply to watch him squirm, for Randall was too smart not to know the value of a school like Wellington. It was a nice piece of one-upmanship. But Monck could play games too. He looked at Randall in plaintive appeal.

"Tell him, Gordon. Tell the old hard-head what the score is."

Randall's eyes lighted up and his laugh was filled with enjoyment, appreciation of Monck's twist. "Mousetrap me, huh?" He looked at Jordan. "What Emory was about to tell you, Sam, is that we can't afford to let a school like this go down the drain. The raiders are already fighting over what top men there are and the American plant needs all of them it can produce. The world competition is getting too keen for us to ignore such a source of potential. Is that the speech you wanted, Emory?"

"Thanks." Monck grinned widely. "I couldn't have done as well myself."

"And here's the catch, Sam. The one million he squeezed out of you is only a teaser. He's got his hand in every one of our pockets."

Joe Thomas was watching, weighing all the words and making his own assessment. He said in a quiet, conversational tone, "How much are you trying to raise, Emory?"

"A hundred million."

Sam Jordan said in explosive admiration, "The hell!"

Monck nodded casually. "Spread over ten years. Ten million a year is about the deficit I have to face. I figure that a hundred corporations . . ."

Price Davis had built a cradle of his fingers and was looking into it hopefully. "I'd like to see a balance sheet . . ."

Emory Monck had the paper out of his pocket before Davis broke off. He slid it across the table, then rose and went around to stand over the small man's shoulder, reaching out to run his finger down the tabulated columns, reading aloud.

"Current income breaks down like this: tuition and fees, nine million two hundred and fifty thousand. Interest on the invested endowment is four hundred and fifty-two thousand, sales and services of the educational departments earned approximately a million, three hundred forty-six thousand last year. . . ."

Davis twisted to look up at him. "What's that mean?"

"Largely services that the departments and labs perform for the government and for business research for various companies."

"You mean the school's in business?" Sam Jordan was beginning to show an interest.

"Certainly. For instance, they ran some studies on oil treatment for us six years ago. And that doodlebug I built; I had help on it from four of the electronics professors."

Davis had looked back at the sheet, reading it with the interest of a horse bettor studying his *Form*. "I see that auxiliary enterprises earned better than two million six. What are they?"

"Semiprivate businesses set up by the school. For one, they run a computer center which sells services to a lot of small businesses in the area, firms too small to afford to lease their own data processing equipment."

"So, current income last year was just over fifteen million." His finger slipped down the opposite column, stabbing at the cost figures. "Operating expenses ran almost twenty-four. They're in trouble right there."

Around the table their attention was sharpening, each of the men thinking ahead, forming his own picture of the situation, and since Monck had mentioned the doodlebug even Larry Donovan had abandoned his antagonism and joined in the concentration. It was funny, Monck thought, to watch the financial wizardry represented in the minds of these people all concentrated on a problem out of which none of them could take any profit. Eli Jordan too had come from the building, a sixth sense having told her that the conference had reached a point at which she would want to listen. Monck put his arm around her, picked the paper from Davis' fingers and put it into her hand, smiling his welcome.

"But this isn't the whole story. The school owes nearly eighteen million on building bonds that it issued over the last six years. Interest, carrying charges, and the fund for debt retirement run near a million annually. Are you satisfied that I need what I'm asking?"

"I'm satisfied of one thing," said Sam Jordan. "The

eggheads don't know the ABC's about running a business. Who would loan those jokers the dough?"

"Banks. The loans are secured by the land and buildings as evaluated at time of purchase. The land runs about four and a half million, the buildings almost eighteen. Since they don't pay taxes, I haven't the slightest idea what the plant is worth today, probably twenty times what's carried on the books . . . a lot of it was built sixty years ago. So the bondholders are certainly protected, but if they were forced to foreclose there'd be a mess. What do you do with a used university?"

There was a perceptible shifting in the point of view of the group. They had listened to Monck's recitation only to try to learn what the lodestone was that could draw him away from their sphere. Now the problem itself began to intrigue them. They could not look at any problem without automatically seeking a solution.

"What about expenses?" Joe Thomas said. "Can't they be cut?"

Monck's expression was pained. "Not without appreciably diminishing value of product. About sixteen million goes for instruction and research. Administration takes two million six and it costs a million four to run the present plant."

Harry Hertz smiled broadly. "I never thought about higher education except vaguely as a home for underpaid professors. Boys, this thing is big business."

Emory Monck watched Hertz massage his hands together like a gourmet sitting down before a table prepared by a favorite chef. The others were moving, standing up, stretching their legs, going to the bar to refill their glasses, wandering without apparent aim a few steps this way across the flagstones, a few steps that. A new force had come into the air around them; it seemed as if their thinking had generated an electrical charge that forced their bodies into physical activity.

Monck raised his voice. "The rest of the expenses are absorbed by the clinic, student aid, auxiliary enterprises, athletics and miscellaneous items. We could throw out athletics, of course, but the department managed to earn a couple of hundred thousand over cost last year . . . and what would we do with the new stadium?"

Gordon Randall brushed aside any notion of curtailing

41

any facet of the school's endeavor with a swinging gesture of his arm.

"You don't grow anything by cutting it down. Emory's school has to go forward, not backward."

"So where do we get the rest of his money?" Sam Jordan did not see anything odd in his abrupt about face.

"We'll have to go outside the family," said Joe Thomas. "There's plenty of dough around."

Where do *we* get it? . . . Emory's money . . . the family . . .

Emory Monck looked down on Eli Jordan and the two of them laughed together without making a sound. The boys had a new toy. They were like fathers on Christmas Day, out in the street playing with the kid's new football. It did not technically belong to them, but they had appropriated it and they were having fun.

Though it would not be aware of it for some time, Wellington University had not simply hired itself a chancellor; it had been taken under the wing of one of the most powerful organizations in the country. This could be a boon of which other institutions of learning might legitimately be jealous. It could also prove that the university had taken a baby dragon to raise under the misapprehension that it was a cute little chameleon. The distinction, Monck knew, would depend upon how fast he could think, how maneuverable he was, how able to anticipate, deflect, obviate, transmute and otherwise stay on top of whatever these benefactors might come up with toward making his school a satisfying plaything. This gift of the gods demanded that the recipient be forever afterward alert.

Price Davis, the man of charts and tables and diagrams, had the ball and was running downfield.

"We can divide the country's industrial community among us," he said. "Joe, you have enough muscle to bring in the insurance field, Gordon and Harry can cover the aircraft outfits. Sam's got oil . . . George Pappas can be had if we mention a study in oceanography. His fishing fleet always likes to know where the fish are likely to be . . ."

"You make it sound mighty simple," Eli Jordan said. "What happens if nobody wants to play?"

Larry Donovan told her as patiently as if she were a

cherished daughter. "We clobber them. For instance, our suppliers like Texas Tool and Drill, sell us an awful lot of equipment. We ask them politely if they wouldn't like to make an altruistic gift to help American kids get an education. They know right away that if they don't, we can always get our tools from Hughes."

The lawyer, Randall, had already accepted as an accomplished fact that one hundred million dollars was waiting to bail Wellington University out of its perplexity.

"We'd better consider how we're going to arrange distribution. We can't just pass these funds over to a corporation that has shown itself incapable of managing its finances, and Emory does not own the school. There's a board of trustees about whom we know nothing except that they're going to want the power of disposition. We'll have to protect not only the money, but Emory's pre-eminence. Nobody's going to just shovel out dough to see it thrown away.

"I suggest that we establish a trust, a foundation dedicated to promoting education generally. We can make Price executive director and the rest of us sit on the board, keep control. We can give whatever grants Emory needs and increase our capital by making loans and . . ."

"Pretty please . . ." Emory had a sensation of drowning. Already they were moving in. He had hoped to raise the money with no strings attached, but you never get anything for nothing. He was caught in the middle and there was really no way he could object to the plan.

Randall was talking on, ignoring him, enjoying himself. "We'll call it the Educational Assistance Foundation. Nobody can question that it's legitimate . . ."

Emory, growing desperate, cut in emphatically. "That's just fine, Gordon, but I need every dollar we can take in. There won't be any surplus for loans, for other operations. Get your hands out of my till."

Gordon Randall looked surprised and then had the grace to grin sheepishly, a small boy caught with his arm elbow-deep in the cookie jar. But he recovered with the agility of a cat thrown out of a window, squirming in mid-air to land safely on all four paws.

"Just trying to help, Emory. Now let's look ahead. You're predicating your fund on a ten-year period. What's

43

going to happen after that? Where's your provision for future income?"

Sam hooted. "You're slipping, Gordon, we just shake the tambourine again."

"There's a better way." Monck had thought this out carefully. "By then I hope to have Wellington on a self-supporting basis. First we'll expand the existing services to industry, triple them, say. We can broaden the use of the computer for one thing. Then we take a lesson from schools like Cal Tech with its jet propulsion lab, and MIT." He looked around the group innocently. "Among our hundred contributors we ought to find enough customers who for self-interest would buy our services."

He saw their suspicion rise again and hurried to head it off.

"I'm thinking that grants could be made profitably for specific research. Consider what we spend at Alcon for research, nearly fifty percent of our budget. And for every commercial product we develop successfully we work on a dozen that never come off, right?"

Hertz was nodding, the rest not committing themselves.

"So supposing Alcon should make a grant to Wellington for the support of research. If nothing comes of it, the grant can be written off against taxes. If something usable is created it can be licensed to producers. Alcon and the school split the royalties and both come out with a profit. Some of the gamble is taken out of private research and development, because the grantor is spending tax money. The school can't lose. It has the grant to run its laboratories, to train its undergraduates. The graduate students get to work on projects of practical value, prepare themselves to go into industry. And from the successful products the school has a continuing income that can run for years."

Sam Jordan came out of his chair slapping his thigh. "Boy, you did it again. Now there's a real idea. But hell, if that would work why do we need these donations to a foundation?"

"Walk around money, Sam." Monck grinned at him. "Front money. I can't set up this program overnight. First I've got to sell it to the school, then I have to sell it to industry. I figure on about two years to implement it, another five or six to bring in enough income to whittle down our deficit.

"Now when you go out asking for the original money you've got bait. The contributors will have first call on the university's resources."

The new perspective of self-interest marked all their faces. Price Davis' smile was thin and amused. It was as close as he ever came to showing excitement or enthusiasm.

"The boy has learned good. He gets it going and coming."

The others hardly heard him. They were already beginning the argument, realigning their thinking, working out the pitch they would use on their fund-raising expedition. They were used to operating on credit. Asking for cash demanded a refined approach.

Eli touched Monck's sleeve and led him, unobserved, into the main building, where the cool air reminded him how hot he had been on the patio.

"How about scholarships, young'un? Aren't there some brilliant students who can't afford to go to a private university?"

He thought of the many he had known, those who worked part time in the mills, or waited table at the fraternity houses, who performed the hundred odd jobs around the campus, and of those he had not known, unable to take even this advantage, forced by want of money to quit at the end of high school and sink into the tar pit of labor, their talents wasted.

"You can say that again."

"So let me in on the deal. I'll put in a million dollars for them. Don't tell Sam. It's my money, but he'd want to tie strings to it, like only giving it to people who promised to go with General Consolidated after they graduated."

Monck reached up, cupping his hands around her small head, bending to kiss her dry lips.

"You just bought a piece of the action. And it will be our secret, until Price worms the next balance sheet out of the trustees."

She swatted him, hard, on the backside. "You'll handle it. You'll hide it so they'll never know. Now I've got to run and stir up the cook."

She left him, a bantam figure swinging down the long room toward the dining hall and the kitchen beyond. Alone, Emory Monck again felt the chill of the room, made more potent by the tiredness that now attacked him, the reaction to the taut strain under which he had been working.

All afternoon it could have gone either way. He had had to outthink them, to keep one jump ahead, to have the right answers at any particular moment, and as in every job of selling he had had to watch for the closing point, the instant, to cinch the deal.

He had won. There was now no doubt that Wellington would survive. He had two things going for him. First there was their self-interest, and he had deflected that so it would not interfere. He had shown them how they could make a profit out of their association with the school without damaging it. He had given them more than a toy. Then, he need not worry that they would back out. They had given their word to raise the money, and these people could not abide failing, losing face before their fellows.

He heard the squabble continuing in the patio and walked back to the door to listen. Now they were arguing, betting on who could raise his quota first, putting a thousand dollars each into the pot, six thousand for the winner. No university had ever had such enthusiastic backers. He wished Strindberg were there to hear it. The old professor had sounded very unsure that he could really deliver, but then, Strindberg did not know the fierce competitive urge by which this group lived.

He had had his own doubts, the doubts of a man to whom success is vitally important, and he had labored under a fear that his true motivation would be discovered. Sam Jordan had touched close to it once, asking for the real reason why he had left industry, but that too he had been able to divert, turning their attention until they had become so engrossed in the *how* that they had forgotten the *why*.

If he had been cornered into answering that question, if he had had to explain that he intended to use his success at Wellington as a power base from which to move into politics, they would have been on him with a whoop and a holler. He would have become their captive tool.

He had to be free of them before he could take his next

46

step. Any associate of Sam Jordan was automatically suspect in the public mind. He must build an image, a background that had nothing to do with business, that could be investigated without any conflict of interest being uncovered.

He needed these men now, but a continued close association with them could become a kiss of death. Even Strindberg, who was neither a businessman nor a politician, had recognized this and made it a telling point in his sales talk.

8

☐ Martin Luther Strindberg had long ago discovered that the head of a department in a university must not only know his subject and the art of administration to be effective. He must also be an accomplished trader. Practically everyone from whom he wanted something wanted something in return. The trick was, not to pay too high a price.

He was not cynical. Cynicism was for the shallow minded. He accepted people as they were and worked with them as best he could. He seldom stood up and fought directly, for in his opinion everyone lost in a knock-down fight, whether it be a lawsuit or a war. His methods were indirect, and his list of accomplishments through indirection was long and impressive.

Thus he approached the problem of Emory Monck. He believed that he knew and understood Monck better than anyone else, and he was fully aware that any appeal not offset by an offer of reward might as well be shouted on the wind. Monck had demonstrated early that in business affairs he was impervious to sentiment. He could be swayed by logic, but only if the premise on which it was predicated was entirely sound.

The boy's success in industry had not surprised him. From the beginning he had watched Emory's development, sometimes in horror, always in fascination, and precocious children were not the kind of novelty that might deceive him. His wife had spent most of her life working with them.

Too often when an individual is markedly advanced in one area it is to the detriment of his other facets, but this had not been a problem of Monck's. In an unusually free childhood he had breezed through his elementary education, which, given his restless mind and ability to learn, had never required more than a portion of his attention. The unusual number of scrapes he had gotten himself into did not stem from any maliciousness in Emory. They came about because he was inquisitive, and because of his boundless energy and lively imagination. He had considered his parents emotionally too close to turn to, and it had been Strindberg rather than Austin Monck who had repeatedly come to his rescue.

When Professor Monck had retired and decided to move to Greece where, he dreamed, he could commune with the ghosts of the men he had for so long interpreted to his students, it had seemed perfectly natural to everyone that Emory should move into the Strindberg house.

The arrangement had worked out well for all concerned, in effect giving Strindberg a built-in laboratory where he could watch a developing mind as closely as he might watch an experimental guinea pig. He had only once imposed his will on Emory during their association, and even then he had had to prove his point by logic. This had come at a crossroad, just before Emory's graduation. He had flung himself into the study that night, seventeen years old, his thin face set, his eyes bright with unshed tears.

"I don't get it." He was too upset for a greeting. "Those guys from DuPont and Allied Chemical and General Electric have been around talking to every one of the graduates except me. So I went up to see the one from GE. I told him I had the highest grades in the class, that I'd made Phi Beta Kappa and I asked him what was the matter, was my hair too blue or something . . ."

Strindberg shoved back his creaking swivel chair and lifted his feet to the desk top, preparing for a long session.

"You know what the jerk said? He said, 'You're too young for us, Sonny, I'll see you in three or four years.' What kind of an answer is that? They're paying Pete Moses seven thousand to start and he got three B's."

"Hold it up," said Strindberg. "Where's the fire? Are you afraid GE's going out of business before you get there? You'll get over being too young soon enough."

The boy perched angrily on a corner of the desk. "Damnit, Martin, I'm tired of being too young. Ever since

48

I can remember that's been the excuse. I was too young to start in Helen's school, so I went through the first grade stuff in six months. I was too young to be business manager of the Annual, but I sold twice as much advertising as anybody ever did before . . ."

"You mean that team of freshmen you put together did," Strindberg said drily.

"I told them how." The voice rose resentfully. "I picked out the storekeepers for them to see and I figured out the pitch that each of them would go for."

Strindberg sighed, accepting a fact that he could not change. He had hoped that Monck would turn to teaching, but it had become more and more apparent that the boy had no interest in the profession. So, if he was headed for a life in industry he had better be prepared.

"Well, while you're sweating out getting old you might as well be working on your master's. You're tired of electronics, I've seen that. Why don't you give business administration a whirl?"

It was a new idea. Emory's eyes widened and then half-closed as his mind studied it.

"That's not bad. I've watched what happened to some of the fellows in science; they wind up doing research on a dull salary and taking orders from some salesman who doesn't know what *pi* means. But gee, I hate to waste the time. I had it all figured out I could make a million dollars before I was thirty." He threw his arms wide to show how big a million dollars was.

"Kid, you've been in a hurry since the first day I saw you, sitting in your gocart crying because your mother wasn't pushing it fast enough. So you want to be the boy millionaire. What are you going to do with the rest of your life? Sit on your butt and count your money? Play golf? Go fishing? Die of boredom?"

Strindberg thought that the thing he liked most about Emory was the surprise element. The anger was washed away by his budding interest in a business master's; the making of his million had been put behind him. His whole young body relaxed and he stood up, walking around, toeing a scrap of litter on the carpet, in unconscious mimicry of some carefully deliberating businessman.

"I've been thinking about that." From anyone else his age it would have sounded juvenile. "I think that after

I've made as much money as I'll need I'll go into politics. That's where the power lies today, in Washington, and it's going to get more so as the government gets bigger and bigger. Some day they'll tell business what to charge for its product and tell labor what wages it can have."

"Sounds like Communism."

Monck shook his head quickly without looking up. "It's not that, but our society is getting so complex that we're going to have to have wider controls."

"And you'll be on the controlling side. You shooting for the White House?"

The face came up, open and eager for a split second, then closing with thought again.

"Quit kidding, Martin. That's a thousand to one shot for anybody, and it's overrated at that. There are other spots nearly as powerful and they last longer than eight years. In the long run they've got more muscle. Some of the committee chairmen carry a lot of weight, and go on and on. And the majority leader doesn't have to take off his hat to anyone, even to the President."

"That depends on the majority leader." Strindberg sounded somewhat choked.

Emory was too caught up in his vision to take offense. "You think I'm talking through my hat again, but look, Martin. If I can figure out a way to get elected while I'm young enough, and can keep getting re-elected, seniority will move me up. That's the great part about the Senate, you don't have to really do anything, you just have to be there."

"Your master's and your doctor's first," Strindberg said. "If you're going that route you'll want all the advantages you can get."

Twelve years later Monck had made no move to step aboard that escalator, and Strindberg could only pray that the interest was still there, dormant.

Physically Monck had not changed a lot. His body had filled out but not thickened, his hair was more carefully groomed, his dress was more artful, but his face still had the thin intensity of his inner drive, his voice still held the bubble of subsurface laughter.

"Martin, it's good to see you. It's been a long time."

It had been a long time, nearly three years since Monck had been lured back to deliver the commencement address, Strindberg recalled aloud.

"It's been a busy three years," Monck said, and because this was his old friend he allowed a note of boastfulness to tell in his voice. "I've been building this plant and getting it open. The whole place is experimental. Come and have a look."

Underfoot there was a constant vacuum system and overhead an air cleaner and fortifier straining out pollution, because, Monck explained, industry could no longer afford dirt.

Strindberg was like a kid in a toy factory, admiring the gadgets, the products being designed and created here, being tested for later commercial uses. There was a great amount of automation, but the doctor felt a real sting of jealousy in visiting the shops, the laboratories where a small army of young scientists worked. They had so much equipment that he dreamed of having at Wellington. But he was not there to be jealous, he was on a selling mission.

The grand tour took on the proportions of a parade as word spread that the eminent man was a visitor, and he began his campaign with those who gathered around him. Gracious, complimentary, he used his opportunities to flatter Monck.

"Great, isn't he? He's an organizer, huh? He's doing a good job?"

It took him two hours to maneuver Monck back into the privacy of his office, but it had been time well spent. Emory had loosened the guard of hard alertness that he had learned to keep up in his business world; he had subtly fallen back into their old association of mentor and protégé, and Strindberg played on this carefully.

Sinking with a sigh into the deep couch, he said, "I'm proud of you, Emory." He was proud, and he was not too far from meaning what he said next. "And if things don't straighten out I may be back, asking you for a job."

Monck raised an eyebrow hopefully. He would give a lot to have Martin Strindberg with him. "What's up? Are you really thinking of quitting teaching?"

"I'm afraid it's about to quit me, at Wellington anyhow, and I don't want to start over at another school."

"What do you mean?"

"School's broke." Strindberg shifted his position unhappily.

Monck looked let down. "Oh, come on, Martin. They always did cry poor. Every time anyone wanted a new lab or new books for the library, they were broke."

"This time they mean it." Strindberg spread his knees and folded his arms on them, looking beaten. "Amos let the strength of the presidency die by default. He's good at Latin but he's no administrator, so the chancellor's office has come to be the power center, and the last one ran us into the ground."

Business oriented as he was, Monck's interest in the subject picked up. "Who was he? What did he do?"

"Jim Dice, a promoter the trustees brought in when he sold them a bill of goods; he said he could make Wellington a rich and powerful institution. All we needed was advertising, he said, and the money would roll in. He got them to hire a big name football coach and put on a recruiting program."

"That must have paid off, they held Notre Dame to a scoreless tie last season."

"It didn't pay for the new stadium, or the three buildings that aren't finished for lack of funds. Dice was a snake oil salesman at handling General Fenton and the trustees, but he never did get around to the big fund-raising drive he had promised."

"And the financial committee didn't do anything about it until now?" Monck was wondering how much of a bite Strindberg was going to put on him. He thought he could stand a couple of thousand. That was what an alumnus was supposed to be good for.

"Dice had Dr. Bellows snowed too. He's financial vice-president, but he didn't come to until the bondholders began to scream. Now it's too late."

"How much do you need?"

Strindberg flapped his hands hopelessly. "Near as we can tell from a quick audit is about ten million to get us through the coming year . . ."

"Ten million." Monck had been opening his desk drawer, reaching for his checkbook. He closed it hurriedly. "Ten million? And where do you expect to get money like that?"

"We don't. That's why I said I might be asking you for a job. It looks like we're going to fold up."

There was no worry about Strindberg finding another

job, but the suggestion that Wellington might close struck Monck as unrealistic.

"Martin, schools don't go out of business."

"You sure of that? More colleges in this country have gone bankrupt than have survived. It takes money to run them."

"Of course, but like Sam Jordan says, there's always a way to find money, with a little imagination."

"I wish we could hire Sam Jordan."

Monck laughed at his mind's picture of Sam running a university. "They'd do a lot of things no school ever did before."

"They'd better if they want to stay alive. You wouldn't happen to know a wheeler-dealer with enough larceny in him to help us out in a hurry, would you? He doesn't have to be an educator."

Monck's smile showed his sympathy at the older man's naïveté. "Not for free, I'm afraid. What could he get out of it?"

Strindberg rubbed the side of his head reflectively. "Depends on who he is and what he wants. The job doesn't pay anything to speak of, per se, but if he wanted public exposure as a hero he'd get the vote for a hundred mile radius . . ."

Emory Monck sat very still, and a smile twitched at the corner of his mouth. His tone was very soft. "Political vote, you mean?"

Strindberg shrugged elaborately.

"Martin," Monck's laughter trembled behind his words, "you wouldn't be trying to con me, would you?"

Strindberg said ruefully, "Well, I was going to try. I remembered that when you were a kid you were going to be the majority leader, but I guess it's no good. You're nearly thirty now, and you haven't made a move in that direction."

"Oh, I've still got plans, although they're going to take longer than I thought they would at first. But what you're suggesting doesn't make sense."

Strindberg drew an uneven breath, trying to cover his sudden elation. "It doesn't seem to, at first thought. You've made a big success in industry, a lot of money, and that takes brains. Brains are a good recommendation for a cabinet post. But I've noticed a peculiarity about people,

53

sort of a superstition. They still seem to believe down deep in their hearts that any man who makes more than a hundred thousand dollars has to be a crook."

"I've got news for you, Martin," Monck grinned. "They aren't too wrong."

Strindberg nodded in sage agreement. "Maybe so. Anyhow, do you think suspicion is an asset in getting people to vote for you?" He gave Monck a brief moment to think about this, then said more briskly, "Well, it doesn't matter if you're going to stay here and pile up more dough and never go into politics. You'll do fine for some years yet. But then it comes back to that other thing we talked about. When you get tired of getting richer what have you got to be interested in?"

Monck picked up a pencil from his desk and twisted it back and forth in his fingers.

"You haven't even got a wife."

"It takes time to get married."

Strindberg thought of his own romance. He had met Helen at a teachers' conference in Chicago thirty years before. She had introduced him as the principal speaker and he had taken her to dinner afterward.

"I don't believe in marriage," she told him. "I believe women are the equal of men in every respect, but marriage still perpetuates the double standard."

"Granted." She was a very attractive woman and he did not argue with attractive women.

"Sex has virtually nothing to do with marriage."

"Granted again."

"And sex is an important part of each individual life."

"I heartily agree."

They were married three days later, and only a very few times had he regretted it.

"Time isn't the reason, Emory, you've just been all-engrossed in the challenge of outthinking the world. But a balance sheet makes a cold bedmate, and when you've got all the money you can use, the challenge of making more is pretty empty. Your mind is too active to put up with that kind of slow death."

Monck's eyes had turned brooding, dark and unseeing. "You think I'd find fulfillment as Chancellor of Wellington University?"

"Only as a first step toward a career in Washington,

54

which could keep you busier than a spider on a hot skillet the rest of your life, with something of real importance at stake all the while. Now you're the big shot of this company here in Ventura, but how many California voters ever heard of you?"

The eyes began to glow, windows through which Strindberg might watch a mind sprinting ahead of the things he was saying.

"California politics is a grab bag, people come out here with no roots, no feeling for the government, mentally disenfranchised. Even party labels don't mean much. Unless you have already held a political office, or are some kind of celebrity you have a hell of a job building a public image. But let's assume for the moment that you came back to Wellington, did the impossible, saved the life of the school. What would you have going for you then? First, you're the savior of the whole community; they'd love you for that alone, and on top of it you're the local boy who made good, which reflects on their pride. Now look at the dividends. You are divorced from industry and the stigma attached to that. You're clean. And you've got every educator in the state throwing his stature behind you.

"Give us a couple of years. Then we'll run you for Congress."

Monck held up his hands, trying to slow down the gathering impetus, but Strindberg overrode him.

"This isn't blue-sky talk, Emory. It's for real. Senator Lightner has just been re-elected. He's sixty-eight years old. The odds are loaded that he will not stand for another term six years from now. He's a personal friend of mine, and we can use this term to groom you to stand in his place."

Emory Monck shook his head as though he were coming out of a trance. "You know, Martin, I've been underestimating you. You ought to be with Sam Jordan. Why don't you go out and raise your money?"

Strindberg grunted. "Because I don't know how. But I do happen to know you, and what you can do, and what you really want, and that's just as good."

"Supposing I fall on my face? Supposing I give up what I'm doing and then can't bail you out. What do I do then?"

For the first time Strindberg looked glum. "That could happen. I know I'm handing you one hell of an order to fill." The eyes he raised to Monck held no sheen of cunning now, there was an honest, desperate pleading in them.

Monck needed to see that, to be convinced. He dug in his pocket and pulled out a folded bill, grinning at the doctor.

"A dollar says I can get your first year's dough in six months."

9

□ Strindberg paid off the bet in two months instead of six, at the rally in the new stadium. He stood on the stage erected in the middle of the field, beneath the *WELCOME HOME EMORY* banner and proved his showmanship, fumbling through his pockets, saying loud enough that the public address system carried the aside to everyone in the crowded bleachers:

"I know I've got a dollar here somewhere . . ."

He found it, waved it over his head and made the presentation grandly, setting the tone for the celebration. It was a gay, noisy, colorful day.

Monck had not been on a football field since he had left the school, but the din of yelling students, the gyrations of frolicking cheer leaders, the excitement of the pompom forest wildly shaking brought the old days rushing back and made him laugh aloud. It did not matter that the ceremony they had come to watch was not a game, it was an excuse to make noise, blow off steam, use up some of the energy that crackled through the crowd. The autumn foliage of the trees beyond the stadium, yellow maple, maroon oak, vermillion sumac, the extravagance of crimson ivy, spread the air of carnival across the hills. The girls' bright dresses, the boys' shirts focused it in the rising tiers of seats, and the October sunshine promised peace and plenty to the school that had so lately been beleaguered.

It was a happy campus; that seemed evident although Monck had not had time until now to notice, but the phrase came to him as he listened to Cec Eliot, the student body president, whipping up the enthusiasm of his audience. He had felt it when the student press had interviewed him en masse and the *Daily Warrior* had run a long, laudatory, and self-congratulatory story emphasizing his Wel-

56

lington background, recalling exploits and escapades, bragging, "Now that we've got Emory back, watch us blast off."

He had not been on the ground much in these first few weeks, what with winding up at Alcon and taking the precaution of sitting in on the establishment of the Educational Assistance Foundation. The *Warrior* had addressed another effusive column to that, singling out the members of the Jordan group for short biographical attention and thanking by name all of the other ninety-four contributing corporate heads.

Also, the news weeklies and the wire services had cut into his time. While less emotional they had been equally interested in Wellington's new lease on life. They too recapitulated the business histories of the incongruously selfless officers of the new foundation. That kind of money was national news. Emory Monck rated a *Time* cover and the artist had demanded several sittings. But it was valuable exposure for him.

In another aside, this one unheard by either the microphones or the university trustees seated behind him, Strindberg told him, "Take a look around you. In four years every one of these kids is going to be voting."

"Pipe down." Monck did not interrupt his waving acknowledgment of the ovation. "I don't want even a whisper of that yet."

Still, it did look like an auspicious occasion. He felt the excitement and it came through his speech, giving it a warm ring.

Even the trustees looked pleased, eight aging men like a row of black crows perched on a fence, and he hoped that the mood would carry over to the formal meeting of the board tomorrow.

Some of them he vaguely remembered; they had been fixtures when he was a boy. But as he talked half of his mind was working ahead, looking at them from the changed point of view, trying to analyze how each of them would react to his reorganization schedule.

He wished for one of the tools of his business days, a staff of investigators who could bring him a dossier on the character and habits of each man. He and Strindberg had talked about them, but Strindberg was not an objective witness and his biases could not be relied on.

57

Amos Wellington, who had let the presidential position sink into unimportance, would not be a factor, and apparently the three clerics—Dr. Townsend, retired, Dr. McKenzie, head of the Council of Ohio Churches, and Dr. Clafflin, a pastor of a church in Pittsburgh—were merely useless appendages. Old Amos had specified the inclusion of three churchmen to insure that religion would continue to be taught, and that, Strindberg insisted, was their only area of interest. Dr. Binford of Cleveland, once a noted heart surgeon, could be counted in a like category of single-minded concern of long standing. He wanted a medical college. Edgar Hyman, who had been the vice-president of an express company, and Don Dundee, president of the alumni association, owner of a wholesale hardware store in Wheeling, one-time manager of the Wellington Warriors, whom Strindberg sneered at as a Joe College, were the only two members that Monck could conceivably associate with business. In them he hoped that he might find understanding.

From Jerome Fenton he expected some argument. They had already had one minor brush over the general's righteous protest that the money was tainted because of the Jordan-Gordon Randall clique. Fenton had recalled a Senate investigation scandal involving the group and their rough usage of another general. Military men, like elephants, do not forget; nor do they forgive. He had finally accepted the rationale that money itself could not be guilty of anything, and that any stigma he felt to be attached to the precious funds would be cleansed by the use to which they would now be put. Another clash would come when Fenton discovered that the military's beloved committee system was not going to prevail under Monck's administration of those funds.

At least, Monck thought, he would have a chance to meet these men individually and size them up briefly at the reception after the rally, a cocktail party that Amos and his daughter were giving.

The last speech was applauded. The last flash card message wished him good luck. The band played and the assemblage rose for a solemn rendering of *Wellington We Will Remember*. Monck sang the words without stumbling. He would never forget the phrases drummed into him throughout his youth.

58

Wellington our alma mater,
Hallowed halls in ivy dressed,
Reigning o'er Ohio's water,
With all glories are you blessed.

Wellington we will remember
Down the corridor of years.
There will ever live an ember
In our hearts to quell our fears.

Wellington we will remember,
Wellington——

As the last strains left the stadium still standing he walked with Strindberg and Fenton, making a slow way through the reporters, photographers, gladhanders, toward the old manse, and there took his place in the receiving line beside Alice Wellington.

There was no reason, he thought, why he should be so agreeably surprised at the change eight years had made in what he remembered as a skinny little girl who had dogged him around the campus. He had not seen her on his single return, to address the graduating class, because she had been in Europe, so that the impact was undiluted, and it took his breath. She was gracious rather than beautiful, but the effect was the same. She was a poised hostess in command of her job, and by all standards the best-groomed woman in the room.

Because it was instinctive with Monck to look first at the distant future and second at the present, it came into his mind without any accompanying emotion that she would make a very fitting wife. He was not unfeeling. He believed that pride in his wife would generate a more solid affection than the passions which he had seen trip up other young executives by saddling them with women who could not keep pace with them.

It was not sheer theorizing; he himself had barely escaped. During his last year at Wellington there had been a Polish girl whose father was a puddler in the mill. Zonia had a fervent interest in politics and a burning determination to change the world for the better, plus an early ripened musky allure, pomegranate lips and purple eyes. The spring had been so ecstatic, the affair so flagrant that Helen Strindberg had tried to interfere. But no personal appeal could have put out the fire, and it had taken the new job with Arabian Southern Oil to rescue him. They would not send a married man overseas. He went, promising earnestly to return to her, but when he did come back Zonia had married a teacher from Riverdale High School and her first baby was on the way. The loss had sickened him at the time, but it had sobered him. He wondered if she still lived down the hill, how many kids she now had in the old red brick, factory-like elementary school in the cramped town.

His memory of Zonia no longer loomed as a romantic tragedy, for in the Sam Jordan league women had a different importance. They were stage dressing useful in business entertaining; they provided warm solace when a man needed to unwind; the wives were women of strong character.

He watched Alice Wellington as she manipulated her party, and knew that it was not an easy task. Most of the department heads remembered Monck with doubtful pleasure, as a boy too smart for his age, wild and unpredictable, "full of the devil" in Amos' words, likable but an unsettling experience, and his reentry into their midst as their superior, their chancellor, apparently was causing uneasiness. They were glad enough for the money he represented but they were fearful of the winds of change he was certain to bring with him.

Conversation lagged. The rooms broke up into small groups seeking safety in familiar company. These people had known each other for a long time; they were not only neighbors but were bound together by their like occupations, their day-by-day, hour-by-hour association, an exposure that made few personal secrets possible.

The campus was like a peacetime army post, the wives restless under the restrictions laid upon their lives by their husbands' status, the men working too close to home, without the safety valve of a daily trip away to break the inevitable tensions. Growing up in its midst, Monck had only occasionally been aware of the explosive situation, when a chance remark, overheard, had whispered of some carefully veiled indiscretion. There had been dismissals, scandals, but these were hushed up quickly and hardly rippled the still water. The prevailing ethical code was a holdover from the days when the school had been church dominated and there had been no major revolt against conformity.

Monck felt the weight of unanswered questions among them, but no one would be so impolite as to ask them in this social atmosphere. He was on view, to be looked at, to be greeted briefly and then retreated from. There was a coldness, made more apparent by its contrast to the hallelujah spirit in the stadium. He could get nothing but banalities out of the trustees, although he exerted all of the charm that usually broke down barriers. He began to realize that he was going to meet resistance at the business meeting. Furthermore, the punch was innocuous and the food too sweet. He felt the need of a drink, of several drinks.

The ordeal eventually came to an end; the Strindbergs were the last to leave. Helen wrapped an arm around his shoulders. To all purposes she was his foster mother, yet his affection for her was not filial. He respected her for her tested ability, but he had never felt any special warmth for her.

"I am proud of you," she said, in much the same tone she had used to congratulate him when in his childhood he had succeeded in reading a full page of *Ivanhoe* aloud. "I hope you'll be happy back here."

She went away then, her hand under her husband's burly arm, and he found himself alone with the Wellingtons. A maid, one of the coeds who worked part time for the family, began to clear away the debris. Amos Wellington came over, stoking the pipe that he had punctiliously reserved for this show of fellowship.

"A highly satisfying evening," he pronounced. His round, slightly baby face looked pinker because of the crown of white hair, and his eyes asked for reassurance.

Put a toga on him, Monck thought, and he could double for one of his well-fed Roman senators. He was having difficulty containing his urge to get away.

"Thank you for the party," was the most enthusiasm he could muster.

"Well, it's my bedtime. Good night, children."

Amos' meaning was clumsily clear; he did not expect Monck to leave yet. He took himself out of the parlor and climbed the stairs deliberately. The maid had vanished into the kitchen. Alice Wellington looked up at Emory with the first real smile he had seen since entering the house, as if she were genuinely glad that he was there.

On impulse he said, "Let's go somewhere and get drunk."

He saw her startled reaction and heard her defensive laugh.

"I saw you making faces over the punch. There's a bottle of bourbon here . . . I keep it for Martin. I'll get it."

"To hell with your bourbon. I want to go somewhere with lights and noise and uncurl my toes. This has been a bitch of a day."

Her tone was uncertain. "Riverdale's still a local option town; there's nothing closer than Wheeling."

"So let's go to Wheeling. You need a coat?"

"Not tonight."

"Then let's go." He reached for her arm, but she still hesitated.

"Well . . . all right. I'll have to tell Father." An obedient daughter, she turned to the stairs.

After she had gone he thought, What in hell have I got myself into? But it was too late to renege, and he was heartened by the eagerness with which she came back down, tying a filmy scarf over her head, a purple accent to the white dress.

By an accident that Wellington found meaningful, the old house that Monck's parents had used had been available, and had been assigned to him, a square yellow box directly back of the manse, hidden from it by the trees in the combined rear yards. Emory led the girl out through the screened porch and across the lawns.

As they passed the old barn that had once housed the Wellington carriages, which were now replaced by a single car, Alice had a spate of giggles.

"Remember how horrified you were the day I caught you stealing eggs from our haymow, and I kissed you?"

He grinned at her. "I'm still shocked. I was fifteen years old and you were about ten. It was humiliating."

"It was exciting. You were my idol."

"Most discerning of you."

Back to back with the barn was his garage, both too short and too narrow for today's cars, and he left her beside the sagging door to bring the Impala out. The Continental had seemed too ostentatious for the campus.

The old, narrow, and winding road down the hill to Riverdale had been widened and straightened, costing more, Monck thought, in the loss of pastoral beauty than the improvements were worth in efficiency. The covered bridge that had spanned the stream which the road had followed was gone, and the stream itself was edged with fresh rubble dumped along its near bank in the only two places where the new road approached it. Ranch-type houses, built since he had gone away, along the rim of the bluff, blocked the once lovely view across the gorge.

The town that climbed the steep hillside in tall, narrow buildings was shrouded in a grimy mix of smoke and night fog rising from the warm water into the cooler air. In the harsh, soot-blackened brick walls, the dull eyes of windows opaque with dirt, or broken, dripped tired drops of black moisture, as though they wept with hopelessness.

"River towns," he said. "They're all alike. There's no greater ugliness on earth. It's criminal the way this country has misused its rivers. This looks even worse than I remember."

"Hideous," she agreed. "How did it ever happen? In Europe everybody glorifies the waterways. And Riverdale is worse than you remember. For a while we had a Navy base and things boomed a little. People got a taste of something better, but now that's gone and they've sunk back lower than before. If the school had closed you could have swept the whole town into the river and forgotten it. You're a local hero, did you know?"

Monck chalked up another score for the image he intended to build, but he did not mention it.

"How come the Navy base closed?"

"Part of the defense cutback, I suppose. The town did everything it could to save it, but no luck."

"How big was it?"

"Well, at the peak it had about twelve thousand personnel plus a lot of local civilian employees."

"And what's happened to it now?"

"Not a thing. The weeds are growing up in the streets and in another year or two the buildings will probably start to fall down. There have been rumors that it was for sale, but so far I guess there haven't been any takers. This is Appalachia, Emory, a dying country. More and more of the steel plants are moving toward Chicago and Detroit."

The river highway had not been improved except for a make-shift widening of the shoulders, leaving the old crown still hazardous. Traffic was heavy, mostly monstrous trucks thundering down grades and crawling up them, and it took nearly an hour to do the twenty miles to Bellaire, where, Wheeling being as depressing as Riverdale, he crossed the bridge with scant anticipation.

10

☐ Papa Perino's was redecorated but otherwise unchanged. It had started as a speak in the roaring twenties and survived as an institution, well into its third generation of family management. It was a long, dark cellar with a smoked-beam ceiling, a bar along one wall, a handkerchief-sized dance floor and a four-piece combo that catered to the musical tastes of a clientele old enough to be financially rewarding. The prices as well as the tempo kept student patronage at a minimum. It was a haven for escapees from four-letter dances and orgiastic rhythms.

In his mood of reaction against the lifeless party, Monck would have preferred a younger crowd. He thought briefly of the old religious sects whose people, after six days of solemn, prudent labor, on the seventh gave themselves up to hysteric possession by impulses they hoped were godly. And he wondered if the frug and its relatives were not possibly the same kind of relief valve for youngsters burdened too heavily by a world in woeful flux. He also wondered if Alice had chosen Papa's as the place they were least likely to run into anyone who might carry gossip back to the university, and decided with amusement that his guess was right.

But the scotch was good. The girl ordered hers with "a little water and no ice," and he made another guess.

"European training?"

"Uh-huh. And it sort of mollifies my father. He has one cocktail before dinner and a brandy after. If I'm going to drink at all it makes him feel better if it looks like an affectation."

"Nice thinking," He laughed with her and then apologized as their knees knocked together under the tiny table.

He discovered that he had to initiate conversation, whether because she was naturally not talkative or had cultivated reticence as a form of flattery, offering others the stage, he did not know. But he wanted to get her talking, to hear her version of the school's undercurrents.

"Do you like Europe?"

"Paris. London was cold and dreary when I was there, but Ireland was beautiful."

"So I've heard . . ." He thought that he should have taken time to visit Ireland, but there was so little time, and there had never been a business reason. He did not make trips for pure pleasure. "Paris strikes me as a tourist trap; I never saw a Frenchman who didn't have his hand out."

"I think it depends on where you stay, and what your own attitude is. My father loved Paris, and it was his dream that I should study there after I finished college."

"Artist?"

"Singer. At least I tried to be, but I wasn't the greatest and I never liked being second-best." Her tone turned lightly bitter. "One generous young man told me I hadn't suffered enough yet to sing with the necessary passion. In spite of . . ." Her voice dried up and she hurried to finish her drink.

For her urge to be the best he admired her. "In spite of what, a sour love affair?"

She was reluctant for a moment, but people talked to Emory Monck and she needed to talk to someone.

"I found the right guy, at least I thought I did, but he was married."

He saw the taut lines drawn suddenly in her face, and motioned to the waiter, indicating their glasses.

"Bad?"

She grimaced. "Bad at times. Maybe it was my own fault, maybe it was the way I was raised, the stultifying atmosphere we grew up in. I was able to cut loose for the first time in my life, but apparently not all the way. I'm not sorry. At least it's something to remember."

"Want to talk about him?"

She shook her head, and when the new drinks were delivered she swallowed hers rapidly, as if to wash away the temptation.

"I'd just make a fool of myself, and I hate women who

65

cry in public. Let me take a rain check."

"Any time. So let's talk about the school. I'd like to pick your brains."

"About what?"

"For instance, the people I'll be meeting with tomorrow."

She looked puzzled. "How do you mean?" Automatically she raised her empty glass toward her lips, glanced at it and set it on the table again.

He caught the waiter's eye and then told her, "Well, in selling anything it's an axiom that the more you know about the man you're talking to the more you can tailor your argument to make him understand, to make him buy. Among lawyers they call it preparation. In business we have staffs of investigators who dig up all the information about a man they can, a biography, if you like. It gives you the advantage of being able to make capital of his peculiarities rather than having those peculiarities crop up as surprise liabilities to spoil a deal."

"That sounds sneaky. That's spying, isn't it?" Outrage coupled with uncertainty gave her voice a comic lift and made them both laugh.

"Technically, yes it is, but since it's practiced on both sides its effect is to save a lot of time and avoid a lot of false starts. It's quite approved in the business world."

She watched his smile for a long moment, sipping her fresh drink and then lifted her eyebrows dubiously. "Well, learn a little every day. And I suppose the trustees do know a lot more about you than you do about them. Yes . . . I guess you'll need all the ammunition you can get if, as Martin says, you're going to reorganize the administration." Her eyes brightened and her chuckle had a mischievous energy, but her tone was fond. "The old dears are a little stuffy."

A new animation made her flush, made her fidgety, but then she caught herself up, still cautious.

"First, you tell me something. General Fenton is very upset because all of the money you raised was put into a foundation. He told my father it ought to be turned over directly to the university, that it was raised in Wellington's name. How do you answer that?"

"Cold business logic. If you had the responsibility for those funds would you trust them to the same people who

66

let Jim Dice bankrupt the school? And actually the school had nothing to do with the money being made available. The men who raised it have never seen the campus and probably never will. They did what they did because I sold them a bill of goods, and even so they didn't even give me a place on the foundation board of directors. Satisfied?"

"Eminently." Her tone was teasing, and she abandoned all pretense of distaste for gossip. "Now, where do we start? I feel deliciously salacious."

"Let's start with the scuttlebutt. What's the rumor factory saying?"

"Well . . . some of the trustees and the professors too have come to see Father. They're worried that you'll try to come in like an iron man. From some hints that Martin has dropped they're afraid you want to turn the school into a business concern. Students are always rebels, of course, and they're keyed up to badger you for changes they want." She stretched her arm across the table, laying her hand over his. "Emory, you are not really an educator. Please think carefully what you're doing before you hack away some wonderful old traditions."

He smiled at her, turning his hand over and squeezing her fingers. "There are good traditions, and there is slavery to habits that have lost their usefulness. Is that sacrosanct to you too?"

"No. . . . But sometimes it's hard to tell the difference, and you're going to have opposition, which can make it harder."

"Thanks for the warning. Now how about the people I'll have to convince?"

They went down the list, but other than the rumors of a few funny peccadilloes involving Dundee and Hyman, Monck learned nothing particularly useful. Alice knew them all, but only by their appearance as her father's guests, and her interest in them had never been analytic. Still, the telling took a couple of hours. Concentrating, mining for information, he was unaware of how drunk the girl was getting. Accustomed to the Jordan crowd's high tolerance for alcohol, he had not given it a thought.

Then a stray giggle alerted him. He got her on her feet and out into the air quickly. In the parking lot she swayed against him and he tightened his support on her arm. She balked, spreading her feet to find a steady footing, shaking her head to clear it and saying in a surprised voice:

"You know something, Emory Monck, I'm looped."

"So I notice. Are you all right? You're not going to be sick?"

"I feel wonderful." She threw her arm in a wide arc. "Feel better than I have since I came home from Europe. Free . . . free . . ."

He piloted her to the car, got her into it and crawled under the wheel with a haunting presentiment. In his present uncertain relationship with the university authorities all he needed was to be seen bringing the president's daughter home pie-eyed.

Her exhilaration collapsed and she slumped into the corner of the seat. He thought, he hoped, that she had gone to sleep, that a twenty-mile nap in the night air would clear her head and rescue her dignity.

He drove more slowly than necessary; the fog had thickened and headlights came out of it at him like tracer bullets, making even normal speed impossible. The cool dampness was refreshing to him, and since there was nothing he could do for the girl for the next hour or so he tried to enjoy the ride, humming softly and remembering other nights just such as this, laughing to himself that the same worries bothering him now had hung over his head more terribly then.

Riverdale was silent and still, even the traffic lights dark, the road up the hill a relief, with no other car on it. Then they climbed above the fog bank and the girl startled him, speaking without opening her eyes.

"We nearly home?"

"Two or three miles."

"Oh boy." She giggled. "I hope Daddy is asleep. He's never seen me loaded."

Fervently Emory hoped the same thing. "Better sit up," he said. "I'll go around the back way and the chances are there'll be nobody there at this time of night. But just in case . . ."

She straightened obediently, plumped her hair up with her fingers and tied her scarf over it, but the gestures had a conscious, now-I-will-do-this quality that warned him she was not yet sober.

There was no one at the rear gate; there seldom was.

And the street winding past the fifty or so houses to his place was deserted. He cut his headlights and coasted quietly into his driveway and on around the house to his garage.

The girl made no effort to get out, but sat as if frozen or paralyzed or asleep again. He went around the car and opened her door, touching her shoulder.

"Here we are."

She blinked at him but did not move. He took hold of her arm, pulling her toward him.

"Come on, kid, let's get you inside."

Like an automaton she swung her feet out of the car, slid them to the ground, and he drew her upright. She hung onto the open door, swaying, and then with a lurch threw her arms up, around his neck, and sagged against him. He caught her around the waist, holding the limp body from sinking to the ground. In a surprise move she stiffened, pulled his head down and found his lips with an unmistakably violent kiss.

At another time Monck would have been glad to cooperate, but not now. He pulled back and held her away.

"Easy, Alice."

She did not resent the rebuff; in fact he was sure that she did not know what she was doing. He stood debating whether to take her to his house and try to get coffee into her or to sneak her home. He decided on her place, afraid that at his she might go to sleep and he would be unable to rouse her.

A light burned in the lower hall of the Wellington house but the rest was in darkness. He picked her up and carried her across the yard. He had a clear memory of the interior of the house; in his day none of the doors had ever been locked, but he held his breath until he had sidled with his burden into the kitchen.

Here there was stygian darkness. Emory Monck sweated, praying that he would not stumble against some obstacle that would sound a clattering alarm. He found the rear stairs and cursed them because they were so narrow and steep. He had to rearrange Alice, throw her over his shoulder with her head and arms dangling down behind, and in this manner he squeezed up the steps to the second-floor hall. This was dark too and he stopped, faced with the problem of deciding which of the several bedrooms that opened on it might be hers.

Balancing the girl, he fumbled his cigarette lighter from his pocket, flipped up the little flame and tiptoed to the nearest door. The hinges were well oiled and it opened without sound, but it was not the right room, and he felt that it would be less than gallant to betray her by depositing her in a place she would obviously not have chosen herself.

He backed out and tried two other doors and behind the second found an acceptably feminine boudoir. He carried the girl inside, closed the door and turned on the light, then bent and rolled her onto the bed. Hurrying now, he pulled off her shoes, turned her over enough to loosen the zipper at the neck of her dress and then the one at the side seam, since the waist appeared too tight for comfort. The house still held enough of the day's heat that he did not think she needed a blanket. He saw that her eyes were open, that at least some of her rag doll limpness was sham, but he was too anxious to get out of there even to be angry. He patted her cheek, switched off the light and opened the door.

He stepped into the hall and collided with a solid but yielding bulk.

A shout of fearful astonishment hurled him back. Bare feet scurried across the carpet and the bulb in the ceiling socket came on, illuminating Amos Wellington in a white nightshirt, his hand still on the switch, his hair tangled and standing upright in a caricature of terror, his pupils dilated from the recent darkness, giving emphasis to the incredulity on his face. He did not look frightened, possibly because there had not been time for fear to register, but more likely because in all of his life there had never been any cause for fear within this house. The bulb also illuminated Emory Monck, rigid in a wrestler's crouch and stamped with guilty knowledge.

Fifteen years were sloughed away and Emory was trapped in the beam of Amos' flashlight, on Amos' roof on Halloween, wiring the skeleton from the art department against a chimney, straddling the gable.

The bedroom door behind him opened and Alice's disheveled head thrust out, pressed against the jamb.

"Who yelled?"

Emory Monck could not help himself. From the bottom of his being a flood of laughter choked him and then gushed out, loud, raucous, unstoppable. It came with sharp enunciation, Ha, ha, ha, and Ho, ho, ho, surging up again and again. Tears blinded him and the convulsion of his face squeezed his eyes shut. His stomach trembled. He leaned against the wall weakly, surrendering to the tempest. When it was spent he felt surprisingly cleansed of all the day's hypocrisies.

Amos Wellington stayed where he was. "I'm not sure that I find this so very funny," he said. "Alice, I suppose you can tell me what's going on?"

The girl stepped into the hall, smoothing down her skirt, but she was barefoot, her zipper gaped and she was wobbly on her feet. Also, Emory's hysteria was contagious and she was giggling again.

"It's all right, Daddy, really. It isn't as bad as it looks. I just had too much to drink. Emory had to bring me upstairs because I couldn't make it. I'm sorry we woke you."

"You didn't wake me." The scholar could not abide a misinterpretation. "I was going to the bathroom. He bumped into me. But where have you been?"

Monck straightened, trying to gather his scattered wits. "Doctor, blame it on me. I was so busy listening to what she was saying that I didn't watch out for her."

Wellington interrupted with emphasis. "Where were you?"

It penetrated through to Monck that the man was more concerned over who might have seen them than he was with his daughter's inebriation, and his cynicism returned.

"You can quit worrying on that score. We were at Perino's in Wheeling, and there was no one else from here. There's no harm done. She may have a hangover, but otherwise she is unscathed."

"I don't need your reassurance that she will survive a binge, Emory. I was a young man something less than a century ago, and not altogether a clod . . ."

The words gave Monck an odd sensation that a veil was being lifted to reveal an unknown personality. It had never crossed his mind that Amos had had a youth.

". . . And I doubt that you are stupid enough to come to this campus and involve yourself capriciously in a seduction that would reflect on your new standing here. You're too cold-blooded. But you appear to have forgotten that in a community as small as ours you can do great harm to my daughter by exposing her to malicious speculation. Now go home and think over whether you admire the risk you took."

Monck took his licking like a schoolboy, because he felt that he deserved it. "You are perfectly right, Doctor. Alice, I apologize, and I'd appreciate a chance to make amends later. Good night. Good night, Doctor."

On the walk across the dark yard he knew that Wellington was right. He was in a different world here, and another careless misstep could trip him up and play hell. As it was, he may have jeopardized any possibility of cooperation from the president, and at the least Wellington would now be on watchful guard, less sympathetic than he might have been. He had lost the advantage of his years away, his growing up. In Amos' eyes he was still a reckless hooligan kid no different from those in the dormitories along the edge of the campus.

As if to rub it in, there was a hullabaloo of some kind going on down there now, late as it was, shouts and screams that sounded like a riot, and he felt a twinge of sympathy for those who would be called on the carpet tomorrow. He grinned, thinking of the times when he had been embroiled in noisy flare-ups and of the trouble in which they had landed him. He was still close enough to the students' age to understand how volatile they were. He began to trot as an explosion of energy hit him, demanding his physical participation.

He ran the last few steps, caught the post that supported the rear porch roof and swung himself aboard. The telephone was ringing inside. He went through the kitchen hurriedly, flicking on the lights, with a growing foreboding that the ruckus had got out of hand, that the chancellor was being called to quiet it. He wondered if he was going to have to make his first official act a disciplinary one.

The voice that answered his hello said, "Kid, is our football team going to beat Syracuse Saturday?"

It took Monck a minute to orient himself. "Sam? Where are you? What's the matter?" The clock on the desk read quarter past three.

Sam Jordan said, "I'm at the Spring. Are the Warriors going to win and if so by how much?"

"How the hell do I know, and what do you care?"

"I got a guy here that graduated from Syracuse. He's offering me six points. Is that good or bad?"

As far as Monck knew Sam Jordan had never seen a football game or shown any interest in them. But again, when Sam associated himself with anything, he leaped in all the way. Now he had apparently adopted the Warriors as his own personal team.

"Sam, I haven't even seen them play."

"We beat the tar out of a Big Ten outfit last week, and this jerk wants to bet me ten thousand, but I don't take that kind of a bet blind. Call up the coach and see what he thinks."

Monck choked on his laughter. He held the phone away from him and looked at it. He had a picture of the coach, being dragged out of bed in the middle of the night to furnish betting information to the university's new chancellor.

"You've got to be kidding, Sam. I haven't even met him yet, and if I had I couldn't ask him that. It would lay us open to all kinds of charges."

"Well, hell," Sam was put out. "Where's the fun of having a team? How can I make any dough if I don't know who's going to win?"

11

☐ The girl on the front porch was petite, her dark hair teased into a round balloon that looked too sleek for anyone in such an upset state, making Monck suspect that it was a wig. Her black eyes were large and full of fury, and her fist was raised, poised to continue her pounding on the old panel as he yanked open the door.

"What is it?"

"They're taking them to jail. They're taking them in the patrol wagons . . ."

She was bouncing up and down on the balls of her feet, about to explode, or, Monck thought, to go into orbit. He had no idea who she was. He had barely hung up the phone on Jordan's call when the hammering had brought him running down the hall.

"All right," he said. "Slow down. Take a deep breath, a real deep one."

73

She obeyed without intending to.

"Now, first, who are you?" He had guessed that she was one of the coeds.

"Denise Dempsey, assistant dean of women. Come on." She reached for his wrist and swung toward the steps, then hauled up sharply when he did not move. "Oh, please."

"Just a second, Miss Dempsey." His hilarious reaction to Sam Jordan's recent demand carried over into his view of the girl before him; she was like a cricket on a burning log, and looked hardly old enough to be out of school. "Who is being taken to jail?"

"All twenty-five girls. Dr. Monck, please hurry."

As if to speed them on their way the yells and screams from the south side of the campus rose suddenly to a higher, more ominous pitch. The girl spun away to run, but he caught her arm and held on, shaking her to get her attention.

"What twenty-five girls? One minute either way isn't going to make much difference. Stand still and tell me what's happened."

After a small moan of impatience and a sigh of surrender, but with no lessening of the rush in her words she said, "Girls from Tathford Hall. They went over to Harner, that's one of the men's dorms."

"I know."

"They all took sleeping bags and spread them out in the upper hall, they said it was a 'sleep-in.' They're trying to protest the late privilege rules . . . they are archaic, you know. . . . They're tired of being treated like delinquent children."

"But what happened? The quicker you tell me the quicker we can do something about it."

She was beginning to bounce again, like a loose lid on a steaming tea kettle. "The proctor discovered them and ordered them out, but they wouldn't leave. He called Pat Crowell, the campus police, and when he came the girls turned the fire hoses and the extinguishers on his men. Pat called the sheriff's office. Now they're hauling the girls out bodily and putting them in the cars. . . ."

She wrenched her arm free, ran to the steps and jumped to the walk, landing lightly in her soft, heelless shoes and racing away up the street.

Monck debated going for his car, decided that that

would take longer than cutting across the commons on foot, and followed the girl. He ran easily, more than half-inclined to laugh at the picture that rose in his mind of the look there must be on Esther Hollister's face. The dean of women had clung to her post for nearly thirty years, inflexible, stemming the tide of changing mores with an indomitable frontal presentation of her awe-inspiring bust. Monck had run afoul of her too often, and he had a deep pity for those who would face her wrath now.

Lights were coming on in the houses he passed and ahead of him the tumult was growing. As he rounded the last building and had a view down the long green swale through the trees he found an eerie, sobering sight. He could see a dozen cars parked haphazardly, in front of Harner Hall, red lights blinking in a frenzy and spotlights poking angry white fingers along the line of the second-story windows. Yellow headlamps and other spots threw a glare over the area around the entrance and against this illumination silhouetted figures leaped and ran toward a churning crowd.

Monck began to run harder. He was now able to make out individuals, boys in shorts, boys in trousers, without shirts, girls in diaphanous peignoirs with their hair rolled around pink plastic curlers, some cruelly exposed and some tucked under spangled, tufted or tulle rosetted coifs. Some were yelling, some were screaming, making a terrific din. The crowd filled the street and spilled over into the lawns and flower beds. There was a more or less stationary fringe of onlookers, but within that circle was bedlam.

Denise Dempsey had vanished behind the human wall. Monck dived after her and broke through into the roiling riot.

By now the sheriff's officers had been supplemented by police from the Riverdale force, and a double line of these had formed an alley leading from the doorway to a huddle of patrol wagons. Through this chute half-dressed girls were being wrestled, dragged, and shoved.

"Oh shit."

Emory Monck said it aloud, as the humor of the situation dissolved. A campus fracas was one thing. But this had gone far past the horseplay stage; it was rushing toward a point where violence would explode and people would be hurt. Riverdale was a mill town and mill towns are not gentle places. Neither are their police gentle. They are chosen and trained to be an intimidating force capable of keeping the lid clamped tight on a community of men of brawny muscle and violent appetites.

Monck headed for the doorway, charging, butting into the dense and angry pack. He heard his name shouted as he was recognized but could not tell if the voices were friendly. A boy spun and without looking drove an elbow into his ribs, then grunted, aghast, and squeezed out of Monck's way. Hands pushed him forward and others shoved him aside. The crescendo of noise rose, but he did not think it had anything to do with him.

He craned to see over the heads, catching a glimpse of the tousled evacuees stumbling through the door. Anger welled up within him. A concert of indignation howled around him. The dormitory hall filled with echoing, hysteric shrieks. Two of the Riverdale police, in uniform, were carrying a girl outside. She was spread-eagled between them, wriggling, kicking out, shaking her head, flinging her long, loose red hair about as if it were a lash, making all the noise she could. She was lugged across the high porch and down the steps. The men carrying her looked unaffected, bored. Tonight's duty was a Sunday picnic beside some of the brawls that erupted along the river front, the battles they had to put down and try to survive without being mutilated.

But the student audience was shocked by this display of brute strength, which looked even more offensive by contrast to the spindly arms and legs of the tender figure thrashing helplessly in the policemen's hold.

Esther Hollister was not in sight. Forcing his way forward with more and more difficulty, Monck could see none of the university authorities on the porch. The stone slab was held by a single, formidable figure, a burly giant in khaki with thick legs rooted solidly and a bull horn against his mouth.

Rocks and bottles were being thrown. Monck caught one on his shoulder. Individual fights made the whole mass move like an ocean, and he was caught up in a general forward surge. The cordon walling off the alley stiffened, linked arms and braced itself against an imminent onrush. There was a threat of immediate tragedy. A battle was closing.

"Tear gas."

Monck had reached the fence of uniforms which was now bending inward under the pressure of the mob. He was at the steps when the order through the bull horn hit him in a deafening vibration. He shouted his name and the word chancellor against the set, red face of a policeman straining to maintain his link in the line. It took a while for the man to comprehend his meaning and another moment for him to bend aside and give Monck room to squirm through under the twined arms.

His clothes showed the mauling he had taken. He ran up the steps and waved his hand before the man in khaki, trying to attract his attention.

"Sheriff," he could not control the tremble that anger put in his voice, "I'm Emory Monck, the new chancellor here . . ."

"Later. I'm busy." The voice sounded flat and small as against the bellow it had had through the horn.

"Now, God damnit. No gas. Hold the gas."

"Nuts. You want a stampede here?"

"Let me have the horn a minute. Let me talk to them."

The sheriff glanced at him, glanced at the mob swaying against the cordon, and passed over the horn.

"Try it . . ." There was little confidence in his tone.

"Cool it, you guys. Cool it." Monck shouted through the horn, waving his free arm, gesturing at them to back up.

From this height he could see the perimeter of the mob, the outbreaks already started there, scuffles, a shoving match toward which a policeman was running, a boy in a white shirt throwing a fist at a blue uniform, a small group making an end run either toward or away from some hot spot. Now he could identify some members of the faculty collaring what people they could, hurling them back, shouting orders that had not much effect. He saw Amos Wellington scampering out of the shadowed trees, and saw Martin Strindberg appear from nowhere, head off the president and lead him out of harm's way.

Across the mayhem, his mind's eye pictured the next morning's headlines: RIOT, POLICE, MANIA AT WELLINGTON.

"Cool it, I said. I'll take care of the girls. They'll be released. If you want to help them let's not have a war. Flake off. Let the cars through. I'll handle it." He kept talking, hoping that the raucous horn would command their attention. They would have to listen to unscramble the words from their gritty echoes, and curiosity and the discipline of listening might stop them long enough to break the mounting rhythm of emotion.

Whether or not it would have worked, he was too late. The order calling for tear gas had not been rescinded. He became aware of the low, warning snarl of a siren and saw the lead patrol wagon begin to move, inching into the mob that surrounded it. Its lights gave a solid look to a sinking cloud of smoke from which the students were recoiling, staggering, bending over and running to escape.

A ragged path was cleared and the cars filed slowly through it. The epidemic of coughing and choking penetrated to the core of the ranks struggling against the police fence. The mob's attention veered, and it turned around, layer by layer. The waterfall of sound diminished, splintered into isolated shouts and catcalls; the pattern of disintegration spread as small groups drifted back and away.

Pat Crowell, chief of the campus security force, came out of the dormitory, a big-shouldered man with thick white hair and a broad red face which he was mopping with the sleeve of his jacket. He was another of the old guard whom Emory had reason to remember. Emory turned his attention from the crowd, which was still large and still dangerous if some new spark should ignite it again. His own anger was not extinguished yet.

"Pat, what in the devil made you call in the law?"

Crowell was tired. "Hello, Emory. Those girls are crazy. In thirty-five years I never saw anything like what they did. They turned the fire hoses on us; they threw bottles and stuff at us; then they threatened to burn down the hall if we rousted them. I believe they'd have tried. I didn't have any choice. I had to yell for help."

"Why didn't you call me?"

"I did, when the trouble first started. There wasn't any answer."

Below them the police cordon was beginning to relax, and Denise Dempsey ducked through, evaded a reaching hand and ran up the steps, asking for the horn. She was not bouncing now. Her hair was wildly disordered but she was intact, and she looked ferociously calm. He passed the instrument to her. It covered her face when she raised it, but the crowd had seen her and they waited.

"Everybody go home now." She said it as quietly as anything can be said through a bull horn. "Chancellor Monck will have the girls released, and he will listen to their request. Don't you think this is a shameful way to behave after what he has already done for you? And with this his first day on the campus?"

She turned to Monck, extended the horn for him to take and thanked him with a solemn nod; then she walked down the steps and through the aisle, facing from side to side with shooing motions of her hands as if she were scattering a flock of chickens.

A queer embarrassed silence trailed after her. The assistant dean of women walked to the one remaining wagon, into which the shrieking girl had been tossed, and stepped inside it.

Pat Crowell went down the steps heavily, circling out into the uncertain crowd. The temper had gone out of them and he coaxed them wearily.

"Come on boys, break it up. Get back to bed, fellas. Let's go home now, the excitement's all over . . ."

The police fence had dissolved. Individual policemen moved without hurry, easing the remnants of the mob back, circling off toward the patrol cars, pulling out. Still the wagon remained, the driver and his partner standing at the rear door apparently arguing with Dempsey. They turned as Monck came toward them and the driver said:

"Okay, Chancellor, climb aboard if you're riding with us."

He looked inside. Dempsey was sitting on a bench beside the long-haired girl. There were four others huddling in silence on the opposite side. Wellington's new chancellor got into the patrol wagon.

12

☐ Riverdale waking up looked like an old, unkempt man with the granddaddy of hangovers. The fog clung, heavy and motionless, cutting visibility to half a block, wetting everything. It made mud of the trash and grit on the street in front of the courthouse. It concentrated the sour, astringent smell of coal gas and chemicals, but even that was better than the smells of the old jail. Trucks bombed past the intersection, leaving the air quaking, and occasionally cars poked like timid mice into the coming day. Yellow oval lights attached to nothing hung in the soup at the second-story level, windows of apartments above stores where people were getting up, getting dressed, getting ready to slink down the rear stairs and feel their way to other holes where their jobs were. The gray dawn spread and saturated the fog with a harsh luminosity that hurt the eyes.

Emory Monck came out of the courthouse, located the orange glow from the all-night Eatery down on the corner, across the street, and headed toward it, frustrated, disgusted, in a mood to match the town.

The windows were steamed on the inside, sooty on the out. He shoved the narrow door open and went into a bright, white room. The floor was made of the small white hexagonal tiles that used to be familiar in men's rooms, slick with the dampness brought in from outdoors and sweating from the inside humidity. The walls to the height of the booths were white plastic tile, also sweating. Above the tile the walls and ceilings were of waffle-patterned tin, painted white a long time ago. The lower part of this was now a cream color; the color deepened through ochre hues as it climbed and became a pale umber near the ceiling and across it. But the total effect was white, lighted by three fixtures with white glass parasol reflectors that dangled on long chains down the center of the room. A short-order counter with revolving stools took up the wall that abutted the next building; a row of ice-cream parlor tables paralleled it and across an aisle a row of high-backed, plastic-covered booths hugged against the windows that faced the side street. Garlic had been a staple of the cooking here for years.

Nicholas, a thick, happy man, kept open for the jail and bail trade and sometimes traded off with his counterman in taking the night shift. There wasn't as much traffic then but what there was had some spice to it. Tonight there was too much spice. Hs had heard the riot squad go out long after midnight, and later Denise Dempsey from the university had come boiling in, phoned Al Conner, and the publicity man had shown up minutes later. Now the two of them sat glumly in the booth waiting for Emory. Nicholas' nose was somewhat out of joint that Monck had not yet been down to see him; he had retired behind his counter, behind his *Form*. But he could not hold a grudge and when the door opened again he dropped the paper and yelled.

"Jesuschrist, Emory. What the hell it takes a riot before you come say hello? Howsa kid?"

He threw an arm across the counter, bare, thick, white fleshed with black fur that ran all the way down the back of the soft hand and two joints of his fingers.

Monck detoured to pump the hand, to grin, to point incidentally toward the coffee urn. "Right back where I started, Nicholas." The man had broken a lot of heads in his battle not to be called Nick. "In trouble with the cops." He squeezed the hand again and went on to the booth.

Denise Dempsey watched him come, trying to read his face, giving him the impression of a large question mark leaning toward him. The man opposite her stood up and Monck shook hands with him.

"Al Conner, public relations. Glad to meet you, Dr. Monck. Sit down." The man slid back into the booth and Monck sat down beside him. "What's the score? You get them out?"

Nicholas arrived with fresh coffee and wedged his bulk in beside Dempsey to listen and commiserate.

Monck's head moved left and right, quickly, in troubled impatience. "All except the girls with us were booked by the time we got there. They can't be bailed out until after a hearing before the judge, and the cops claim the judge is out of town until around nine o'clock. I don't believe it, but that doesn't help." He looked across at the girl, seeing her mouth open and knowing what her first question was going to be. Where were the four from the last wagon, in which he had come down? He beat her to it. "Your redhead . . . Martha Yates? . . . didn't hear a thing you told her. She put on quite a show." In spite of his anger with the coed the funny side of it forced him to smile. "I could have kept her and the other three out, but she got on a soap box. She was the leader of the movement, she said, this was the best break they could have, the publicity would force us to meet their demands, they were not going to be divided and conquered, and all of them, by God, were going to jail for what they believed was right.

"I tried to tell her that she'd already made her point, but she wasn't about to trust me. Then the others backed her up and they all sprawled down on the floor. The cops laughed like hell, but they wouldn't put the kids back in the wagon and haul them up the hill again, and I'm just a suspicious enough old bastard not to want them loose over there on the outside of the bars.

"So we booked them and locked them up. I did make sure they were all in a tank by themselves; they moved the other women down the hall."

Beside him, Conner had his arms crossed on the table, leaning his weight on them. His body was shaking with deep mirth.

"Too bad. The whores might have learned something."

Monck glanced at Denise Dempsey to see if she were offended, but she puckered her face and stuck the tip of her tongue out at Conner.

"Well," she said, "if you hadn't been in such a hurry to rush me out of there, if you had let me phone Al from the station instead of dashing over here, I might have been able to do something with them."

Conner was not in the least excited. He winked at Nicholas. "I think he did it on purpose, Dempsey. The way you sounded they'd have locked you up too."

Her mouth twisted, acknowledging the charge. "Anyhow, I can understand how Martha felt. She doesn't know enough about you yet, Dr. Monck, and she hasn't got anywhere trying to talk to Esther Hollister . . ."

"By the way, where was Esther tonight?"

"In Pittsburgh, visiting her sister. She'll be here in the morning."

"Just as well she wasn't around. Now, Conner, I have to meet with the board at nine. Suppose you can be at the girls' hearing and bail them out?"

The public relations man moved his cup in a circle, dragging the wet ring after it. "Depends on how much the bail is."

Monck found his checkbook, signed a blank check and left it on the table. Conner picked it up, pursed his lips and raised his thick eyebrows in admiration.

Without any real hope Monck said, "What do you think the chances are of blowing down the story? It's too late for the morning papers . . ."

82

"Nil. You think a wire editor is going to pass over a riot about twenty-five girls in a men's dorm? There were half a dozen people down here to cover your show in the stadium, and a couple of them stayed over. You'll get coverage . . . maybe I can tone it down some . . . I dunno." He looked up at the clock above the door. "Let me out, I'll go camp on the jail stoop in case some joker gets up early. But don't hope for too much. This town will buzz like a hive of wasps."

Monck stood up, letting the man pass him, then sat down again and watched him ramble to the door. Conner was squat, square, his head chunky, his black hair thinning and graying, his face brooding, long but squared off at the jaw. He really looked like a newspaperman. Monck decided that he liked him. An early customer came in as Conner went out, and Nicholas excused himself to go make a breakfast.

Monck looked back at the girl. "Dempsey, it would help me if you'd start at the beginning and tell me what made this thing happen tonight, last night."

"Do I keep calling you Doctor?"

"Try Emory. Monck, if you want."

"I don't like the sound of that. It doesn't fit the way you look. I'll use Emory. It happened last night because everybody was keyed up at the stadium and it carried over. They had a bonfire there right after dark, and there were a lot of parties. But mostly I think Martha planned it like a general . . . hit the enemy before he gets organized, get to you before the status quo people do. She's such an anachronism, so young, idealistic, vulnerable, but so shrewd in her militance. Her father is an editorial writer on the Detroit *Press* and she knows how to make publicity work for her. She's got the students behind her partly because she's a very good folk singer, partly because she wants to fight all their battles."

Her eyes came up to meet his in a way that made him see her with her fists doubled, in a John L. Sullivan stance. Unfortunately he laughed.

"It isn't funny. The kids have several legitimate gripes."

"I was laughing at you. Your name fits you all right, but you're not big enough for the shoes."

"You want to bet?"

Her smile, the first time he had seen it, changed her face entirely. Her small chin jutted out, asking to be hit; her cheeks turned into little red crab apples and her eyes squinted into two long slits deep behind her long, dense lashes. Her mouth lost none of its full bow as it spread, and it tucked in at the corners the same way Monck's did.

"Okay, tell me about the gripes, starting with the hot potato in our hands now."

"This I am going to enjoy; I've been muzzled a lot longer than I care for. Do you remember, when you were in school, that the girls were allowed to be out until ten-thirty only two nights a week, and once a month until twelve-thirty?"

He nodded and she returned the nod.

"Do you know how long that rule had been around then?"

He shook his head.

"Forty years. Fifty years now. And if Esther Hollister has her way it will stay around. It's too ridiculous. Martha and a committee went to the old dragon the day after registration and asked for a change. Hollister said she would take it up with the faculty committee, but she hasn't done it. So the sleep-in was a protest. The girls are tired of being second-class citizens."

It was the kind of call to arms that Monck had thoroughly enjoyed in his undergraduate years. He had been a rebel then, and the time spent with Sam Jordan had not changed him. He wished that he could have seen the defiant entourage lugging their sleeping bags across the dark lawns, bedding down in the male sanctuary, not, he thought, that there would have been any objection from the boys.

He missed some of what she was saying, but he picked up the thread again. It was a night for soap boxes.

"Protest is the American way, Emory. Civil rights, anti-war, anti-this, and pro-that. Look at the demonstrations women had to put on to be allowed to vote. It's a hundred years now since American colleges began admitting women, and since then we've made our place in industry, politics, even in the armed forces. The eastern colleges are beginning to admit that coeds are grown-ups capable of making decisions. They can visit the men's rooms there. Men and women can talk to each other as equals,

84

without the insidious distinction between a supposed higher and lower intellect . . ."

"Intellect, huh? Somewhere I got the idea that libido was involved . . ."

She was so wound up that she took the interruption at face value. "Of course it is. When wasn't it? But sex is a lot more comfortable in a bed than it is across a console and two bucket seats or in a wet haystack in some farmer's muddy barnyard. And the kind of trauma, the criminal syndrome that goes with sneaking around in dark corners is the worst thing that can happen to a girl. With that beaten into her she may never have a decent orgasm, not in all of her life. Do you know how many American married women never do, never, never? More than twenty-five percent. And that, Mr. Emory Monck, is sin."

Monck reached hastily for his handkerchief and trumpeted into it. When he could, he said, "Have you spoken to Esther Hollister about this aspect?"

"Hollister. I'll lay you ten, five and even she's never had a man in her life."

"Dempsey, you do have a flair for phrase making."

13

☐ He stood under the shower, as hot as he could tolerate it, until the hot water gave out, then turned it off and let the cold spray jolt him back into human shape. He dressed carefully to create an image of de facto dominance and durability, and two cups of hot black coffee helped to restore the inner man. He picked up the sheaf of presentations, got in his car and turned it toward the administration building.

After the night's hiatus he doubted that the meeting would go as he had intended, with his taking up the points of his program aloud, expanding and elucidating them, countering the objections that both Strindberg and Alice Wellington had warned him would be raised. He had no doubt that, talking to them one by one within the group, he could bring them around. He had been up against harder cases at Alcon, and if he could hold his own with Sam Jordan's crowd he could certainly handle this dilettante board of directors. But he guessed that their minds would not be on any long-range program today.

Thank God he had made up the presentation. It was printed and it was bound, which in itself, experience had proved, was an effective conditioner. Whatever the matter might be, if it was printed it carried authority.

His proposals were broken down into specifics with a time table for each: for securing grants from industry for research; for creating the facilities in which the research would be conducted, for borrowing specialists already noted in their different fields as lecturers, demonstrators, visiting experts who could guide and stimulate the work; for a schedule of royalties on successful products by which Wellington could build an income which would make the school self-supporting.

Newsweek had already got wind of the idea and the involvement of the Sam Jordan wheeler-dealers. It had dubbed Wellington the Wheeler-Dealer University, and Monck knew that this was going to draw fire from the conservatives. To counteract this he had thought it necessary to lay out in black and white the assurance that he was not turning Wellington into a trade school. They were justifiably proud of their academic standing and the high quality of the faculty, for which Martin Strindberg was largely responsible. They had struggled out from under the demeaning nickname of "cow college" and the provincial image that embarrassed so many Midwestern schools, and they were just as suspicious of the trade school label.

Therefore, the presentation included Dr. Binford's new medical college, hospital, and an ambitious medical research establishment. It was not only bait, it fitted naturally into the new pattern.

According to Strindberg, Don Dundee, the alumni association president, thought the rest of the school was there to support the football team, so that came in for mention. And it belonged because it earned its way, not necessarily financially, but because it was their window to the non-academic world. Bucky Buckhorn, their middle guard, a giant Negro who tipped the scales at two hundred and sixty, had made All-America and gone on to sign with the New York Jets for a reputed thousand dollars a pound, giving Wellington more newspaper exposure than all the scientific breakthroughs ever would.

86

But all of this meat Monck had placed at the back of the book, and led up to it through a short course in the history of American education that he thought would pull the teeth of anyone who wanted to resist change behind a mask of preserving tradition. There had always been change.

Change had dragged its feet, but it had come inexorably, and Monck traced it. The original nine colleges in the colonies had been patterned on Cambridge and Oxford, simply because the men responsible for them had been educated in England. But the training of young gentlemen in languages, religion, and history proved irrelevant in a pioneer land where a settler family's pressing concerns were to kill game for food, clear forests, grow corn and potatoes and hold their ground against Indians. Education was theoretically only for the sons of rich men, and the so-called physical arts were looked down upon.

It took Jefferson and Franklin, both non-college men, to force a grudging acceptance of the more practical sciences that were valuable to a developing industrial society.

Even the study of agriculture was ignored, although for the first hundred years farming was the country's major occupation. But the Morrill Land-Grant College Act of 1862 changed that; the A and M schools were established and degrees were given in fields other than the liberal arts.

After the Civil War the university at last made a break with the past. The emphasis on time spent in class, on rote learning, the looking backward gave way. America leaped to the German point of view: research, the discovery and creation of new knowledge turned the face of education toward the future.

The battle was still engaged, the schools still lagged behind industry in innovation, the professor still distrusted the man who worked from the profit motive, but further change was inevitable. Industry and education joining hands in partnership was the next step, already well under way. Hardly a recognized school in the country was not engaged in some kind of R and D activity for the government; eleven hundred were participating in the work-study set-up under the anti-poverty act. Tulsa had been given a laboratory by one of the major oil companies, to establish a petroleum institute. Emory Monck's proposals no longer looked wildly revolutionary, but instead hardly in advance of present-day practice.

And education was no longer for the wealthy few. Any number could play and there was increasing room for more; any bank would loan a qualified student all the money he needed for his schooling, loans guaranteed by the government.

Emory Monck did not see his job as focused on the students. Financing and teaching them was outside of his province. In an economic analogy, business and government were the consumer, the school the supplier. As the consumer demanded more products and higher quality, the supplier must produce them. The supplier's plant must expand, and expansion cost money. Emory believed that he was on the campus purely to manage the plant.

This was the second phase of his argument. The school had to have money for maintenance and development. Again he pointed to precedent. Early schools had tried to finance themselves in many ways, some through lotteries, some through business enterprises. He cited the California college that had embarked on a hydroelectric program to build a dam which hopefully would have furnished light and power to the city of Claremont, and he could not resist recalling the two Ohio schools that planted mulberry trees in the fond expectation that they could finance themselves on a skein of silk.

No sound came from the board room as he reached for the door, and he wondered if the trustees had not arrived. It was precisely nine o'clock. He had lingered in the car, timing his entrance.

The room was as silent as dust when he went in, but they were all there, sitting around the table, all except Don Dundee who stood at the water cooler drawing a paper cup full of what, to judge by his face, he hoped would turn out to be pure alcohol. They all looked at him, over his head at the clock, and back at him. There was a murmur of greeting that sounded more like a response in a litany.

Monck did not smile. He went around the table briskly, dealing out the presentation, a copy laid before each man, and took his chair at the foot of the table, pulling it forward with an emphatic tug. Perhaps after all he could beat them to the punch and side-track talk of the riot.

"Gentlemen," he said, but Dundee's voice rode him down.

"What the hell went on here last night anyhow? The Wheeling papers got me out of bed at five-thirty this morning and caught me with my pants down. I didn't know what to say."

He walked to the table as he talked, watching Monck to discover if his worst fears were true, feeling for his chair and slipping sideways into it. He was dressed in a business suit, white shirt and tie, but if you closed your eyes the after image would be of a turtle neck sweater, a red, round, overstuffed face and a bush of white hair too big to look like an organic part of him. He might have dealt in hardware for many years, but it had not erased the stamp that nature had put on him. He was an athletic coach.

Monck began again, but Dundee was not finished, he was so deep in his own woe that he probably did not even hear.

"I'm just glad it's an out of town game this weekend and not here at home, that's all I've got to say."

This time Monck waited to be sure, taking the opportunity to look for signs of the reaction of the others. General Fenton, he noted, sat at the head of the table. Amos Wellington was president of the university, but Fenton was chairman of the committee, and Monck thought that here was a pretty good example of the mechanics of power play, whether or not the military man was aware of the symbolism. Fenton looked the very model of the presiding officer at a court-martial. The three ministers' expressions deplored. Edgar Hyman, the express man, a sharp-billed tomtit, waited on a twig for something to peck at. His small body dipped forward when Fenton cleared his throat.

"I now call this meeting to order, and I would like to ask Mr. Monck for a report on last night's violence."

"Gentlemen." Emory waggled his copy of the presentation and dropped it back to the table. "I had hoped to discuss the business of administration with you this morning, but I guess the other matter does take precedence. It may be better at that if you will read this at your leisure, and we can talk it over another time. As to last night, Amos, you were there, what's your picture of the story?"

Fenton did not like it, but he did not object aloud, and Amos Wellington waved his hands in small, helpless circles in the air.

"I really don't know anything about it except that it was a shocking thing. Dr. Strindberg thought that I should not, ah, intrude my presence at the heat of the disturbance, and convinced me that you, Emory, were better able to control it."

Monck wondered if the man was remembering that a scant half hour earlier than his appearance on the fringe of the demonstration he had been dressing Emory down as a miscreant schoolboy hardly worthy of the faith he was professing here. It was less faith in him, Emory decided, than a tacit unwillingness to take responsibility, and the next plaintive words shored up that opinion.

"Properly, it was Esther Hollister's obligation to put a stop to it. I don't understand why she was not there."

"She was in Pittsburgh," Emory said. "I don't know that she's back yet. But I doubt that even she could have done much. As I understand it, a blow-up was due."

Dr. Binford dropped his glasses to the bulb of his nose and looked over them. "Do you mean that there was a reason behind such a disgraceful performance?"

"Are you unaware that the students have been asking for an updating of campus rules? Apparently they haven't even had recognition."

"That is no excuse," said the general. "A committee should be appointed to make a full investigation and punitive measures must be taken at the chancellor's level."

There was a nodding of agreement, not even a show of curiosity about the forces that had broken loose. Dr. Townsend's question sounded more like the salacious eagerness of a gossip than the concern of someone charged with the governing of a university.

"Is it true that the girls were taken to jail?"

"Twenty-five of them," said Monck. "They were thrown into the tank. The prostitutes were moved to another."

A night without sleep was not the best fortification for sitting in on such a tea party as this, but he knew that he should not be letting his impatience show. He had better get out of there. He said rapidly:

"They were to have a hearing about nine o'clock, and I left Al Conner, our publicity director, to post bail and try to keep them from talking to reporters. News coverage is unavoidable, but we're doing our best to prevent sensationalism. General, a committee isn't necessary, I'll undertake to look into the background and send each of you a written report.

"Now, I'd like to get back on it. Good morning, gentlemen."

He stood up and left, giving them no opportunity to hold him, knowing that none of them was going to do anything toward resolving the underlying causes of friction. Whatever was done he would have to do himself, and he discovered that he had been naïve in believing that the business end of the university was the only area he would have to deal with.

He did not know whether the girls had been freed, whether Dempsey had taken them in hand, or where Conner was now, and he guessed that the best place for him was in the chancellor's office, where he could be reached. He turned toward it, down the long hall.

The administration building had been built thirty years ago, and the architect had been a traditionalist. It was an oblong box with three stories above ground and a basement beneath. Like the other buildings, it was yellow brick, compact to conserve heat because the winters were cold here in the mountains, and for the same reason the window space was sparing. A central hall divided each of the floors lengthwise, and wide stairways connected the floors at either end of the building. The basement was crowded with files, and the odor of dust rose from there up the stair wells. The business offices, registration, accounting, and bursar, the detail crews needed to run a community of eleven thousand people, occupied all of the ground floor and overflowed onto the second, sharing that with the vice-president in charge of finance, the dean of men, and the dean of women. The conference room where the trustees met was at the head of the stairs at one end of the top floor, the chancellor's office at the other, and between them, on both sides of the corridor ran the offices of the president and the chairman of the trustees.

The walls were uniformly plaster above and wood paneling below, tough, enduring yellow oak. The furniture was oak; the desks were oak. The building presented a grim, unyielding face and its constant silent presence exerted a pressure, an influence on the people who worked there year after year. The greatest change that had ever been made in the building was the installation of a telephone system with its own switchboard.

Emory's secretary was on the phone when he opened the oak-paneled hall door and came into the antechamber. She was listening without interest, the receiver and a cigarette in one hand, the other hand sorting through the morning mail, filing most of it in the wastebasket beside her chair, opening other envelopes by anchoring them with an elbow and sliding a pencil along under the sealed flaps.

Vivienne Krump did not match the building and did not belong in it. She already had a vendetta going against its constricting force. A tall, heavily feminine woman in her mid-forties, an orange blonde wearing an orange dress and a bracelet of multiple strands of large brilliant beads, Monck had taken her with him from General Consolidated to Alcon, and had now brought her here. She was a businesswoman, able and valuable in screening out irrelevant material and people, capable of carrying a constant heavy work load, out of her element and bored in this rural setting. As one part of her battle against the room she had filled a corner of it with an enormous floral arrangement, extravagant with out-of-season iris, gladioli spears, sweet fern, ranunculi, carnation. It was a burst of springtime and did indeed drive back the blue-lipped ghosts that haunted here.

Monck put the tips of his thumb and forefinger together, stretched the rest of his hand like the barrel of a short gun and drew a bead on the flowers, an old signal of approval between them. Vivienne took the receiver away from her ear and covered it with the heel of her other palm; a voice was still coming through it. She smiled because he liked the flowers and then made a face that spelled trouble.

"The assistant dean of women is on fire. She wants to know the second you come in." Her brows went up to ask whether he wanted to talk to her now.

He reached for the instrument and said, "Dempsey? I just got here. Something wrong?"

"I'll be right up," she said, and broke the connection.

14

□ She must have run up the stairs. She bolted in from the hall just as Monck was sitting down at his desk. He had been through an exhausting thirty hours without rest, and he wished that she would stop acting like a tornado. But come to think of it, she had not had an easy night herself.

"Esther Hollister is back." She said it as she came through the inner door, closed it and leaned against it. "That woman . . . that woman . . ."

At another time it would be funny, this small, cute bundle of girl filled with a wrath and indignation too big to stay inside her and too tumultuous to find an orderly expression, but now it was tiring just to watch her. He leaned back in the swivel chair, as far as it would tilt.

"Dempsey, for God's sake, have a heart. Make sentences that I can understand."

"I'm sorry." She came forward, a little less precipitate. "We got the girls out and brought them up the hill, and they were pretty well cooled down. I guess that jail is something."

Monck remembered a night he had spent in it after a party at Revere House, and if it had not changed he knew what she meant.

"But Esther was already here and she'd heard the story. If she'd kept her big mouth shut I think everything would have quieted down, but oh no. She was breathing fire and not about to listen to anything. She suspended them. All of them. Ordered them off the campus. She's going to the faculty committee to get them expelled."

"Damn. Where are they now?"

A wicked humor made her dark eyes brighter. "In their dormitory, barricaded on the second floor, naked. Esther sent Pat Crowell to get them out and they threw their clothes out of the windows at him. He won't go in. She's down in the yard screeching at them and they're up there hooting and throwing pillows and clothes at her. She ordered Pat to seal off the building so no one can go in or out, says she's going to starve them into submission. You can guess the effect that had, every male on the campus is scratching around for a way to sneak food in. The reporters are . . ."

"The what? Where did they come from?"

"From the hearing. They followed us."

"Okay, let's go."

"What for? There's not a damned thing you can do. Esther told me it was my job to get the girls off the campus, and I'm not even going to try. I came up here to resign."

He was already at the door, with her following, and he waited until they were in the hall to answer.

"Hell with that. The first thing is to get the campus cops away from the building."

"Esther won't let you." She trailed him down the steps, running to keep up.

"Hell with Esther. Get in the car."

He ran toward the parking circle and held the car door for her, then climbed in and drove toward the dormitory.

The crowd was not as large as it had been the night before, and it was in a better humor. That at least was a relief. They were laughing, recognizing that the girls had the upper hand and enjoying the discomfiture of the authorities. The car was an advantage in forcing a way through; he pulled it to the curb, left the girl in it with orders to stay there, and headed for Pat Crowell who stood on the steps with two of his men, guarding the front door, looking embarrassed and unhappy. Strewn around the porch and the ground along the front of the building lay a limp clutter of clothing, dresses, skirts, capris, sweaters, blouses, slips, with a predominance of briefs, brassieres and bikini bits. Monck had trouble keeping his face from coming apart.

"Pat, get your men away from here and keep them clear of all dormitories and fraternity houses until you hear from me."

The security man shifted from one foot to the other. "Emory, Esther told me not to let anybody go in."

"I am the chancellor, Pat, not Esther. Where is she?"

"She left."

"I'll see her later. Now get your people moving."

The man was piteously relieved to have the burden

94

lifted from him. He gathered the men deployed around the building and herded them toward their car under a barrage of yells and cheers. Monck watched until they were gone, then lifted his face to the upper windows. There was no one visible but he knew that the girls were watching, listening, waiting for the next move.

He cupped his hands and called upward, that the guards were withdrawn and would not be back, that the girls were free to come or go as they chose, that he wanted to talk to their spokesman in his office later.

A panty girdle expertly thrown sailed from a window behind him. It landed on his head and the dangling garters wrapped around his neck in a stinging embrace. A shout of pure ecstasy erupted from the audience. Monck's temper blazed and for a moment he poised on the verge of charging into the building. Then a chill of sanity washed through him. If he broke he would be the loser; it was just what the crowd wanted. He pulled the girdle away and waved it over his head slowly, as if it were a trophy, and went deliberately down the steps to his car.

A tall man shoved away from it as he came up. "Chancellor, I'm Arthur Reedy of the *Press*. We'd like . . ."

"See Al Conner at the publicity office."

"We want a statement from you. Are you going to expel the girls?"

"No comment." Monck brushed around the man, got the door open and slid under the wheel.

Reedy's hand was on the window ledge. Monck started the motor and touched the control to raise the window, forcing the reporter to move his hand or get it caught.

"You'd better give me a statement, Chancellor . . ."

The car moved ahead. The girl said, "Is that smart?"

Monck had not wholly recovered from his flash of anger. "Hell with him."

"The photographer got a picture. You did look funny when that girdle hit you."

His laughter came with a rush, as sudden as breaking glass. "Good. That's all right. We can use a little fun around here, maybe it will loosen things up. What's so God damned serious?"

"The papers will laugh, you can bet on that."

"Fine. That ought to take the curse off the riot. But

we're going to have to wind up this revolution pretty quick or else lose a lot of face. You have any ideas?"

"I don't know. I can't see that much is changed. The girls are still suspended and they're still huddled up there in the altogether. They have a cause, or at least they think they have, and you're going to have to settle that before they quit. Maybe then . . . there's no real fun in fighting unless you have someone to fight against."

"Dempsey." He took a truly relaxed breath. "You not only swing a mean left, you throw a beautiful curve."

"How do you mean that?"

"Like you just came up with the answer, if I can bring it off. You go on and wait in my office, I'll stop and see Esther. Here, take this with you." He shoved the girdle into her lap. "It may be the only one the kid's got and I don't want her to have to come asking me for it."

He parked in the circle again, escorted her to the second floor and turned down the hall.

There was an owl-faced coed in the reception room of the office, a girl who drew back when Monck asked:

"Is Esther here?"

"I'll see, sir," she said, and started to rise.

"Don't bother." Monck waved her down, found the latch of the gate in the picket railing and went through to the closed door. He knocked but did not wait. Still, he did not think he surprised Esther Hollister.

The dean of women sat stiffly behind her desk, which faced the door from the far side of the room leaving a long no-man's land to be crossed in full exposure under the guns of her awesome glare, a chilling gamut for any girl called to account. The Hollister prow was tightly jacketed but still strained mightily against the mauve wool bodice of her dress and overthrust the hands knitted into a double fist on the edge of the desk.

"Emory." She opened the attack as if he were still an undergraduate within the radius of her domination. "I have just had a call from Pat Crowell."

"I rather thought you would, Esther. That's one reason why I dropped in."

He dropped further in, ambling forward with his hands shoved deep in his trousers' pockets, sitting down on her desk, smiling down on her as if she were the most beautiful creature in the world.

"I think we'd better get together on a reassessment of tactics, don't you?"

But there was no relaxation in the square, heavy cheeks. Instead she physically recoiled because he had used her given name. "Since you have seen fit to countermand my authority I don't know that there is anything we can discuss." The hurt to her pride quivered in her voice; she clearly expected him to apologize for wounding her.

His smile did not waver. "I didn't have much choice, Esther. We can't have the campus turned into either a battleground or a concentration camp. We've already had some unfortunate publicity, which we can ill afford while we're trying to rebuild our image, and the kids have got a point."

Her face reddened. "Martha Yates is a nasty little Communist out to make whatever trouble she can."

"I'm not interested in her politics, I'm interested in the school's policy, in keeping communication open between the students and ourselves. They have the right to be heard."

She became even more rigid. "Do you intend to let them run freely through each others' dormitories, cohabiting like wantons and profligates?"

"Now, Esther." He was glad that he was already smiling. "Let's not get our imaginations all inflamed. With the heavy work schedule in college today there just isn't enough time or energy left for sex to be the dominant reason why they want more freedom. Young people all around the world are terribly serious about the life climate they'll soon be moving into, civil rights, the preservation of freedom of the individual to function in a more and more controlled society. That's where you are casting yourself in the role of villain. We're not here as policemen, but to help, guide, advise when we're asked. Unless they trust us, they won't ask, and then we have failed in our primary reason for existing as a school: to provide a transition from childhood dependence into responsible adulthood."

"Emory Monck, don't you lecture to me about children. I have spent forty years handling them, and they're no different now than they ever were. They come in here like wild animals and they have to be taught discipline. The Lord knows they don't learn it at home any longer.

This is their last chance to learn it before they're turned loose on the country."

There was enough truth in that to remind him that any question can be argued from more than one side, but her totalitarian rule was not going to work any longer. He tried once more to get through to her.

"If you're talking about self-discipline I'll agree with you that they have to learn, but they have to learn it for themselves. They'll make mistakes, sure, and that means problems for us, but they're safer making them here than later. If we stifle all their initiative by dictating, permitting no freedom of choice, then we rob them of the chance to learn to make their own decisions."

He was talking to a stone wall. He saw it in her opaque stare.

Again she tried to club him. "Emory, you're too young for the job you have been given here, but since you have the title, and if you are going to insist on turning the campus over to these radicals, I have no alternative but to resign."

"We'll be sorry to see you go."

He stood up and left the room. He knew that she must have used the threat before and that she could not have visualized anyone actually calling her bluff. He closed the door on her dumfounded silence.

At Alcon he had had to clear away dead wood, to drop men who had built up the small companies of which the complex was composed but who were unable to readjust to the new broad conception, to keep up with the pace of change. Esther Hollister was dead wood in that she had failed to distinguish between today and forty years ago. Today it was an achievement for a student to maintain a grade level that permitted him even to enter a university, and such achievement bred a sense of individual importance as well as a sense of responsibility to the world that had been unknown a few generations back. Naturally such people felt that they should have more control over their daily lives, the right to learn by listening to diverse views and to say what they thought. How did she expect an inquiring mind to grow in a social or political vacuum? But it still saddened him to know that he had destroyed this woman. Even though she had destroyed herself by her inflexibility, it had been he who had taken advantage

98

of his knowledge of her and had jockeyed her, herded her into making the move he wanted made. That he had not fired her was a pure technicality.

He put the unpleasant thought aside. The road was cleared now for quieting the furors of the student body, not only the tempest over visiting and hours, but whatever other little bombs the kids decided to throw, and he was whistling when he came into his own office.

He expected to find Denise Dempsey in the front room with his secretary. Vivienne had a knack that she called getting acquainted; in a short time she could pump an amazing amount of personal information out of anyone she cornered, and he had not thought she would let this opportunity escape, but she was alone.

"Dempsey didn't come in?"

Vivienne aimed a thumb over her shoulder toward the inner office. "She's got a short fuse, hasn't she?"

"What happened?"

Vivienne pinched her nose and tilted it into the air, giving him a small, unfriendly laugh. "I got as far as finding out that her daddy trains race horses and won the Belmont Stakes last year; then she told me she was sure she was keeping me from doing something important and that she'd wait inside. Brush off."

"Forget it, she's upset over her girls. See if you can locate a boy named Cecil Eliot, he's president of the Student Senate, and ask him to come over here right away. And bring Martha Yates."

As she reached for the phone and a flip-up directory, he went past her and through the inner door.

The assistant dean of women turned away from the window and looked at him solemnly, ready to commiserate with another of Hollister's bruised victims. His smile confused her.

He said at once, "Esther decided she couldn't work with me. She's resigning."

"What . . . ?" It was a long-drawn, incredulous sound and it took her until he had crossed the room and sat down at his desk before she could find other words. "That's hard to believe. It's hard to imagine Wellington without her."

"Yes. But I think we'll survive. Sit down, Dempsey, and let's get reorganized before Cec Eliot comes up. I've sent for him. First, you will replace Esther immediately as acting dean. We'll get your official promotion later."

She dropped into the chair across the desk, aghast, repeating, "What . . . ? But that's impossible. I haven't the experience. I'm only twenty-six; I've only been out of school four years. It's too much responsibility."

She was gasping and he laughed at her. "You'll live through it; I'm only three years older than you, and I know you've got the kind of ideas we need."

"Yes, but . . ."

"Just relax and listen. Authority is not synonymous with age; it's only a matter of thinking a problem through to a workable solution and then implementing that. This is your chance to prove your ideas. We're going to make Wellington over, give it a new, young look to fit in a young age. By nineteen seventy, half the population of the country is going to be under twenty-five; it's going to be their nation and they've got to be ready for it. The people who will help them get ready have to think young enough to comprehend what motivates them, because, if the kids are going to run the country I live in, I want them to know what they're doing."

He watched her as he talked, wondering if he were overdoing it, and decided that he had when the enthusiasm he was trying to generate in her, which he saw rising in the new sparkle in her eyes, stalled and turned to calculation.

"You sound good," she said, "but at the back of my mind I have a feeling that a lot of it is window dressing, that you only mean half of what you're saying and that there's a reservation, something you keep holding back."

"You see too much." He was not displeased; it showed that she was thinking, but he wanted the conversation kept away from that area. "You're looking at the undecided part of me, but it's not a part I'm ashamed of. I don't like a man who thinks he's got all the questions answered. He's quit learning. I'd rather bet on someone like Sam Jordan. Old as he is he'll always listen to a new idea from anybody. And use it if he thinks it's good. For instance, when I quit Alcon he thought first that I'd been recruited by the opposition; then he thought I was crazy for quitting an assured future in the oil business to come back here. But in just a few minutes he got interested in the school's problems and took off running. Without him I never would have raised the money we needed."

If he thought he had sidetracked her, he was mistaken. "I'd like to ask just why you did come back. Nobody on the campus can figure it out."

So he had to meet it head on. "Sometime I'll answer that. I had what I considered a sound reason."

She did not appreciate being put off and it showed in the asperity in her voice. "I'm certain you did. I'm beginning to believe that you never did anything in your life without a reason. It makes me wonder why you want to appoint me dean."

He grinned at her. "I need you to hold my head."

"Oh, sure you do. And that's the last reason you'd do it. Now I want a straight answer."

"All right. Last night I saw how the students reacted to you, and how mad you were about the police intervention. I want you because the kids trust you; they'll feel free to bring their troubles to you, and you won't let them down."

She put a hand up quickly to stop him. "Don't get it into your head that I can talk those girls out of their protest."

"You won't have to."

Her eyes narrowed, looking straight into his as she tried to figure out just what he was doing to her.

"You're a con artist," she accused.

He shook his head. "Snake oil salesman."

Her feathers ruffled, she prepared to do battle against his trifling with her intelligence, but that had to be postponed. There was a short knock on the door; it was opened and Vivienne Krump admitted Cec Eliot to the room.

Monck had met him the day before at the stadium ceremony. He had been impeccably polite then but he walked in now with a belligerent caution. He was about six feet five, probably a basketball player, strong boned but very thin. His face was long and narrow, hollow cheeks and pointed chin showing through patches of a scraggly, dark beard. The eyes were arresting, very dark, set deep behind a high-bridged, thin nose, alert and intelligent and overzealous. This was a young man who espoused positions without due regard for their tenability, and who would not find compromise easy.

Monck was grateful that he was this easy to read. He

saw a small reflex of relaxation as Eliot recognized Denise Dempsey, but the boy tensed again with Monck's first words.

"Sit down, Mr. Eliot."

"I'll stand." The voice was higher than the speaker wished, but the challenge was there. He was not going to be intimidated.

"Suit yourself," Monck said agreeably. "You know Miss Dempsey, don't you? She's now our acting dean of women." He stopped to watch the reaction: a flicker of doubt and then a renewed look of truculence. It was not hard to guess that Eliot had been rehearsing his position and his speech all the way across the campus and that he did not intend to be thrown off stride. "Didn't Miss Yates come with you?"

This was closer to what the boy had expected and his arrogance was more secure. "She is not leaving the dormitory."

"Oh? Are they all still there? How are we going to get them out and get classes back to normal after the little trouble we've been having?" The last half of the sentence was added carefully, a drop of combustible chemical deliberately measured into a hot test tube.

"The little trouble?" Eliot caught his opening and pounced. "Do you call it a little trouble when twenty-five women are man-handled and dragged off to jail like victims of a concentration camp?"

Denise Dempsey started to speak but Monck, without looking at her, lifted a single warning finger. He sounded interested, equable, honestly questioning.

"What would you call it, Cec?"

"An outrage."

"All right. It's a broad word, but I'll agree that it applies. It should not have gone that far, and I stepped in where I didn't really belong because I was afraid someone would be badly hurt. Sorry about that. But it's over now, and the girls' suspension is lifted. They're in the clear."

"There's nothing over, Chancellor. What do you propose doing about their demands?"

"Me?" Monck's surprise was mock-innocent. "That's why I asked you to come over, to tell me what action you
102

and the Senate mean to take. It's your problem, Mr. Eliot, not mine."

Cec Eliot, a professionally angry young man, had built a successful career in college politics by opposing the entrenched order and what the students considered its abuses of them. His strength was in protest, and he had a store of grievances with which he had intended to inundate this new chancellor.

Emory Monck was no stranger to the technique. As an undergraduate, before Eliot was in grammar school, he had employed the same tactics to effective advantage, and he intended not to be backed into taking a stand that could be successfully attacked by the student leader. He saw with warm approval that Eliot was smart enough to realize what Monck was doing, and was selfishly glad that the boy had not quite enough experience to counter skillfully. He watched the studied calm crack apart.

"Chancellor, you can't shuck this off on us. We didn't make the idiotic rules, and the girls were forced to act after they had exhausted every other avenue to relief."

"You aren't blaming me? I've been on campus less than forty-eight hours."

"I am blaming Miss Hollister."

Monck was bland. "Miss Hollister is no longer dean of women. She retired."

Eliot shook his head a little like a baffled bull not certain which way to charge. "It won't wash, Dr. Monck. You are the chancellor."

"And you are president of the Student Senate. We established that way back in my day, and under the bylaws the student body is supposed to govern itself by democratic vote in everything except classroom activities."

The boy wavered and now sounded defensive. "It's never worked that way since I've been around. Dr. Dice only allowed us to recommend, and when anything was important we were overruled by the faculty committee."

"Jim Dice is no longer chancellor. As you said, I am."

The student president was nonplused, hanging, the solid footing cut out from under him. Monck bored in with a show of man-to-man equality and an embracing smile.

"Cec, you and I each have a job to do, and both jobs have the same purpose. We want whatever is best for the students of Wellington."

Eliot was not ready to capitulate. "How do I know that if I go along with this you won't do just what the other chancellors have done, grab for power? That's the pattern every place today, a big paternal government with a bureaucracy that pats our heads and says it knows just what's best for us all and if we are good little children they'll allow us a few little privileges as long as we don't break their rules."

"You don't know. But how do I know about you? When you accepted the presidency of the Senate you took on the responsibility of looking out for the students' interests."

"That's what I'm trying to do."

"By a negative approach. You're against. You're the opposition. It's easier to try to knock down an established structure than to build a better one, but that kind of destruction is not progress, it's retrogression. If you want to go ahead you have to construct your own program."

Monck stood up and paced before the boy, letting Eliot's greater height serve to support his dignity and cloud the fact that he was again listening to the voice of authority.

"I was brought in here to raise money to save the school . . . for what? So you people could stay out of classes, break down the public's faith in Wellington? Make it the laughingstock of the nation by crying how put upon you are? Why don't you take the initiative to correct the conditions you object to? You're the student leader. Go get them together, draw up a reform program, lay out clearly and fairly the individual rights involved, balanced so that the desires of the few don't transgress on the rights of the majority. Lay it on the line. It won't be as easy, but the reward will be a lot greater."

He stole a glance upward and decided that it was time to stop. In Eliot's face was the look of a boy who has climbed to the top of a hill and found the view from there entrancing. Monck took his hand and shook it, and with practiced expertise issued him through the door.

Denise Dempsey sat in silence for quite a while after the door had closed, then she took a long breath, as if she had forgotten to take the last few.

"Remind me never to listen to you unless I'm ready to believe."

104

Monck thought that indeed she did see too much. He gave her a crooked smile. "You make me sound like a phony."

"No," she was thinking it through, "but you do twist people into seeing through your eyes. And you very neatly slid the university out from under. You said the problem didn't belong to the administration and dumped it in the students' lap."

"What's wrong with that? Isn't that where it belongs?"

Her words were still measured. "Probably. But Cecil Eliot did not originate the problem and it wasn't because of his doing that those girls went to jail and are still holed up in that dormitory."

"Nevertheless you have just witnessed a transformation, the end of a politician and the beginning of a statesman. Eliot's got ability and his vision will grow. In a sense the future of Wellington has been delivered into his hands. He knows it and he will live up to it.

"Eliot will get those girls into their clothes and out of doors. He'll talk to the reporters and put a new face on the story: that it's a family difference not between arbitrary authority and captive kids, but between the students themselves, a policy matter to be put to the vote."

"I still don't know . . . you convince me when you're talking, but I have that funny feeling that it isn't honest talk, that you're manipulating people. Cecil Eliot has been a rebel all of his four years on campus, and in ten minutes you send him out of here all fired up to do exactly what you, the figure of the authority he's been fighting, want him to do. Will it last? Will he carry it through? Or now that he's away from you will he do a double take and realize that he's been had?"

Emory Monck felt an exhilaration going through him. That had been part of the zest of his life with Sam Jordan's group and he had not expected to find anything like it on this campus, but here in this girl was a brain that he would have to pay close attention to; he would have to think carefully if he did not want her to pierce as far into him as to discover his personal motivation.

"It will last, because it dawned on him that a rebel never creates anything. He can destroy an existing situation and create a vacuum, yes, but it takes a positive power to come in then and fill the vacuum, and that's the important man. Cec Eliot has just quit being a rebel, because he caught a glimpse of positive power and what it can mean to him. He wants that power.

"Let's go eat."

15

☐ As a young child Cecil Rhodes Eliot had been painfully thin, subject to colds and violent sinus attacks, growing too fast for robust health to catch up with him, giving his mother the excuse she wanted to baby him.

His father prided himself on being a typical American. An automobile dealer with three stores, on Euclid and Hayden avenues, in East Cleveland, and in Garfield Heights, Gilbert Eliot was active in the Chamber of Commerce, Rotary, and the American Legion.

Through the early years Cecil hardly knew the man with the broad, heavily tanned face and clam-shell mouth who seemed to use their home to sleep in and for little else. Not until he was in high school, had stopped shooting up and begun what slight filling out he would ever do, and showed an unexpected promise on the basketball court, did his father really discover him. By that time it was too late; whatever communication they might have developed was defaulted. They were courteous, restrained in each other's presence, embarrassed, two men who felt that they should like each other but could find no common viewpoint.

To Gilbert Eliot his son appeared as a visitor from another planet, and although the boy never showed open antagonism toward him there was an underlayer of passive resistance which the father neither comprehended nor was willing to accept.

"God damn teen-agers," he groused to his sales manager, his confidant. "What the hell do they think they're doing, that crazy music, jumping around like monkeys when they're not yakking on the phone . . . for Lord sake, do you know I had to put a separate phone in the kid's room? I couldn't get an incoming call through."

The sales manager nodded his understanding. He had a sixteen-year-old daughter. "They live in their own world, Gil. Don't ask me what they think about . . . I can't understand their language or their ideas or their hairdos. Mary isn't a bad-looking kid, but she gets herself up like a witch. Hell, the other night I caught her and one of her girl friends ironing their hair, Gil . . . ironing it, like a shirt . . . what can you make of that?"

Gilbert Eliot squinted at the used car they were checking. "I don't get it. We were all that age once, but we were still part of the human race. I used to go hunting with the old man, and to see the Browns and Indians play, and when I was at Michigan we were too busy chasing broads to go around waving banners or wondering what was going on in darkest Africa. . . . You know what that kid of mine pulled on me last night? I had him set at Michigan and the old house was going to pledge him, and he comes in and announces he's going to Wellington. . . ."

"Where the hell is that?" The sales manager bent to examine the dented fender more critically.

"God knows . . . down on the river someplace south of Pittsburgh. Seems his physics professor graduated from there and there's some old monkey named Strindberg who won a prize for cracking an atom or making a bomb, or maybe he flew to the moon for all I know . . . anyhow, we had a knockdown dragout argument; at least I argued . . . Cec didn't say a word until I'd talked myself blue in the face, then he just shrugs. 'It's all arranged,' he says, 'I've passed the college board and I went down last week and talked to Dr. Strindberg.' How do you like that? Never a word to me. I got a little bit hot, believe me. I asked him who he thought was going to pay his bills, and you know what the punk said? He thought I should but if I didn't see it that way he'd make other arrangements."

"He wants to be a physicist?"

"That's what gravels me. Here I've built this business up and who do I have to leave it to? He wants to mope around a laboratory in a white smock like a service man and use atoms for peace . . . that's what he told me, use atoms for peace. Shit."

"What are you going to do?" The sales manager had decided that the bumper would have to be replaced.

"What am I going to do? What can I do? I can't stop him. He got a straight A average his last semester." Unnoticed, a note of pride crept into his voice. "Imagine a kid of mine getting even one A. I was lucky to pull down

C's. If I hadn't been able to lug a football they'd have tossed me out on my head. He can get a scholarship without trying, but I'm not going to have it said Gil Eliot's boy went to college on a charity deal."

"That's not charity, Gil." The sales manager disagreed with Eliot for one of the few times in their association. "That's something the kids earn."

"I don't care what it is; nobody's going to tell it that Gil Eliot didn't educate his kid right, even if he is a goon."

Never had Cecil Eliot considered himself to be a goon, although he confided the worry to his closest friends that he simply did not know who he was, and had spent his high school years in a search for his identity. The knowledge would have astounded his father. It was not at all the picture the father had of him: a cocky brat who needed more discipline than the mother would permit.

Cec's arrival at Wellington had marked the beginning of a change that would be even more incomprehensible to the parents. He had resisted Michigan for a negative reason. He foresaw no pleasure in following in the footprints of a father who had made All-American there. He had chosen Wellington positively, because Strindberg had become his idol, and there he was under no man's shadow.

He was on his own, a member of a freshman class that numbered nearly three thousand and submerged the average youngster in obscurity. But Cec had something extra going for him. He made the freshman basketball team with astonishing ease. And he had more money to spend than most of his classmates. He was not ostentatious with his allowance and Gil Eliot was not an extremely wealthy man, but on campus where half the student body had to earn some part of their expenses, Cec had a distinct edge.

He did not try for a scholarship, either academic or athletic. One thing that had seeped through his consciousness was his father's rancorous shame that football had paid for his education; and his single certainty was that he did not want to become like his father. The fact that he was not on scholarship puzzled his classmates and drew further notice upon him as they discovered that he was a fast study, had no need to grind to maintain his high grade level. Added to these assets was his instinct for turning his

108

nervous mental energy into the channels of student affairs. Taken all together they left little room for surprise when in his senior year he was elected student president. It was a position he relished, a compensation for the knee injury that had retired him from basketball in his first sophomore term. He resented the stiffness of the knee, but at least it would exempt him from the draft and it gave him just enough limp to be dramatic.

He left Emory Monck's office and cut purposefully across the campus toward Tathford Hall, ignoring the circular walk, plowing through the grass that was brittle now from early frosts.

There was still a straggle of younger men around the front of the dorm, held by the delicious knowledge that the heads visible just above the window sills were supported by a shoulder to shoulder picket line of birthday raw female figures. The invisible fact was testified to by the clothes gathered and piled on the raised porch as if it were a sacrificial altar. An exchange of banter, some hairy suggestions, some morale building, helped to fill the intermission while the girls waited for Authority's next salvo. Cec was welcomed as the bearer of tidings.

"What's the word, man?"

Cec stopped where he could look up at Martha Yates, a new Rapunzel, her long red hair falling across her bare shoulders and arms where they rested on the window sill, crouching low enough that the low wooden ledge hid her breast line. He cupped his hands and called up.

"You did it, Marty. Hollister's gone, booted. The Dempsey chick is acting dean of women as of now."

Behind him whistles and catcalls drowned her answer.

"Hard to believe, Cec."

"You sure? It isn't a come-on?"

He turned, flapping his hands for quiet. "It's for real. Shut up."

They did not shut up.

"It's bitchin'."

"It's too much."

"Cool it. I got business with Martha. Get lost."

They did not leave, but they did fall silent enough that he tried again to talk with the girl.

"Can you hear me now?"

"Loud and clear."

"I have their promise that we'll make the rules. Get some rags on your birds and come on down. I'll pitch the stuff in." He had already started for the porch when her voice, angry and frustrated, screeched at him.

"Don't you touch them. Don't be a clod. This war isn't finished, it's just begun. What's their promise worth?"

He wished that he had a little privacy. But maybe it was better with the audience. If they watched the wheels of government turn they might more readily believe.

"Marty, you're thrashed. It's time to negotiate."

Martha flung her red hair, a waving banner. "Monck's got you jazzed. He'll do like all the rest, con us into submission and then clobber us again. I've got too much invested . . . you didn't get hauled off to jail last night, slammed into a filthy bucket."

"You loved every minute of it. You're Joan of Arc without the armor, Eleanor of Aquitaine all revved up, marching your Britons out to fight the French."

"I'm Martha Yates at Wellington, and I'm staying right up here until I see a paper signed by everybody."

"Don't you trust Dempsey?"

"She's not all ape." Her voice was grudging.

"You trust me?"

"What have you got to trust?"

"From now on the Student Senate says what goes."

"Who says?"

"Monck."

She laughed down on him. "He's not big enough. The trustees are too square. They'll have his blood."

Cec Eliot had begun to sweat, but now he was again on solid ground.

"Use your head, duck. He's got the bread. One hundred million bucks. Sure, the trustees won't listen to us, but they'll listen to bread, they were raised that way."

She was still not convinced, at least she did not want herself to be. The taste of power was too exciting and had been too brief. She did not want the shooting to be over so soon.

"We're staying here until I see something on paper."

With the chorus behind him rising again, Cec spurred on. "You're coming out if I have to drag you." Even as he said it he wondered if he had the nerve, but he could not back down now.

"You wouldn't dare. We're naked."

"I've seen you in a bikini, where's the difference?"

Cec went through the door into the lower hall before he gave himself a chance to think. He was halfway up the stairs before she capitulated.

"All right." The words came down amid a shower of shrieks and giggles from behind a barely cracked door on the upper floor. "Go on back outside. Throw in our clothes and then get away where we can watch you. But I'm going to talk to the chancellor myself."

Cec stopped, raising his head to have the last word, to call that this was just what the chancellor wanted. Then with a stroke of new statesmanship he let it ride. Let well enough alone.

16

□ Martha Yates was two years younger than Cec Eliot, educated to believe in the dignity of man, a red-headed, conforming rebel.

Her father was a rangy, indecisive man who sublimated a deep feeling of lack of personal achievement by espousing the causes of the helpless and inarticulate. He was a Voice of Protest, not an Activist. He had never marched in a civil rights parade, never sat in a drafty corridor waiting to be dragged out by police. He had never joined the Communist Party, was not a member of any inter-racial council, gave no allegiance to any of the crusades for World Peace. He was a loner, a one-man aristocracy whose credo was that the words he pounded from his beaten typewriter were more effective than any physical commitment of his single, indistinguished body. In this isolation he was free to damn the Capitalists on one page and on his next, to drum out a message crucifying Organized Labor.

As a result he had few enduring friends. Men avoided him in bars, wearying of his arguments. More and more he retired to the shady, unpainted house in the weedy lawn that was separated from the hot traffic of Telegraph Road by seriate piles of rusting iron in the junkyard next door.

He was an entertaining editorial writer and he had sense enough to keep his personal and political opinions out of his paper's columns, but at night, behind the book-lined barricades of his workroom sanctuary, he indulged himself with diatribe pieces for any organ that would print them.

His wife had died when their daughter was seven, and a large, bosomy colored woman "did" for them, came twice a week to wash and iron and do what cleaning the old house received.

From her Martha absorbed an emotional knowledge of social injustice that backed up her father's more abstract fireworks, and precluded the development of any suspicion that her father was not an oracle.

He shared a privileged closeness with Martha. When he did not feel like writing he would join her at the scarred dining-room table and help with her homework. Then over his can of beer he would try out on her his latest theory concerning the brutalities joyfully heaped upon mankind by mankind. Her sense of history ranged from cannibalism among the troglodytes through the Roman sport of matching unarmed Christian against lion to the projected Day when someone must use the Bomb because he has it.

Tuesday nights he reserved to himself to visit a house on Temple Street, but even that he shared with her in a sense when she became aware of the pattern of visits followed by Wednesdays of mental refreshment and physical relaxation. She asked him why, when she had heard that it was a shameful place, it made him feel so good. He attacked her informant's narrowness with the same steam that he brought to his broadsides.

"You're pretty young to be told about sex, but you're smart. You'll be hearing more and more about it, and I'd rather tell you now than have you get a sick picture from the Philistines and bigots.

"I don't know when you'll feel its power, not for a couple of years yet at least. But it is powerful, it's one of the great life forces, which is why people in this country have been scared to death of it. They've called it sin, which is rot. If you read dangerous for sinful, you can put it where it belongs, in a category with alcohol, gambling, the automobile, LSD, atomic power. They're all good, useful tools for living, but when you handle them remember that you're handling a bomb. Put it by for now, but when you begin to have special feelings about boys come to me and we'll talk about it as we do about everything else."

She had promised, trusting him, and in time she had come to him; there was a boy who wanted to put his hands on her and it gave her goose pimples.

"You'll be happier if you wait." He wondered what made him start off that way, if it were simply old male jealousy shuddering down the eons, and decided not to trust himself now that the chips were on the table. He stood up and reached for the Kinsey Report, ran his fingernail across the backs of the other volumes, hesitated over the new *Human Sexual Response,* then included it in his gesture. "Get as much perspective as you can from books and do some thinking ahead, but for God sake don't allow yourself to be brainwashed by anybody. Make up your own mind and then fight for what you decide."

She had taken the words literally and applied them to a wider scope than sex. But they left her disappointed in him. She had expected something more personal and positive after his build-up, and as she puzzled over the defection she came to know that with all his protests he would never take a concrete action in any direction. Rebellion was demanded. Martha Yates was through with tempests in a vacuum. Whatever decisions she made, she would commit herself wholly to them.

But overcoming at Wellington was a midnight walk through a quicksand swamp. She came prepared, her red hair elbow-length and loose, her guitar mastered and her repertory of songs practiced with tapes of the greats who originated them. Yet she was inundated with three thousand freshmen, all confused, all desperate to adjust to the new environment, flowing around her without pause to listen. Instead of achieving immediate prominence, she seemed to herself as pointless as her father, flailing at vapors.

She finally managed to rouse the ire of and a warning from Esther Hollister for making an impassioned speech outside the Student Union, defending the right to be heard for a speaker from the Student League for Democratic Action who had been barred from the campus. That was her breakthrough. It was the speech that attracted Cec Eliot's attention.

He stood on the steps of the Union building, his mind half following her words, half amazed at the fire issuing from the pale-skinned, fragile-looking orator. It left him

113

gaping, staring out from behind his patchwork of straggling beard.

She flung her last outraged sentences at him, meeting his stare with defiant green eyes. "Take a picture, turkey, it lasts longer."

He started, knew that he had been looking stupid, and laughed at himself and at her truculence. "Look, duck, take off the armor. I'm in your corner."

She considered him then. In these first few months on campus she had found, as her father had found before her, that men melted away from the intensity of the dedicated. While this one did not exactly stoke her, he was male, and he seemed uncommonly certain of himself, as if he were somebody. She lifted and dropped her shoulders and jumped down from her chair, then caught her breath at having now to look up at him as far as she had just looked down.

"Mind if I walk along?"

"The grass is free." She hoped that her tone sounded as careless as she tried to make it.

He came off the steps, matching his stride to hers and they headed across the commons.

"That was some soapbox you were on."

"Somebody had to speak out."

"Why?"

She craned her head sideways and tilted it to look at him. "What gives with these clods? I thought there was a law about the right of free speech in this country."

"There is. But this Student League guy is a square. I heard him in Pittsburgh."

"So why don't they let us find it out firsthand?"

"A newspaper called him a Commie. That's enough for Estherester. Wave a red flag in front of her and she goes ape. What do they call you at home?"

"Martha Yates. Who're you?"

"Cec Eliot."

He sounded surprised that she had not recognized him and she damned herself for once again saying the wrong thing. She was always embarrassed at being caught not knowing something she might be expected to know. She was still burning when he said:

"How about we go down to Nicholas' and eat?"

She brightened instantly. She had not been in Riverdale

except at the Greyhound station where the school bus had picked her up on registration day. She did not know what Nicholas' was and she could not ask, but the mention of food was enough. She nodded with emphasis and he led her to the student parking area, stopping beside a sixty-four Olds.

"Super," she said on a long breath. Several of her friends in high school had had wheels, but nothing so elaborate as this.

Cec Eliot was always uneasy about appearing ostentatious. He said in haste, "The old man sells them. I got it off the used car lot."

He opened the door and handed her in. Her opinion of Eliot was escalating second by second.

"This is too much."

His grin made him look exceedingly young, incongruously so, and that gave her the courage to ask, when he had folded his long legs under the wheel, "Ought I to know you?"

"I play basketball. Where you from, bird?"

"I haven't seen a game yet. Detroit."

"I'm from Cleveland. We're neighbors."

How come you're at Wellington?"

"Because my old man went to Michigan. What about you?"

"My dad went here."

"You ski?"

"Once. I didn't do so good."

"I'll show you sometime. Where'd you get your convictions?"

That touched the sore spot of loneliness, of strangeness, and she reached with a rush of warmth for her father. She talked about him all the way to the parking lot behind the Eatery, first in a gush of love and then deliberately critical, to recoup her image. She broke off only when they pushed through the rear door into the steamy room. She did not want to talk so personally with a crowd around, and besides, she would have had to shout above the conversations and the jukebox.

A foursome got up and emptied out of the front corner booth, and by the time the waitress had stacked the thick dishes along her arm, mopped the table and cut an expert, swaying swath, a broken field dash through the jumping mob, Martha had her ear attuned so that she could hear Cec's voice.

He helped her into the bench and was still getting himself comfortably settled when the waitress came back with fresh place mats and menu folders, which he waved away.

"Hi, Dotty. Make it a pair of steaks, well done, french fries, sliced tomatoes. Coffee later. Right, Marty?"

She nodded, dazed. She had not tasted steak since coming to college. The food at the Union was ugh, and steak was to dream about.

Half a dozen men stopped to pass a word with them, but her speech was not mentioned, whether they did not know about it or preferred to keep off the subject she could not guess. Then the steaks came and they concentrated on food. Cec seemed to be as ravenous as she was. When her plate was cleaned and the coffee mugs arrived, Martha sat back in euphoria.

"That's the first time I've been full since I got here. Thanksarot."

He leaned forward, anchoring his sharp elbows on the table, his eyes on the paper napkin as he scientifically tore it into bits. His long torso brought his head close enough to her that he could lower his voice to a confidential level and be heard, and he returned to the theme that had first interested him, his curiosity as to the depth of her dedication.

"So your old man is a talker but not a doer, and you're antagonistic about it. You're going to be different. Is that what you were doing, making with the speech?"

She started to agree, to bare to him her decision of total commitment, but a wayward wisp of female adulthood drifted into her and stopped her. She had driven other men away by the exposure of too much truth. A secondary truth might win more approval. Her face reddened.

"I guess I was just trying to make some noise and say, 'Look, I'm here,' to establish an identity, if you dig what I mean."

His smile was encouragingly understanding. "I kind of got a break, making the basketball team."

"And you've got a dreamy car, and you must have bread, to be putting out like this." She gestured at the empty plates, then noticed that he flushed and hurried on. "But me . . . there are about eighteen hundred freshman girls.

116

How do I get to be somebody with that kind of competition?"

It relieved her that he laughed. "Don't you do anything special?"

"I sing a little, folk music. But who doesn't here?"

"I want to hear you. Let's split; I've got a three o'clock." He rose and waited for her.

She trailed him through the thinning crowd, feeling that the sun had come out, that a hole had been made in the roof of obscurity through which she now might rise and be recognized, that a step had been taken toward belonging, which was the necessary precursor to total commitment.

17

☐ The Martha Yates whom Cec Eliot led back to Emory Monck's office was a year older than the fledgling who had made the speech that first brought her athwart Esther Hollister.

She was still groping, but she was no longer a lonely unknown. Through Cec she had become a Little Sister for the Delta Gamma Rho house, and she was as certain of her place on the campus as any member of the faculty. With an instinct for taking up a cause at the right moment she had built up a wide undergraduate following. She had refused the invitations to rush, since to isolate herself in one sorority would remove her from too many possible disciples, and for the same reason she had shied away from doctrinaire labels.

In her own mind she was a Marxist of the ideal interpretation, yet she was as opposed to Communism as a John Bircher. She feared its totalitarianism as much as she feared the encroachment of the federal government into personal liberty. She was not certain at what point governmental interference should be stopped, believed passionately in the benefits of a welfare state while being unwilling to accept its constrictions. That was a gray area she preferred to ignore.

Her battle focused on faculty authority and her battle cry rang with indignation: the individual was being brainwashed into a slave herd nonentity. Esther Hollister made an excellent example and target, and their feud had simmered on just below the point of boiling over until this last

117

week. With the change in chancellors she had reasoned that the administration was at least temporarily disrupted and so weakened that it was time to test her power.

That Hollister had been so quickly vanquished, removed from the field, left her with a sense of loss and confusion. She knew that she should be happy with the apparent victory, but a feeling persisted that she had somehow been cheated.

Martha Yates had savored the fight. She had looked forward to the ridicule that would be heaped on the university by the press. She had enough sense of news value to realize how tickled the American reader would be at twenty-five naked and helpless girls defying the police power of the school, the town, and the county.

Now Cec told her that the new chancellor had sidetracked the whole issue by dumping it into the lap of the Student Senate. Only last night she had thought she had beaten him by successfully resisting his efforts to keep her from being locked up in jail with the others. Today he had even stolen away her most important ally; Cec Eliot had gone over to the enemy camp.

What made all of it worse, the new chancellor was sexville. He had something for her. It was an unfair weapon.

She called up all her grievances against the office to armor herself against the man, steeled herself to fight down any butterflies that might rise when she faced him, and marched into the office as Cec held the door.

Their arrival was anticlimactic. Vivienne Krump looked up and smiled impersonally. In no way did she reflect her knowledge that Emory Monck was in trouble and that these kids held the key, or her distaste for the long red hair that hung uncombed down the shoulders of the man-sized sweater, the tight black capris and the bare feet thrust into all-but-invisible sandals. She showed no reaction to the girl's angry attitude.

"The chancellor went down to the faculty dining room for a sandwich. He'll be back in a few minutes. You can wait in his office."

The situation was too delicate for her to risk any probing other than what she could learn by watching, but she saw the girl's eyes flick at the word sandwich. Whatever the outside might look like, they were all the same in the stomach.

118

Martha Yates had not eaten since the night before, and the picture of Monck stuffing himself while she waited on his whim was one affront too many.

"Hell with it. Let's go."

But having got her this far, Cec Eliot did not mean to lose her. He took a firm grip on her arm and steered her toward the inside door.

She tried to hold back. "I'm hungry."

"That's news? After we talk to Dr. Monck I'll take you down to Nicholas' for a steak."

The very thought of a steak, brown and chewy, of a basket of still bubbling french fries, was more than she could resist. Besides, she did not want to lower her dignity before the secretary by fighting openly with Cec. She allowed him to push her through the door.

Only after he closed it did she wrench free, and now she needed to get back at him somehow. The empty, high-backed chair behind the desk pulled her like a magnet. She stalked to it, flung herself into it, pushed it away and crossed her feet on the desk top.

"Mr. Eliot." The timbre of the voice was Esther Hollister's. "It has been brought to our attention . . ."

Cec gaped at her. "What gives with you now?"

"As chancellor of this university, with the power vested in me by the trustees, I must request your resignation from the presidency of the Student Senate. Lack of cooperation, Mr. Eliot . . . you have violated your sacred oath to uphold at all times the magnanimous restrictions bestowed upon you by our omnipuissant faculty committee. What in hell do you think this is, Mr. Eliot, a democracy?"

"Oh-oh. Shut up." Cec was not looking at her. He was looking past her, down the room, at the open door where Denise Dempsey had stopped with Emory Monck close behind her.

Martha was late in getting the message. By the time she turned she had seen Cec bow his head and wrap his arms up over it, covering his face and skull. She tried to leap up, but too late.

Emory Monck poked a gentle forefinger into Dempsey's spine, prodding her on.

Dempsey was caught between the tableau in front and the chancellor, whom she could not see, behind. She did not dare to let her face come apart, to let the violent giggle

119

rise past her chest. She did not know how he was reacting.

Monck walked past her with his easy, well-oiled step. He dropped onto the couch, extended his legs and crossed his ankles, leaned against the back and tipped his head toward the ceiling.

"Sorry, Martha. I should have knocked. Thanks for coming over."

Cec Eliot had disguised his pantomime of ducking to receive a thunderbolt by combing his fingers back through his hair.

Dempsey moved to stand at the girl's shoulder, to let her hand brush the small fist pressed against the chair arm.

Monck continued to stare at the ceiling. "I think you put in a nutshell what's wrong around here. I hope you're taking drama?"

Martha Yates was caught off balance; she had expected a Hollister-type diatribe, and the chancellor's approach puzzled her. She had lost the advantage that she thought had been hers when she walked in here, and she was still frightened at being discovered in the act of mocking him.

"No, sir." She sounded very meek.

"I think you'd like it. Has Cec told you that Miss Dempsey is now acting dean of women?"

She nodded carefully.

"Good. And that the Student Senate is going to draw up a code to be ratified by the student body?"

She glanced toward Cec but found him giving her no help. Rather he seemed to be hanging on Monck's words. That helped her to recover. Cec had gone over to the enemy, and this was the enemy before her. The awful paralysis ebbed away and her suspicion returned, bringing strength with it. She gathered herself like a spring.

"That's what he said, but how do I know the trustees will let us do it?"

Monck lowered his eyes then, judging that the critical moment of vulnerability was passed, and smiled like a small boy on the carpet himself.

"I don't think they like the egg on Wellington's face."

It was hard to believe it. She had won, really won, and he was admitting it in front of everybody. It was too much.

"I'm not interested in Wellington's image, Dr. Monck," she said. "I'm interested in results, and I want to be sure. I don't want all of our efforts wasted."

120

"I shouldn't think so, any more than I want mine wasted. Have you seen the papers?"

She had not, and she could not stop her eager words. "Did we make it big?"

"Big enough. Denise, poke your head around the door and ask Vivienne for the clippings, will you?"

When Dempsey spread the front pages across the desk the redhead had trouble choking off a squeal. All of them carried pictures of the girls being dragged out to the patrol wagons, of the rioting students. The Pittsburgh *Times* featured the shot of Martha spread-eagled in the arms of the two policemen, writhing in martyred agony. A boldface caption above read **FOLK SINGER GETS HEAVE HO FROM LAW**.

It was exciting proof of her effectiveness. She flung her hair back and looked up, gloating. "How about that?"

"It certainly makes a laughingstock of the school. I hope it doesn't hurt us too much."

"Hurt what? The precious image? The precious traditions? Who cares? What matters is that we've won freedom for students."

Monck burrowed in his pocket for cigarettes, offered the pack to Cec, who started and shook his head, then held it forward toward Martha. She drew back and he lit one for himself.

"I wasn't thinking about tradition in the sense of outworn restrictions . . . you had a valid beef there . . . I was thinking about the value of the school to you, as a sort of supermarket where a young person can find in one place the things he or she needs, a place to make the transition from family life to independent competence, to take advantage of what men like Martin Strindberg can offer."

She was indignant at being so misunderstood. "That's different. I'm not against that."

"Oh, I didn't think you were." Monck sat forward, pulling in his legs, crouching over his knees and supporting his arms on them, cupping his hands around the cigarette, a man in unhappy thought. "But that's my problem, to keep that part of the school alive. I don't imagine you know that I was asked to come in to raise money, that there wasn't enough to keep going through this year?"

She felt a warning twinge of guilt and a mysterious dismay. It was not the old Hollister flat accusation, but it did hint that now he was going to try to put her in the wrong, and she fought against it.

"I heard rumors. But what's that got to do with freedom?"

"Not with freedom. Call it credit rating. You see, I raised operating capital on the proposition that Wellington would establish a combination university-business research program. Business would supply the funds and we would do the research. I thought the students would like working on projects that might develop something really useful.

"But publicity is tricky stuff. Did you notice there"—he gestured at the papers on the desk—"it's suggested twice that the demonstrations here had Communist backing . . ."

"That's not true." She flared, resenting that anyone should think she was not the sole organizer.

"I'm sure it isn't. But how do our business people know? They're going to watch us a lot closer now, and it will be harder to sell the program to them. We may lose some of them. If we lose enough, we'll be out of business. You tell me you're fighting for freedom, but what good is it going to do you if there's no university to exercise it in?"

It was a new thought. "Well, tell them." She hesitated. "Tell them that the girls will get a better break because of my sleep-in."

"I can't tell anybody anything. Neither can you. It has to be proved. Cec and I were talking a while ago. Tearing an old way down isn't enough, you have to be ready with a new way. You've been looking for a way to go and you've got it. It's up to you leaders to work out your own rules of conduct, get them voted on. Go prove to the skeptics that Wellington isn't Commie run, that anyone who wants to support our program will be doing a service to a group of sober, intelligent young adults, not the nursery school crybabies those papers make you out. I believe in you, or I wouldn't bother talking to you. And I'll back you up."

Martha Yates got to her feet slowly. The way he sat there, hunched over, looking up at her, she wanted to wrap her arms around him and protect him.

Following Cec Eliot down the echoing stairs she sighed deeply. "How neat. How absolutely neat. Sexville."

"Huh?" Cec Eliot gaped at her.

"Emory Monck. He's dreamy. I think I'm in love. In fact

I know I am. Cec, I'm stoked."

Back in the office Monck stretched and winked at Denise. "Dempsey, do you know any harder job than growing up? I don't."

The acting dean of women did not answer his question. She said simply, "God."

18

☐ A female animal pregnant for the first time builds a nest in instinctive anticipation of an event which it may not comprehend. The ancient chemistry of even a false pregnancy stimulates the built-in urge, compels the animal to change the habits of its life and directs the appropriate action.

Some years back Esther Hollister had begun preparations for her retirement. She talked about it, and she built a house on a lot while ground was still moderately priced, a view lot on the rim of the gorge. She moved into it. It did give her a more tangible feeling of security to live in a house that belonged to her, not to Wellington; but between the strata of instinct and of professed reason in Esther's being there burbled in an undefined channel a continuing flow singing that she would never retire. Without really recognizing it she had bridged it with a rationale. She had told Amos Wellington that she wanted a place to live out her days far enough from the campus to be uninvolved but close enough that she could keep her contacts.

The campus was the sum of her life. She was not overburdened with sexual demands. She remembered as lovers those men who had spoken kindly to her at faculty socials. Men like Amos Wellington leaned upon her strength. She approved of women as long as they did not gush.

She had moved up from the ranks, from a position as English assistant, and she had been a good dean of women. Under Helen Strindberg's prodding she had fought for equality for her girls, against the tendency of the male faculty to consider them secondary citizens. They could thank her that they were accepted into the science courses, that their athletics were given stature and that they were admitted without prejudice to the Student Senate. But years had eroded the lively path that Helen had cut. The fresh trail had become a rut. She still pointed west but she wasn't going anywhere.

She had for years considered herself indispensable to the university. Emory Monck's treachery was a mighty blow. She appreciated how Bertha Tilden felt, wan, drooping, sniffling in the kitchen. The child had, in effect, been summarily dismissed with the dean.

They had grown to be close in the two years since Esther had taken her into the office. Bertha was not the brightest student, but she was obedient, she had learned neatness and she was useful without being intrusive. She was grateful for the small scholarship that Esther had been at pains to arrange for her, and for the job without which she could not have stayed in school. And living in Tathford Hall she had proved valuable as an extension of Esther's eyes and ears. In the office too, for that matter, for she could report on the attitudes of girls on their way in to see the dean and again on their way out. A lot could be told about a girl from her reactions when she thought she was not observed.

When Esther moved into her house she had taken Bertha along as part-time help. Long evening talks made the girl seem like an adopted daughter. It was fortunate now that Bertha had this haven to come to for comfort. Yet after an entire afternoon of listening to her, Esther Hollister was getting impatient with the child.

She went through the louvred door into the kitchen to check on the marination of the steak, the progress of the salad, the warming of the rolls.

"When you hear the door chimes, Bertha, you can just slip on out the back door. If you haven't finished, never mind, I can pop things together in a jiffy."

Normally she would have entertained without even noticing that the child was underfoot, and her guests were used to speaking freely in front of the little shadow; but tonight was quite different.

This was not the first crisis among the Wellington coeds that she had experienced. When you had under your control four to five thousand girls just emerging from teenage into womanhood there were bound to be problems. Girls, frustrated by their changing body chemistry and the uncertainty of their future, disturbed by their widening perspective, were more difficult to handle than boys,

124

which Denise Dempsey would shortly find out. Boys had the advantage. A male student could work off his energy in fighting, drinking, athletics; and in sexual relations the advantage was always with him. She had so far managed her exacting job without any man's help, but the present challenge went beyond the problems of girls and boys and she needed the reserves.

Amos Wellington was about as decisive as mush. Dr. Strindberg never looked at anything seriously. But General Fenton she could rely on. The general was one of the few men she admitted admiring. He had a clear purpose, an ordered mind and an understanding of the meaning of authority. He was an advocate to whom she did not hesitate to present her case.

She had gone to freshen her hair when the carillon sent its tinkerbell sound through the house. Esther's footfalls were characteristically heavy as she hurried toward the thick slab door.

The house had been built to her specifications as translated by an assistant in the architectural department. That had been one of the satisfactions of living in a tight-knit university community. You could always have the best professional services free. The living room was twenty by thirty, with one glass wall decorated at night by the distant lights of the West Virginia shore. The rest of the house was not large; there were the kitchen, a single bath between her bedroom and the spare, planned for her sister's occasional visits, and a dining nook off the window wall, modern but cozy.

She pulled the door open and the cold evening wind struck her full in the face. It had been getting colder all afternoon but she had been too preoccupied to notice the change. She should have had Bertha light the logs laid ready in the roomy fireplace.

"Come in, Jerome, come in. It smells like snow."

She caught his wrist in one hand, his shoulder in the other and possessively pulled him inside, where she helped him to shuck his light topcoat.

"I hate to drag you out on a night like this, but I thought we should have an uninterrupted talk."

When he was free the general made her a military gesture, half bow, half salute.

"My pleasure. It's good of you to invite me. I've always been partial to a home-cooked dinner."

They chuckled with the easy manner of old associates sharing a mutual trust. In his early years Fenton had been something of a ladies' man, indiscreet enough that had not the First World War come along when it did a nasty scandal would have destroyed his career. But in 1917 every line officer was needed in France, and the fact that he had seduced his commanding officer's wife did not, in the eyes of the War Department, lessen his ability to kill Germans.

At war's end he had visited the widow of a dead buddy and married her, but she had been gone for five years, and he looked back on the marriage much as he looked back on the posts from which he had been transferred. Now, like others who have been profligate in their youth, his sex drive had faded away, in the tradition of old soldiers. Certainly Esther Hollister had never struck the slightest fire from him; he viewed her as a dependable staff officer who could be trusted in emergencies, but a home-cooked dinner was not to be lightly dismissed.

Obedient to her order he lighted the logs, and was relieved when she brought him a bourbon and water and directed him to a deep, soft chair at one side of the blaze.

"What in the devil happened this morning?"

Esther sat down in the chair opposite, empty-handed although she had been known to sip a cup of punch at Alice Wellington's teas. Alcohol even in small doses made her sense of stability uncertain and tonight she wanted to be very certain in all she said.

"Emory Monck is just as devious now as he used to be when he was in school, running wild."

"But he doesn't have the authority to fire you, Esther."

"That's what I mean. He didn't fire me, he tricked me. I was trying to shock some sense into him. I said I'd resign, and he snapped me up before the words were out of my mouth. That was just what he intended. Jerome, I don't think he is going to work out as our chancellor."

The general began to feel the warmth of the room and the drink.

"We're in rather an awkward position there. I don't like his high-handedness either, nor his plans; but without him we simply do not have the resources to keep going."

"Well, he's going to cause a lot of trouble, with Denise

126

Dempsey and that radical Yates girl leading him around by his nose."

After the steak Martha Yates and Cec Eliot lingered on in the Eatery, ignoring classes, working up the new bill of rights and limitations. Nicholas' place was as good as any to take a sampling of student opinion. They buttonholed students and filled a notebook with suggestions, taking down everything, no matter how way-out it sounded. Later they intended to whittle the list.

Martha wanted sweeping changes, a whole new deal for Wellington. Cec argued for moving slowly, beginning with the three or four most pressing inequities.

"Let's not turn up with a goon program just when we're getting the chancellor's confidence. I think we'll get farther if we don't try to do everything at once. We ought to make a start that can be handled, and add amendments later, otherwise we're going to have every kook on campus fouling up the real issues."

They stayed on to catch the evening crowd. Al Conner, the publicity director, ambled through the door and pushed across to their booth.

"Thought I might find you here. Mind if I sit down?"

The girl slid over to make room. Only that morning she had deeply resented Conner's bailing out the girls but now she said in a voice diffident enough to draw a look from Cec, "I didn't thank you this morning. I guess I was a little on the rude side."

Conner waved his hand. "Forget it. You were pretty upset. I wouldn't have felt any better after a night in that tank." He accepted the cup of coffee the waitress put before him. "Dr. Monck wanted me to get together with you and set up a time for you to talk to the press."

Cec Eliot felt a small, cold chill run down his spine. It was the same every time he got nervous, as if someone rubbed an ice cube along his back. This would be the first real action he would take under the new authority the chancellor had handed him. He simply could not goof off on it.

He said, hoping that he sounded confident, "Martha and I are working on the new program that the Senate will present to the student body next week. We haven't got it firmed yet." He thought the word had a businesslike sound to it.

"Okay," Conner said, "I'm due home now so I'll shove, but when you get it set—I don't care how late it is—I'd like a copy. Right?"

"Right."

Nervousness made Cec Eliot hungry again, and he knew about Martha without asking. He flagged the waitress and ordered another steak.

The plates arrived and with them, Nicholas. He slid his bulk into the seat vacated by Conner and smiled at the kids. Nicholas was very fond of the kids from Wellington. Sometimes they got out of line, of course, like the mob scene after the football game when they broke three tables and a front windowpane, but usually they were only noisy, and Nicholas loved that. Besides, over half of his business stemmed from the campus, and business was good, good enough that he might long ago have followed his original intent and returned to Corfu had he not learned to read by deciphering the *Form*.

Nicholas Bates was a confirmed horse player and a loser. He had married one of his waitresses, a strong-boned redhead, and taken her name, abandoning his original string of consonants over which the American tongue tripped. She had borne him a strapping son and he remembered her with pleasure. The redheaded girl in the booth reminded him of his wife and was one of his pets. He liked it especially when she brought her guitar in of an evening. He had tried once to teach her some of the old songs, but that was not what she understood of folk music. The kids now all had new ways. So be it.

Everything about Wellington touched Nicholas deeply. His son Steve was the only sophomore on this year's starting varsity football team, and to his amazement and joy had been pledged by the Delta Gamma Rho's. That alone was an almost unheard-of honor. The DGR house was the foremost on fraternity row.

The Eatery serving as an unofficial forum for the students, Nicholas had heard many things discussed over a cup of coffee or a Coke; he knew the campus politics better than most and he was perfectly aware that the fact that Steve had made All-State fullback in high school and was likely to become Wellington's second All-America had much to do with his being pledged. That was an understandable principle. Even so, Steve's acceptance into the house might not have come about without Cec Eliot's one-man campaign on his behalf.

Nicholas loved Cec Eliot. Cec was his boy almost as much as Steve was, and he could communicate with Cec as he had never been able to do with his son. Steve was impatient with his father's English which had never lost the old world taint. Cec was the only boy not bound by Nicholas' strict rule of no credit to a student. Eliot blithely charged his food from one quarter's allowance to another, and lost nothing in esteem. He always paid up as soon as his check arrived.

But Nicholas was not concerned with Cec at the moment. His melting chocolate eyes searched the girl's face.

"You got trouble with the cops?" Nicholas knew about cops, from back in the prohibition days when the product of the Kentucky hills had found its way into his cellar. "Sonsabitches. I see your picture on the paper. Whassamatter they got to haul you around like sack potatoes?"

It was the first chance Martha had had to talk about the horrors of the tank, the obscenities flung at the girls by the evicted familiars, and Nicholas was militantly sympathetic.

"Them whores, don't you pay them no attention, Marty, like me. I don't even let them in my place, only way late when there's no ladies here."

Cec Eliot did not listen. Martha's protest had brought results and it was past, he was not interested in hashing it over. The room had filled with the dinner mob and was jumping, but he saw no one they had not already queried whose ideas on the new constitution he cared about having. He ate in silence, musing upon Nicholas. The man had intrigued him from their first meeting. Beneath the scrambled syntax he sometimes caught a glimpse of extraordinary comprehension.

Where had it come from? How did it arrive in such an unlikely vessel? Nicholas was big with powerful shoulders and a deep chest; his head was large but bullet shaped, with a round bald spot pale as a newly grafted skin patch in the middle of a mass of black wire hair, long and standing out, each hair waving independently of the others.

The back of his head, as is common with modern Greeks, rose straight up from the bunched neck to the top.

Cec had wondered if Greek babies were bound on flat boards while the skull was soft enough to take the shape of its support. He thought this theory had some substantiation because Steve Bates' head was as round as his own, while otherwise Nicholas' son surely showed his Greek blood. He was as dark as his father with the same heavy features, a far cry from the golden-haired, blue-eyed warriors and poets, philosophers and scholars of the classical age.

Still, those were not the native stock, those heroes of the Homeric legends, so where had they come from? Out of the north somewhere, to the leisure of a softer, easier climate, bringing energy to burn. And what a blaze they had made, all that building in so few short years, with the light still making a beacon across the centuries. Where did they go? Nowhere. Just sank into the populations they had conquered, the dark-skinned men who had once ringed the Mediterranean with their trading cities and their naval power. Phoenicians they, the durable traders out of the Near East who fought Greece and then Rome and watched both fall before they were themselves submerged under the tidal wave of Islam.

The migrations of early man, the development of peoples and cultures, of trade and power were an old love of Cec's. As electives he had taken Anthro One and Two, and in the summer of his freshman year he had gone on a dig to a site in New Mexico. But the tedious, meticulous work of brushing out an artifact had been too much for his patience. His mind was too thirsty; there was too much else to explore. He had read a lot, everything from Hrdlička to Leakey and the heretics Velikovsky and Brennan, but as the press of his laboratory work rose and his student activities increased he had had to abandon electives. There just was not enough time to cover all the bases.

But here was Nicholas before him, suggesting some ancestral gene from the golden time, a thinking man in a nonthinker's business, an aware brain in a Homo Habilis skull warped out of shape. Still, hadn't old HH been a thinker? How else had he picked up one rock and banged a piece off another, made a sharp edge, made a tool? How

130

else had he survived and changed himself and become man?

Cec Eliot jumped almost a foot when Nicholas flung up a thick arm and shouted.

"Emory, Chrissake, there's my boy."

Cec had to twist his head to see the door. The chancellor had just followed Denise Dempsey inside, stopped her with a hand under her elbow and was already turning her to leave. There was not an empty seat in the Eatery. He looked tired, but as he heard Nicholas' hail and recognized the group in the front booth his face came alive with that quick glow that made you feel he was really glad to see you. He steered the new dean of women toward them, winked at Nicholas and smiled at Cec and Martha in turn.

Nicholas heaved himself to his feet. "Nice to see you, Miss Dempsey. Whatya think of the little girl here getting tossed in the clink? Thas no good, is it? Looka how she been working all afternoon onna new rules, eh?" He waved at the notebooks, the papers and pencils shoved aside on the table. "Hey Emory, you really start the fireworks up onna hill, got your name in alla papers already. This school politics kinda different from business politics, ain't it? Never mind, never mind, you fix it the school don't close and they quit laughing. They make you governor, by God."

Emory Monck was jolted by the remark. Hearing Nicholas talk about politics and governorships made him feel as if he had waked up naked in this crowded room. He patted the restaurant man's shoulder and looked at Cec Eliot.

"Did Al Conner catch up with you?"

The boy nodded. "We hope to have a program ready by tonight sometime. He said he wanted to see it."

Nicholas was making shoving motions with his hands. "Whyn't you kids move around and make some room in here for the boss?"

But Emory shook his head. "No thanks, Nicholas, never stop a man with a shovel. Let them work, they don't need us."

"Okay." Nicholas cast a practiced eye around his room. "That bunch in the back is done, they're just clowning around now. I'll heave 'em out."

He headed for the rear. Denise and Monck said a

friendly good night and followed slowly, Denise pausing for a word with other girls along the aisle.

Cec Eliot watched after them thoughtfully. "You know, snook, that begins to look like an item."

Martha Yates had sat there stone silent. Now her voice had a ragged edge. "I don't know what he could see in a dean."

Eliot's eyes came back to the girl. "Boy, you are jazzed. I never saw you like this before. Well, let's go up to the Union and wrap up the bylaws."

He unfolded himself from the booth but it was a long minute before she stood up, outside she climbed into the car and sank deep into the seat.

"I don't feel like making any rules tonight."

"What am I going to tell Conner?"

"Anything you want."

She was indifferent, as if she were exhausted. The drive back to the campus was made in a strained silence very unlike their usual easy comradeship. The night had turned very cold, so it was not odd that she hurried across the grass to Tathford Hall, but then she ran up the steps and inside without a parting word.

Watching after her, the cold moved into Eliot's chest. Martha Yates was in trouble; he knew it certainly and he did not like it. And he did not know what to do about it.

As he crossed toward fraternity row he scuffed the side of his head with the heel of his hand. He'd phone Conner from the house; the bylaws would have to wait. He was not going to move while Marty was so obviously upset. He had never seen her like this although he had watched her go through several "in-likes" as she called them. They had had a short romance in the beginning, had gone steady for a while, but there had been more talk than action. She had not been ready for an affair and he had not pushed; he had not been that sent emotionally. Then that had petered out as each found other partners and their relationship had centered around their mutual activities. Cec had decided not to get serious about any girl until his professional life was settled. Martha had claimed to feel the same way, but there was no dispassionate objectivity in the way she had just behaved.

In the Eatery, insulated from eavesdropping by the general noise level, Monck looked speculatively at Nicholas.

"By any chance do you still keep a bottle hidden under the counter? A drink would save our lives right about now."

Nicholas cast a quick, suspicious glance at the new dean of women, but saw only pleased surprise. As they settled into the booth he went away and returned with thick coffee mugs filled with ice and a rich amber liquid. He grinned and bent over the girl.

"The kids don't know about this, Miss Dempsey. I keep it for just special people, like Emory, and sometimes an emergency."

"I won't breathe it to a soul, Nicholas, and I think tonight qualifies as an emergency. I've never spent a longer night and day."

Monck sagged back, lifted his cup, and closed his eyes. He was tired through. Martha Yates's publicity, if he had not got it checked, could have played hell with both his program for the school and his personal image building. As it was he felt sure that he would have to backtrack to at least some of the subscribing industrialists and reassure them of Wellington's solidity. But he thought he had the campus under control now. All he wanted was to eat a little, drop Dempsey off and go home to the bed he had not seen since night before last.

There was a whipping wind and a halfhearted sprinkling of snow when they left the Eatery. Dempsey was hardly awake as he drove up the hill. She bid him a sleepy good night at the door of the apartment building used by single faculty people, and he went off, anticipating a couple of quiet drinks and blessed solitude.

He put the car away, ducked his head against the wind, and hurried in through the kitchen door. He switched on the light, got ice from the refrigerator, a glass and a bottle from the cupboard and was at the sink when the rear door rattled. He thought at first that it was the wind and paid no attention, but then he heard Alice Wellington's voice. It was so unexpected that he jumped.

"Hello the house. May I come in?"

She did not wait for an answer, but turned the knob and came through with the door, pushed by a gust. Her cheeks and nose were red and her eyes bright with tears started by the cold. Her hair was prettily blown into wisps that

133

clung against her face. It made a very enticing picture.

"Get in this shanty before you freeze." Monck turned to get another glass. "You're just in time for a nightcap with me."

She closed the door and leaned against it, her smile rueful. "Didn't you have enough trouble with me last night, plying me with likker?"

The memory of the scene in the upper hall struck them both at once and they broke up. It felt good to Monck to laugh aloud, as though it took the tiredness out of him.

"Don't worry, you only get one this time, then I'll throw you out. I'm bushed." He made the drinks and led her through into the dark living room, waited while she turned on lights and passed him to sit on the couch, then dropped down beside her, giving her a glass. "Boy, what a day." He stretched his long legs before him and rested his head on the couch back. "You know, kid, innocent me, when I took this job I figured all I had to do was raise some money. What have I been doing? Stopping riots, springing girls out of jail, canning little old ladies, insulting trustees . . ."

"You really walked into a buzz saw, didn't you? And you don't know the whole of it. That's why I came over. I've been waiting over home like a spy for your lights to come on so I could warn you. You've really started some hell popping."

He raised one eyebrow at her. "What don't I know?"

"There was quite a meeting at our place tonight . . . after General Fenton had dinner with Esther Hollister . . ."

"Oh-oh."

"Oh-oh is right. The general is in a perfect stew. He's trying to find a way to get Esther reinstated."

This he had not foreseen, had not had time to think about, that they would go behind his back to abrogate his decisions. Anger rose in him. He fought it. This was stupid. Had he expected Martin Strindberg's road to Washington to be a rose-strewn path? He waited until he could trust his voice, then shook his head.

"Not while I'm here he won't. I'm sorry about Esther, but it's either her or peace on the campus. We can't afford a repeat of last night's performance, and that's exactly what we'd have if she came back."

134

"I know. But it was the way you handled it that shocked people. You couldn't do much else at the moment; I see that, but it's the wider impact that I'm worried about. With the general as mad as he is I'm afraid he'll try to block your research program. He didn't like it to begin with, and the other trustees are pretty shaky."

He rolled his head to study her face, searching for some sign of confidence there. "How do you feel about it?"

Impulsively she put her hand over his and squeezed it. "I'm in your corner. I wouldn't be here if I weren't. I feel a little like 007, carrying tales to you."

He smiled at her. "You don't look like him, you're prettier." Abruptly he twisted toward her and kissed her.

"Emory." She colored, pushing him back. "Be serious. This is important talk. I'm trying to make you understand that we'll have to move more slowly."

"I don't want to move slowly. That tasted like more."

He reached for her shoulder, but her face pursed up with impatience and she slapped at his hand.

"I didn't mean it that way, nut. I meant about the school. Listen to me. Even Helen Strindberg was upset about Esther, and Helen has always been progressive."

Monck sighed and leaned back. "She used to be, but if she still thinks Esther belongs here she's atrophied. What was your father's reaction?"

He had no real hope of any positive action from Amos Wellington, but with Alice prodding him the president might possibly back him up.

"You know Papa. He likes things to stay the way they are, and Esther is a very old friend. But I think he realizes deep down in his heart that there had to be a change."

He rose, restless and frustrated, and took the glasses to the kitchen for a refill, thinking about Fenton. If he chose, the general could play the devil, could make Monck's position untenable, and if that happened the whole game would go out the window. When he came back the girl was frowning in thought.

"There's one thing that might help. The Dempsey girl. From what Fenton said, Esther blames her and Martha Yates mostly. She told him that the two of them were winding you around their fingers."

That at least he could get a chuckle from. "Do you think I'm the patsy type?"

135

She was a little late in shrugging, and surprisingly hesitant. "I wouldn't think so, but Dempsey is pretty young to be a dean, and Esther is intimating that she's a radical."

"Everybody who doesn't kowtow to Esther is a radical. And yes, Dempsey is young, but she turned in one hell of a job last night. Furthermore, the kids trust her."

"Which is just what Fenton is afraid of: that she's too close to the students, that she couldn't maintain discipline. Don't you think it would be smart if we brought in someone from outside, someone who isn't all involved with the faculty family?"

It nettled him to find her maneuvering him. "Kid, in business when a man gives way to pressure to replace someone who's doing a good job because of someone else's spite, he's less than no good to his company. He's dangerous. He destroys the confidence of the whole personnel. Either I am Chancellor of Wellington and I do the job, or I'm not. They can fire me if they don't like my way."

At once she was on her feet, her voice suddenly warm and protective. "Of course you are. Poor Emory, what a baptism of fire." She bent over him, took his face in her hands and kissed him, her lips soft and parted.

Monck pulled her down onto his lap. "Just you stick by me."

"Always." She slid her arm around his neck and tucked her head into his shoulder. "Just keep in mind that everybody likes to feel important. Give a little, dear; that's all I'm asking. Just a little. Please?"

"I'll try."

She twisted and stood up, patting his arm. "You're dead tired, I know. I'll run on and let you go to bed. Don't bother seeing me home."

"You know, kid, I'll take you up on that. Thanks for coming. I'm a lucky guy, having such a beautiful spy."

19

☐ Delta Gamma Rho was the oldest fraternity on the campus, founded as a local in 1879 by three farmers' sons. According to campus gossip the chapter was, like Gaul, divided into three parts: the jock straps, the brains, and the bread.

136

This heterogeneous society managed to exist under one roof without too much internal friction for two basic reasons. First, whether a man got Charley horses or straight A's or touched for loans, he felt a pride of identity with the leading house, and second, the house itself was the last word in luxury.

The building was less than six years old. It had such conveniences as four color-television sets, one for each of the two main floor reception rooms, two for the basement recreation areas.

Downstairs there was also a record player, its music piped into every bedroom. There were two pool tables. There was a bar. The bar had not been drawn into the original plans but had been assembled later by the brothers in honor of the product Wymer Edwards concocted in his still.

Edwards, a short, chunky chemistry major, had perfected a mash consisting principally of corn sugar stolen from the laboratory, to which he added raisins and yeast and set the whole to work in a large crock in the furnace room. His still, a maze of copper coils, wound through the heating ducts and into a cooling apparatus and dispensed a potable, potent liquor. Gabe Glasscock, the house president, had named it the Delta Brew.

Glasscock, one of the bread men, was the son of a Philadelphia lawyer with a national reputation as a personal injury advocate. Gabe was a slight, quick boy with an intense face, a shock of yellow hair and remote, very light blue eyes, who took life and his responsibilities with a deep seriousness.

Normally he had few qualms about his future or his identity, and he would instantly veto any suggestion that he suspected might detract from the Delta image. Thus he had peremptorily dismissed a proposal that Wymer Edwards turn his talents toward lysergic acid. He was not going to permit his chapter to make itself vulnerable to the nickname Acid House or Travel Bureau as some of the other fraternities were disrespectfully called.

But since the night of the September pledge party Gabe had wrestled with a personal decision that disturbed him and defied solution. Cec Eliot had requested that they pledge two Negroes.

As the only declared member of the Birch Society in

the chapter, Gabe was nicely trapped. Had he not been president he would have fought as an individual for their exclusion, but his pre-legal training had given him a dogmatic reverence for Robert's Rules of Order, a conviction that any presiding officer must maintain an impartial attitude toward any important question brought before the membership. He was under further pressure because of his high regard for Cec Eliot's political know-how. And his certainty that in this case Cec had been influenced by Martha Yates helped to complicate matters even further.

To him Yates was a dangerous and disturbing element. Everything she stood for was opposite to what he believed, and he could not comprehend Eliot's interest in the girl. She was too skinny to be attractive and he guessed that she was a virgin, probably cold. Yet she definitely had some kind of pull for Eliot, and Glasscock, as his best friend, resented it.

Gabe had been feeling great after the pledge party until Cec had come in with the pledge list and asked him to go upstairs to their room to look it over. Cec had seated himself at his desk, switched on the Tensor light while Gabe had stretched himself on his bed. Cec had read the list slowly, pausing to comment on the proposed names. Gabe had kept a mental tally: eight athletes, twelve grinds, seven boys with acceptable financial backgrounds.

"That all?" He was disappointed. They could not, of course, hope to get the full complement.

"Two more. Harold Polly and Lin James." There was a defensive inflection in Cec's voice as if he expected an argument.

"Who in hell are *they?*"

"Both of them made the freshman basketball team last year. They both have A averages."

Gabe sat up abruptly as he got the message. Now he understood why the names sounded familiar.

"Jigs."

Cec came to his feet. "Don't call them that. They're nice guys."

"What do you want me to call them, Muslims?"

"Don't call them anything. You didn't call Van Rothal a Dutchman when I read his name."

"For Christ sake, Van's granddaddy owns half the real estate in midtown Manhattan."

"Meaning that if instead of being a veterinarian Polly's father owned the National Security Bank you'd think he was okay?"

"I didn't say that." It bothered Gabe to argue racial relations, and instinct told him that this could not be Cec's idea. It had to have come from the Yates girl. "Who started this foolishness, Marty?"

Cec hesitated. He hated the suggestion that he was merely parroting Marty, yet that was exactly what he was doing. They had had a hot exchange over it that afternoon.

"You're out of your mind," he had told her at first. "The chapter would never do it. National would cut us off at the shoelaces. Polly and James wouldn't want it; they don't make waves; they won't trade on the fact that they're black."

"You're missing the point." Marty sounded like an exasperated mother. "The campus is talking. You Deltas didn't send one solitary worker South for the civil rights jazz last summer. Is it a racist image you want for the chapter? You could take the lead and pledge these boys. You claim to like them."

"I do like them." As student manager for the basketball team the last season he had seen a lot of them. "But Marty, it wouldn't do any good and it might do a lot of harm."

She was adamant. "It would prove that the Deltas aren't afraid to stand up and be counted. It would be a break in the wall. How do you expect ordinary people to accept integration if we leaders don't make the effort to show the way?"

As an institution, Wellington had been integrated from its inception. This was historically abolition country, and Riverdale had had a station on the Underground Railroad before the Civil War. Still, for some reason there had never been many Negroes on campus, and Cec could not believe that her idea would work.

"Even if I got it through the chapter I don't believe Polly and James would buy it. They strike me as not wanting to stick their necks out, attract personal publicity."

"What's happened to you?" She was disgusted. "Has the Senate presidency made you reactionary? Are the

139

Deltas fogging you up? You used to be with it."

So he had added the names to the pledge list and then browbeat Gabe into letting them stand for the vote. And now the hour of decision had arrived.

To Gabe's consternation Cec's wild idea had garnered backing from a number of the brothers during the interim. It had been discussed and rediscussed at the chapter meetings, and each time the number of supporters had multiplied. Kurt Pfiester had assumed the leadership of the pro group. He was talking now, and even Gabe listened.

"The way I see it, what have we got to lose? Everybody knows this is the top house, and no one's going to turn down the opportunity of going Delta if it's offered. The other houses couldn't take in these people; they'd kill themselves on campus right now. But we can do it and get away with it."

Gabe tried to sound impartial. "The question is, do we want to? National will raise a stink for sure. They might even kick us out."

Kurt laughed at him. "Man, you're not thinking. That's the last thing they'd dare do. They may haul us personally on the carpet, but don't you think they'll risk being called racist by the press. Me, I'm for it. I think Cec had a good idea."

"It wasn't his," Gabe insisted. "It was that Yates bird, and look at the hell she's raised around here in the last two days. Getting all those broads to strip naked up there this morning." He had a happier thought. "Jesus, how I'd love to have got up in that dorm. What a run through the daisies that would have been."

Some of them thought it was funny, but Joe Turner said in Martha's defense:

"You have to admit she got rid of Esther-ester. Where is Cec? He ought to be here."

"Down at the Eatery working on the new rules, last I saw him. Maybe he forgot about tonight."

Cec Eliot had forgotten, in the excitement of the day. It was only luck that brought him through the door now.

"It's about time," said Kurt Pfiester. "We're getting ready to vote on the pledges. Do you want to say anything before we decide whether to go with Polly and James or not?"

Tathford Hall was still trying to sort out its wardrobe, which was in no greater disarray than Martha Yates's emotions. She needed a physical outlet for the pressure inside her. She took the long flight of stairs on a run, two at a time, ran down the hall and burst into the room like a bomb.

Jane Cullen, her roommate, was at the wall mirror. She wore bikini briefs and a bra; her body had a golden warmth, all lush, magnificently apportioned six feet of it. Her dark, thick hair shone even under the unkind ceiling light and the shoulder-length flip swirled as her head came around. She had a high, brunette coloring and discharged a kind of amorous electric field.

"What's with you?"

Martha slammed the door, spread her feet for balance and threw her thin arms as wide as they would go.

"Jazzed. Stoked. Oooh. I've found him. I'm in love. Hey. Whoever thought it would happen to me?"

"You're not drunk?" Jane prowled forward, sniffing suspiciously. She had come near to believing it, she had heard it so many times. Martha was never going to marry. She would travel, she might join the Peace Corps, she would have affairs, but never would she subjugate herself to one man.

"I'm drunk on love, that's what I am." The redhead cast herself across the nearer of the twin beds, landing on her stomach, her arms dangling loosely over the far edge. The long hair wrapped around her face and spilled to the floor. The sandal soles flapped as she kicked her heels in the air.

"What a wonderful word. Love, love, love. He's so groovy. He's fab. I can't stand it."

Jane Cullen eyed her roommate, scratching at one breast where a rough seam of the bra made the nipple itch. Had Martha finally wised up to the way Cec Eliot was always around when she wanted him? She did not believe that, and she searched for other names that Martha had mentioned with anything except scorn.

"Well, who?"

"Emory. Emory Monck." Martha rolled onto her back. "What a silly name, Emory Monck. He's no monk, believe me."

"For God sake." Jane's normal serene composure was

shattered. "Did he make a pass at you?"

"Indeed not." Martha sat up, shocked at the suggestion.

"Then what are you trying to say?"

"I told you. It's a real happening. He talks to me as if I were an adult."

Jane had followed Martha's leadership not because she shared the redhead's impassioned convictions but because it was fun; it put her in the middle of a stream of activity that, left to herself, she would not make the effort to enter. Martha was a one-man amusement park. At the moment the big girl did not dare laugh aloud.

"Aren't you? You're always claiming to be."

"Well sure. But most of the faculty pats me on the head. Jane, I keep expecting one of them to offer me a lollipop."

"This really happened sudden, didn't it? As late as noon today you hated Mr. Chancellor Monck with a pure and burning passion that only murder was going to cool."

"That's the way love comes." Martha became theatrical; it was the only expression she knew strong enough to do justice to her ecstasy. She pulled a pillow from beneath the spread and sat up, hugging it against her. "One moment you are free, the next you are a slave. It is so written. It is my destiny."

Jane turned her back quickly. "Nuts. All you need is some sulphur and molasses."

She opened her closet door and pulled out a dress, looked it over critically and exchanged it for another, draping it against her and weighing the effect in the mirror. Martha watched, unthinking until the meaning worked through her daze.

"Where do you think you're going?"

"Out."

"Do you know what time it is? It's after ten."

"So?"

"If they catch you you'll be campused until Christmas."

"I thought you'd heard. Queen Esther is no more. The new dean hasn't any rules. The students are supposed to make up their own."

"All right. We're going to. Cec and I spent all afternoon on them. But I was so shook at seeing Emory bring Denise Dempsey into Nicholas' that I couldn't work any more. You don't suppose he could go for an old hag like that?"

142

Jane considered Denise Dempsey anything but an old hag. In fact she had admitted to herself that if she were interested in other women, Denise would be her type. Martha, though, was having a bad time at the moment, and she rose to it loyally.

"I can't see how he could possibly be interested in her. He's barely seen her."

Martha took this as reassurance and returned to the crisis at hand. "I don't think it's fair, you going out tonight just when the Student Senate is on trial, as it were."

Jane had chosen a third outfit and was rolling a tight skirt up over her hips. Getting into a new skin would have been no greater problem.

"Honey, you take care of your politics and I'll take care of my love life. Fair?"

"It puts me in a very bad light."

"Ho ho. Now you've joined the cops you're going to be worse than Esther-ester? I went to your sleep-in and I went down and spent the night in that tank, and that was something for an outsize bird like me. So I fought in the war. Now I'm going to collect my medal."

"Who are you going out with?"

"That town boy the Deltas pledged last semester."

"Not Steve Bates? Not the Greek's son?"

Jane Cullen stopped in the act of pulling her fur coat from the closet. She turned on her heel, looking as though she had been betrayed, her dark eyes darker still.

"You got something against Greeks I don't know about? You got brotherly love for Negroes and Jews and all the little people in the world, but Greeks are poison, is that what you mean?"

It had not been at all what Martha meant. Jane Cullen's father was a member of one of Washington, D.C.'s best law firms; her grandfather had been a U. S. Senator from a New England state; her mother's father owned a chain of women's magazines. Jane was society. The picture that had shocked Martha was of Nicholas, his fleshy, black furred arms, his heavy features, his sickly bald spot and his stained apron, of Jane married to Nicholas' son, brought down, impaled for public ridicule on the stool behind the cash register at the Eatery. It was not a matter of ethnic origins. It was a class distinction. Martha recognized it with horror. But it was there. And it would not go away, because it involved Jane Cullen. She sat, her face stricken. In that one moment she had smashed her whole vision of her life, her battle against prejudice, her clear belief that everyone had equal dignity. When she found her voice it was clotted with tears.

"I didn't mean it that way, Jane. I meant, it would be an awful waste, you in a hash house in Riverdale with a townie."

As quickly as she had become angry, Jane turned sympathetic. Martha looked like some small, starved waif that she had stepped on with her big foot. She sat down on the bed and wrapped her arm around the thin shoulders.

"Take it easy, baby, and thanks for caring enough about me to worry. Maybe I got rough because I'm a little doubtful myself. But I've got to find out. I've been watching him. He's so big, he's the first man who ever made me feel small and feminine."

Martha still had not found her bearings. "You never mentioned him before."

"Good reason. I just met him. He was in the line behind me in the cafeteria tonight and he said he thought it was lousy that we all were arrested. He thought the sleep-in was a fun gag. So we ate together and finally he told me he'd been wanting to date me and didn't have the nerve to ask."

"But why so late?"

"He had to take his aunt to Wheeling and couldn't get back any earlier."

"Where are you going?"

"I don't know, Little Mother. I'm meeting him behind the parking lot at eleven. From there we'll play it by ear. I sort of think we'll go have a look at the old Navy base. That's kind of In."

Martha looked at her quickly with new concern. "You really mean it?"

Jane shrugged her shoulders and stood up. "He sends me. What's to quibble about?"

She got her coat, opened the door and peered around it, then slipped through and pulled it closed silently. Martha sat on in misery, feeling all alone in the world.

Tathford Hall was one of the newer dormitories, built during Jim Dice's tenure. The chill efficiency of the room was disguised by Jane's collection of Navajo rugs and
144

their souvenirs, but without the big brunette's presence it felt like an empty refrigerator. Martha had the sensation that Jane was not coming back, that she would never see her again, and on a frightened impulse she ran to the window.

She was in time to see Jane come onto the porch, then a further fright struck her. She heard the soft hiss of Pat Crowell's bike chain somewhere close, coming closer. She wanted to shout a warning, but apparently Jane heard too. She jumped for the shadow of the shrubbery that would cover her escape around the corner of the building, and was gone.

Martha stayed at the window, watching as the campus security man came into sight, stopped before the walk and moved up to check the dormitory door. Here was the familiar symbol of the enemy to reassure her. The disturbing talk with Jane had made a shambles of her certainty. Her clean charted path had been broken, leaving her with an unease, a rolling of the drums of doom, a dread of the unknown.

Pat Crowell was a reminder that brought her comfort. It was because of the authority he represented that Jane, a perfectly competent, intelligent woman, had to sneak out of the house at an hour that no adult considered late. Because of them she was shut up in here, a prisoner in a concentration camp. But tomorrow, oh tomorrow, she would break the bonds, write the new rules, and they would all be free.

Warmth returned to Martha Yates. She stuck out her tongue at Pat Crowell and shook her hair until it pulled at her scalp.

But no, he's not my enemy. My enemy is faceless.

That would make a good new folk song. She hummed a few experimental bars. My enemy is faceless. My enemy is uncaring selfishness, is greed. My enemy, the throttler of the free.

But for some reason she could summon no fire to the composition tonight.

Pat Crowell did not know that he was observed and would not have attached any unsettling meaning to it if he had known. He pedaled slowly down the maze of walks on his solitary night patrol, a ritual begun forty years ago when he had first been hired as the single security officer. Even as the force expanded and he rose in rank he never delegated the night tour to any of his subordinates.

Nothing very drastic ever happened during the daylight hours. Whatever mischief the students plotted was logically reserved for the shelter of darkness. That was the time when the hand of experience was needed.

Besides, he liked to be by himself, to savor the rolling lawns and ancient trees that were his alone only at night. He liked the feeling of forest silence. That was the reason why he had resisted all attempts to supplant his bicycle with a motor bike.

The campus was unusually quiet tonight which he sensed was a reaction from last night's hullabaloo. Apparently, from the small number of lighted windows, there was nothing stirring, no cause for alarm. It looked like the fraternity houses had even shut down their poker games.

He made the call box at the far end of the parking lot, yawning as he dismounted and kicked down the support rod. Emory Monck must really have thrown the fear of God into everybody. Monck was smart all right, always had been, even if Pat had had to hop lively to keep up with his shenanigans when he was a kid. He grinned in wistful regret for those times. So much was changed now. Not just at Wellington, but all over. The vogues that had started in the universities of a bunch of unstable little foreign countries had been picked up in the States: long hair for boys and pants for girls and all the other crazy stuff, this wild-eyed shouting and marching, going off half cocked over matters that oughtn't to concern school kids who ought to be learning all they could before they had to go out and scramble for a living. It made it rough on a man trying to do a job.

He sighed and turned his bike back toward the guard post at the east end of the administration building. He had two more years to go before retirement. But then what would he do? He thought fleetingly of Esther Hollister. He had respected her without liking her, with a policeman's appreciation of the need for public order. She had held a tight rein, but age was the great leveler. She was gone and he would go, and new mobs of students would come in with their restless impatience to grow up, but the school would stand.

146

With that astronomical amount of money Emory Monck was bringing in, it would last, and that was a good thing. For a while he had really despaired of its surviving. The school was the part of his life that had stature, importance. If it had failed, he would have failed with it.

He dismounted, thrust the front wheel into the rack and went into the small office, into the little island of light given off by the single hanging bulb, and closed the door against the increasing cold. Wellington slept, the uneasy sleep of a volcano perhaps, but Pat Crowell was on guard to watch over it.

20

☐ Thanksgiving was past. Christmas was almost upon them. The leaves were gone, fallen, gathered in by the lonely snuffling tractor rake and mulched around the roots of the rose bushes, mounded and weighted down on the flower beds. The ivy made a vein pattern, black, up the faces of the buildings, and all of the faults of the architecture were exposed to cruel view. The ground was alternately crunchy and sponge soft as thaw followed frost and early snows fell and melted. Color for the next months would be in the girls' legs, red, blue, black, harlequin leotards, in the bright skirts.

The day had been sparkling, warm with Indian summer, as if it would impress on the world a pleasant memory to last it through the winter. It was lost on Ward Perry, crossing the campus, dodging bicycles, oblivious, bent on his errand. He came into Denise Dempsey's office at three-thirty, looking harried.

He was a tall man with a skullcap of tight curling black hair and a long, white face. He was not handsome but he had a driving vitality that attracted people. He was thirty-five, a graduate of MIT, and three years ago Martin Strindberg had chosen him as assistant dean of the Physics Department. More recently Emory Monck had appropriated him from Strindberg to help get the research program into gear.

It had not taken Monck long to decide that Perry was the man he would train to step in as chancellor when the time came for him to stand for Congress. But he had not told this to Perry. He wanted the spark of administrative initiative that he saw in Ward to grow, wanted Ward to discover it for himself, to develop a taste for management. If Monck judged right, one day Ward would wake up, recognize his potential and take off, bucking for Monck's job. If he judged wrong, Ward was not the man for the spot; but then he did not think he was wrong.

Perry stopped in the anteroom and asked the new girl if Dempsey was alone, received a quick smile and a nod, knocked on the door and opened it without waiting for an invitation.

Denise Dempsey was pleasantly surprised. She liked Ward. She had gone out with him several times in the last two years. After the third date she had had to use finesse to stall off his asking her to marry him. In the beginning she had entertained the idea, but then shied away from it, seeing indications of a stubborn streak that she did not want to fight for the rest of her life.

He crossed to the desk and sat down on one corner of it. His face cleared as if a happy thought had just come to him.

"Did I tell you how pretty you are today?"

She simpered. "You haven't seen me today."

"So I haven't. This Monck character is ruining my love life. He keeps me so busy I'm spinning."

"I've heard the complaint from others."

"No complaint, really. But brother, he's stirred up more business than we can handle in a year. You ought to watch him operate with these corporation muckymucks." He pinched up his face and drew in a whistle. "First time I went with him I was scared spitless. But learned something; you can talk to those people easier than you can to our own trustees. . . . What I came in for: Didn't you say the other day you had to meet your father in Pittsburgh tonight?"

She nodded. "Between planes. He's going West."

"Maybe I lucked in. Monck's due on a nine o'clock plane from Houston . . . you know that joker telephones me every cotton-picking day, doesn't matter where he is. Calls Al Conner too. . . . Well, I was supposed to meet him, but now I have to be in Wheeling. Could you maybe pick him up?"

She wondered at the small lift of excitement she felt.

148

"Sure. Pop's plane takes off around ten, the timing's fine."

The drive to Pittsburgh was fun, with Monck to think about, to laugh about. She had hardly seen him since the Eruption, that Marathon day. He had been on and off campus like a yo-yo, had taken Ward Perry along on several trips to sell the research program to industry. And then there were the speeches . . . he was making more speeches than a presidential nominee. At first that had puzzled her, but now she knew a secret. It gave her a feeling of intimacy with him, a glow.

"Quit it," she told herself. "Stop kidding yourself. If that man had the time for any woman it wouldn't be you, it would be Alice Wellington. You just stop thinking about him, right now."

It had snowed in Pittsburgh; there was an inch of slush at the airport and she had not brought overshoes. Her feet were sloshing in her shoes by the time she crossed the parking lot and came into the waiting room; she found a heater and sat by it, trying to dry out in the twenty minutes before her father's plane was due, but her shoes were still wet when he walked in.

Carl Dempsey was little bigger than a jockey. He had a sharp pointed nose and jug ears, a deeply weathered face and a thatch of unruly gray hair. He had been a good rider until weight took him out of the saddle, and now he trained a large public stable. Everybody liked Carl for his pixy quality and his kind humor. He was a happy, gregarious man with a gentle understanding of men as well as horses.

He kissed his daughter without fuss, and the time that they had been apart disappeared.

"Hope you didn't eat. I thought we could go uptown and have some dinner together."

"Let's eat here. I have to meet Emory Monck at nine."

"Monck? Oh, your new chancellor. I don't know if I wrote you, I met him once when he was working with Sam Jordan."

She tucked her hand under his arm and started him toward the restaurant. "Small world department."

Racing was a small world. Carl Dempsey had run across Eli again and again and liked her, but about Sam he had reservations. Monck he remembered only as a big, good-looking boy, pretty sure of himself but more head than heart.

"How's he working out in the job?"

"Lots of excitement. I'll tell you about it."

They found a table, ordered dinner, then the girl began to talk. She had not known there was so much bottled up inside her, but at Wellington she had had to be careful of what she said. She told him about the Eruption, about Monck's research plans and his campaign to enlist industry, about his shoving his program down the reluctant throats of the trustees, about the changed, charged atmosphere of the campus. It was pure luxury to talk this freely, to let go. She felt stimulated and knew that she was flushing, but she did not want to stop.

Her father finally interrupted. Something did not fit. "What's a man like Monck doing, fiddling around with a school job?"

She had been bursting to talk about that, and she lighted up further.

"Everybody wants to know the same thing. Well, I caught Al Conner in a slip of the tongue and made him tell me, but don't you repeat it. Emory wants to get the school on its feet, build it up, make himself a reputation and then run for Congress. He wants to go to the Senate eventually. He's very smart. He figures that the seat of power is more and more in Washington, and he wants to be in on it, without any strings tied to big business. He'll do it, too."

Carl Dempsey's reaction did not show. He said quietly, "Kind of interested, aren't you, baby?"

It was like cold water in her face, and her laugh was short. "He doesn't know I'm alive. It's Alice Wellington he takes out."

"He made you dean of women."

"That was an accident. He needed someone in a hurry and I was there. I don't even think the job will last; there are several people after my scalp."

"You'll make it. We're a tough breed."

The outpouring had abruptly dried up. Carl Dempsey knew why, but he waited until he was certain, then began to talk casually about the coming season at Santa Anita. He had two three-year-olds that he was high on, and she had always liked the racing world. They had had a lot of

150

good years together, following the tracks. She began to look interested again, and he leaned toward her wishfully, persuasively.

"Why don't you come on out with me? It's warm and the flowers are blooming and the park's prettier than ever. You weren't cut out to shut yourself up indoors with these petty intrigues and conniving sharks. Come on back and live."

Denise caught her breath. The old outdoor, horsey smells, the sounds, the excitements rushed through her. A homesickness for the old life with him hit her. But after a moment she closed her lips firmly and shook her head.

"Nope. I loved it when I was a kid, but I've got to hoe my own row, Pop. You understand, don't you?"

"Sure, honey. It was just a thought. Maybe you'd come out for the opening though. Doesn't your Christmas vacation start this week?"

The temptation was strong, but then Monck's plane was called. She hurried Carl to the in-bound gate.

Monck came through with the long, deceptively relaxed step, searching through the waiting crowd for Ward Perry's tallness, and did not see the girl until she spoke to him. Then surprise, and his quick warm smile.

"Dempsey. You meeting somebody?"

"You. I'm a substitute. I was meeting my father anyway and Ward asked me to pick you up." She introduced her father and Monck put out a hand.

"I remember you. Funny the name didn't ring a bell with me before. You got a horse for the Derby this year?"

Carl smiled up, a sleepy, withdrawing smile. "A couple, I hope."

Monck put an arm around Denise's shoulders and pulled her against him briefly. "You've got another winner here. Can I buy us a drink?"

Carl said, "We just ate."

"A brandy then?"

Monck ignored the small man's reserve until they reached the bar, but then automatically, as they waited for Carl's plane, he made an effort to talk about horses, about Eli Jordan, to listen to the trainer with more apparent interest than he really felt. He was bushed. When the loudspeaker called the flight he went with them to the gate, shook hands and then moved back while Denise kissed her father goodbye.

The older man looked at him once more, his face telling nothing, then turned and swung away down the boarding ramp. The girl watched him out of sight, then came to Monck's side.

"I always feel bad when I see him take off that way, alone. He looks so lonely. As long as she lived my mother went everywhere with him."

His smile had a hint of a nip in it. "I don't think you need to feel sorry for him. It strikes me that he's pretty certain his kind of life is the only way. And I suspect that he doesn't approve of mine. Are you ready to head for home?"

At the curb Monck looked at the brown mush of the road, at Denise's shoes, and hailed a porter, handed him a bill.

"Give him your keys and tell him where the car is."

While they waited he wondered at his use of the term, home. Had he meant it as applied to Dempsey, or was something within himself recognizing the return to Wellington as more than a transient step on his road? He was, he admitted, glad to be here in spite of the foul weather, glad that Dempsey had met him instead of Ward. It was a welcome break after the weeks of travel, of concentration. Keeping so many balls in the air was a strain. He had been from one end of the country to the other, reassuring the heads of companies that were on the fence about coming into the program of industrial involvement with an educational institution, finding new organizations and interesting them. He was already trying to broaden the initial base with related types of research, in effect to diversify, to bring under the umbrella of the Educational Assistance Foundation such diverse interests that a slow spell in one type would not affect the whole. He had, for instance, a good list of customers for the data processing department and in chemical research, and he thought he had sold two of Johns Hopkins' most cherished people on the idea of jumping to direct his medical expansion. He was, he thought, becoming a pretty fair raider in his own right.

And on top of this activity, pressing as it was, he had started in on his political career. Al Conner had jumped like a trout when he had outlined for the publicity man his personal long-range schedule. He had had his old team of investigators from Alcon run down Conner's entire history before he had opened his mouth, and Conner had come out smelling like the ideal man to handle his campaign. He had cut his teeth on Ohio politics, grown from a cub on the courthouse beat in Cleveland into a respected political reporter. He knew everybody in the league for thirty years back, and all doors were open to him. Jim Dice had conned him into coming to Wellington after a year of illness in his family had cost him all of his savings and more; a newspaperman's salary hadn't been enough to get him out of debt. Dice had proved a dud and Conner was bored to death, but trapped at the school. He had accepted instantly when Monck had asked him if he wanted to manage his entry into the arena.

Monck liked the way Conner thought. He was shrewd and he had enthusiasm without being precipitate. They had worked out the timing together. If Monck's Wellington program went smoothly enough, they would enter the primary a year from the coming May. If the program lagged they would delay for another two years. In either case, he would be in Congress when Senator Lightner announced his retirement.

In early November he, Conner and Strindberg had had a conference with the Senator in Washington and made their deal. When the time came, Lightner would throw the weight of his political organization behind Monck, first in the race for Congress, then for the Senate seat. Monck was not so naïve as to believe that anyone could win without the backing of the state machine, and Lightner had been assured that he would retain control of the party for as long as he wished if Monck were elected.

But until he actually entered the primary race no mention of politics would be made. The emphasis would be on speeches, which Conner was writing, ostensibly to explain the school's new concept to the people of the state. The line was that education today had both a new need and a new responsibility. With the cost of educating an individual rapidly rising, already putting a strain on the tax dollar, and with the certain prospect of the strain increasing, the schools could not morally continue to demand that their total support come from the burdened taxpayer and private donation. They must to some extent pay a part of their own way. Also, with technology pro-

153

liferating like gerbils, it was unrealistic and wasteful to dump a graduate into the economic world without a grounding in the functioning of that world. There must be an easy continuum between school and profession. Liberal arts must not be lost nor trade schools become a substitute, but they must be integrated to the benefit of both.

Conner knew his people well, chambers of commerce, service clubs, professional and educational groups, anything that could not be tabbed as partisan. Monck was to become the advocate of a marriage between the increasing sophistication of adult occupation and the preparation of youngsters moving toward full participation in the nation's life.

In another detail they saw eye to eye. Conner took delight in slanting each talk for each group, needling them with controversial twists. Go in and mouth happy platitudes, he said, and nobody will know you've been there. Make them mad and they'll raise a howl, they'll whistle up a storm and it'll rain publicity on you. When we're ready to throw your hat in the ring you'll be the best known name in Ohio, and your hide won't be nailed to any party's or interest's barn door.

All of which was fine, but the pace was strenuous. Emory Monck was going to be glad to sit down quietly for a while, watch Ward Perry manage the meshing of the new programs, watch Alice get used to the new tempo, just watch. Starting with Denise Dempsey, now. It was a real pleasure to be with Dempsey. Dynamo as she was, she also gave off a quiet, warm sparkle that oddly reminded him of Eli Jordan.

He could see her measuring something about him as she looked up when the car came; then with the shadow of a shrug she started around it. He stopped her before she stepped off the curb.

"You want me to drive?"

"I thought you looked pretty tired. Or does a woman driver make you nervous?"

He nudged her lightly. "Sure does. No, not really, but I like to drive, it puts me to sleep."

"Oh, fine. Well, have a nice nap. My feet are wet and I'd appreciate getting out of my shoes."

He helped her in, then put a hand on the hood and

154

vaulted around the front of the car, leaped again, landing beyond the door and so stepped into the slush only twice. The porter had put his two pieces of luggage into the rear seat, and as he climbed behind the wheel Dempsey was already peeling off her hose, draping them across her shoes beneath the heater and wiggling her bare toes in the warming current of air.

When they were out of town, across the river and heading south down the highway she spoke for the first time since leaving the airport.

"I'm lousy at keeping secrets behind people's backs," she said abruptly. "Al Conner accidentally let a couple of words slip and I caught him up on them. I browbeat him into telling me what your soapbox circuit is all about. I told Pop, but I threatened him with boiling oil if he let the cat out, and I know it won't go any further there. And I promise not to say a word to anyone else. Don't blame Al; nobody but a very nosy busybody would have thought anything about his slip. Now, that's off my chest."

Monck found that he was not even surprised. It was almost as if she had read his mind, back at the airport. He said so.

"I'm glad you brought it up; now I can use you to test some of my ideas. What do you think of the scheme?"

"A lot. I think Wellington's very lucky to be so important to you at this stage. I don't know of anyone who could have done for it what you're doing, and I'm sure it couldn't have got you to come for any other reason . . . I'd been chewing my nails wondering why you did come. . . . But now I'm wondering what's going to happen when you leave. Are you going to walk out and turn the school back to the kind of administration it had?"

"Ouch." He took his eyes off the road and looked at her. "Is that what you think of me, Dempsey?"

She was unhappy, but she did not retreat. "I just don't know. I want to believe in you, but I keep getting the strong sensation that you're really a robot, a computer, that when you're turned on you're operated by a bunch of pre-programed electric circuits."

Emory Monck whipped the car onto the shoulder of the road and stopped. He knew that he could not drive and laugh the way he was going to laugh. He lay back against the seat and roared. When his control returned he reached for her face, held it in one hand and kissed her mouth with hard possession.

"Dempsey, I love you. Where the hell did you come from?"

He sat back, letting the car idle in neutral, not attempting to drive on, resting his elbow on the seat back between them. Dempsey sat in shock.

"You just bought another secret, but I'm surprised you haven't already ferreted it out. I'm building up Ward Perry to take over for me. By the time I leave, he'll be able to do everything I can. But this you don't talk about either. Even Ward doesn't know it, and I don't want him to until he learns the job, knows he can handle it and gets hungry for it. Does that ease your mind, little worry-wart?"

She looked at him squarely and he watched dampness gather in her eyes.

"I am going to cry now," she said. "And you're no gentleman if you look."

Obediently he faced forward and put the car back on the road. "When you're finished, how about telling me what the state of the campus is from your perspective; what's with the kids and how you're doing?"

She nodded and turned her face to the window, but after a mile she began to talk.

"So far I haven't been knocked off of the rock. But things do come up, and sometimes I catch myself reaching for the phone to call Esther and ask her what to do."

"That's all we'd need. You mean there's been more trouble?"

"Not concerted, no, just the usual run of personal problems. Cec and Martha called a Senate meeting, read their proposed rules and let the floor debate them and suggest others; then they took an item-by-item vote. I was surprised at how conservative the end result was. For one thing, they tied late privileges to grade averages and the progression of terms, and so far the record is pretty good. Then they laid down regulations about visiting speakers and of course the faculty and trustees do not approve of those."

"What are the regulations?"

Her lips tipped up at the corners. "Anyone may speak at Radner Hall if three hundred students signify they want

156

to hear him. They had that man from Yale last week, on Vietnam. I'll admit I held my breath, and Pat Crowell had his men alerted, but everything went pretty quietly. About three hundred turned out to hear him, and a few hecklers gathered outside—several of them didn't belong on campus—but the Senate had a corps of boys moving through the crowd and they broke it up without any excitement. You were right about Cec turning into a statesman. You've never seen a more ardent constructionist than that boy is now."

She interrupted herself with an impulsive laugh. "That day of the riot when I watched you conning him and Martha; if I had known about your political plans then, I think I'd have wet my pants."

"No, you wouldn't. You've got too much fight in you."

"Now you're conning me."

He turned his head to wink at her quickly. "How do you know?"

Then he had to give his attention back to driving. The night was black and the headlights of the trucks lumbering toward them made a baleful, blinding threat on the dark, narrow road. Talk was exhausted for the time being; they drove on in comfortable silence until they turned the main corner in Riverdale and saw the isolated lights of the Eatery.

"How does a coffee stop sound?"

"Just fine. That kind of driving hypnotizes me; I need a break."

Monck raised an eyebrow, although she could not see it in the dark car. "You had trouble keeping on your side of the road?"

She nodded and then sat up sharply. "You darn fool, you're driving."

He turned the corner into the side street, parked at the curb and got out, laughing as she continued muttering indignantly. Dempsey picked up her stockings and slung them across the back of the seat, slipped her feet into the warm shoes and reached for his hand as he opened her door.

Nicholas was alone and eager for company, but when he brought cups and plates of berry pie he sensed that three would be a crowd, and diplomatically retired behind the counter to his stool and an absorbing comic book.

Outside, Esther Hollister had just come from the YWCA building when Monck parked and got out of the car. To avoid any chance of having to speak to him she stepped back into the shadows of the entrance, saw Denise Dempsey get out of the same car and stayed where she was until they were out of her path, inside the restaurant. Resentment at both of them, especially the girl who had pre-empted her job, flared into an angry, giddy weakness. She wondered if it were a heart attack. Then she rallied and marched stoically on toward her coupe. Passing Denise's car she looked inside, as if thereby she might poison it. She saw the girl's stockings, impudently molded to the shape of calf and foot, and saw Monck's luggage on the rear seat. At once she compromised them in her mind's eye. The Young Turk who had cheated her of her job and the Jezebel with whom he had replaced her; how brazen they were, sitting together at this moment, hidden from her sight by the malicious screen of steam on the inside of Nicholas Bates's windows.

Emory Monck and Denise Dempsey could see Hollister no more than she could see them, and they were unaware of the ominous chill wind that now blew through the street. Nicholas had thought of something he wanted to ask Emory about, had returned to the booth and uncorked a recent problem that Denise had not intended to mention.

"Emory, what's the lowdown on the rumble between Polly and James and the Deltas? I hear some talk and I ask Steve, but he tells me to keep my nose clean."

Monck looked at him blankly, then raised an eyebrow at Denise. She made an unhappy face.

"I wasn't going to tell you because I think the crisis is past. There was a flap, but it seems to have subsided by itself, so why bother you. A rumor got started, I don't know how, that the Delta house was going to pledge two Negro boys from the basketball team. Amos Wellington heard it and reported it to the trustees, and they went up in smoke. They thought it would ignite a lot of ugly activity. Finally, I understand, the men's dean called in Cec Eliot and Gabe Glasscock. It was a relief when they showed him their pledge list and the names weren't on it. Of course he couldn't have interfered; it's the chapter's business, but it would have meant a lot of touchy publicity."

158

Nicholas snorted. "Whassa matter with you up on the hill? Them two boys come in here like everybody else; the kids don't act no different with them. The Deltas and them sit and eat together right here in this booth. I give Steve hell; what's his ritzy house think, the color's gonna rub off on the sheets?"

Dempsey puffed up, shaking a spoon at the restaurant man. "Before you get so charged up, Nicholas, why don't you think a little bit about those boys? If they had been pledged they would instantly have been made the butt of all kinds of embarrassing attention, just when they stand a fine chance of making the starting team, just when they've made friends and have a secure place on the campus. No boy who has done so well in overcoming his handicap should be asked to throw everything away and become a guinea pig. It's hard enough, being eighteen or nineteen, without having the trauma of being gaped at by the whole country. They don't need that fraternity. They're already respected, because they've earned it, and if the Deltas did start the rumor I think it was damned selfish."

Nicholas had taken a backward step, looking at Monck with a silent plea for help. He got a wink and with that support lifted his shoulders and spread his palms before Dempsey.

"Holy smoke. Excuse me for misunderstanding you. I can see your point, sure." Then he beat a retreat to the safety of his counter.

Monck said quietly, "Do you think it was only a rumor?"

"I don't know." Dempsey shook her head impatiently. "But whether it was or not, we nearly had a Brannigan, and the two boys vanished from the campus for a week. Anyhow, Al Conner was able to keep it out of the papers, and I'll admit I'm selfish enough to be glad it didn't flare up during my first year as dean. It appears now that it's all forgotten, and for everybody's sake I hope it stays that way."

21

☐ Vivienne Krump's current floral pyrotechnic was in chrysanthemums, gold, bronze and lavender, with a four-foot wing spread. It would pale an Aztec sunburst shield,

159

solid gold and in the sun. Her smile was just as brilliant when Monck surprised her by walking in at nine o'clock.

"Welcome home, believe me," she said. "What's going on in the living world?"

Monck dropped his briefcase on her desk with a small flip, a satisfied finality.

"Business. There is the contract from the Houston space center for two-and-one-half-million-bucks worth of research. We lifted it out from under the noses of three other schools. I am especially pleased, after one of their representatives twitted me about our wheeler-dealer university.

"On this one we have to get to work fast. The trustees made Don Dundee chairman of a new contracts committee, so I'll have to go to Wheeling and get his signature and shoot it back to Houston. I don't want to lose the time fooling with the mail. Will you phone him and tell him I want to see him around noon?"

Vivienne's face had changed from radiant pleasure at having Monck in front of her again to a congratulatory glow over this newest feather in his cap, and now it pinched into a grimace as against an offensive odor.

"That All-America charmer. Really. Emory, how long are we going to have these goons on our necks? I don't know that Washington is worth the price."

He laughed at her. "What's Dundee bugging you about?"

"He's not to believe. He strutted in here the other day and wanted to know if I was buying these flowers out of office funds. I told him politely that you gave me an allowance personally and do you know how he translated that? He said that with you gone so much, he'd take me to Cleveland for a weekend."

"That was thoughtful of him. What did you say?"

She was reaching for the briefcase and did not look up. "I asked for a rain check. I told him my syphilis was having a little flareup."

"Mrs. Krump. Remember the Wellington image, please. Call your playmate for me, and then get hold of Cec Eliot. I want to see him before I leave."

He went on to the inner office, and sat at the desk mulling over what approach he should take with the student body president. Having successfully, he had thought, gotten the students' governmental problems delegated to the Senate, he did not want to step back in and give them a

160

chance to accuse him of reneging on his word. Yet he wanted to know what was behind the rumor. That could be a bomb.

It was not a question whether integration was right or wrong. It was an approaching fact. Someday there would be Negroes in the Wellington fraternities and sororities. What Monck did not like was the timing. There was national focus on the school now and there would be more as the experimental program got rolling and as he stumped the state talking about it. He thought that possibly if all of the houses got together quietly and made the break as a united front there would not be too much friction; it could pass as a matter-of-fact policy decision. But if one faction made the gesture it would unavoidably look like a dare.

His own tenure was too new and there was too much at stake to risk the almost certain howl from the trustees and the uprising of opposing campus groups.

The buzzing of the intercom made him jump. The box had not been there when he had last sat at this desk. He flipped the switch, said yes, and heard Vivienne's voice.

"How do you like your present?"

"I like it. Thank you very much."

"Miss Yates and Mr. Eliot are here."

"Yates too? All right, show them in."

The door opened and the pair came in looking expectant but a little diffident.

"Marty was with me when I got your call," Cec said. "We guessed it was about student business, so she came along, but if . . ."

"No, I'm glad she's here. Come on in and sit down. Miss Dempsey tells me you've done a very good job on the new setup; so, congratulations and my personal thanks."

He watched the girl blush and waited until they dropped self-consciously onto the couch.

"How's it going? Is there anything you want to talk over with me? I don't want to butt in, but I think we can all operate better if our departments keep an open flow of communication. I've been away so much I feel like I'm losing touch."

Martha Yates said primly, "We've missed you, Dr. Monck."

But Cec Eliot's face had tightened and Monck thought,

161

He knows what I'm asking about; this kid doesn't miss much. He smiled his thanks at Martha and waited for a moment, not long enough to be obvious but long enough to be pretty certain that neither of the two was going to volunteer information. That he did not like. He was going to have to work on them. He looked secretive, but pleased.

"I'll let you in on something that's just happened for us. It won't break for a couple of days, but I think you'll like it. I went down to Houston and got us a big contract from the space people. We're going to do a two-and-a-half-million-dollar job for them. That's not bad, huh?

"Oh, Cec, I heard something about the Deltas planning to pledge a couple of Negro boys, but then they didn't. You're a Delta, aren't you? What's the story?"

Cec Eliot frowned uncomfortably. "The chapter decided that we wouldn't talk about it, Dr. Monck."

"Oh?" Monck sounded surprised and disappointed. "I'm sorry to hear that. I don't like secrets between business partners, which is what I envisioned the three of us as being."

"Well, uh, all right. The house talked it over, but they aren't on the pledge list. That's all."

"So . . . lots of things are talked over within the houses, but isn't it supposed to be privileged talk, not to be repeated outside? How did the rumor get started?"

Eliot's head whipped around, his eyes, angry and accusing, on the girl. Her chin tilted up and she refused to look at him, looked at Monck instead, defiant of Cec.

"I started it, on purpose, to try to put some backbone into Mr. Eliot after he chickened out. He'd promised to put those boys up and then he let Gabe Glasscock and that bunch of Birchers scare him out of his principles. It's about time somebody around her stopped talking big and did some acting. What's so awful about pledging a Negro? Eastern colleges are doing it and living through it, but oh, no, not our lily white Deltas."

As she talked, Cec Eliot was lifted out of his seat by the power of his sudden fury and he stood over her, shaking.

"You don't know what the hell you're talking about, so shut up. You jump to conclusions without any facts." He swung toward Monck, pointing down at the girl, gasping for words, and then turned to pace up and down the green carpet. "This rattle-brained female gets me into the
162

damnedest messes. I told her I couldn't tell her what happened because the house voted not to talk. So she decides she knows all about everything and goes blab blab blab. . . . Well now I'm going to tell you, Miss Smart-ass, and I hope it makes you real happy.

"No, Gabe Glasscock did not talk me out of any principles. He presided at a meeting where we voted to ask Polly and James, and I was appointed to make the invitation. I did ask them. And they turned us down. And if you'd kept your big yap shut . . ."

The redhead had sat through the beginning of the tirade in numb astonishment, but now she was getting madder by the second. She leaned forward, her fists doubled on her knees, and shouted at Eliot.

"I don't believe it."

"You'd better believe it, because I made a damn fool of myself and I do not appreciate that a bit. Now you listen good. I told you it wouldn't work. I told you Polly and James didn't want to make waves, but I let you bug me into it. So I went up to their room and I told them we wanted them in the house. You know what they said? They said, thank you very much, Whitey, no. They were insulted. They said, did we want to pledge them because they played basketball or because they were black. That's exactly what they said. . . ."

They had forgotten Monck. The girl bounced to her feet, jumping up and down without leaving the floor, pounding the air with her fists. "Oh, shut up shut up shut up . . ."

"I'm going to shut up in just one minute. For good. But first I'm going to tell you what you did, starting that talk. You embarrassed the whole Delta house and put me in a ridiculous position. And Polly and James packed up and left school. They went up to Cleveland and started looking for jobs. I had to chase after them and argue like hell. It took me one whole day to talk them into coming back. You know the only reason they did come back? The basketball team. They're on the team. That's their edge to get where they want to go. That's their wedge to drive a place for themselves where they can make a white man's wages. So they came back and took the whispering and the funny looks and the standoffishness and the cover-up

163

heartiness . . . which they had never before had to take on this campus. Goodbye."

Discoordinated by his anger, Eliot stumbled on his way to the door, jerked through it and slammed it behind him. Emory Monck sat still, watching the girl. She took two steps, following Eliot, stopped with one hand extended after him in the pose of a discus thrower just releasing his quoit, stayed so for an instant and then whirled on Monck. Her face was bloodless, her eyes fiery. A moment later they filled and spilled abundant tears.

"Did you hear him? That jerk. That stupid, conceited, blind, dumb clod."

She broke now into a quick, driven pacing, her fists raised and shaking.

"Why didn't the imbecile tell me before? Why didn't he say they didn't want to pledge? Oh, damn. After all my work. All wasted. Everything spoiled. Everything twisted around and ugly. Oh, I can't stay here. I can't work in a place with people like that. Not after this. I've got to get away. I'll leave. I'll join the Peace Corps, where somebody appreciates what somebody does." She stopped before Monck with terrible resolve. "Right now. That's where I'm going. Right now."

Monck waited until she pivoted to face the door, then he said, "I think that takes a little time."

She jarred around, her sobs working toward hysteria. "So what? I'll go home and start. I'll get a bus in Riverdale."

Monck nodded slowy. "Home is Detroit, isn't it?"

She bobbed her head.

"The express bus doesn't stop in Riverdale, but it does in Wheeling."

The words did not make sense to her and her mind paused over the puzzle. The effort brought her slowly aware of where she was, who was speaking, but it still made little impression on her.

"What's that mean?"

"I'm going to Wheeling this morning. I'll drive you over."

Again she bobbed her head.

"Go get your clothes. I have to leave pretty soon."

"I don't want them, they can give them to the Good Will. I just want to go."

164

Monck got to his feet and came around the desk. "All right, come on."

Only as he stood up did he notice that the intercom switch was still open. In the outer office Vivienne Krump held his briefcase up for him to take, saying nothing. She did not need to. In the way she looked at the girl Monck saw her longing to turn the redhead over her knee and whale the daylights out of her. Monck coughed to draw her eyes, gave her a bland, smug smile and blew her a kiss to comfort her.

He held his breath until he got Yates into the Impala and they were well past Riverdale. His luck lasted. She had not remembered that she was not carrying a purse. From then on he felt free to try to establish a two-way communication, the trick of a good teacher. Strindberg he remembered as a prime example. Old Martin would make you so mad that you began to think in order to fight back, and making you think was what he was after.

He could not lecture the girl, he knew, and it was not his way to make people mad. He decided that his best chance was to talk about the school, his plans for it and what they could mean to the institution and the students; ask her advice. If he could get her interested in the full scope of the changes and convince her that he needed her help in stirring up the enthusiasm of the kids, he thought her bruised confidence would heal itself.

By the time he reached Wheeling he knew that he had never worked so hard at a selling job. He felt wrung out. But the tears had stopped; Martha's feet were curled under her on the seat and she sat facing him. The rigidity in her backbone was gone and her normal eager intensity was back. She had refused the twenty-dollar bill he had extended for bus fare, and she was impatient to return to school and fight her weight in wildcats.

He parked in front of Dundee's hardware building and left the girl waiting in the car. Crossing the pavement, between the restored redhead and the unpredictable trustee, Emory Monck had a wistful longing for the simple days of Sam Jordan and Alcon Electronics. Could it be that his secretary was right, that Washington was not worth the effort?

The interview with Dundee, which should have been no more complicated than the man's signing his name,

165

stretched into a picayune go-round.

Don Dundee sat at his desk turning the pages of the contract slowly but too quickly to be reading them, and fiddling with his pen as if to put off the act of commitment.

"General Fenton see these?"

"I stopped by his office this morning. He was on campus."

"What did he say?"

Monck kept his patience. "He said you had been made chairman of a new contracts committee and I'd have to get your signature."

"But he didn't object?"

"Would I have driven down to Wheeling if he had? It is important to get this in the mail this afternoon so it can be signed in Houston before something can happen to upset it. Don, this is bigger than just the original research. If we can solve the problem for Houston we'll have a new type of fabric with wide commercial uses. Royalties on its manufacture could bring us a hell of a continuing income."

Don Dundee was a success in his own line. This year he would clear something like thirty-five thousand before taxes. But he actually disbelieved that any research project could earn such amounts as Monck discussed so casually. It led him to circumambulate, to approach this piece of paper as if it would blow up in his face. Then too, he had a habit of ending most of his sentences with "huh?"

"Jeeze, Emory, I don't want you to misunderstand what I'm going to say, but you've gotta know that the board and the financial office are getting nasty about some of the spending you've authorized . . ." He pulled open a lower drawer and brought up a sheaf of papers. "For instance, seven hundred and sixty-five thousand dollars to convert those buildings Jim Dice started."

Monck counted to ten, studied the corners of the ceiling and paced his voice to an idle conversational tone.

"Sure. The shells weren't any good to us the way they stood. Two of them didn't even have their windows installed, another winter would have wrecked them . . ."

Dundee said hurriedly, "Of course, I understand that; you don't think I'm stupid, do you, huh? And I'm a hundred percent behind your concept, you know that, don't you, huh?"

Monck chose not to comment.

"The only thing is, don't you think we're moving a little fast? Why do we have to do everything at one time?"

Monck said nothing about his personal reasons for haste. Instead, with a perfectly straight face he said, "We have to strike while the iron is hot. Right now, with all the favorable publicity we're getting, industry is watching us. We will be judged on our performance, not our promises, and the people I'm talking about are interested in speed. Then there's the competition. Other schools are beginning to see the possibilities of what we're doing. We've got the jump now, but we won't have it long."

This was something Don Dundee understood. He signed the papers. Then he said in half apology:

"I hate it to look like I'm all the time dragging my feet, but after all, Jim Dice made us a lot of big promises, and a burned man kind of backs off from the fire. You don't blame me, huh?"

Emory said that he did not blame him. He would have liked to get away, but Dundee was not finished.

"The idea of spending more than we have sort of bothered all of us. Just when we got the money for current expenses. And it still doesn't go down with some of the board too well that . . . well, it seems like industry is going to come in and tell us how to run things."

Emory smiled at him. "You needn't worry, they won't. We will furnish the facilities and the graduate students to work on the projects. They'll send in their top research men to set the projects up."

"That's what I mean. Those men won't be under our control. They won't be under the same rules as the rest of the faculty. It's bound to cause jealousy and some friction."

Monck was pleasantly surprised. Apparently under the Joe College exterior there was some perception after all.

"That's a stream we'll have to cross when we come to it, but I have already set up one of our own people, Ward Perry, as a coordinator."

"Who's he?" Dundee did not recognize the name.

"He's in the Physics Department; he was Strindberg's assistant. He has his doctor's from MIT, but he understands the way industry works too."

Dundee's mouth drew down. "I think I know him, dark haired, about six feet? Yeah. We've been having a little trouble. He's kind of stubborn."

167

Monck folded the contract, placed it in the envelope Vivienne had prepared, and sealed it. "I think Ward's loyalty to Wellington is beyond question, and his firmness may come in handy in integrating our business partners."

He turned toward the door and Dundee followed him out to the entrance of the building. Martha Yates was watching through the window of the Impala. As she caught sight of Monck her smile broke, wide and unrestrained. Don Dundee clutched at Monck's arm.

"Zowie. Is that yours?"

"My car?" Monck was forced to stop.

Dundee whistled. "The redhead."

Monck moved his arm, indicating that he would like to have it back. "She's one of the student leaders who rode over with me to discuss some campus business."

Dundee leered. "Some dish. Hey, uh, that reminds me." Having said this much he plainly wished that he had not, then apparently decided that he must go on. "Hell, I wasn't going to say anything, but maybe you better see something. You got another minute?"

He let go of the arm and beckoned, hurrying back into his office. Monck followed with little patience. Dundee returned to his desk, took a folded letter from the center drawer and extended it.

"This came in, special delivery this morning, from Riverdale."

Monck unfolded the paper casually and read the single typewritten sheet.

Dear Mr. Dundee:

You as a Trustee of Wellington University should know certain things about the actions of certain faculty members and their relations with subversive organizations of national scope. It is a fact that during her residence at Columbia University Denise Dempsey attended a number of study groups which by their own literature are obviously Communist fronts. In the recent rebellious demonstrations on Wellington's campus she openly sided with the radical element, as she has done consistently ever since her arrival at that school.

That in itself is cause enough for alarm, but more dangerous is her intimacy with the new Chancellor.

They have been seen often in each other's company off the campus, and it might be illuminating if you asked her where she spent this last weekend and why she returned late last night with luggage in her car, which was being driven by the new Chancellor.

A friend of Wellington.

Monck read it through twice, the second time to give him a moment to get hold of his blaze of anger.

"Where's the envelope?"

"I chucked it, I guess. Wait a minute." Dundee scrabbled in the wastebasket and came up with the envelope.

The name and address were typewritten, and it had been mailed early that morning in Riverdale.

Monck noticed that the paper was trembling in his hand.

"You know this is hogwash, don't you?"

Dundee did not quite look at him. "Well, jeeze, Emory, I wouldn't blame you. That's a lot of broad. But you're in a pretty exposed spot . . . I know, you're a little young to stop and think how things might look . . ."

"Miss Dempsey was asked to meet me at the airport in Pittsburgh when I came in from Houston last night. Yes, I drove her car back to Riverdale."

"Christ, Emory, I believe you; you don't have to bite my head off. But that's beside the point. The thing that worries me is, what do you know about these things she joined at Columbia?"

"Nothing. And I am not interested. Undoubtedly she went to all kinds of meetings during her college years. So did I. So did every kid who ever went to school, out of a healthy curiosity."

Dundee moved his shoulders uncomfortably. "I didn't."

Looking at him, Monck realized this was probably too true. Dundee must have been growing up in the days of the Oxford Movement, and the other movements now nearly forgotten, but Don had been too busy counting sweat shirts and assigning lockers to football players to have much comprehension of what else was going on. He said more quietly:

"May I keep this letter?"

Dundee hesitated. "I don't know. It was addressed to me. I only showed it to you in confidence, just trying to help you out."

Monck did not press the point. He left and took Martha Yates to lunch at Gorman's, over her half-hearted protest that she could not go into a place like that the way she looked. He was too disturbed by the letter to be amused or, on the drive back, to tailor his conversation to her age. He was raging, and to counteract it he talked a good deal, flatly, about the technical specifics involved in reorganizing the school, good, solid, factual, unemotional stuff to bring his thoughts back into focus.

22

☐ Monck pulled into the parking circle before the administration building and automatically went around to open the door for Martha Yates and offer a helping hand. The girl accepted it with self-conscious delicacy and went floating across the campus toward Tathford Hall, filled to bursting with a new dream that must be told to Jane Cullen in luxurious detail.

Monck headed for his own office and threw himself into the chair, gripping the edge of the desk until his knuckles showed white. He was too upset even to see the mail stacked in his basket.

"That God damned old busybody." He said it aloud. He had no doubts about who had written the letter. He was not afraid of the personal attack; he thought that he had squelched that with Dundee. It was the nasty tarring of Dempsey that mattered. Nothing would erase the hardware man's suspicion of her character, political or personal, and Monck did not trust him to keep the slurs to himself. He was helpless to prevent the man from gossiping, and he would gladly have thrown both Dundee and Esther Hollister into the Ohio River. He reached out and slapped the switch of the new intercom.

"Find Al Conner and tell him to get his butt over here."

Vivienne's voice was sharp. "Emory, are you all right?"

"I'm all right."

"You looked like a thundercloud when you stormed through here. Did you have trouble with Dundee?"

"No, I did not have trouble with Dundee." He said it very carefully.

"Then it's that little redheaded bitch."

"God damnit." He seldom swore at her. "It is not that little redheaded bitch. I'm all right. Will you please get Conner."

He closed the switch and sat there, the back of his shirt wet with sweat.

"Come on, you jerk." He was still talking aloud. "Get a grip on yourself."

He came out of the chair like a fighter from his corner, strode to the water cooler and drank three paper cups full, spacing his swallows, fighting the grip that anger had on his whole system. By the time Conner arrived he was back at the desk, going through the mail with his habitual speed.

The publicity man came in unsmiling, his greeting almost too laconic. "Good trip?"

Monck's nod was jerky. "I'll dictate a release for you when I get through this junk. But what I called you for was to tell you about a letter Don Dundee got this morning."

Conner's voice was an animal growl. "He got one too?"

Monck's head snapped up. "There was another one?"

"Others."

"How many?"

"I don't know yet. I got one. Strindberg did. Amos Wellington. He had me in his office for an hour with the screaming meemies. He wanted me to hire private detectives to go back over Denise's record at Columbia. I blew that down, told him I had a couple of friends in New York who would look into it."

"God damn Hollister. I'll kill her. Doesn't Amos recognize a smear when he sees one?"

"That isn't the way his kind thinks. Now, I can slap Hollister down if you want me to."

"How?"

"I can turn the crap over to the postal inspectors."

"No."

"That's about the only way I know to shut the old bag up."

"Murder could be effective. Damnit, this is going to be a mess. For a nickel I'd toss their lousy school in the ash can and bail out of here."

There was a silence while Monck gave the idea consideration, during which Conner watched him with close attention. Finally he said decisively:

"Kid, you know something? You need a few days off.

You've been batting the ball around like crazy. Why don't you go someplace over Christmas? Vacation starts Friday. Nothing much will happen here until after New Year's, and you sure as hell can't do much business during the holidays. Go on out. Get drunk. Find some civilized people to talk to. Get laid. Anything, just forget this rat race for a while. It won't look so bad when you come back."

Emory Monck went to Geronimo's Spring. He called Jordan as soon as Conner left, and when he hung up he went out into Vivienne's office.

"I'm leaving in an hour. That junk on my desk can pretty well take care of itself. I've got to breathe some air."

"Take me with you," she said. "I'm stir crazy too."

He looked at her, realizing how the campus was getting her down, and gave her a warped smile. He took out his wallet, pulled two one-hundred-dollar bills from it and dropped them on the desk.

"I don't wonder. Go to New York for the holidays, see some shows, get yourself plastered. I'll see you after New Year's."

Sam Jordan met him in Phoenix, which did not make him too happy. Flying with Jordan was a harrowing experience. Sam had been over sixty when he took his solo, and he still handled the sleek Humming Bird as if it were a bronco.

Sam looked at Monck with shrewd, searching old eyes that had seen more of the world's chicanery than one man usually does. His voice was grudging; he talked as if he had expected Monck to have wasted to a quaking shadow.

"You look pretty good, maybe a little thin. I thought you said the joint was bugging you."

The hot Arizona sunshine had just begun to loosen the tight band around Monck's forehead, and now it tightened again.

"Forget it, Sam. I want to enjoy the visit."

Sam squinted, nodded, making a deduction. "Okay, start enjoying. You want to fly her?"

It was a concession that surprised Monck. Sam loved to fly. The freedom of the air was to him like the old freedom of the empty plains, a man and his horse, a man and his plane, and no barbed wire.

Monck felt the same exhilaration as he lifted the ship

172

off the runway, a clean, buoyant expansiveness, with the tentacles of frustration loosening and falling behind. He played with the plane, making detours, trying out some maneuvers, a couple of slow rolls, some evasion acrobatics, like a boy turned loose in a field of deep grass in the spring. Sam let him alone, pulled the long bill of his cap down over his eyes and pretended to sleep. The change from the chill, withering weather that he had left at Wellington to the sharp, bright clarity stretching infinitely away around him here, seemed to lift him out of the mean world of little minds and flip him back into the extravagance of Sam Jordan's world. He had not realized how much he had been missing it.

He grinned at the man beside him and took the ship in for a landing as hot as any Sam Jordan had ever made. The rest of his black mood evaporated when Eli met them with the jeep, hopped down and threw her arms around him, trying to lift him off the ground.

"Emory," she laughed, "this is the nicest Christmas present we could have. Some of the others are coming in a day or two, but until then we'll have you all to ourselves, and I want to hear all about your school."

Sam cut in to head off the questions on what was so obviously a sore subject. "Jesus, woman, let him catch his breath and get a drink under his belt."

At the ranch they dropped him in front of his old bungalow with instructions to climb into some trunks and meet them in the patio, and he wasted no time in complying. He ran barefoot across the hot lawn, swinging a towel, and hit the water in a long dive, churned down the length of the pool and back, and felt vigor and pleasure in living fill his dehydrated being.

Sam wandered onto the flagstones, pushing the portable bar into the shade of the table umbrella and Eli followed with a tray of crackers, cheeses, nibbles. Monck heaved himself and a lot of water up onto the deck and collapsed in a plastic chaise. He stretched back, closed his eyes again the sun and felt its heat settle into him.

"God, this is good."

Sam built him a drink and brought it over, resting the cold glass on his bare stomach. Monck tensed against the shock, reached for the glass and swallowed thirstily, extended his hand for a refill. Sam brought the second drink, snorting to Eli, "I believe that herd of ponies back there have got him all tuckered out."

Monck moved his head slowly from side to side. "Not that jail bait. I've stayed as pure as snow."

Jordan screamed. "What the hell, ain't you having any fun at all?"

"Fun, yes, but not that kind." Monck's lips began to twitch at the corners, to bend upward. "I won a bet from Harry Hertz. Did he tell you?"

"Nope. What was it?" Jordan made drinks for Eli and himself and sank into a chair, sighing mightily.

Monck raised his head only high enough to sip from his glass and then lie back.

"Harry looked up Alf Perkins of Genoa Plastics. He'd heard that they've been trying for three years to develop a thread. The specs are that it has to be pliable, weave like cotton, fire resistant, non-stretch. They haven't got it and Harry tried to talk Alf into a grant for us to work on it. Alf told him to go to hell, he wasn't giving away any grants. So I bet Harry a plane for the school that I could make the deal."

Sam said lazily, "Perkins wouldn't give his mother-in-law a dose of arsenic."

"He gave. I told him that if he'd set us up for the project we'd put a raincoat made of the stuff on every coed on the campus. I had Al Conner plant it as an advance tip in all the garment industry magazines. Genoa got a bale of publicity. Even if we don't lick the problem he's had more inquiries for his synthetic fabrics in the last two months than he's ever had in his life. So he gave me a quarter of a million, sent in extruding machinery and loaned us his research chief."

"Hot damn," said Sam. "What plane's Harry giving you?"

"The new Humming Bird President."

Monck stood up, stretched, did a small soft shoe step and built himself another tall drink. He knew that he was bragging, and he needed to brag, to crow before these receptive minds, after the months of battling the obstructionists. He laughed.

"I've run into some real funny ones. A man called me up last month. He's working on a new mousetrap . . . yeah, really. It's based on the theory that rodents are attracted by certain smells. He wants us to make him a sex smell to impregnate the traps with, and he'll spend twenty-five thousand on it."

"Lousy trick."

Eli slapped at Sam's leg. "Will it work on gophers?"

"That's a thought. Then, the agricultural college wanted a couple of new tractors. I got them from Mark Dinning, sold him on the idea of letting us experiment with an attachment that would shape a hedge on both sides at once, for highway departments and big installations.

"We've dug up a lot of oddball stuff, outside of ordinary research areas. How's this one, a non-slip necktie? That one came out of the suggestion box."

"The what?" Sam Jordan dragged out the last word, giving it two notes, high and then low.

"By request of the students. I put one in the hall outside my office, and you'd be surprised at some of the ideas the kids have come up with."

He kept talking, trying to uncoil. "I just signed a sweet contract with the space people, and I think that's all I'm going after this winter. This next semester we'll get what we have organized and see what our publicity will bring in. . . . Speaking of publicity . . . I went to Hopkins Camera because one of the boys in the Physics Department came up with an idea for developing pictures. It involves an entirely new emulsion, and they laughed at me.

"So we took a hundred pictures and printed up a supplement. We photographed the whole school, two pictures of each building, one on regular film, one on the experimental stuff, and laid them out side by side. Under each pair we ran a quick description of what the building was used for. They wouldn't listen to my sales pitch, but they looked at the supplement and were impressed in spite of themselves. I think we're going to get a grant and a contract for all their research."

"Sneaky, aren't you?" Eli grinned at him.

He reached for her hand. "I learned from a good teacher."

She shook her head. "You're operating in a way Sam never did. I don't see where you find the time for it all. I subscribed to the Ohio papers to keep track of you, and it seems every time I open one it's reporting on a new speech you've made. You'd think you were running for office."

Emory Monck sat down deliberately. He had kept his plans secret from them in order completely to divorce himself from the Jordan organization, but now the divorce was an accomplished fact. He would only hurt them by waiting until his direction became obvious to everyone, and that would be a stupid mistake.

"You're pretty smart." He smiled up at Eli fondly. "That's exactly what I'm doing."

He talked fast now, trying to get the whole thing said before Sam should think to take offense at having been kept in the dark, watching Jordan's face for reaction. The older man was puzzled at first, but then as he saw the scope of the plan his eyes lighted with glee.

"What a way to go." He sat cackling, rubbing his hands together and pounding his feet on the stones. "I wouldn't want it for myself, but for you it's a natural. You give the word when, and the boys and I'll get behind you and . . ."

Emory Monck put up both hands in a restraining gesture. It was a moment he had been dreading, had sweated over, trying to think how he could say what must be said. If he fouled it up he could be in deep, deep trouble. If Sam got mad nothing could keep him from bitterly turning his considerable power toward wrecking not only the political career, but anything else Monck might try to do. He made his voice as earnest, as heartfelt, as sincere as he was able, and took the dive.

"Sam, you can think better than that. If I go into public office painted with the wheeler-dealer brush there won't be one damned thing I can do to help you. Any move I make will be suspect. I've got to stay loose from anything that John Public can possibly construe as a pressure group. That's the only way I can be effective. And we're going to need somebody effective in government, you know that as well as I do."

He watched the antagonism gather in Sam's sunken cheeks, in the chilling of the hawk eyes, and thought, Oh my God, I've blown it good.

But then there was Eli, Eli to the rescue. He should have remembered that this was the softening hand. Eli began to giggle.

"Sam Jordan, stop looking like he stole your new rattle. Me, I'd rather see Emory in a position to do something good for all of us than wasted up there with his hands tied.

176

You trained him, now let him make his own deal."

Jordan looked up at her for a long, rough minute; then his mouth relaxed and he put his club aside for the time being. He wrinkled his nose.

"I knew you were up to something from the first. I never bought you wasting your time on that school for love."

Now Eli asked the question that Denise had asked him. It was strange how much the two reminded him of each other.

"Emory, I think your political ambition is fine, but you've already done so much to put the school into the vanguard. You aren't just going to turn your back on that?"

He had wanted to forget the school, indeed to turn his back on it for this week, but Eli was too valuable an ally to put off. He told her about Ward Perry, without, however, being able to keep the sourness out of his telling.

"He's taking hold fast. At first I thought I'd have to bring in someone from the outside, but this works better. The faculty and the board already resent the industrial men coming in, but Perry is one of their own, and I see signs that he's beginning to make the current changes more palatable. God knows I'm having trouble enough with that crowd without asking for more."

Sam cawed, happy again at Monck's discomfiture. "That riot, I never read anything as funny. It must have been like the night the girls took apart that whorehouse in Fallon when Amy decided to take a bigger cut of their graft. Jesus, I like to died laughing."

"The riot wasn't bad, the kids were honestly trying to get a bum situation changed, but it touched off a chain reaction."

In talking about Hollister's poison pen attack on Denise Dempsey and himself, Monck's throat constricted.

"You asked for it," Sam's snaggle-toothed mouth spread in a raw grin. "You sure asked for it. What you going to do?"

Once more Eli turned aside the collision course, whether deliberately or not, as she made a discovery.

"That Denise Dempsey, is that Carl's daughter?"

Monck nodded, still caught up in his anger.

"I remember her. She was a cute youngster. If she'd been a boy she'd have made a great jockey. What's a girl like that doing at a university?"

"She's got too much brains to hang around a stable all her life."

"Oh? You've got something against racing horses?"

Monck blinked at her, coming out of his red haze. "From your angle, no. But without money behind her, where would it get her? She's got too much on the ball to waste it on animals when she can handle kids like she does."

Eli looked off into blue space, saying casually, "You've been dating her a lot?"

Emory Monck could hear wedding bells in her wistful tone, and he looked at Sam blankly. Sam snuggled happily deeper in his chair.

"You better watch out, she's ganging up on you."

Monck was surprised to find himself embarrassed. He did not know how to answer, but he did not dare laugh at Eli in this mood. He had to play it straight.

"No," he said. "Honey, when I choose a wife it will be a quiet, refined girl I can take to Washington and know she can handle herself as a hostess. As a matter of fact, I've been thinking about one I've known all my life, Wellington's daughter. She already has some experience, giving teas for her father."

Eli Jordan, used to the men around Sam teasing her with straight faces, looked at Monck very closely, then she said in disbelief, "He sounds like he's buying a horse."

Sam was still having fun. "Smart. There's plenty of sex laying around; he don't have to tie himself to one piece."

Eli ignored him, worrying about the boy she had in a sense adopted.

"Emory, you don't seriously think you can be happy with that kind of a marriage, do you? You don't really think you can file your life in a card index, run it with a computer? You're talking like some machine."

He stood up and folded her into his arms. "And you're talking just like Dempsey. You two could be mother and daughter. You know something? I'm starving. When do we eat?"

"All right, I'll get the hamburgers. Sam, you make us a fire."

She freed herself with a tart impatience and went toward the house. Sam chuckled after her.

"Every once in a while the old gal acts like a woman. They just can't let a man alone. Make us a drink while I
178

start the barbecue. Hamburgers. God damnit, my teeth; I can't chew a decent piece of meat any more. It's hell to be trapped in a worn-out body. Can't eat. Nothing in my pecker . . ."

He went away muttering. Not since very early in their acquaintance had Monck thought of Sam Jordan as old and Sam had never spoken of it. It made him distinctly uncomfortable. He mixed the drinks absently, trying to drag his mind away from the pictures that rose unwanted, but his thoughts clung to Sam and Eli, and, oddly, to Dempsey. Restless, he dropped into a chair at the table and reached for the deck of cards in the box that had its permanent place there. He shuffled them, riffled the edges with a smart splatter of sound.

Sam was already back; there did not seem to have been time for his chore. Monkey-like he scrambled into the opposite chair, clapped his hands and rubbed them together briskly, reached for the box and counted out chips. Monck suddenly felt better. Sam might be old, but head to head stud with Sam Jordan was the most wicked game in the world, and Monck was ripe for it.

"My money's back in the cabin. You want to trust me or make me walk?"

"Trust you. You can't get away from the ranch without I know it. Deal."

Monck dealt, one card down to each of them, then one up. "How'd you make out in England?"

Jordan tipped up the corner of his hole card and tossed a blue chip to the center of the table. "Got my company set up and my own duke running it."

Monck met the bet without looking. "What do you mean, your own duke?" He dealt two more cards up, giving Jordan a pair of deuces showing, peeked at his hole card and found that he had the third deuce, an ace and trey showing.

Jordan raised the bet to five. "Kid, you wouldn't hardly believe this guy, he's right out of a book. But he ain't dumb and he knows everybody over there. You ask him if he can get to someone and he stares at you through his little glass eye and says, 'Rawther, cousin of mine, y'know.' The son of a bitch is related to half the House of Lords."

Monck met Sam's five and in reckless, juvenile defiance of reason added two more chips, a bet Jordan did not understand. "How'd you happen to get him?"

"Got him with the company. Only way I could swing the deal." Sam added the two chips and waited for his fourth card. It was a six and he looked at it spitefully and passed, dumping the onus of betting or taking a free ride into Monck's lap.

With an ace showing, and the four he had just caught, Monck elected to bet the seven chips. Sam had him beat on the board, could have a pair of sixes or could have the fourth deuce. Against that Monck could only hope to fill his straight, which was unlikely, or catch another ace which would stand up if Sam had nothing but the single low pair. It was a suicide bet, but it fitted his present frame of mind.

Sam scared him by staying, and scared him further by catching a king as his last card. Monck did not fill. He got the fourth deuce, which would beat Sam unless Sam had that second pair.

Sam's hawk head jutted forward, his eyes squinting, peering at the potential of Monck's hand, then he shook his head and folded.

Emory Monck was disappointed. He had hoped Sam would bluff his exposed pair, that he could then clobber him with his matching pair and high ace. And then he realized something. This was not the smart poker he should be playing. The thought chilled him. He should know by now never to let his guard down with Jordan. He would, he thought, have to straighten up. He could not afford to start making mistakes at this point.

Sam reached for the cards, gathering them up, and sneaked a look at Monck's hole deuce, then grunted.

"You're shook, boy. What's eating you?"

"Nothing I can't cure in a couple of days with you. Tell me about the English company."

He played better then, more carefully, dividing his mind between the cards and Sam's joyous recounting of the English deal.

"They had these three hundred gas stations, see, and an old refinery that was worse than the piece of junk I bought down on the Gulf years ago. I didn't want it, but you couldn't separate it from the stations any more than you could separate the duke from the company. It was a family concern. The duke and a brother and a couple of cousins were happily running it into the ground, and at first they wouldn't even talk about selling. But then they got to fighting among themselves."

Monck saw the quick glint in Sam's eyes. "You wouldn't have had anything to do with the fighting, would you?"

Jordan looked hurt. "Me? All I did was send Larry Donovan over there to make a survey, and he told the cousins the duke was killing the company, which he was. The cousins put up a squawk and then I went over and sympathized with the duke. I told him his cousins were talking to Shell."

"Were they?"

"How the hell do I know? By that time none of them would speak to the others. Anyway, I went to their banker and made an offer through him of five million dollars American. That figured out about ten thousand a station, with nothing for the refinery. They squawked to heaven. Well, by then I'd learned that they had nearly a million in cash in the till and another million owed them by some French companies, so I raised the offer to eight, and they bit. That is, all but the duke. He owned fifteen of the hundred shares of the company, so he couldn't block the others from selling, but I'd said all or nothing.

"We had to try it another way. Make me a drink. Larry managed to buy twenty shares from one of the cousins, then we borrowed six million from the bank in the name of a trading corporation we set up. We used that to buy out everybody except the duke. He damn near wrecked the whole deal. I was sure he'd sell when we waved the extra cash under his nose, but he didn't.

"So there we sat. The trading corporation, which Larry and I owned jointly, had sixty-five shares, Larry held twenty and the duke fifteen. What we'd intended to do was to borrow money on the ground the stations were built on, use that to have the oil company buy up the shares held by our trading corporation and so retire the bank loan. That way Larry's twenty shares would have owned the whole thing. We could reorganize, incorporate British General Consolidated, have Larry transfer his shares to that. It would have meant we'd bought the company, which I figured was worth about ten million, for one million six plus the mortgages we'd given on the service stations.

"But we couldn't go ahead with the old boy blocking our way. If we did, his fifteen shares would have wound up worth better than four million bucks."

"So how did you get around him?"

Jordan chortled. "Simplest way in the world. He wanted to stay in as chief executive officer. I told him if he'd turn his shares in to the company we'd pay him a hundred and fifty thousand a year for the rest of his life. I pointed out that he had no direct heirs and that anything he left would just go to those cousins, and he hated the idea. That did it.

"We retired all the stock, reincorporated for fifty million, put the stations and refinery in at ten million, paid ourselves that ten million of the new stock, sold the rest to the public, paid off the mortgages on the stations, junked the refinery and built a modern one, and still had some twelve million in the treasury for expansion.

"So, for a million six investment we control a fifty-million-dollar corporation. The duke is happy as a clam as managing director and I've got Jack Finney over there as head of the financial committee to ride herd on him."

Emory Monck laughed, feeling the old zest that Sam's deals always gave him.

"Are you going to branch out to the Continent?"

"Maybe, but not to France. Those crazy frogs have the silly idea that the country belongs to them."

That night Monck got gloriously drunk. After Eli and Sam had finally gone to bed he spent an hour in the pool under the low arch of the dazzling desert sky, and slept until noon the next day. For the week and a half he had allotted himself, he played. He and Eli rode in the mountains. Hertz, Price Davis and Gordon Randall with his handsome wife arrived. They played a lot of poker. They talked about deals. It was wonderful. Toward the end Monck thought about Ward Perry and what his reaction would be to this group.

"I wish Perry could hear you tell that English story," he told Sam.

"Call him up, tell him to come on out, I'd like to meet him."

So Ward Perry came to Geronimo's Spring. Monck watched him recognize the names as he was introduced and watched his eyes glaze as he listened to the talk. Ward licked his lips over the poker game and Sam invited him to sit in. Monck warned him, but Perry waved it aside.

"I can afford one shellacking if I take it," he said, "but

I'm a pretty fair mathematician too."

He was a good mathematician, but not the equal of the Jordan crowd. Still, they liked him, gave him no quarter, and he ate it up.

He and Monck went back to Ohio together, Monck freshened and relaxed and ready to return to Al Conner's schedule of speeches and to take the next steps toward redesigning Wellington, Perry with a new image of life that enthralled him and pointed the way that he would go. Perry, Monck thought, was coming along faster than he had hoped for. It might be that he could leave the school and give all of his time to the campaign earlier than he had planned.

23

☐ Martha Yates, barefoot, in a terry-cloth mumu, her hair hanging in a straight sheet still damp from its weekly shampoo, balanced on tiptoe on the back of a couch in Tathford Hall, sticking the latest newspaper photograph of Emory Monck on the wall above her head with bits of Scotch tape.

There was already a large collection of the chancellor's portraits on display. The *Time* cover held the place of honor, directly above the Beatles and Batman.

Twenty or more girls were in the room, practically everyone in the dormitory who did not have a date. They had been watching Peyton Place. It was an hour of lull, a time for doing nails, rolling hair onto plastic curlers, investigating skin for blemishes, changing hems in skirts, knitting on sweaters. It was a soft, scented, pastel scene of languorous peignoirs, pale bare arms that had lost the summer's tan, bright toenails luminous in the subdued light, of diagonal figures draped crosswise over chairs, flowing pyramid forms cross-legged on the floor. It was a brief time, with studying to be got back to at any moment.

Jane Cullen rose to shut off the television, then walked on to appraise the new item of Monckiana. It was a good, sharp picture, Monck smiling strongly into camera, inviting confidence and affection. Below it a caption read Wellington Chancellor to Address Ohio Educational Association at Columbus.

"God, he's handsome."

It was the consensus of the campus, but particularly of this dormitory. Thatford Hall considered Emory Monck its personal property and idol.

"Wouldn't I love to be on a desert island with him."

Someone across the big room hooted. "You haven't got a chance. He's Martha's."

Martha had talked a good deal about the trip to Wheeling, basking in the certainty that any of the others would have given up her hope of heaven to have been in her place. The conversation had been gone over word by word and the general deduction made that Monck had indeed accepted Martha as an equal, to be talked to on an intellectual parity. Further, he need not have taken her to such a place as Gorman's for lunch; a hamburger stand would have been sufficient if he had not considered her to be special.

Only Bertha Tilden did not enjoy the romance.

"If he's so gone on you why hasn't he taken you anywhere since vacation? Or has he?"

There was a vitriolic probing in her voice, as she searched for a sore place. She was a member of the hall without being a part of the group. She did not attract friends, she disliked everyone, but she had a particular and lively hatred for Martha Yates. She blamed Martha for getting Esther Hollister fired.

As Hollister's secretary she had enjoyed a comforting measure of power. Over her desk had passed all requests for off-campus permits, class attendance cards and disciplinary injunctions, and she had made the most of it. The girls had resented her but had feared her too, and the fear had made for a passive acceptance in the house. But now that Hollister was no longer dean and Tilden in no position to do them harm they had by mutual consent excluded her from their circle.

Martha Yates debated whether to trouble to answer, but this was a vulnerable point. She had not heard from Monck since the holidays and had taken refuge in wishful dreams and rationalizations. The oftener she went over them the more factual they became. She jumped down from the couch.

"He's got to be careful." She said it as much to convince herself as to answer Bertha. "The faculty isn't supposed to date undergraduates. You know that."

184

Tilden spoke with bitter logic. "I don't question that he took you to Wheeling, but it was only to keep you from running away from school. You go around looking like a beatnik; you think he wants that when he can have Alice Wellington?"

Jane Cullen swung around. She wore a light robe with nothing under it and she was never concerned with keeping it closed.

"Split. Who asked you into this anyhow? Get lost."

"I've got as much right here as anyone." Jane frightened Bertha; she was bigger than anyone else in the dorm; she was more mature emotionally and more experienced. She frightened her and drew her to try to curry approval. "I'm just asking a reasonable question. How do you think she'd look up there in Columbus with him making a speech to all those respectable people? But the way she talks you'd think she was sleeping with him or something."

"So what if she were? It's none of your damn business."

"And anyway, I can't see what you're all so stokered about. I don't think he's so much."

A chorus of mockery drowned her.

"All right, all right, then make her prove it. Make her go to Columbus and prove it. She won't do it. She's too chicken." Her thin voice carried above the rising sound level.

Martha Yates pointed a shaking finger at Tilden. "Who's chicken? Who went to jail to get some decent rights for everybody? I didn't see you riding downtown in any patrol wagon. Where were you?" She raised her arm. "Upstairs there hiding under your bed, that's where."

"Because I had better sense." Tilden appealed to Jane Cullen. "Look at her, chickening out, changing the subject. Now how do you like your fearless leader?"

"You've got rocks in your head." Martha overrode the noise. "I'm going to Columbus and I'm going to shut you up for good."

The silence of shock echoed in the room. Jane Cullen took a fresh look at her roommate.

"You mean that, Yates?"

"I mean it."

The noise began again, excited, expectant, uneasy, cautioning, urging.

Tilden laughed. "Like a witch on a broomstick. He'd

185

spank you and send you home."

Martha Yates flipped the pennant of her red hair. "No. Just because I'm free to wear what I like here doesn't mean I can't conform to what he likes." She turned to speak to the others. "Somebody lend me some clothes."

There was a race for the stairs. Whether they believed she would go, whether they approved of her going or disapproved, whether they would have gone themselves or backed away, whether they thought it logical or adventurous or foolhardy or wrong, made no difference; each girl urgently wanted Martha Yates to wear or carry something that belonged to her. Each would find a special thrill in sending something of herself on the symbolic trip. Tathford Hall belonged to Emory Monck, and each of her young bodies, at least tonight, quickened with visions of Yates and Monck in love's embrace.

Underwear, slips, hose, scents, make-up, dresses, coats, handbags, overnighters, jewelry, shoes, hats, gloves, arrived in the Yates-Cullen room. They fought over whose this and whose that she should take. They manicured her, pedicured her, dressed her hair and undressed it and dressed it again. A wardrobe was agreed on. A case was packed. The halls whispered with a going and coming of bare feet stepping lightly. A watch was kept for the house mother. But nobody noted that Bertha Tilden had slipped away to her bed.

It was three o'clock before the last of them left. A chill wind blew through the barely opened window and moved the drapes in sluggish unrest. The cold touched Martha's feet and slipped up through her body. She looked up at Jane with dilated eyes.

"What if I'm wrong? Jane, what if he doesn't want me?"

Cullen turned a chair around and straddled it, resting her chin on her arms, crossed on the back.

"You really want him?"

"I get wobbly inside when I think about him."

"Then go. You'll never do it any younger."

"But if he doesn't . . ."

"Baby, in that peignoir of Helen's the man isn't born who can walk away from you. If I'd waited for my Greek god to wake up by himself he never would have."

"I wonder what it will cost. I mean, if I'll have enough money."

Cullen watched the dark eyes, the face, pale beneath the hint of rouge.

"Honey, are you afraid of going, or of not going?"

The head shook quickly. "Only that he really doesn't care."

Cullen got up and got her purse, took out three twenty-dollar bills and then went into the bathroom. She came back to Martha, shoving the cap onto a small plastic bottle.

"You can't wear my clothes, so here's my contribution. Here's sixty bucks, and take the pill the next morning."

Martha drew away. "That doesn't do any good, you have to take them on a schedule."

"Not this one. It's new. Works differently. Good up to six days afterward. Only don't you wait that long."

Down the hall Bertha Tilden slept uneasily, worried by the enormity of what she had started, although she did not really believe that Martha would go. Not until morning did she learn that Cullen had taken Steve Bates's car and driven Martha to the bus station.

She did not hear it directly. She was not being spoken to. But there was an air of excitement all through the dormitory and she overheard a whispered report in the upper hall. She moved restlessly around the empty lounge.

Finally she could stand it no longer. She got her bike from the rack behind the building and rode it through the deep slush of the highway, down to Esther Hollister's.

She was gone for two hours, and when she came back into the lounge she was giddy with success. Cullen and the half dozen girls with her stopped their speculations and waited for Tilden to pass on through, but instead she paused, unable to keep from favoring them with a gloating smile. It was so unlike her usual sullen glower that Cullen straightened.

"Well, what have you been up to?"

Bertha had meant for it to come as a surprise, but she had waited so long for this chance that she had to hint.

"You'll find out."

"Find out what?"

"I don't think Martha Yates will be here much longer."

The game of Assassin, which had grown out of the Gold-finger-Double O Seven excitement, was popular in Tathford Hall. A good deal of time and ingenuity was given to inventing ways of killing a victim, by poison, by impreg-

187

nated notes, by invisible traps on the stairs, by doors opening lethally, by simple, unexpected garroting. Jane Cullen considered several methods briefly and found them wanting now. She got out of her chair, restraining herself until she was close enough to Tilden and then with a swift hand closed her fingers in the mouse-colored hair and twisted it.

Bertha Tilden came up on her toes and her mouth opened to gasp against the pain. She turned her body in the direction of the twist but Cullen wrapped the hair again and yanked it.

Bertha yelled and tried to sink away from the excruciating feeling that her scalp was being pulled loose from her skull. Sudden fright gave volume to her cry.

Doors opened on the upper hall and an audience jammed down the stairs. They misread what they saw, the Tilden girl on her knees with her hands around her head trying to tear free from Cullen's grip. They thought it was the game and made a joint sound of protest. Jane was being too rough, you weren't supposed to hurt your victim. But Jane did not look as if she were playing.

Jane shook her hand and Tilden's head wobbled. Jane had said something but the words were lost in the general noise. Tilden cried out again, a high-pitched shriek.

"Nothing. Nothing."

The crowd quieted to listen. Tilden kneeling, her spine arched, her head pulled back, her nose red and her eyes flowing, made mewling, hurt sounds with a quaking mouth. Cullen jerked the head forward.

"You went to Hollister."

Tilden made a whining sound, an inarticulate yes.

Cullen growled, a jungle cat when her cub is attacked. She shook the head sideways.

"What did she do?"

Tilden raised on her haunches and Cullen took it as a signal that the girl would talk if she could get her lips together. She eased the head forward.

"What did Hollister do?"

"She phoned General Fenton."

Now there was no sound at all in the hall. Cullen moved around in front of Tilden and squatted, a mother goddess even in this position looming above Tilden, her grip on the hair looser but still a threat, her voice as patient as the rattling of a coiled snake.

188

"Tell me exactly what went on down there. All of it."

Bertha Tilden, hurt and frightened, could think of nothing now beyond immediate release from this torture.

"All right. Let go."

"Not until you give." But she did relax her hold enough to let the girl concentrate on what she would say.

The girls groaned as they listened to her confession. Don Dundee had been in Fenton's office and had come down with him. They had listened to Tilden's story. Hollister had suggested that the two men go to Columbus and catch Monck and Yates in their hotel room. Monck would be fired, Hollister would be given back her deanship, Martha would be expelled.

Cullen let her hand fall out of the hair slowly and felt the need to wash it immediately. Tilden bent forward, folding herself over her knees and cried into her hands. Cullen stood up, caught her by the back of her shirt and hauled her to her feet, pushing her toward the stairs, raising her eyes to the ranks packed on the steps.

A narrow path was made and Cullen half-pushed, half-lifted Tilden up through it, then down the hall and shoved the girl away from her into her room. She closed the door.

"Somebody keep an eye on that thing. Don't let her move out of there."

If her voice sounded absent it was because most of her mind was jumping from one course to another, searching for a way to scotch the calamity.

She could phone the bus station in Columbus and have Martha paged as soon as the Riverdale connection came in, but she did not know whether Yates would ride clear into the depot or drop off somewhere along Broad Street. She did try to phone Monck at the hotel where the Educational Association meeting was scheduled to be held. He had a reservation there, but he had not yet checked in, and they did not expect him until evening. Other ideas flung at her by helpful house mates were wild to the point of frenzy.

She went in search of Cec Eliot, caught him in the chemistry lab and dragged him outdoors to privacy.

"She did what?" Cec was incredulous.

"You know Martha and a dare, and you know my ideas about sex. She had a right to go. But that God damned weasel Tilden."

Martha with her chin out. Cec thought that he knew her very well. A victim of her unchanneled energy. But analyzing her was no help now.

"How do we get to her in time?"

"You and I can drive to Columbus."

Eliot started to agree, but had a second thought. "That puts all our eggs in one basket. We could have car trouble. We need somebody else, Cullen. I'm going to Dempsey."

Jane Cullen did not normally confide in the powers. She went her own self-sufficient way. But if anyone could be trusted in this emergency it would be the dean of women, this dean of women.

Denise Dempsey listened incredulously. What they were saying was just too fantastic. But the faces, both the Cullen girl's and Eliot's, convinced her that it was really happening.

She took a moment to reorient herself, to rest her elbows on the desk and massage her temples with her fingers. She felt a watery weakness that drained her of thought, but then she got her second wind. She phoned Vivienne Krump.

"Something urgent has come up," she said. "Do you know where I can reach Dr. Monck immediately?"

The other woman could barely keep her dislike out of her voice.

"What is it? I'll be talking to him this evening."

It occurred to Denise that all she needed to do now was tell Vivienne Krump that Martha Yates had gone to spend the weekend with her boss. The secretary was jealous enough as it was. Fifteen years older than Monck, she probably was not romantically interested, but she surely showed a distaste for anyone who might attract him.

"It cannot wait until evening, Mrs. Krump."

"Well, I don't keep a schedule on him hour by hour. If he calls I'll have him call you. Or you might phone the hotel and leave a message."

What kind of a message could she leave? That a child in a dream world was about to descend on him? That might solve his side of the problem, but what would he do to the girl, with only a cold, cryptic message to guide him? It was Martha she was the more worried for.

"Ask him to call Jane Cullen at Tathford Hall."

It caught Jane unprepared. With the responsibility passed into the hands of authority a dazed inertia had taken

190

hold of her, a passive force that had dulled her reasoning.

"Me?"

"You go back to the dorm and keep that phone open. Stay close to it until you hear from Emory or me. I'm going to Columbus. Cec, you drive me. We'll take my car; it's downstairs."

24

☐ Before the big mirror in Emory Monck's hotel room Martha Yates turned slowly, drawn by the dramatic change to look herself over once again. The reflection was not of the sexless campus Worker for the Movement. She definitely did look older. Her long red hair had been wound in a turban on top of her head, revealing a delicate, proud neck rising from pale bare shoulders. The shadow around the eye make-up added depth to the pupils, which were as enlarged as if she had dropped belladonna into them, and Helen's loosely falling, softly swirling lace promised a figure beneath it had no need to apologize.

There was only one touch of Marty-the-sophomore still with her, a kind of hand to hold onto. She had argued with Jane about bringing her guitar, but she had won when she quoted the adage that music is the language of love.

She had almost lost her nerve when she first came into the busy lobby and went to the room phones. She called the hotel operator and asked for Emory Monck's room number, asked that they ring it. The waiting made her dizzy. The lines of greeting she had been rehearsing all sounded corny now that they were about to be used. She had clung to the receiver, immobilized, but then she had got a reprieve. The room did not answer.

That looked like a bad sign. She hung up, poised to run, but when the idea occurred to her she shook it off. Martha Yates did not run. And it was not a bad sign, it was a good one. She was supposed to get into the room and make herself ready for his arrival. That was the picture she had brought with her, she and Emory facing each other, alone, free to come into each other's embrace, sheltered from prying eyes.

She went to the desk with her head up.

"My husband, Mr. Monck, in eight-fourteen, is apparently out. He did not expect me until later tonight. I wonder if someone could let me in?"

'The clerk was busy. She was well dressed and although she looked young, he remembered Monck and that he seemed pretty young himself. He swung the register 'around, motioned to the bell captain and turned to answer a phone.

In the elevator and going down the hall she debated over the tip and settled on fifty cents. She thought that the boy looked at her strangely as he closed the door, but that was pushed out of her mind by the momentous fact of actually being there.

The room was silent. It was a large room, with a king-size bed, two armchairs upholstered in a Hawaiian floral pattern, a low lamp table, a long bench below a wide mirror.

She stood listening, looking at the impersonal furniture. Then Martha went forward and placed her guitar case on the bed with deliberate emphasis.

On the bench lay his open bag, a used shirt tossed across it. His dark suit, that he wore when he made speeches, hung in the wardrobe. She recognized it from the pictures. A tray near the bathroom door held a container of melted ice, a glass half full, a whiskey bottle half empty. That seemed more intimate to her than even the shirt. She had not known that he drank. It was odd how one could love a stranger so wholly.

She put her blue airplane case beside his bag and zipped it open. She hung the peignoir on the bathroom hook, undressed and pulled the plastic shower cap down over her face. The make-up needed freshening, but she did not want to disturb the basic job the girls had done.

He had not come by the time she was ready. It was another good sign. It gave her a little extra time to get used to the room, to arrange the lighting, to establish a mood. With everything else in order, with another reassurance from the mirror, she reached for her friend and companion.

Coming along the hall, Emory Monck was whistling absently, silently. He had spent the afternoon with the governor and the heads of the legislative educational committee, fleshing out for them his plans for Wellington. If the evening speech went as well as his reception of the afternoon things were moving smoothly.

He had his key in his pocket and so had not stopped at the desk. He had not got the message to call Jane Cullen.

There was the soft sound of music coming from behind a closed door somewhere near, a guitar well played, the haunting chords of the Israeli song *Erev shel Shanim (An Evening of Roses)*. He had heard it sung in discothèques, but never translated. He liked it.

He put his key in the lock and swung the door open. The sound of the strings continued, louder, within the room. There was a light on at the head of the bed and a young woman sitting under it, her legs curled out of sight beneath the flimsy thing she was wearing. She was bent over the guitar with her head tipped to one side, listening to the low, clinging vibrations. She made a very attractive picture, colorful and warm. But she should not be there, or else he should not. He had not asked for a girl.

He backed a step away from the door and looked at the number. It matched his key, so it was his room.

In Sam Jordan's world pretty young girls were no strangers. Sam loved them. They were a part of every business entertainment. Briefly he wondered if this could be a present from the governor, or someone on the arrangements committee for the evening. But it did not fit. Was it a gag of Conner's?

Whatever it was, it teed him off. This was no place and no time for hanky-panky, no matter how enticing the girl. He had had problems enough with the poison pen letter about him and Dempsey.

The girl on the bed caught his movement in the corner of her eye and turned her face. Her expression was withdrawn, bemused with the music, and her voice told him that she was not totally present.

"Hi."

He had seen the face before, but he could not say where.

She put the instrument aside quickly and rolled across the bed. Her bare legs showed as she slid her feet to the floor and stood up. She took a step toward him expectantly and then stopped abruptly, the strange light in her eyes fading.

Knowing now who she was, Monck slammed the door shut.

"What in the name of God are you doing here?"

She stood still. He thought she was starting to cry. Then she set her small chin, ran at him and threw herself against him.

"Emory. Don't be mad. Oh, please. I had to know."

He reached behind himself for her wrists, threw them wide, then caught her arms above the elbows, pushing her back into the room. There he let her go and stepped behind a chair.

"Whose idea was this? What's going on?"

The girl's hands hung at her sides, the palms toward him, trembling. "Don't." She was as shocked as if he had hit her with his fist. "I'm in love with you. I thought you liked me. After our Wheeling trip."

He knew that his anger showed and hardly cared. But also, it was pretty obvious that this was not after all a put-up job. The crazy kid was serious. And he did regret hurting her. He would have to do some tall talking to remedy that, and he would have to find out in a hurry what else had come out of the Pandora's box with her.

He took his handkerchief from his pocket and rubbed it across his face; his smile was one of self-ridicule.

"Martha, honey, you scared the daylights out of me. I like you, indeed I do. But this way isn't right for you and me. Now get your clothes and run in the bathroom and dress, then we'll talk it out."

Still she stood there, with her make-up beginning to look like a mask as she lost color, her mouth trying desperately but unsuccessfully to say something.

"Go on, honey. We can talk through the door."

She bolted, turned to the blue case and flipped up the top, snatched out handfuls of clothing, yanked a dress from the wardrobe and disappeared in a billow of lace into the bath. Monck came around his chair and approached the door, saw the whiskey bottle and reached for it, then stood with his fingers around its neck, not lifting it.

"Martha?"

She did not answer.

"It makes me very proud that you thought enough of me to come."

She said nothing.

"Please forgive me for being so rough. I didn't understand.

"You're a brave girl. I like people who have the courage to do what they believe in.

"Martha, I'm not the right man for you. You deserve someone who will love you. I'm too old to give you that.

194

"Martha, I'm afraid that I'm not capable of that deep an emotion."

It was too early still for anyone from the coming meeting to appear, but if someone did show up it would be sweet, just sweet. He remembered that he had automatically switched off the lock on the outer door and started across to secure it, but Martha Yates's appearance stopped him. He dared not make a move now that was not directly concerned with the girl.

She came quietly, still pale, without expression. He went to her and put his arms around her, pulling her head against his shoulder, and kissed her temple.

"Don't let it throw you, kid. I really meant it that I'm proud, and proud of you. We'll stay good friends, won't we?"

To his relief she nodded. He tipped her face up with a finger under her chin and kissed her gently.

"Now let's go sit down and find out what your visit is going to mean from a wider angle."

She went obediently to the chairs and sat down primly. He pulled his chair around to face her, their knees almost touching.

"How did you get into the room, Martha?"

Her mouth twitched painfully. "I told them at the desk that we were married."

Monck's stomach knotted. "Did anyone know you were coming here, and why?"

Her voice was hardly more than a breath. "Yes. The girls in the dorm."

"How many?"

"Thirty, forty."

He sat back, filling his cheeks with air. "How did that happen?"

Her eyes had no life in them, only an anxiety to be understood.

"A girl made me mad and dared me. Everybody was there. But that wasn't why I came. I wanted to come."

He reached for her hand and held it. "Thank you, Martha. Now let's think for a minute what will happen to both of us at Wellington if the girls are left to believe that we were partners in a clandestine night in a hotel room. You know they would talk about it. And when the board of trustees heard it I would lose my job. They would have

195

to fire me to protect all of the students. They can't afford to have a chancellor who takes advantage of young girls. And I'm sure that they would not let you stay in school. They'd be afraid that someone else might really hurt you. I certainly do not want you to be hurt or to leave either."

He watched the girl's reactions to what he was saying, and knew that the ideas appalled her.

"So here's what I think we'd better do. Since the hotel believes we are married, I'll pack and we'll check out. I'll put you in a cab for the airport. I can't take you out there myself; I've got a speech to make. When you get to Pittsburgh, go to a hotel and get the bus down in the morning. Tell the girls when you get to school that you realized the jeopardy in the situation and changed your mind. I think they'll see that you're right."

She was nodding monotonously. He stood up, drew her to her feet and patted her shoulder.

"Are all your things in your bag?"

She continued to nod, and he went quickly to the wardrobe, pulled down his suit and put it with his dark shoes into his overnighter, stuffed the soiled shirt in a corner and closed the sides together. He was fastening the catches when a knock jarred the door. He gave the room a fast glance, hoping that it was Al Conner, although the publicity man was not due for another hour.

"Who is it?"

"General Fenton. Open the door, Monck."

He stopped in mid-step. He looked at the girl. She was staring at the door, her eyes wider than ever. He started to point to the bathroom, but even as he thought of trying to hide her he knew that this would only make a bad situation worse. The very fact that Fenton was in Columbus was warning enough that something had gone wrong, someone on the campus had spread the news of Martha's trip.

He saw his plans vanish. He visualized headlines. UNIVERSITY CHANCELLOR CAUGHT WITH COED IN HOTEL ROOM. It was the end for him at Wellington, and the end to his political dreams. And what would it do to the girl? God knew she was insecure enough. This would be disastrous for her. They were registered as man and wife. He could only try to brazen it out.

"Don't look so scared," he whispered. "Let me do the

talking. Just look relaxed." Thank God her bag was closed, the lace affair out of sight.

"Come in," he said. "It isn't locked."

He watched the door swing open, watched Fenton stride into the room and then saw that the general was not alone. Don Dundee was at his heels.

Dundee was self-conscious and ill at ease. He would much rather have been anywhere else in the world, but he could not refuse Fenton's demand. He did not dispute Monck's right to live a little if he chose, but he should have had sense enough not to get caught. It looked bad for the school. From the first he had not doubted Monck's guilt. He had seen the redhead in Monck's car that day in Wheeling.

And he subscribed to Fenton's intention as outlined on the drive to the capital.

"We'll face them," Fenton had said. "We'll allow Monck to resign and let the girl withdraw from school. I don't want to wash the dirty linen in public."

"What about the money Monck raised for us?"

"I think Mr. Monck will be glad to cooperate, that he'll arrange for the funds to be turned over directly to the school in return for our keeping silent about his slip."

So they were armed and ready. Dundee had not known precisely what to expect when they broke in. From his own convention trips to Las Vegas he could make some guesses, and he had read enough news stories about people being surprised by detectives to expect a chaotic reception. He felt let-down, finding that the culprits were both fully dressed.

Even Fenton was nonplused by their welcome. He had pictured Monck embarrassed, making excuses and wild explanations.

Instead Emory Monck was smiling warmly, offering his hand. "This is really good of you. I had no idea either of you was in Columbus. Did you come over for the Education meeting?"

"We did not." The general's voice was icy. "We came on a most unpleasant errand."

Monck raised an eyebrow in sympathetic question. "I'm sorry. I'll be with you as soon as I see Miss Yates out. She came up to wish me good luck from the students. I think that was a very nice gesture." He handed Martha Yates toward the door, but Fenton lifted a hand.

"She'd better stay. This concerns her as much as . . ."

Denise Dempsey swept past his hand. For one horrid, fleeting second Monck thought she was a part of the Fenton entourage. Then she was beside Martha, apologizing breathlessly.

"I'm sorry I kept you waiting so long, Marty, but I had to find Cec, and there were so many people in the lobby, even as tall as he is . . ." She laughed lightly and looked back at the door.

Monck looked too, and saw Cec Eliot just behind Dundee's shoulder. He could have kissed them both.

25

☐ "I love you, I love you, I love you, in front of witnesses," said Emory Monck.

He had recovered from the near calamity in the hotel and had had time for some private laughter. It wasn't just everyone who had scantily clad young women casting themselves so eagerly upon him. He could anticipate Sam Jordan's reaction, the howls of glee. It was too good a story to keep to himself, and the only thing Sam would not understand would be why he had not bedded the redhead.

He and Denise Dempsey and Al Conner were having a late dinner after the educators' meeting. The speech had gone well. At least he thought it had gone well, but after he had relinquished the mike and sat down his mind had gone totally blank, and he could not remember now anything he had said.

"Watch what you're saying." Dempsey did not sound as lighthearted as he felt. "I'd think you'd have had enough of that subject for one day."

He shuddered deliberately and laughed. "Never will I forget Fenton's face when you breezed in. He looked like he'd swallowed the hottest chili pepper in history. He knew it was rigged somehow, but he didn't know what to do about it."

Conner grunted.

"He hates you, Emory," Dempsey said soberly. "Jerome Fenton cannot abide looking the fool, and he had egg on his face. And he knew it. You'll have to watch out for him from tonight on."

"I've had to watch him from the day we met. Stuffed shirts are always dangerous. They take themselves so damned seriously. But God, it was funny. There wasn't a thing he could do. Unless he'd had the brains to look at the hotel register."

"He might yet."

Conner grinned. "Forget it. I used to know the manager when I had the legislative beat for the Cleveland *Press*. I had a talk with him, told him the whole story. I said, the hotel doesn't really want that kind of publicity, now does it? He said he thought they could get along without it very nicely, and gave me this."

Conner handed Monck the registration card Martha had signed, and Monck made a ceremony of tearing it into small bits.

Denise said, "I hope she'll be all right with Cec."

"She'll be all right," Monck assured her. "That Eliot kid, I'll go a long way for him. They can use him at General Consolidated as soon as he graduates. I told him to rent a car in Pittsburgh and drive on down. They're probably back on campus by now. She's better off with Eliot; they understand each other's language and she doesn't have to be on the defensive the way she would have been if you'd taken her home."

"I feel so sorry for her. As you said once, it's mighty hard to grow up."

She spoke, Monck thought, from a lofty old age, but she was grown up. Both he and Dempsey had grown up early, and he considered it a distinct advantage.

Al Conner, fifty-two, choked. "Okay, you smug octogenarians, you want to break an arm patting yourselves on the back? The battle's won, but you've still got a war to fight. You can relax and philosophize when Emory's safe in the Senate with Denise running a salon on Dupont Circle." He was a little drunk and feeling reckless.

Dempsey's face reddened. "Al, you're a little out of line."

Conner was pleased with himself. "Oh come on, don't kid an old man. It's bad enough to kid yourselves, but don't teach Papa a class he invented. I been married to the same woman for twenty years."

Denise looked at her watch. "It's way after twelve. If

we're going to get my jalopy back to Riverdale we'd better start. Who wants to drive?"

"I'll take the first trick," Monck said. "You two can toss for the next."

Al Conner was asleep in the rear seat before they cleared the town. Denise curled into her corner, her head on the seat back. They went out Broad Street through quickly thinning traffic. The night had turned cold but the road was dry and Monck made good time at an even cruising speed, driving by habit, his mind looking to the next day.

He planned a showdown with both Hollister and Fenton. He was going to scare hell out of them. He was not going to tolerate their harassment any longer. One more play like today's and they could land him in some mess from which he could not extricate himself. Only Dempsey had saved him this time.

He looked over at her. Her hands were cupped in her lap, her head dropped forward. He had a feeling of comfort, of warm companionship just at having her in the car.

Not once when he had needed help had she failed him. He wondered if Conner was right in his blundering crack, wondered what she really thought of him. Living on campus was so much like living in a goldfish bowl that he was not likely to find out. And it did not really matter as long as she continued to do the job she was doing.

He drove the whole way, glad to be alone and let his mind sort its own quiet way through the maze of his affairs.

He pulled into Riverdale and parked before the Eatery. He touched Dempsey's shoulder, felt her start and straighten quickly.

"How about some coffee?"

Her eyes, still dull from sleep, went to the lighted sign and blinked at it.

"You drove all the way."

"No problem."

Her hands went to her hair in an automatic gesture to arrange it. In the rear Al Conner yawned loudly and sat up.

"Did you say coffee?"

Monck got out, flexing the stiffness from his legs, and looked through the window at the clock. It was six-thirty.

200

He'd done pretty well. He went around the car and helped Dempsey out.

"We might as well make it breakfast. As I remember, Nicholas' sausages and hot cakes were one of the brighter spots of my youth."

Nicholas and the day chef who had just come on duty were busy discussing the merits of the horses in the fourth race at the Fair Grounds in New Orleans and he did not come to the table until the three were settled. He arrived with a long face.

"Shame about the kid, Emory. How is she?"

"What kid?" Monck looked up.

"The one tried to kill herself. Little Marty."

Denise Dempsey's breath rushed in with a rattling sound. Monck came rigidly to his feet.

"What the hell do you mean?"

"You don't know?" Nicholas was confused. He thought they had come from the hospital. "She took a bottle of sleeping pills. We had excitement around here most of the night. Where you been?"

"Out of town. Where is she?"

"Down at the hospital. They pumped her stomach."

Dempsey sounded as if she were praying. "She's alive? She's all right?"

"Last I hear. It was maybe twelve-thirty, one o'clock. My boy Steve comes busting in. He's been running around with Marty's roommate."

"I know. Go on."

"She phoned him. She's having hysterics, says get a doctor, get an ambulance quick. So the ambulance goes out and brings her down. The driver was in here for coffee after the run. Then Steve brings his girl and Cec Eliot in for a thermos of coffee. I hear them talking, then they go back to the hospital."

The Riverdale Community Hospital was an antique, an old red-brick square sitting on the shoulder of the hill above the sprawling freight yards. Attached to one side of it was a modern wing of glass and shining metal, a single story building less than ten years old, which the university operated as a free clinic.

Emory Monck whipped the car into the hospital parking lot, yanked open the door for Dempsey and with a firm grip on her arm hurried her across the icy pavement. Conner followed at a dog trot.

"Damn, damn, damn," Denise continued to swear under her breath.

She slipped on the steps and Monck hauled her upright without losing stride. They went into the big reception room of the old section. It was a cheerless place of scarred, dark-varnished furniture and brown linoleum that had lost whatever luster it had had through constant mopping. The sharp, acrid smell of disinfectant permeated even the plaster of the walls. There were three people there. Jane Cullen, her round face sagging and gray, Cec Eliot hunched wordless, deep in a wicker chair, and Steve Bates standing above the girl, talking to her in a quiet voice as solid as his big muscled body.

There was a reassuring quality about Steve Bates, a kind of low-keyed self-confidence as if by his very size he had gathered emotional strength and positiveness.

He turned as the three came through the door, bringing the winter air with them, and it was he who moved forward.

"How is she?" Denise put her hand on Bates's arm.

"Sleeping. The doctor says she'll be okay. She was pretty beat. I guess having your stomach pumped is no picnic."

Monck said, "I want to see the doctor," and went back to the receiving desk.

Denise went on and sank to the hard seat beside Jane, saying quietly, "Tell me what happened."

Jane's eyes filled with thick tears, easily, the ducts already lubricated to a quick flow.

"It's my fault. Martha came in about midnight, just after I'd got to sleep, and I was dopey. I wanted her to tell me about everything then but she said nothing had happened, it was all right and she said she'd tell me in the morning. I must have dozed off. I heard her go into the bathroom and then come back and climb into bed. Pretty soon I had to go, and I went in and found the empty bottle. It was on the wash basin. It was mine and I keep it in the medicine closet. I knew what had happened right then. I went right to her but she was already asleep. I called up Steve and he got the ambulance and Cec and they brought her here. Miss Dempsey, are they lying? Is she going to be all right?"

"I don't think they'd lie, Jane, and you have no reason to blame yourself. How many did she take?"

"I don't know exactly. Better than half a bottle. My doctor gave them to me because I haven't been sleeping so good."

Denise looked up at Steve Bates. "Supposing you take her back to the dorm. And kids, the less this is talked about the better it will be for Martha."

"You can say that again. Come on, baby." Bates lifted the big girl from her seat, sliding his arm around her.

As they started for the door Denise turned to Cec Eliot. He had not yet spoken.

"You'd better go with them."

"I'm staying here."

His sensitive face was resolute and she did not argue. Monck came back across the wide room with Conner under Eliot's unwavering stare.

"The doctor says she's safely out of it. They caught it within the hour of when she took the pills. If it had been later there wouldn't have been any point in pumping her stomach. As it is she'll feel lousy for several days, but there's no physical harm done."

Cec Eliot stood up, pulling at his knuckles. Monck had hardly noticed him, sitting so still in the corner.

"It's my fault. I drove her to it."

"No you did not." Monck's voice was sharp. "I should have thought of it in the hotel. I should have recognized shock. I was thinking about other things and let it get by me."

There was a stubborn, fanatic light in Eliot's eyes.

"I opened my big mouth. I told her off all the way home. 'You raised hell, didn't you?' I said. 'You had to prove something and you nearly fixed things good.' That did it. God damn me."

"Cec," Dempsey said, "don't torment yourself. I'm at fault too. I was so relieved to get there in time that I didn't consider how she was feeling. I doubt that anything you said made any difference."

"It did too." His tone was dogged. "She didn't argue with me. She didn't fight back like she always does. She just sat there with that white, frozen look and I kept talking. I couldn't stop. I didn't mean to hurt her. When I thought she was going to die I couldn't take it. I just couldn't." He turned and went blindly down the long corridor toward the girl's room.

Monck started after him. Denise caught his sleeve.

"Let him go."

"He's going through hell."

"It's his hell," she said, "and he's got to fight his own way out of it. I've watched those two kids together for months. Neither would give in to the other. It was kind of a battle to prove who was superior. Maybe this will change things. Maybe they'll learn that they're attractive to each other as human beings, not as sparring partners." She looked at Al Conner. "Al, what happens now? How much of this is going to make the papers?"

Conner said tiredly, "There had to be a police report. I'll do what I can to kill it." He went out slowly, walking like a middle-aged man whose feet hurt.

"We'll have to wire or phone her father." Denise was thinking aloud. "I'm not sure he should come down here, I'm not sure he won't do more harm than good, but it can't be avoided."

"I'll talk to him," Monck said.

"No, not you. You may be the bright young man with all the answers in business, but what has to be said to Mr. Yates is going to come better from a woman. There are some realms that men can't share with other men. I'll see him."

26

☐ Denise Dempsey met Hugh Yates in Pittsburgh and drove him to Riverdale through a sleet storm.

She did not know what sort of man to expect. On the phone he had sounded remote, unsurprised, had asked no questions other than to make the arrangements for coming. She had bridled when he seemed so uncaring, and yet his reaction could be that of someone instinctively marshaling himself against coming apart. She reserved her judgment, and was relieved by his first words.

"How is she now?"

His voice reminded her of his daughter's, flutelike, uncertain, as if he put more feeling into his speech than his inner stamina could sustain.

He came through the terminal gate and by some instinct singled her out in the waiting crowd. He was about six feet, looking thin in contrast to his bulky overcoat. The face was not unhandsome; there was an indecisiveness about the mouth although the chin seemed firm enough.

She nodded to him. "All right. I saw her two hours ago. She's still weak, a litte groggy and not very happy, but she will be all right."

"How in the world did it happen?"

"Wait until we get in the car."

He fell obediently silent, but his impatience showed in his long, hurried steps. As soon as they were headed south Dempsey began at the beginning and told him everything she knew about the episode. He listened quietly, without interrupting, but she knew from his tenseness that he was deeply affected.

"This Monck, did he, did he do anything to lead her on?"

"Emphatically not," she said quickly. "Emory Monck has a great deal of personal charm. He attracts women of all ages. At the moment he is the campus god for all of the coeds. It's a mass hysteria, like the crowds that screamed at Sinatra and the Beatles and Bob Dylan. I'm going to be blunt with you, Mr. Yates, because we're both here for the one purpose of helping Martha, and we can't do it by being polite to each other."

"I thank you for it."

"In many ways Martha is mature for her age. She has a social conscience and awareness beyond a lot of people older than she is, but emotionally she is a romantic, not very well developed. I think part of it is because so much of her attention has been focused on the wrongs of the world. She has built herself a character deliberately and left out of it her real individuality."

"I'm afraid that's my fault." Yates sounded remorseful and subdued.

"Undoubtedly, in part, although I suspect that's her normal bent. Her mother is dead, I believe?"

"Yes."

"And you raised her?"

"As best I could, God help me. The only way I knew to handle it was to talk to her as if she were an adult, to talk about the things that interested me. I thought that would ring truer than if I tried to talk on a child's level when I no longer understood that. It used to worry me that she didn't bring many friends to the house. She never seemed to make really close friends of her own age."

To Denise that fit the emerging pattern. "She thinks a great deal of you, that's obvious. And it's natural that she should transfer her father image to another older man, in this case to Dr. Monck. When she wanted to run away from school he drove her to Wheeling, where she intended to catch the bus, and talked her out of leaving, and she apparently mistook his friendly interest for a deeper affection."

Yates shook his head unhappily. "I just don't know what to do about her."

"Actually I don't think there is too much you can do."

"Is she in love with the man?"

"Love? What is it? I don't think Martha loves Dr. Monck in the way you mean. She's romantic, as I said, and she's combative, a real competitor, and she was dared in the presence of a lot of her friends. Without that challenge I don't believe she would even have thought of such an intimacy with him.

"But I'm afraid that now she is going to feel that she has been rejected, and I know she's going to be enormously embarrassed, not only with him but with her peers."

"I'd better take her out of school."

"I was afraid that would be your attitude. I don't know . . . I can be wrong . . . it's hard to say what is best for someone in such a circumstance as this. Maybe a psychiatrist would help. Lord knows I don't pretend to be one, but it seems to me it would be the opposite of a solution to take her out of Wellington. What would you do with her? Let her sit at home and cry over her failures until they loom too big for her? Send her to another school? I think that would seem to her like running."

"But how can she stay here? How can she face the notoriety?"

"Al Conner kept it out of the papers. Of course there's talk around the campus, but that will die out if she has the guts to face it down, and I'm betting that she has. She's got a lot of friends here, and an esteem as a leader. And there's a boy."

"You mean Eliot?"

"She's told you about him? What has she said?"

"Not too much. I know she admires his brains and his involvement with campus politics."

"I think this business has shaken Cec Eliot to his roots. I think he's in love with Marty but never stopped to think of it until he thought we were going to lose her. If she comes out of this I believe it will be because of Eliot more than anyone else. I think I'd like to ask you not to rock the boat."

Apparently Hugh Yates did not. He stayed in Riverdale six days and then took his daughter to New York for a holiday. They went to plays and the Museum of Natural History, the Museum of Modern Art and repeatedly to the United Nations.

Martha came back to school subdued but determined. Within a few weeks she was voted to lead the song festival sponsored by the Music Department, which toured Cleveland, Cincinnati and Chicago and was a spectacular success. Emory Monck wrote her a letter of congratulation, thanked her on behalf of the administration for the acclaim she brought to her school and added a note about his warm personal regard and pride in her friendship.

27

☐ Wellington University was still in the winter doldrums. Below-zero weather had put a crust on the snow that blanketed the hills and muffled the campus. The corridors of leafless trees led to views of distant wonderlands. A freak ice storm had swept the valley the preceding night and left the bare limbs thickly coated with crystal that glistened with a dull luminescence under the low gray sky.

It was late for such weather; the heating pipes pounded metallically again through the administration building.

Basketball season had ended, mid-terms had been survived, yet the last of the snow had postponed the beginning of baseball training.

Looking out of the window at the bright ranks of sweatered figures following the cleared walks from class to class, Emory Monck felt isolated, completely divorced from the rest of the world.

In many ways Wellington retained the clannishness of a small college. It did not have the diffusion of the big universities like Columbia and UCLA, since ninety percent of its undergraduates were housed on campus, and the school's activities were not diluted by the accessibility of a large city's multiple interests.

Wheeling and Pittsburgh were too far away to offer much entertainment, and with the stubborn snow the trip to the movies in Riverdale was less than inviting for bicyclists. A relatively small percentage of the students had cars. Almost everyone had dug in to wait out the immobilization. Faculty row had been forced back on its own resources for leisure occupation. Nicholas and the Eatery had felt the pinch. Nothing much was stirring yet.

The campus was in hibernation, recharging its vitality, looking forward toward an explosion of excesses in spring, the Easter vacation. It had been this way every year that Monck could remember, like a car idling in neutral, and he welcomed the rest. He was tired. He was glad that the round of speeches too had slacked off. Now that he was well known Al Conner had become more selective in making his appearance dates, following a suggestion of Senator Lightner's.

Lightner had been careful not to associate himself with Monck publicly, relaying his advice through Conner.

"Lightner warns us against overexposure," Conner had said. "If you keep talking so much now people won't turn out to hear you when we start our campaign in earnest, he says, and I agree with him. The Senator is a shrewd old hand at this business. I've known him a long time."

It made sense, and Monck had always listened to those who knew more about a subject than he did. He had a lot to learn about politics and he was thankful that he had such competent teachers.

But though he appreciated the pause, Monck was bored. Everything was so quiet. Esther Hollister had not made a sound since he had threatened to take her into court. The student body was making no agitation. Cec and Marty were more concerned with their personal readjustments than with remaking the scholastic world.

As chancellor, Monck could not avoid the rounds of faculty entertainment and he faced each new dinner with an increasing feeling of claustrophobia. He and Alice Wellington were now automatically paired at these affairs and Alice had adopted a possessive protectiveness that made him uneasy.

He knew that he should be happy. The way toward his goals was ordered and open, without a roadblock. The research program marched forward without noticeable hitches.

True, General Fenton had not spoken to him directly since the night in Columbus and pointedly evaded any gathering at which Monck might be present. But he lost little sleep over this. The less he saw of the general the better.

"I'm a damn fool," he told the empty room. "Like a crap shooter kept away from the tables. I don't seem to feel right unless I'm where the action is."

Part of the action he missed was Denise Dempsey. He had seen her only on business since the night of Martha's attempt at suicide. She was conspicuously not included in the faculty parties. It might of course be because she lived in the apartment house and had no facilities for returning hospitality, but it was more than obvious that the wives as a group held Hollister's retirement against her.

Monck returned restlessly to his desk, wondering if it were safe to take her to Wheeling for dinner. He had no anticipation that the sky was going to begin falling on him in large chunks. He was only pleasantly expectant when the intercom buzzed and Vivienne said that Martin Strindberg was there to see him.

The physicist strode in looking more than ever like a bear, bundled in his heavy fabric fur coat, and Monck knew at once that he was upset. But the man took time to peel off his wrapping before he said, "Ward Perry just quit."

Monck came out of his tower of security with a jolt. "What? You've got to be kidding."

Strindberg sank heavily into the chair beside the desk. "I wish to hell I was. That God damn Fenton. He's got a head like a block of concrete."

"What happened? I was with Ward most of yesterday afternoon and he didn't say anything to me."

"Perry's close-mouthed." Strindberg rumbled like a volcano. "He fights his own battles, and this one he lost. So he quit."

"What battle?"

"He won't publish. You know what that means on this campus. Publish or perish. It's an apt alliteration."

Monck knew. All of his early life he had watched his father publish a book every second year to hold his place here. The elder Monck had grumbled and Emory's mother had fumed helplessly at the time wasted, because the books never earned more than a pittance. But Austin Monck had not fought. He had accepted the trustees' dictum as a part of his job and spent many hours that could have been given to teaching doing research for what he called his paste and glue jobs, culling the writings of other men to fill his own volumes.

"You mean they still make you do that?" Monck had been preoccupied with his own area and believed that he was not expected to interest himself in the faculty's functioning.

Strindberg had been rooting for his pipe, a certain indication of his troubled state. He saved smoking for a companion to hard thinking. He packed the burned bowl with unnecessary force.

"They've left me alone since I got the prize. I've written three books because I had something to say, not because I had to stay on the payroll. It isn't a bad idea for younger men who have the time . . . you can consider it part of their education. But hell, a man like Perry can tell off most of the men whose books he'd have to read. The program has outworn its usefulness. It was needed at one time because so many of the available teachers didn't have enough background and it was a goad to make them keep abreast when everything started popping.

"But education has changed a hell of a lot. Our department heads are leading men in their fields. When they turn up something fresh, sure, they ought to broadcast it. Publishing for its own sake, though, shouldn't be a sword hung over their heads.

"Still, the board insists on it. They act like they think the quantity of books we issue is the measure of the school's quality. Why don't they get it through their skulls that the quality of the graduates is what counts? And those people are cheated as undergraduates when the department heads who ought to be teaching, lecturing, sharing what they know and stimulating youngsters to get interest-

210

ed and think, are hogtied, turning out a mess of drivel."

He struck a kitchen match across his teeth, an angry exclamation point, and applied the flame to the pipe.

"God damnit, to lose a man like Perry because old Amos laid down the law that every faculty member's got to make a book every second year. It's ridiculous. And those numbskulls that call themselves trustees prattle about maintaining the academic image of the school. Hell. They wouldn't know an academic image if they met it on Main Street."

Monck only half-listened. His mind was on the implications of what Perry's departure would mean to him.

"When did he resign?"

"This morning."

"I'll go talk to him."

He did not send for Perry to come to his office. He judged that in the man's rebellious mood he would resent anything that smacked of command. He shrugged into his coat, left Strindberg to talk out the rest of his bile with Vivienne, who insisted that Martin was the only human being in a fifty-mile radius, and cut across the quadrangle to the Physics Building.

The wind knifing out of the east whipped his coattails around his legs and made him shiver, made him regret the sunny warmth of Ventura County. Why wasn't he back at Alcon? Why in the devil had he ever come here to play with juveniles? In thinking of juveniles he was thinking not of the students but of the intransigent trustees.

Perry was at his desk but not passively there. He had piles of papers before him and was separating them, slamming them into a different order of stacks. He looked up as Monck came in but he did not rise. There was a subtle change in his manner.

"Strindberg see you?"

Monck dropped his coat and sat down. "He did. Why didn't you tell me? How long has this hassle been going on?"

"Months. It came to a head this morning."

"Christ, this is the silliest thing I've heard yet. You can't walk out now. What happens to the program?"

"Get yourself another boy. If I stuck around I'd break Fenton's stupid neck."

"Not a bad idea. Listen, Ward, I know the rule is nuts,

211

but there are a lot of things in this world we have to live with, nuts or not. Why don't you stall them? Tell them you'll write their damn book as soon as you have time."

"Because I don't lie, to them or to anyone else."

Monck held his rising temper, debating whether to tell Perry that he himself was moving out, that he was grooming him for the chancellorship.

He decided against it. Not that he did not trust the man, but he was certain it would do no good. Perry could not be bribed that easily, and in this mood probably not at all. Perry could get a job in industry without trouble, a job that would pay more than most schools could match. He loved teaching, and the challenge of reaching young minds, but now that he had been introduced to business life he was more than likely to turn that way.

"Okay, you don't have to lie. Go ahead, write the book. When I was in school a lot of department heads had their assistants doing the research. They didn't do much more than put their names on the finished work."

"I don't play that way." Perry ducked down to dredge another load out of a lower drawer. "Anything my name goes on, I write. And it isn't fair to the assistants. They have their own stuff to research and if they had mine to do on top of it they'd have to slough off their classes.

"Sorry, Emory, I know this leaves you in a bad spot, but I can't help it. There just isn't the time to work with you, try to teach half a dozen classes and still sit around reading stuff that's already out of date. Science is moving too fast. Books published five years ago are already bypassed by later discoveries. If I'd come up with a breakthrough worth passing on I'd write about it, believe me, but I'm not about to rehash what somebody else has recorded just to satisfy those jerks on the board.

"You know something, my friend, you know what's wrong with the educational system today? It's being run by a caste of fuddy-duddies who haven't stuck their heads out of their ivory towers for thirty years, or had a new idea of their own. Social systems have changed. Technology has changed. And all those antiques can do is sit on their backsides like a police court hanging onto the status quo. If it was good enough for grandpappy it's good enough for them."

He slammed the drawer, then said with an attempt at

control, "I didn't mean to climb on a soapbox, Emory, but the whole setup has been graveling me for a long time. I'm getting out. I've turned down several offers from industry in the last five years. Now I'm going to take one of them and go where I don't have to kowtow to this crowd."

"I know how you feel." Monck did know exactly how he felt, but he did not intend to lose Perry if he could help it. "Do me a favor, will you? Just sit tight until I can talk to the trustees."

Perry's laugh was short and mocking. "Jesus Christ couldn't talk sense into those muttonheads."

"Just hold off until I can try. Is that too much to ask?"

Ward Perry took a deep, gusty breath. "I owe you a lot. You've given me a new concept of what business is and how it's done, and those men I met at the Spring are like nothing I'd ever seen. Okay. I won't walk out until you make your pitch. But I know even you can't budge them."

Perry was right. Not only could he do no good, the situation actually grew worse. Monck took Strindberg with him to face the hastily assembled trustees. He thought he had a trading lever if he could make them aware of Ward Perry's importance as liaison between the school and the businessmen. He tried to seem friendly and reasonable.

"The position on publishing is outmoded," he said, and dressed the points Ward had made in less inflammatory language. "Even if Perry were only an example I would feel it necessary to protest an unhealthy rigidity of viewpoint. But Ward Perry is not simply a symbol. He is an integral and necessary cog in the machinery of the program to make Wellington financially secure and a leader among the nation's institutions of learning. It is not as simple as the fact that I have spent months in training him. He is a unique combination, a teacher of proven ability who also can get along with the industrial leaders on whom we must depend for help. Do any of you believe you could fill that spot?"

He made them uncomfortable, to be sure. He wanted to. To stir them up and break them out of their hidebound complacency.

General Fenton had not looked at him directly but now he lifted his head like a cavalry horse that hears the bugle's call to charge.

"Dr. Monck." It was formal, disapproving. "You are

213

being emotional because this man is a friend of yours. You are not being reasonable. If we made an exception in this one case we would undoubtedly be asked to relax the requirements for others. Amos Wellington, Senior, specifically directed that every teacher must discharge his duty in periodic publication. We are not the only school to use this standard. In California where, I believe, you spent some time, no teacher may advance without regular publication. Several years ago one of the oldest and most respectable schools in the East dismissed a department head for refusing to conform. The board here has taken its position, and we will not be backed down, even if Mr. Perry is joined in his insubordination by every member of the faculty."

Strindberg brought his doubled fist down on the table. "That's not a bad idea."

The attention jumped to him. The heavy voice raked over them.

"Last fall when we were up against the wall Emory came here and bailed us out. And if he has to he can club us down. All he has to do is walk away with the money we're living on."

Fenton did not bend an inch. "Martin, I can't believe the school is worth saving if we have to surrender the very principles for which Wellington stands."

"Oh hogwash. You don't know what the hell you're jibbering about. You mouth platitudes like a ventriloquist's dummy, and you've got just that much brains." Martin Strindberg poured out his accumulated frustrations. "There isn't one man on faculty row who hasn't squirmed under that idiotic, dogmatic nonsense, and it's time to get rid of it. If we all stood together and said shove it, what do you think you could do about it?"

Fenton's cheeks shook with his outrage. He had eaten out subordinate officers in the same tone.

"Martin, you have been given extraordinary leeway because of your reputation and your tenure, but I warn you, there are limits to our patience."

As a matter of good sense Martin Strindberg avoided controversy when it served no purpose, but he was past caution now.

"This is not the Army, General, and there's no way you can court-martial me. I don't know any law that says

214

I can't suggest to my colleagues a school-wide protest."

"Are you threatening a strike?" Don Dundee was incredulous.

"I don't give a damn what you call it."

The board fluttered in consternation, but Fenton never hesitated.

"Martin, either we are running Wellington University or you are. You force us to ask for your resignation."

28

☐ Martin Luther Strindberg fired! The mushroom cloud spread over the sky and the sheet wave crossed the campus. Nothing in Wellington's history compared with this. In the minds of the faculty, in the doctrine of the students, Strindberg was Wellington. There was no envisioning one without the other.

The faces of the students gathered in the Union after supper were dazed. Cec Eliot arrived looking more like an undertaker than a student leader. The focus of the group was on him.

"Is it for real?"

"Did you see Monck?"

"Is it true the Doc hit old Fenton in the nose?"

He climbed on a chair and from there to a table, shoving ash trays aside with his toe, and waited for attention.

"I saw Monck. It is true. Strindberg is out."

"Why . . . ?"

"Something about the publish or perish jazz. Monck didn't elaborate. He told me to tell you to stay cool, to turn in, there'd be a formal announcement in the morning."

A meeting was held at the house of Harold Keller, dean of the Mathematics school. All the department heads except Strindberg attended, and most of their assistants.

"The way I understand it," Keller said, "the trustees landed on Ward Perry to publish or else and Perry told them to go to hell and resigned."

Dean Sloan of History wanted to know, "Why shouldn't he publish? We all have to."

"We could resign too, if we had the guts. But to go on, Martin called Fenton on it; I guess he read the riot act, and you know Fenton. Our fearless leader blew and fired Martin on the spot."

"What does Monck intend to do?"

"I don't know yet. He said he'd get back to me in the morning."

Emory Monck did not know himself what he was going to do. He was baffled by the inanity of the whole uproar. Denise Dempsey and Al Conner sat side by side on the couch, looking blankly across the desk at him. Ward Perry stood like a wooden Indian, staring out of the window across the snow. His voice was stricken.

"Damnit, I wouldn't have had this happen for the world. The school is Martin's life. And to be fired at his age, what's he going to do?"

"That's the least thing to worry about. Martin can have any job he wants."

"Can't you make them reinstate him?" Ward Perry was feeling the weight of guilt for the entire mess. "After all, you still control the dough. They can't operate the school without that."

"They think they can. I spent an hour with them after Martin stormed out. They kept coming back to the research grants you and I got from industry, which are signed by the trustees and made out directly to the school."

"Who's going to run the program?"

Monck shrugged. "They're pretty smug, Ward. They argue that there are hundreds of men in the country who could handle the job if I walked out. There are, of course. But what the dumb bastards won't get through their heads is the acute shortage of trained executive personnel available. By the time they find that out it may be too late, but that's beside the point. Fenton hates me personally and he'd love to show me up."

"Why should he hate you?"

Neither Dempsey nor Conner chose to explain.

"It doesn't matter," Monck said. "What I want to know is, what are your plans?"

"To get out of here as soon as I can."

"Have you talked to Martin? I haven't."

Perry nodded. "He's still boiling, and I don't blame him. He was all for packing up and clearing out tonight. Helen talked him out of that."

Monck had tried twice to call the physicist. Helen had refused to put him on the wire.

216

"Let him alone, Emory," she had said. "I've never seen him take anything so hard. He doesn't want to see anyone. Wait until tomorrow."

Everything seemed to be waiting now, stunned and inert.

"I don't know of anything we can do tonight," Monck said.

He watched Dempsey and Conner stand up. He spoke to the publicity man:

"I hope this doesn't hit the papers until we get it straightened out."

Al Conner looked pained. "Have you any idea of the news value of Martin Strindberg's name?"

"Do the best you can." He felt sorry for Conner. It seemed that the man spent more time trying to keep stories out of the press than he did planting them.

Ward Perry came from the window and took Dempsey's arm. "I'll walk you home."

The girl glanced at Monck and then quickly away; she nodded. He saw them leave with new irritation. He had planned to take her out himself, take her to Wheeling for a therapeutic night on the town, but he didn't want to risk any further friction now.

Conner waited until the door closed and then paced the room.

"This is a real hot potato. From where I stand it looks like you're in the middle. You can't take a walk, ditch your program, and get elected to anything."

"I know it."

"And if you stand behind Strindberg . . ."

"I'll stand behind him. I've got to. I simply can't show weakness with the trustees. I do that and we can forget the whole business."

Conner made a long, weary grunt. "Well, I'm going home and get my shoes off. It looks like an interesting day tomorrow."

Monck sat on, trying to think, trying, as Sam Jordan put it, to come up with an angle. The more he thought the less he saw. To put it simply, it was one hell of a hog wallow.

He switched off the light, got up and went through the door; he was surprised to find Vivienne still out there. It was after eight o'clock.

"What are you doing here?"

"Waiting for the dynamite to go off."

He touched her shoulder. "Don't let it throw you. You and I've been in tighter spots and squirmed through. All we can do is keep punching."

"If we don't get punchy first. How long are we going to hang around this chicken shit operation?"

"Washington. Remember?"

"Balls."

"The trouble with you is, you've been cloistered. You've only known the kind of people who play in the majors. Did you have dinner?"

"Who needs it? I didn't feel like cooking and I damned well didn't want to show up at the faculty club and listen to the yakking."

"Come on, I'll take you down to Nicholas'."

She wrinkled her nose.

"So I'll take you to Wheeling and get you plastered. I could use a couple of belts and some clean air."

She got her coat with alacrity. "How are you going to get to Washington with this crowd dragging you down? It's a losing fight. Every time you've had anything set up some idiot has knocked it down. None of these mules is going to give in, and you know it."

At the back of his mind he was afraid she was right, but he put it away from him for the night.

Vivienne loved to dance. He had not known that. In the ten years she had worked for him he had never before taken her out.

At twelve o'clock she said, "Why couldn't I be fifteen years younger or you fifteen years older? This is fun."

She had drunk drink for drink with him without noticeable effect. Monck grinned at her.

"You're good medicine for a man's ego. How come you didn't get married again?"

She made a sour face. "One louse in one life is enough. Let's talk about something pleasant."

On the drive back to the campus the only pleasant subject they could find was the weather. An unexpected warm front had pushed up the valley and the snow was melting under the wheels of the trucks; water was running from the soggy drifts into the road. In another two days, they agreed, it would be gone. It would be none too soon for Vivienne.

218

He dropped her at the faculty apartment house and drove on to his house, put the car in the garage and slopped through the slush to the rear door. He turned on the kitchen light but did not make himself a drink. He had had just about enough and he wanted to be clear-headed in the morning. It did not surprise him to hear the light step on the porch, the knock, the opening of the door and Alice's voice. The visits had become as regular as neighborhood coffee klatches.

"You still awake?"

"Come on in."

He knew that he had been subconsciously expecting her and realized with a kind of horror that this was the reason he had not wanted to come home. He had not wanted to face Alice Wellington tonight.

I've got to quit ducking, he thought. I never ducked before and there's no need to start now. He met her at the doorway as she hurried in. He had never seen her as grave.

"Emory." She came to him extending both hands, and gripped his fingers hard as if she found comfort in touching him. "This is the most awful thing I ever heard of."

"I agree with you." He said it as if he meant it.

"Uncle Martin fired. What's got into everyone? I think they're all going crazy."

"Who, the trustees? They didn't have far to go."

It was as if she did not hear him. "I'm talking about the faculty. They're insane." She saw his puzzlement and rushed on. "You haven't heard?"

"Heard what?"

"They had a meeting. They decided to strike. Strike, do you hear me? As if they were garment workers or truck drivers or grape pickers."

"Oh for Christ sake."

"They did. They came to Father an hour ago with an ultimatum. Unless Uncle Martin and Ward Perry are reinstated and the publishing clause stricken from the contracts they are refusing to conduct any classes."

Monck was seized with a violent impulse to laugh. He thought he knew the faculty so well. Though good men in their fields, most of them still tended to be stuffed shirts, fat cats grown sluggish toward life beyond their immediate professions, self-satisfied in their niches, secure with their tenure and fringe benefits. It was one facet of the picture that had disturbed him all along, that they were too bound by inertia to come up with the aggressive leadership his program would demand.

It seemed that there was more life in them than he had guessed. Without having been at the meeting he knew that they must have been rocked to the bottom of their souls to have taken such a suicidal step. And the girl's face warned him that he dared not laugh.

"I thought Father would have a heart attack. I could just shoot Dempsey and that crowd that hangs around her. You know the older people would never have considered such a thing."

"Dempsey, was she there?"

"She must have been. That's the only explanation."

Monck let that pass. "You mean it's only a group?"

"I wish it were, but Emory, almost every faculty member on our rolls signed that paper. You know they had to be brainwashed. Nothing like this has ever happened at Wellington before."

Here was backing that he had not in the least expected. He had thought that he would have to face the trustees single-handed, with precious little hope, and here came the reserves, the entire faculty in rank behind him. When he gave way to a small chuckle, she gasped.

"Emory Monck. How can you laugh?"

"I was thinking of Fenton's face when he hears."

"That is not funny. Don't you realize that this is hitting at the very foundation of the school?"

He realized more than she. The new development could break the log jam and immensely facilitate his revamping of Wellington.

He said, "Don't worry so. The trustees can't afford to ignore the unanimous opinion of so many people of our faculty's caliber. They know what they're talking about, and they'll all do a better job with their hands untied. Now come on, relax. I'll walk you home."

It was warmer out than it had been before, balmy even. The clouds had thinned and stars appeared and disappeared as the vapors ran silently before the wave of southern heat. There was an orchestration of dripping sounds, a high metallic rhythm as drops fell against tin, a flat beat as they struck concrete and a soft slushing as icicles rained from the trees into the rotting snow.

His hair and coat were wet when he came back into the house. He shook his head, spraying the kitchen, caught up a towel and mopped at himself on his way to the phone. He dried his hands and then dialed Denise Dempsey's number.

"Did I wake you?"

Her voice lifted when she heard him. "Who can sleep on a night like this?"

"Then you have heard about our strike?"

"I heard. They called me about ten and asked me to come over and sign."

"Did you go?"

"I did. I hesitated. In fact I talked to Ward first. I didn't know whether an administrative official should sign, but all of the other deans did, so I went along. Shouldn't I have?"

"You should have, if they're serious, if it doesn't collapse as soon as the sun comes up and they begin to wonder how hungry they'll be without a pay check."

"They're serious. I didn't know that crowd could get so worked up. If it had been about anyone but Strindberg they would not have taken the action, but this was the attitude, that Strindberg has been fighting their battles for years; he's thrown his personal prestige on the line time and time again. They said it aloud, that in trying to protect Ward, Martin was fighting for all of them against compulsory publication. There isn't a man or woman among them who didn't speak out in resentment against being told that they have to write."

"That's what I wanted to know. Thank you I didn't feel free to call anyone else."

"Thank you, sir. It will work, won't it, Emory?" There was concern in her tone now. "The trustees surely aren't going to let the school close for pure pigheadedness?"

"That's what I'm going to ask them in the morning. I've got a stake here too, if you recall."

He hung the phone up slowly, then went more quickly to the kitchen, poured himself a drink, and toasted the good teachers of Wellington.

29

☐ Cec Eliot waked Monck at seven-thirty, pounding on his front door with unnecessary vigor. Monck called through the open window, slipped on a robe, and went downstairs.

"What got you out so early?"

"I haven't been in bed." It was easy to believe. Eliot's thin face looked drawn beneath the scraggly beard and the slump of fatigue was in his lank frame. "The Senate has been in meeting all night."

"Let's get some coffee."

Monck tramped down the corridor to the old-fashioned kitchen and plugged in the percolator, then dropped into a chair at the round table across from the student leader.

"All-night meeting, huh? Decide anything?"

"That we will support the faculty. If they strike, we strike too."

"The whole student body?"

"The works."

Monck was flabbergasted. "It can't be too popular if it took all night. What was the vote?"

Eliot's eyes gleamed. "The faculty didn't vote until after midnight. By the time we got everybody routed out there wasn't too much night left. Then everybody wanted to get his two cents in. They're still debating, but it's clear enough how they'll go. The vote is scheduled for nine-thirty."

Monck thought it was very funny. This wasn't the reserves arriving, it was the whole damned army, and it put him in a most peculiar position. Here he sat in complete agreement with both the faculty and the students, yet he was being forced into the rôle of mediator. A shutdown like this would mean a shutdown of the research work.

"I appreciate the showing," he said, "But let's not go off half-cocked. I'm going to see Fenton as soon as I think he's in his office, and see if we can't work out a compromise."

"They won't compromise." Eliot was scornful. "They don't know the meaning of the word. They're too old. They're not with it. They're calcified."

Monck looked at him keenly. "Never trust anyone over thirty, you mean?"

Eliot flushed and then grinned self-consciously. "You can't really blame us, Dr. Monck. It wasn't the kids who set themselves apart, it was the older generation, snowing us under with no-sense rules."

"It always was that way, Cec." Monck got up to pour the coffee now that the pot had quit its happy muttering.

"Sure it was, but there are a lot more of us now and the world is changing. We've got to defend ourselves. If they can shove us into uniform and ship us off to a war they're going to have to give us a voice in the decisions."

Monck sounded half-mocking. "What do you want, a seat on the board of trustees?"

"You could do worse. You might find us more flexible."

An hour later, with Fenton and Dundee in Fenton's campus office, Monck wished there were seven kids on the board.

"This has gone beyond personalities and individual prejudices," he said. "I've talked with two of the faculty leaders and they are adamant, they're not going to back down without at least some show of reasonableness from you."

Fenton was frosty-eyed, his tongue sharp. "You know, Monck, that you're to blame for this insurrection. That's exactly what it is. Ever since you came back here you've been coddling the radicals, siding with them against con-stituted authority."

Couldn't the man talk without sounding like a pam-phlet? Monck thought in exasperation that none are so blind as those who will not see, and kept his feeling out of his voice by conscious effort. He was not cut out to be a conciliator. He was schooled to quick action, quick deci-sion, to dealing with men who did not need to be babied.

"No matter whose fault it is"—his tone told that he was not accepting the blame—"we've got a nasty situa-tion, and Wellington's future is at stake. Last night you made the point that our development contracts were signed in the school's name and I could not as an indi-vidual withdraw them. But there is a performance clause in every contract, and we can lose them oh so easily if there's no faculty to implement them."

Dundee began snapping his fingers, jiggling nervously, but no matter how much he weakened, Monck knew that

223

he would not cut loose from Fenton's lead. And Fenton was crowing with confidence.

"We'll have a faculty. When they understand that we are not going to be intimidated they'll come around fast enough. What choice have they got? Where could they go? What school would hire them at this time of year, and after the spectacle they're making of themselves here?"

Monck swore to himself. The general was probably right in that. Few were the teachers who put aside enough money to support themselves for long periods of unemployment. Still he butted ahead.

"Supposing you're right; the publicity can only be bad for us. If industry can bargain with organized labor certainly the trustees of a great educational institution can discuss and compromise with its faculty."

"I do not bargain with traitors. I will give them just twenty-four hours to return to their duties. If they refuse I will ask the court for an eviction order to clear them out of the houses and we will begin recruiting a new staff."

Monck's hands tightened into fists. "For God sake, Fenton, use your head, if you have one. Every man worth his salt is already teaching somewhere else. Competent men don't grow on bushes. It takes years to build a faculty comparable to Wellington's. What are you gaining? And what about the students? Do you want them deprived of their education while you hang onto a point that nobody else agrees with?"

"That's quite enough, Monck. If need be we'll call a holiday until such time as we . . ."

"You won't need to." Monck's voice was flat. "The student body is voting at this minute on a motion to support the faculty action by a strike of their own."

A white line rimmed the general's suddenly compressed lips. "They wouldn't dare."

Monck laughed unpleasantly. "Take a look at other campuses. The students today dare do anything they believe is right."

"I'll close the dining rooms. I'll communicate with their draft boards. I'll have them reclassified."

Monck did an about face and got out of the ugly room before he must start swinging. He was too blinded by anger to see Denise Dempsey waiting on the steps outside the administration building, waiting to be the first to hear his

224

report. One look at his stony face and she fell into step with him without speaking.

It was unseasonably hot. The campus was cleared of snow except for shrinking, discolored patches on the north side of the hillocks. Spring was miraculously in the air. But Emory Monck had no time for the annual miracle as his long stride took him toward the auditorium.

The girl trotted alongside. When they were halfway across the quadrangle and he still had not slowed, had not by any sign recognized her presence, she touched his arm.

"Emory, take a deep breath. Cool off."

He stopped without warning. He turned to look at her and scrubbed a hand across his face.

"Dempsey, you're a real St. Bernard. You're always at the right place at the right time with a keg of common sense."

"I judge your interview with the general was not constructive."

"That bastard. That drill sergeant. The only way he knows to deal with people is with a club. He says he's going to evict the faculty, close the dining rooms, and if the students strike he's going to have them reclassified."

"Oh no."

"Oh yes."

They went on, Dempsey now as wrathful as Monck. There was a noisy crowd milling around the front of the auditorium, students who had not been able to force a way inside. Signs waggled above the heads.

STRINDBERG YES, FENTON NO.

TRUSTEES GO HOME.

NEVER TRUST A MAN OVER THIRTY.

WE'RE WITH YOU ELIOT.

There was a strong mood, different from the free-for-all violence of the autumn riot, a glowering, growling resentment running like a rip tide, an air of union and determination. Monck did not even try to make a way through them. He turned aside, down along the building to the stage entrance.

Inside, the clamor was loud even in the wings, and it rose as he and Dempsey stepped from behind the curtain. The hall had been designed to seat twenty-five hundred.

225

At least five thousand were there, and woe to anyone who mentioned the fire department's restriction. The aisles were crammed. The rear behind the seats was a solid phalanx. Most of the seats were doubly occupied as girls crowded onto the laps of boys.

On the stage were the officers of the Student Senate, a group tight around Cec Eliot. Martha with her folk singers surrounded one hanging mike, their voices amplified above the hubbub. *We Will Overcome*. Monck had never heard it sound more patient, more inexorable, more warning. Behind him he heard the thunder of footsteps as the mob outside discovered the side door and followed him to fill the backstage area.

Cec Eliot saw him and pushed out of the official circle. "I'm glad you're here; we've been holding the vote to hear what Fenton says." His voice was urgent.

Hanging from the flies was a gallows rope knotted around the neck of an effigy dummy wearing a cardboard sign: FENTON.

Monck looked away from it, back at Cec.

"He says a lot, and none of it very good. I warned him about your meeting, but I don't think he understands the depth of feeling. He threatened to close the dining rooms if you do strike. He also threatened to have the boys reclassified. I think you'd better get that across to these people . . . the fool would do it. They ought to know exactly what they're going up against. You've all got a lot to lose."

Eliot's eyes changed, retreating into disappointed suspicion. "You mean we should cave in quietly and let him get away with it?"

Monck was torn. All that he had worked toward here could go down the drain if the rebellion became a stalemate, if neither side would give. He knew that Fenton would not. Fenton was secure.

"Why don't you stall? Fenton is feeling very pushed right now. If the students follow the faculty he's going to bow his neck and never budge. Easter vacation starts next week. By the time it's over I'll have had time to talk to the other trustees individually, and maybe I can get the faculty to soften some. Keep your people out of it for now, will you?"

226

Eliot shook his head. "Sorry about that. Look at them. I couldn't stop them if I wanted to. Every one of them feels that Strindberg belongs to him. He represents something they believe in and they won't stand by and watch him be kicked around."

He crossed the platform, purpose stretching his stride, and commandeered the mike from Yates's musicians.

"Quiet." He had to repeat it three times before the room responded, but then its attention was complete. "The trustees have refused to settle. Fenton sends word if we strike he'll cut off the food."

A rising howl from the packed rows, an animal yell of protest not unmixed with a call for blood, drowned him and he waited, waving both arms, until he could be heard again.

"More. He'll pull our 2S cards, throw us to the draft. How about that? Do we chicken or do we stand up to be counted?"

They were stamping, yelling, whistling. Sound raged in a monotonous roar, then settled into a jarring rhythm, and a chant took form.

"Strike. Strike. Strike."

Emory Monck wrapped his fingers around Dempsey's arm. "There's a way out through the basement dressing rooms and the heating tunnel. We don't belong here now. It's their party, God help them."

They worked through the crowd in the wings and went down the narrow stairs. The tunnel was a small passage, bricked, through which the steam pipes ran from the central station to the auditorium. It was hot, airless, dusty, and without light. Monck used the flame of his lighter to pilot them down the tomblike corridor, and they came out finally in the power plant.

The girl had collected a smudge of dirt across her cheek and he used his handkerchief to wipe it away.

"Whoo," she said. "I'm glad I'm not a miner. I get claustrophobia. How'd you ever find that?"

He relaxed for a moment, remembering. "A guy named Peterson found it. Little kids are curious about closed doors. We used it to set off a stink bomb during the graduation exercises when I was about thirteen."

"Sounds like Pat Crowell was right; you must have been a real brat. Do you happen to know a secret passage

227

into Fenton's office so we could strangle him? I'm getting scared for those kids."

"So am I."

"If Fenton closes the dining halls they'll have to give up or leave, and if they do that I think it will be the end of the school."

She was wrong. They found another alternative. She and Monck were still together in his office half an hour later when the phone rang. It was Pat Crowell, and he was breathless.

"Emory, the students have seized the kitchens."

Monck held the instrument away from him and looked at it. "They've what?"

"Taken over. About two hundred of them. They pranced in and told the cooks they were giving the orders now. What do you want me to do, call the sheriff?"

"I do not. Let me find out about it."

He rang off and told Dempsey, who broke up.

"What are you laughing about? This is getting worse by the minute."

"I can't help it. Oh Lord, that's funny." Her laughter was uncontrollable. "The general maybe isn't as great a tactician as he thought. This looks like an attack on his exposed flank."

"So have hysterics. I've got to go."

He headed for the door but Vivienne caught him as he went through, distraught, covering her phone receiver with her palm.

"Newspapers. They're going crazy. What do I tell them?"

"That I'm out. Shunt them to Conner."

He ran down the stairs, paused at the second floor, considering telling Fenton, then shook his head and ran on.

The main dining hall that housed the kitchens and the huge cafeteria stood behind the Student Union. He found the double doors guarded by a squad of fifty or more. The boy in charge was nervous at stopping Monck, and stuttered.

"I . . . I . . . I'm sorry, Chan-Chancellor, but but but you can't go in without a p-p-pass."

"Where do I get a pass?" Monck was aware that they all watched him closely. At least they were businesslike.
228

The boy appealed to another behind him. "Get-get-get Cec."

Cec Eliot appeared, his manner as decisive as a command officer. "It's all right. Let them in."

Monck turned around. Dempsey had arrived, running on silent feet. The guard unit parted and they filed through into the cafeteria. It was busy but surprisingly orderly. Kitchen employees were filling the long steam tables with the noon meal and aside from the small groups of watchful students everything appeared normal.

The chef, moonfaced, burly shouldered, with a ponderous gut, came from the kitchen when he heard Monck's voice.

"Doctor, what the hell goes on?"

"I guess you'll have to ask Mr. Eliot. He seems to be in control."

The chef spread his thick white arms, palms up. "They busted in here and said everything would be okay if we'd go ahead as usual and do what they told us. I'd already had a call from General Fenton ordering me to close up after lunch. Now these kids won't let me call him back, call anybody. They just stand around and watch."

This time Monck joined Denise's infectious laughter. It was hard not to, she was making no attempt to hide her amusement.

"Go ahead and do what they say until you hear from me. All right?"

The fat man was obviously relieved. "You're the boss." He lifted his shoulders and ducked back into his bailiwick.

Monck turned to Eliot. "How long do you think this can last?"

Cec was grave. "We took inventory of the storerooms, the freezers and the kitchen. There's a lot of food and Marty is having a ball making up menus."

Monck had a picture of that, having seen the girl eat. She was as near hollow as anyone he had ever met.

"I'd guess the supplies won't go far then. But seriously, this is kind of a problem."

"Why?" Cec was genuinely puzzled. "I've got nearly six thousand men for guard duty to make sure the cooks stay in line. We're not fooling, Chancellor. If anyone tries to throw us out bodily there is going to be real trouble."

Monck believed him. "Well, do you think you can keep

things from getting out of hand?"

"No problem. We're organized. We've taken control of the dorms and put men in the records department. Fenton had ordered them to make up a grades list to send to the draft boards. No one is going to send anything anywhere until we give the word."

Monck accepted the situation because there was not a thing he could do to change it just then.

"It seems to me that you people are running the school," he said. "I wish you better luck than I've had."

He started for the door but Cec stopped him. "You'd better hear the rest of it, Dr. Monck. We've also got guards on the gates. No one comes on campus without a pass signed by one of the Senate officers. We are not going to let any of the faculty be served with eviction orders. You might tell Fenton that."

30

☐ The sun, almost at the meridian in a bright, intensely blue sky, gave the day a midsummer feel. A holiday air made the campus festive. The trees might be naked, the lawns soggy, yet the grounds resembled a Pacific beach. Colorful knots of girls and boys sat on plastic bags from the cleaners, plastic tablecloths, raincoats. Groups with guitars played and sang folk songs sad or militant. Others played cards. Some read, some lay flat and dozed. Some made light love. Some made speeches. They bloomed like flowers under the trees, in shadow and sun, perched on walls that bordered walks, on the steps of buildings. They danced to transistor radios, listened to ball games, practiced tumbling, rode bicycles. The sounds of music high and piercing, nasal voices raised in love's laments and the raptures of youth made islands that overlapped with other islands of low, slow, soft balladry and deep-toned strings. The surface scene was idyllic.

There was a larking atmosphere that did not match with the heavy mood the word *strike* brought to mind. They might be facing expulsion, they might be called into the armed services, the courses of their lives might be approaching major disruptions, but to Monck it appeared that these people felt they need not waste precious moments while they waited. Waiting was the job to be done. They were doing it. But they took it for granted that it was foolish to let pass unused the opportunity to enjoy a beautiful day.

He looked at Dempsey. Dempsey was smiling and humming. She caught his glance and shrugged.

"They've got the right idea. When it's inevitable, relax, and make the most of it. Save your energy until you have something to work on."

"You have anything to do for a while?"

Her head tipped. "I'm on strike too, remember?"

"Come on upstairs with me. Let's do some thinking. Maybe we can come up with a gimmick."

As they came into the office Vivienne flagged him. "The governor has been trying to reach you. I told the operator you'd call back as soon as you got here."

She reached for the phone and Monck was hardly seated when his instrument buzzed.

The governor's voice said, "Emory, for God sake, what's going on down there?"

"A little family misunderstanding." He was glad that he had gotten acquainted with the man and that Sharkey had a wider than average comprehension.

"Little misunderstanding? Sounds more like a siege. I had a call from General Fenton. He says you've got a state of anarchy, that it's passed the point where the local law can handle it. He wants me to call out the Guard."

"I don't think that's necessary. There's no violence."

"I checked with Sheriff Fulton. He says armed students turned him back at the gates. He hasn't got the manpower to force an entry."

"Governor, if I'm any judge the Guard is the last thing we need. You would have a mess if troops came in. More than likely it would mean a pitched battle, with people hurt. As of now there's no damage. The kids have taken over, but it's orderly. I'm going to see Fenton now. I'll get back to you when there's anything to report."

Fenton was like a statue in his chair. He did not even look up as Monck came in.

"Don't you think this had better be settled pretty quick?" Monck said.

Fenton's voice had a military chill. "The Guard will settle it."

"The Guard is not coming. I've just talked with Sharkey. I told him troops weren't needed."

Fenton went livid. "You dared countermand my order? Monck, I've had enough. You're fired. Get off the campus and stay off."

That solution had not occurred to Monck. It startled him as much as if he had run into the edge of a door in the dark. With his breath still drawn in he swung out of the room.

By the time he reached his office he had his fury under rein. Denise was sitting on the corner of Vivienne's desk, the first sign he had seen of anything more than civility between them; probably the common danger and their desire to help him was drawing them closer. They waited for his report and a foolish smile answered them.

"He fired me."

For a long count none of them moved. Vivienne recovered first. With a whoop she swiveled, and sprang to her feet. She fastened on the symbolic floral fantasy, listed it high, then crashed it on the floor.

"Now we're cooking. Let's get out of this insane asylum." She flung herself into the chair again and began pulling out drawers, grabbing handfuls from them indiscriminately and jumbling everything together on the desk top.

Dempsey twisted off the corner of the desk and stood watching her for a moment; then she looked at Monck in growing disbelief.

"You're not going to quit?"

"The hell I'm not. Fenton is paranoiac. I've had it."

Her head was shaking rapidly from side to side. "You can't do it. No, no, no. You can't let those kids down now. You can't abandon everything. You can't just walk away and forget all the things you've started."

Her excitement triggered his anger again and now he let it go.

"Oh yes I can. Why the hell can't I? Everybody in this place has fought me tooth and nail from the day I walked in here. My hands have been tied behind my back every time I made a move. The trustees dug their heels in. The faculty won't listen to me. Nothing I say has an ounce of weight, and I've been fired. The kids have taken control. All right. Let them manage it. Let Fenton bring in the

Guard. At least it will let off some steam, but I don't want to be here to see it."

"Emory Monck." Every time the girl got mad she bounced and whistled like a small tea kettle on a very hot flame. "You're just proving what I've thought from the first. You don't know the meaning of guts. It'll all been easy for you, always, just use your superintelligence, just use Sam Jordan's crowd's muscle and everything falls down in front of you just the way you want it. Always a winner, you. You don't know, you just don't know how to fight when the odds are stacked against you. A fair weather genius, that's what you are."

"Sure. Great. Skin me alive. What do you suggest I do?"

"I don't know. I'm not a genius. If I were I'd go out and do something. It's your motto that there's always a way. I heard you sit in there and lecture Cec that anybody could tear things down but it took a man to build. Well, what are you building now, Dr. Monck? Those kids out there are trying. Maybe their way isn't the right one, but they're laying it on the line, they're fighting, and it can mean very serious sacrifices for a lot of them. I'm beginning to think they're right; they shouldn't trust anyone over thirty, or maybe over twenty-five."

She slammed out of the room; the jarring of the door rattled the wall.

Vivienne gaped after her. "Brother. Now I've heard it all. When do we leave?"

"I don't know. I want a few minutes to think."

Monck went into his office and closed the door. He went to the water cooler and found that his hand shook enough to slosh water out of the half-full cup. He threw the swallow down, crumbled the paper and pitched it viciously away. He lay down on the couch and laced his fingers under his head, tightening them, flexing them to stop the trembling.

Dempsey's blow-up was acting like a line reeling in a fish, drawing him, compelling him to think about himself more consciously than he had done in years. Yes, he was an opportunist. He had grabbed at what chances came to him and made the most of them for himself. And his record showed that he had ducked those situations that offered little personal reward. What was wrong in it? Only damned fools and Don Quixote butted their heads against the immovable.

What did she expect him to do, perform a miracle? There was no way to remove Fenton unless all the trustees turned against him, and that was a fatuous hope. No, he did not want the faculty or the students to have to crawl back and suffer whatever indignities the general would choose to impose upon them.

So what was there to do if he stayed? What was he if he left? He sneered, listening to himself through the years insisting smugly that there had to be a way. It was not a satisfying moment of truth.

The intercom was as welcome as the rattlesnake it reminded him of. He got up and grunted into it. Vivienne's voice was unusually uncertain.

"The Eliot boy is here asking for you."

His impulse was to bar the door. For the first time in his life he was afraid to face someone. The boy's being there mocked him. Whether or not he could help it he was letting the kid down, letting down others who had depended on him. Strindberg, Perry, the industry men who had already poured a lot of money into the school. He was trapped and he hated it.

"Send him in," he said, and closed the key.

Eliot looked more like a stork than ever. He must have lost weight since morning. Above the frazzled beard his eyes were sunken by loss of sleep. But he carried himself with a strong confidence that was new.

"Sorry to bother you, Doctor."

"You're not bothering me." Monck flapped a hand toward the couch. "But I'll tell you before you start that I can't help you. Fenton just fired me, told me to get off the campus, now."

He had expected Cec to be disconcerted. He was not.

"You don't have to go anywhere, Doctor, until you want to. We're running this campus, now."

It was true. At the moment Cec Eliot was Emperor of Wellington by right of conquest. What would happen tomorrow or the next day was unknown but irrelevant, and the regal way in which Eliot granted him the privilege of staying restored his shattered humor.

"Thanks."

Eliot nodded absently. "I came up here to ask a question." He leaned forward on his stiffened arms, resting his

234

fists on Monck's desk. "What constitutes a university, Chancellor?"

Monck started to make a wisecrack about this one no longer being constituted, changed his mind and played it straight, adopted Eliot's serious manner.

"Well, I'd say a good faculty is one of the prime requisites."

"We've got one, barricaded behind closed shutters up on faculty row, chewing its nails and waiting to be evicted." Monck smiled harshly.

"What else?" The boy prodded him.

"A student body."

"We've got that. Ten thousand of them sitting all over the grass, also waiting."

Monck began to see the train of the boy's thought. "It takes money."

"You have your Educational Trust Fund. I understand that you, not the trustees have control of it."

A dragon of excitement stirred in Monck. "I do, and I get the idea. We just move the school. But Cec, you need a plant, and even if I could raise enough money to build one it would take too long. By the time we could get it open a lot of you would be drafted or shifted to other schools or off making a living."

"There's that abandoned Navy base six miles away. I'll grant it's run down, but there are a hell of a lot of buildings, if you could get hold of it."

Monck sat looking at him. Just looking. Loving him, the way he loved Sam Jordan. Vivienne heard Monck's laughter through the closed door and bolted in to see if he were as insane as he sounded.

"There *is* a way." He shouted it. He waved a clenched fist at Vivienne. "Cec just showed me how to steal a university. Come on, kid. Let's take a ride. Let's go see what our new campus looks like."

31

☐ It felt good, cleasning, to walk fast. It even brought the first pang of appetite he had had in two days. They went to the student parking area, got Cec's car and followed the curving drive around toward the east gate.

The campus was crowded but more orderly than on any ordinary day, self-consciously orderly. Besides the host on the lawns there were a few men in the entrance of every building. They stood quietly, they gave the campus the air of an alerted military installation. Monck did not see a single faculty member or any of the administrative personnel. It was as if Eliot's description were true, that they were huddling behind their doors chewing their fingernails. It was as if the kids had taken over the world.

The illusion of military occupation was heightened when they reached the gate. Here a squad of boys in ROTC uniform, armed with rifles, patrolled the entrance, Gabe Glasscock in command, wearing a lieutenant's bars. Over their heads Monck saw on the outside a cluster of cars and a group of forty or fifty curious spectators.

Cec slowed for a word with his roommate, his eyes on the audience.

"Any trouble?"

Glasscock spat delicately. "There's several reporters out there. We had to get a little physical with one of them. He wouldn't respect the order."

"Keep them out. You're in charge until I get back. Marty's at the cafeteria. Polly's taken over the administration building. You got your walkie-talkie?"

Gabe held it up.

"I'll get back as soon as I can."

Cec put the Olds in gear and pulled through the gate. There the reporters made a tight group trying to block their path, calling Monck's name as they recognized him. To the side two television trucks taped the scene for national coverage.

Cec accelerated the engine in neutral as a warning, then pushed slowly through until the crowd split. Men caught the door handles and ran beside the car, demanding interviews, but Cec picked up speed steadily until they were forced to let go. When they were free he gunned forward, out past the stadium to the new highway.

Behind them motors snarled as the newsmen dashed for their cars to follow. Cec had an eighth of a mile head start and a determination not to be hampered by a troop of reporters. He drove with the confidence of one who knows every turn, twist and chuckhole. The Olds was doing ninety, its tires screaming on the bends and Monck clung to

236

the edge of the seat, trying to keep his balance.

By the time they reached the lip of the bluff where the new highway dipped to drop into the river valley there was no one in sight behind them. The old road had made a series of tight switchbacks down the bank of the gorge, the new pavement cut obliquely through these in a more direct descent, but vestiges of the loops remained, unused and overgrown. Cec spun the wheel, turning into one of these in a skidding swirl that dropped Monck's stomach through the floorboards.

They pulled over a small ridge, dropped into a clearing through a clump of trees that hid the car from the highway, and there Cec braked to a stop and cut the motor.

Neither of them spoke. The sound of pursuing cars came in a rising whine that flattened to a fast swish as they passed the intersection and then receded as the reporters sped down the grade and on into Riverdale.

Cec grinned at Monck in satisfaction. "That'll hold them for a while."

He started the Olds and drove on down the loop to a dirt track that took off from it and wound across the face of the bluff. This took them past the campus on the south and into another secondary road that eventually led along the rear line of the abandoned Navy base. Cec drove fast but well, following the metal fence around two sides of the depot, arriving at the main entrance. Before the wire gate he stopped and got out.

There was a chain around the center pipes, padlocked. It presented no problem. Cec had a key. He pushed the gates apart and climbed back in the car.

Monck flicked a finger at the key and raised an eyebrow. Cec's lips twitched.

"They're not hard to come by around school."

"No watchman?"

"Old Ferguson. He only shows up about once a week."

He pulled through, closed the gates and then drove rapidly down the wide concrete street between rows of warehouses. A regular gauge railroad track ran down the middle of the street with switch lines veering off into each building. The doorways, fitted with sliding metal doors, were large enough to admit a freight car.

They made a grand tour with no need to consider other traffic. Cec called attention to each feature of the base, the administration building, four huge barracks, three hundred houses that had been used by the officers and administrative personnel.

"You apparently know your way around," Monck said.

The boy glanced at him, then away, saying indifferently, "It's a good place to park. A lot of us use it now and then."

In Monck's day there had been no such grandiose facility. They had used an alley below the switch yards.

The tour continued, past the elaborate Officers' Club that boasted a swimming pool and a nine-hole golf course, out along the weed-grown runways that were long enough to accommodate a Navy jet. Below them was an athletic field with concrete bleachers.

"There's plenty of room," Monck said. "You know how much ground there is?"

"Somebody said there's about three square miles. There's some sixty warehouses, a lot of ammunition igloos, quonset huts. . . . You name it, you'll probably find it. They left a lot of trucks, tractors, there's even a diesel switch engine and a couple of flatcars."

Monck laughed. "We could start a course in railroad management."

"Sure could. Old Ferguson says there's more than sixty miles of track. He's the one we've got to get hold of. He knows where everything is and he's got the keys."

"Let's go."

"You think it will work?" The boy sounded hopeful but anxious.

Monck had seen other deactivated military bases. They all looked much alike. Paint was peeling from the wooden barracks; a lot of windows were broken. Brown grass tufts filled the cracks in the broken pavements.

"What do they do for water, heat, electricity?"

"There's a heating plant. They have their own electric system with diesel powered generators, their own wells. See that water tank?" He pointed across the warehouse roofs to a large tank mounted on high steel legs. "They even have their own telephone system."

"Sounds good. It will take some fixing up. Can you find Ferguson?"

"He's usually in Gimpy's Tavern, about ten miles down the river."

They found him there, a friendly man of sixty-five. He

238

had been head of the civilian guard during the years of the Navy's tenure; he knew every corner of the big installation and he dearly loved to talk about it.

"She was a dinger. Captain Cole—he was the last CO —he said we wanted nothing but the best, nothing but the best."

Monck bought sandwiches and a six-pack of beer and they took Ferguson back to the base.

They walked miles. The mess hall could feed at least two thousand at a time. The big ranges were still in place in the enormous kitchen. Piles of china filled the shelves, bins held thousands of knives, forks, spoons bearing the imprint USN on their handles.

"It's got everything," Ferguson eulogized. "You could move in tomorrow if you had a mind to and Washington gave the word."

Cec Eliot looked at Monck. "You think they would?"

"I know who can find out. Drive me over to Wheeling. Then you'd better get back to Wellington and sit on things. We can't afford trouble there if we're going to try this."

"There's not going to be trouble, not when they hear."

"And you keep close to a phone where I can get hold of you. You've got to be my liaison on campus."

Emory Monck's excitement was building. He had not had this much of a lift since Jordan had first sent him to Arabia.

"We're going to need a lot of clean-up crews. Do you think the boys will turn out to help?"

"You know it. The girls too." Cec's voice cracked. It was as if he had advanced the idea without really believing it was feasible, and was now catching the fever from Monck. "You really think you can get the government to let us use it?"

"I'll do my damnedest. I know a man with a lot of contacts in Washington, and this administration is hipped on education."

The clerk in the Wheeling hotel goggled. "You want a full floor? I think you'd better talk to the manager."

The manager was torn between caution and grabbing Monck around the neck. Business was not that good in older hostels like the Reid.

"We'll have to move some of the guests," he lied, "but I think we can accommodate you."

"I won't need all of it until tomorrow but I need a suite

now, something I can use for an office. Get the rest lined up as soon as you can."

The man coughed. Monck fished for his checkbook and wrote a check for five hundred dollars.

"Let me know when you need more."

The manager picked up the check gingerly, hesitantly. "If you have some identification?"

Monck offered his Diners' Club, American Express, Air Travel cards. "I am, I *was* Chancellor of Wellington University."

"Oh, sure." The man shook his head emphatically. "You've got a mess up there, haven't you?"

"It'll straighten out. When may I have the suite?"

"Right away, sir."

He was ushered to the fifth-floor quarters, got rid of the manager and put in a call for Senator Lightner in Washington.

The Senator's usually measured tones were missing. The man was excited.

"I'm glad to hear from you. I've been trying to reach Conner all day. What is this about a strike? The papers are asking me for comment."

"What did you tell them?"

"Nothing. I didn't know what was going on and I figured I'd better stay out of it. This kind of thing is politically tricky. What's the story?"

Monck told him. "But there's something new now, sir." He outlined the idea of moving the school, feeling a rising impatience with the politician's cautioning interruptions.

"We need the base, Senator. We need it now, if we're going to save the school at all. Do you think you could call someone in the Pentagon and implement the transfer?"

"Your best bet would be to go to the White House."

"Would you do that for us?"

There was a marked pause. "I will if it becomes necessary, Monck, but don't forget this. I belong to the wrong party. I hate to ask favors; those people over there are horse traders. They'd want something in return. I'll do it if there isn't any other way, but isn't there someone in the Jordan crowd who can get to the man?"

Monck found that he was relieved. He had felt obliged to work through Lightner to keep his own fence mended, but he would prefer to use more familiar channels.

"That's not a bad idea," he said. "Let me see what I can do."

He rang off and put in a call for Gordon Randall at the Jennifer plant in Winston, Kansas. It was reassuring to hear the cultivated voice. He had not been certain Randall was there. On any given day he might be anywhere, in or out of the country.

"Gordon, I need help. I want to steal a university."

"Air freight?" The words were dry.

"I've got a four-alarm fire here."

"Looks that way on television."

"There's a Navy base I want to move to if I can pry it loose from Washington. I figured your contacts there are better than Sam's."

"Could be." Randall was noncommittal.

"I need action fast. I've no doubt the Pentagon will sell, but the regular route takes too long, and this is a good year for education."

"You'd better call Harry. He's at the Hay Adams. If he hits a snag, get back to me."

Monck called Hertz. The production man listened and had hysterics. "What have you got to trade with? You need a reason for them to move fast."

"Me nothing. You maybe. Didn't you tell me last month that Dick Garmon was nosing around for a spot at Jennifer? Doesn't he still have that secretarial appointment at the White House?"

"That's right. I think we'll hire him. We need a new contact now that Pete McNally's gone over to Boeing."

"So he ought to be willing to put out a little to get some action. Nobody else wants the base, so there shouldn't be any difficulty, but I'm in a bind for time. The kids are holding the campus by force and every day multiplies the chances of an incident with the sheriff's office, the Riverdale police, or Fenton could possibly put enough pressure on Sharkey to send the Guard down."

Hertz's laughter was syrupy. "That's the kind of spot I like to see my friends in. What do I get out of doing it?"

"You son of a bitch." Monck returned the laugh. "If you don't do it Jennifer's research investment at Wellington goes up in smoke."

"That'll do. Where do I call you back?"

When Monck hung up he breathed in relief. The first

hurdle was crossed. It was one thing for Hertz to ask a favor of the White House, quite another for him to try it on his own.

He called room service for a double martini and food. He was hungry again and he did not know when he could get out for dinner.

There was not much he dared do before he heard from Hertz, but there were a few things. He called Vivienne Krump. She took a dim view of the project, but when he offered her the chance to quit she called him names.

"Then go over to my place and pack me a bag, get my car and collect what you need, and get down here. This will be our base for a while."

He called Denise Dempsey. He ignored her chill greeting and felt rewarded when she gasped at his outline of the proposal.

"I never heard of such a thing."

"You told me to do something. Will you run some errands for me?"

It sounded as if she giggled. "I can't. The kids won't let any of us in or out of the building without a pass from Cec."

"So get one, he's your buddy. I want you to contact the faculty, tell them what I'm doing and see how many will come with us. Call me back here."

He called Ward Perry. Perry was disturbed at first about losing all the new installations he had sweated over at Wellington, but Monck did not give him much time to bemoan that.

"You've got about an hour of daylight left. Go over to the base and make a snap survey. Decide which buildings we can use for classrooms, which for labs. Detail someone to assign the houses to faculty people in order of seniority; check with Dempsey as to who will move. Then bring your notes down here. You and I have to draw up a master plan tonight. If you're with me?"

"It's crazy, and I love it," Perry decided. "I'm on my way."

Lastly he called Cec Eliot.

"How's it going?"

"Pretty quiet. The reporters are still trying to crash in."

"Don't let them in. Don't talk to them yet."

"I'm for that. There's another item. Fenton tried to

storm out without a pass. The boys put him back in his office and cut his phone off at the switchboard."

"Damn. Well, anyway, I may not hear from Washington until tomorrow, but I think we'll take a chance."

"Right with you. What's to lose?"

"Okay, so you call a meeting tonight, better hold it at the stadium so everybody can come. Tell the kids what we're doing. Tell them we want to open some kind of classes after Easter vacation so there will be no argument about their academic standing. Tell them that we'll need everyone's help to do that. Right?"

"Right."

"Tomorrow morning take the school buses and haul everybody who will work over there. First we clean it up, then start painting and moving in."

The hotel operator cut in to say he had a call coming in from Washington.

"Hot damn," said Cec. "Wait a minute. What do I do with Fenton?"

Monck made up his mind hurriedly. "Better keep him there until tomorrow if you can. He'll cause us less trouble if he can't get outside to stir things up."

Harry Hertz sounded relaxed, unemotional as always. "You're in luck, boy. You've got the base. Terms will be worked out later. It's wonderful how a word from the White House makes the fur fly."

32

☐ To Emory Monck it looked as though a giant ant hill had been disturbed. The base that had been ghostly empty yesterday teemed now with throbbing activity. And it was ordered. Much as he had counted on the students, this amazed him. They had entered into the reconditioning with a scientific approach that bode well for the future of the land.

A lot of credit was due to Cec Eliot and the Senate. Eliot had set up a command post in the old Officers' Club, and here they were bringing to life the chart developed the night before.

Monck had watched for months for Ward Perry's initiative to awaken, as he had watched for it in others in the business world, as his own had come. All the long apprentice period seemed to be getting nowhere; all the learning seemed to go into a bottomless dark pit. Then one morning you woke up and it was all there, meshed and ready to be used.

Perry had waked up with the phone call. On his own he had collected the head of the Engineering School and a carload of senior engineering students, taken them to quickly survey the base and then hauled them to Wheeling. Through the night they had worked with Monck, plotting the base out on a rough scale drawing that covered one wall of the suite's main room, sketching in every building, noting its size and type of equipment. Each had been given a number.

This morning each was being inspected and catalogued as to its need for paint and windows, its roof condition and the use for which it was suitable. The drawing now hung in the command post at the base and crews were arriving, thumbtacking cards of specifications against the appropriate locations on the plot. Clean-up crews were then dispatched.

First to be attacked was the mess hall and kitchen—cleaned, inventoried, freezers and refrigerators turned on. By ten o'clock trucks from the food suppliers of Wheeling growled up the hill. Lines of students unloaded them under the eye of the chef and his kitchen staff. By one o'clock lunch was being served in the improvised cafeteria. People, the command post decided, worked better on a full stomach.

Concurrently the barracks came in for attention. They were long, two-storied frame buildings divided into rooms which had each housed six servicemen. Scrubbed and sprayed, they had presented other problems. Winter freezing had broken water pipes; wash basins and shower heads and toilets leaked.

Harold Polly arrived at Cec's post to volunteer the information that he had worked with his uncle, who was a plumber, during vacations. He was assigned coordinator for repairs.

Walking through the second barracks at three o'clock Monck found Polly on his back under a maze of pipes in the basement. He waited until the boy wriggled out and uncurled to his full height, nearly seven feet, his dark face

244

streaked with sweat and war-painted with dust, rust, and sludge.

"How bad does it look?"

The boy raised a hand that held a wrench and wiped his sleeve across his forehead.

"She's coming. Man, most of this junk is sick, but we got the water on. The cans are working. A bunch can move in by tomorrow. Of course it's going to be weeks or more before we get all the little things fixed . . . we're just kind of touching up the surface now."

"You're doing one hell of a job." Monck said it with immense respect.

Polly's face was unreadable for a moment, then his teeth showed in a wide smile.

"You know something, Doctor, this is fun. Every cat out here is having a blast. This place belongs to us, for real?"

"For real."

"Wellington, it was all right, wasn't nothing wrong with old Wellington, and I got treated nice. But it didn't seem like it was any part mine. I was just a hungry man playing basketball to get an education I couldn't get any other way. But here"—he paused, swinging the wrench in a long-armed arc—"every time a can flushes I can say, Polly, you did it, it's yours.

"You maybe don't know what I mean, Doctor, you always had things that were yours, but me, I had from nothing and not much hope of it ever being different. A man's got to have something, own something, something he can touch and feel."

He stopped in embarrassment, then went on stubbornly. "A man's got a house or an office or a school that's his, he ain't going to make trouble. It's the cats that got nothing who make the waves."

A yell from one of the plumbers upstairs demanding more pipe summoned him. He waggled the wrench in salute and galloped away.

Emory Monck followed more slowly. He had the curious feeling that he was not needed. His was the over-all generalship; he had come up with the money for the thousand and one necessities from beds to desks to books to laboratory equipment.

But the kids were doing the work, making the reality.

As he came out of the building he could see squads of twenty, thirty, moving earnestly about their appointed tasks. Walkie-talkies directed them. A third of the student body must own them, and the orders came direct from the command center.

It was a miracle, all right, and an emotional thing to watch. The faculty was here, the wives at the houses to which each had been assigned, measuring, planning, arguing. The teachers had found the classrooms and labs delegated to their departments. It was, Monck thought, probably the first time in history that the professors had a say in how their working facilities would be arranged.

A diesel horn bawled behind him and he jumped. The switch engine snuffled through the main gate and toward him along the track in the center of the street. Behind it bobbed the two flatcars, loaded with beds, the collection of which had exhausted the stores of Riverdale. Monck had thought it would be more efficient to use trucks, but he had not objected when Steve Bates had asked eagerly if he could take the little train down to the main line connection and pick up supplies.

But Steve was coming too fast. His labor battalion swarmed, shouting and waving on top of the swaying cars and the gangs in the street were scrambling to get out of the way. The horn continued its long-drawn bawling. Monck had a surge of anger. This was no time for horseplay especially with a locomotive for a toy.

Then he caught himself up. Why shouldn't the kids play? He had played at their age, enough to give his elders some bad times, and he had never worked this hard. They were earning the right to fun.

But it was not Steve Bates running the engine. At his side in the cab a gnome was perched on the high seat. Sam Jordan hunched at the throttle, the long bill of his sunbeater jutting out like the jabbing beak of an angry bird, his thin mouth stretched in a grin of pure ecstasy.

He spotted Monck at the same time Monck recognized him, braked the switch engine to a sliding stop, waved an arm at the cheering audience on the cars and on the ground, and swung down the steps with the spring of a man a third his age.

"Hi, boy."

Monck crossed to him and grabbed his stringy shoulder.

"Sam, you bastard. Where did you drop from?"

"Flew into Wheeling an hour ago and asked a guy how to get here, and the jerk drove me to Riverdale. I saw the kids loading the train. God damn, I always did want to run a train."

"You're a menace. Where's Eli?"

"She went on to the hotel from the airport." He made a full turn, surveying the hurrying scene. "So this is the new school. Christ, I haven't seen this many people working since we opened the Kyruit field and every Arab in the country descended on us. Who are they all?"

"Free labor, Sam. Building their own world from scratch." He knew that would appeal to Jordan. Sam liked nothing so much as getting something he did not pay for.

"Let's have a look."

Sam in his unchanging uniform of khaki pants, took off with an energy and pace that made Monck increase his stride. He was inquisitive as a chipmunk, poking his nose in everywhere, listening to Monck's explanation of how he intended getting the juggernaut program under way in the least possible time. He gloated over the Officers' Club, the pool, the golf course. Monck took him on a fast tour in the Impala. Passing the runways Sam sounded cheated.

"Hell, I could have landed up here."

"There's a lot of trash on them, we haven't tried to police the grounds yet."

Sam brushed aside the hazard of trash. He had been landing on desert strips all over the west for years. He followed closely as Monck pointed out which buildings would be used as laboratories and named the companies from which he hoped to borrow equipment.

"You got a lot more floor space than you need."

Monck admitted it. "My hope is that some of our participating firms will lease and open pilot plants here. There's plenty of labor and it would be a godsend to the whole section. We've got the power, and there's a high tension line down along the river. We've got water, everything they'd need. And it would make part-time work for students."

Sam was nodding, visualizing the growing industrial center. "You haven't lost your touch, boy. Let's head for the hotel, I'm getting dry."

They stopped and went into the command post. "I want you to take a look at some organization," Monck said. Busy as Eliot was, Monck wanted to show him off. The place purred with a smooth flow of traffic, crackled with the steady exchange of communication through the walkie-talkies. Eliot saw them come, threw the hair out of his eyes and got up. Monck introduced them.

"This is the genius who thought it up. He's running the show."

Jordan looked the boy over with avaricious eyes and ran his tongue around his mouth.

"You graduate, you come see me at General Consolidated. But you gotta shave off that damn beard."

Cec touched his face tenderly, then turned to Monck, soberly. "I'm glad you came in. They just called me from Wellington. Fenton got away. They don't know how, or where he went."

"Forget it. We couldn't keep him on ice forever, and I don't see how he can hurt us now. How many people do you figure you can be ready to move tomorrow?"

"About two thousand. With luck we'll move the rest within the next couple of days."

"Good. Pick the ones you want moved first and I'll have every van in the area out there by seven in the morning."

The spring weather was holding and Monck put the top down, knowing Sam's appetite for air and wind. The reporters were still at the gate, still denied admittance by the guard. He had held a press conference in Wheeling, and talked to the field men when he arrived at the base, but now they were demanding admittance, surrounding the car, shouting questions at Sam Jordan.

Sam merely grinned, disclaimed any part in the activity, insisted that he was only an observer.

Monck promised them a full tour of the base as soon as it was organized, and at last they escaped.

Sam was chortling happily. "I ain't had this much fun since I stole the packing company from Gordon Randall."

That was one story Monck had not heard, and Sam told it with glee as they dropped down the hill and turned south toward Wheeling.

"Gordon was a young fella and feeling his oats, and he and Price Davis tried to hang one on the old man. I made them sorry. Scared the hell out of them. Just don't you get overconfident like they did. In this business you can get the rug pulled out from under you the first time you look the other way."

"I'm trying to keep on top of things."

"Don't let your guard down. I made that mistake with Gordon and Davis. They had a partner named Paxton and damned if he didn't bugger me just when I thought I had them all by the neck."

It was a funny story and Monck appreciated the warning. Sam was not often so generous. But he did not think that he was being careless, nor that there was any danger.

"I don't see what can happen to us now. We've got the base, and it's reasonable to believe I can get the people who signed development contracts with Wellington to transfer them to us as soon as they are voided by the non-performance clauses."

"That sounds all right, but what's the move going to do to your political game?"

"I can't see that it will hurt. It ought to help. I straightened out a mess when it looked impossible."

Sam Jordan licked his lips thoughtfully. "Politics is something I won't even guess about, boy. Business is kind of predictable. You can figure pretty close what people will eat and drink and wear and maybe the kind of car they'll go for this season. But I never can dope out what makes them vote the way they do. I think maybe because voting is so emotional; they vote with their feelings, not their heads. It's the only way I can explain the jerks they put in to run their lives. Me, I'll stick with business. It's based on some kind of a logic, not on a popularity contest."

Monck smirked. "I don't see why I shouldn't stay popular. The kids love me."

"How many of them vote?" Sam's warning tone was still there. "And how you going to know how the people around here will react? You upset tradition when you lifted the school from Wellington and moved it somewhere else. Maybe it's good, but it's change, and the human animal tends to resist change. All you can do is wait and see."

Monck fell into silence. A small cloud passed across the sun. In the fast kaleidoscope of recent events he had given no thought to his own position, and he had too much respect for Sam Jordan's judgment to ignore the low sound of thunder behind his words.

"You still want to go to Washington, don't you?"

"I want to go to the Senate. I want it very much."

Sam was feeling magnanimous. It was a rarity, but he liked Emory Monck more than he had allowed himself to like anyone since he had picked up Larry Donovan as a nineteen-year-old roughneck in a Texas oil field with a chip on his shoulder and his chin stuck out a mile.

"I hope you make it," he said. "But I wouldn't bet on it. I never bet unless I've got a sure thing."

33

☐ The clan had gathered. The fifth floor of the Reid Hotel had blossomed into headquarters for the associated members of Sam Jordan's business syndicates.

Gordon and Marilynn Randall, Fred Thomas, Harry Hertz, Price Davis, George Pappas. Through the night they had straggled in, flying from the corners of the country, Pappas from overseas, drawn by the news that Emory Monck had stolen a university.

They were interested each in what profit he could discover for himself, and as attentive as pioneer women at a neighbor's birthing.

In the living room of the corner suite Vivienne Krump handled the nerve center with unflustered efficiency. This was an old story to her. Over and over these men established temporary bases from which to develop one deal or another.

Vivienne ordered the placement of commandeered desks, the location of the portable switchboard, the buffet tables and bar. The two bedrooms of the suite became work rooms. From the larger one Emory Monck and Ward Perry fielded questions and made decisions. In the second room Al Conner appeared to be running a bookie's phone room; a team from the *Wellington Warrior* was reeling out news releases, trying to keep up with the omnivorous press.

It was all very businesslike, even to the poker game down the hall, a circumstance that gave Conner extra trouble, since the press spent most of its energy trying to arrange interviews with Sam Jordan.

Monck had a visit from Eli Jordan and took her to the far corner of his room to avoid disturbing Ward Perry, on the phone to Akron and Cleveland, sweating to line up more beds for the dormitories. She was glowing with excitement and he kissed her.

"If you're looking for Sam, he's in a game in five-ten."

"Not now he's not. He took off with Price Davis for the base."

"Have you been out there?"

"Marilynn and I are going this afternoon. Emory, this is more exciting than horse racing. And Sam's fascinated. He's talking about moving all of General's research to the base. That's what he and Price are doing, picking out a site."

"Hallelujah. But I hope Price doesn't forget he's due in Washington at four to sign the papers and take over in the name of the Foundation."

She mocked him. "Did you ever know Price to forget a decimal point?"

"You're right. Eli, that million you gave me for scholarships, I've kept it in a separate account to use next year, but right now we need a library."

"I told you to use it any way you want." She stretched to brush his cheek with her dry lips. "Take it a little easy, young'un, you're going like a steam engine."

"You ought to watch the kids." He sounded personally proud.

"I want to. I'll run now and let you get back to work."

He walked with her to the room door. Vivienne Krump signaled that she wanted to talk to him. He hesitated as Ward Perry's voice behind him rose in frustration.

"But there has to be nine thousand of that type bed somewhere in the United States. All right, that's better. Get hold of Flying Tiger and bring them in."

Monck grinned. Perry was coming along fast. He motioned that he would be with Vivienne in a minute and turned back. Perry was slamming the phone down, glaring through Monck, breathing fire, reaching for the instrument again. Monck held up a delaying hand.

"When you get a minute call the base; find the head librarian. Have him check with the department heads, make up a list of what books they need right away, and tell him to send us a material bill for stacks and shelves."

Perry winked at him, he was proving to be a born co-ordinator, even under this pressure. By tomorrow or the next day the new administration office should be set up and functioning, and once the personnel was shifted they could take over a lot of the detail. There was so damned much detail, much of it overlooked in considering the wide picture. At least the dining room was operating and today a couple of thousand boys were moving in. Some of them had sleeping bags to supplement the initial crop of beds.

He went out to Vivienne. For the moment the outer room was empty. Even so Vivienne lowered her voice.

"Alice Wellington has been trying to reach you again."

There had been three calls from Alice the night before. Monck got the messages when he returned from dinner with the Jordans, and had purposely not answered them. He did not want to talk to her, not yet. He guessed that her nose would be out of joint since he had moved without first consulting her.

"What did you tell her?"

"That I couldn't locate you." Her face twisted into a grimace. "She told me she didn't believe me. She said she'd be at Gorman's at twelve-thirty and that you had better be there."

He was not pleased, but he looked at his watch. It was quarter to twelve.

Vivienne said, "Forget it. Stay as far away from her as you can."

"I can't do that. She's an old friend and so is her father. I feel sorry for them; they're caught in the middle of an upheaval they couldn't possibly stop."

He left her and went to Conner's room. Denise Dempsey was there. She had left Martha Yates as lieutenant in charge of the dean's office and made a flying trip to bring clothes to the two girl reporters who had come in such a dither they had neglected to bring anything with them. Of course she could have sent an emissary, but she was too curious to see what was going on in the hotel. Monck chatted with her while he waited for Conner to get off the phone.

The publicity man hung up and mopped the back of his neck with a handkerchief that was already damp.

"Brother, she boils. The governor's secretary has called me every hour on the hour. You ought to see some of

252

the crap the papers are running. They're calling it everything from armed rebellion to a Communist plot to take over education in Ohio."

Monck laughed at him without sympathy. "That's your problem. You asked for the job."

"Little did I know. You been out to the base this morning?"

"Haven't had time."

"You wouldn't know the joint. Cec got the Navy trucks out to move the administration people into the office building. He took ten loads of records from the files, every transcript of every student on the old campus."

"Good, I was worried about that. The trucks run all right?"

"Seems we have an oversupply of natural mechanics. Cec has started a motor pool and he's keeping the roads hot. They had one close brush with the files caravan. The sheriff tried to keep them from taking out the records. Seems Fenton went into court and got an injunction to prevent anything being removed from Wellington."

"Was there trouble?"

Conner's sour newspaperman's humor came through his laugh. "Half the squad guarding the gate just walked ahead of the trucks. There were only half a dozen deputies, and I guess they didn't want to take on something they couldn't finish and start a snowball of real trouble. They did try to serve the paper on Gabe Glasscock, but our young lawyer refused it, said he wasn't named in the injunction."

"Cute. Who is named, do you know?"

"You, and Cec as student body president. The deputies went over to the base to serve Cec but the sentries there wouldn't let them in."

Monck did not like that. He did not want the press to report that they were resisting a court order. He would have to take care of it himself as soon as he had seen Alice. He said so and Conner shrugged.

"Anyhow, it's locking the barn door after the horse is stolen. The records are at the base, all carefully stored in their original files in the basement of the administration building. You want me to do something about it? Denise and I are going out in a few minutes."

"No. Let it alone; I'll go out later." His watch read quarter after twelve. "I've got to run now."

"One thing more." Conner's voice turned a trifle plaintive. "What's the name of our new school? It would help if I knew. I keep calling it the base in our releases and it's awkward as hell."

Monck's expression was foolish. "Yeah, that's a good question." He thought of Eli Jordan and her million-dollar library. "How about Jordan University?"

Conner made a face. "That will get you some great publicity. Jordan's crowd being associated with your Wellington business got us called a wheeler-dealer school, and their clambake here has the papers all stirred up again. They're saying it's a Jordan take-over. I know we need the dough, but . . ."

"We need a lot more than dough. We need brains and influence. How do you think I got the base from the government in three hours? And there's going to be a lot more to getting us off the ground than cleaning up buildings."

"All right," said Conner. "All right, all right. I was just warning you on the reaction we're going to have."

"So we'll put it up to the students. They may decide to call it Eliot. It was his baby. Call him and dump it in his lap. I've got to go."

They had two students stationed at the elevators to keep unauthorized visitors from getting off at the fifth floor, and a girl at a desk in the lobby below to interview and sift those trying to get in touch with Jordan or his associates. There was a television crew down there interviewing everyone they could nab. Monck could not walk through the lobby without being waylaid by newsmen. He used the freight elevator, but he was still five minutes late when he turned into the restaurant's parking lot.

He saw her through the window, sitting alone at a small table, her back very straight, her head up, impeccably groomed, isolated from the crowd by her manner. Staring at nothing, she did not see him until he stopped at the table.

"Sorry I'm late. I came as soon as I got your message." He slid into the facing chair.

"I called you last night."

He said evasively, "I've been moving too fast in the last twenty-four hours for calls to catch up with me."

The waiter materialized at his elbow and Monck ordered drinks automatically.

"Why did you do it?" She barely waited until the man had left. "Why did you do it without telling me, without listening to my opinion?" The hurt in her voice was deep.

"It happened so fast, Alice, I didn't plan it this way. It just broke and ever since I've been on a dead run. Events are pushing me, I'm not pushing them."

"I don't believe you." She leaned forward, her hands twisting in her lap. "You couldn't have done a thing like this unless you had been planning it carefully for weeks or months. General Fenton told Father that it takes a long time to get government property released for sale."

The mention of Fenton made his lips tighten, but he said with restraint, "Ordinarily the general would be right. In this case the circumstances were not quite usual. Shall I say that we didn't go through channels. We went to the top."

Her head was shaking, scolding. "Whether that's true or not doesn't matter. You have done a terrible thing, Emory, destroying a school that is over a hundred years old. Don't you realize what that does to me and to my father?"

He wondered why he was not surprised. Her primary concern was that something she had regarded as a family possession had been snatched from her. He was grateful that the drinks arrived, giving him a moment to formulate an answer.

It was time now to weigh and decide whether he could still have any interest in Alice Wellington. She was certainly equipped to function well as a Washington wife, and as his partner she would be as loyal to him as she was now to her father and her background. But he was afraid that she was too rigid. Change was difficult for her, and he needed flexibility. He said in appeal:

"The last thing in the world I could want would be to hurt either your father or you. I thought you would understand that."

A voice inside him said that if Amos Wellington had used his authority with any rationality there would have been no moving. But recriminations were pointless.

"I couldn't do anything else except put on my hat and walk away. I'd been fired even. But there were ten thousand boys and girls who needed help, and a faculty that deserved more consideration than they were getting after their years of dedicated service. Don't you see that, Alice? Don't you comprehend that I took the only course open to me?"

She did not. She had closed her mind. She saw the problem from one position only. What had appeared in her as adaptability was after all a mere veneer of cultivation; she paid lip service to growth and new ideas, but did not honestly accept change.

"The faculty," she said, "should not have struck in the first place. It was inexcusable and degrading."

"So was Fenton's zealotry."

She jerked back as though he had slapped her, then counted off points on stiff fingers.

"They knew the rule about publishing when they were hired. They signed contracts agreeing to write books. They knew that the board of trustees must have the governing power. You cannot simply usurp authority, that's plain anarchy."

He gave up trying. The lunch had come but neither of them made any move toward touching it. Her face was stony. No matter what anyone else had done, the unforgivable fault was his. He had stolen the school. He had deprived her father of a post that she honored and valued and she would hold it against him forever.

"This is pretty pointless," he said. "I don't know what the trustees will do with Wellington, but . . ."

"They are offering it to the state. The state is short of facilities. General Fenton and Don Dundee went to see the governor this morning." She might have been reading from a dictionary.

He supposed that he should have expected that, and it did not actually matter, but the idea gave him a twinge of regret. Wellington was as much a part of his background as it was of hers. He now realized that even as they had been moving to the base he had hoped against hope that the action would force a sensible compromise, that the students could return to their campus. Whatever the base offered did not include the solid dignity of the old school or the flowing continuity of its tradition. Such a patina, such an aura was not created overnight. The physical structures of the base would never be beautiful; a sleek factory perhaps, but never an Alma Mater.

The barren, naked ugliness of the place struck him with even more force as he drove past the wire fence toward the main gate. It was a military post, a place for fighting men.

The uniformed ROTC guard was a punctuation point to his thought. There was a corps of them holding the entrance against a small army of reporters and cameramen. Television cables lined the ditch at the roadside and their equipment trained on him as he stopped outside the barrier.

NBC and CBS stormed the car with protests that they were being kept away from a story of national interest. Monck apologized for the delay, and promised to set up a press tour with Eliot. He wondered why Marty Yates, with her sense of news value, had not already made them welcome.

He found out a moment later. A man with a press card in his hatband shoved in against the door, said, "Emory Monck?" and put a legal paper into his hand.

A boy in uniform caught the man's arm. "That's why we didn't let anybody in, Chancellor. Shall I shove it down his throat?"

Monck smiled. "It's all right. Let him go."

He drove through the gate, cruising slowly, and shook the paper open. It was signed Joseph T. Byrne, Common Pleas Judge of Riverdale County, and enjoined one Emory Monck from removing any property belonging to Wellington University from the campus of that institution. He was ordered to appear at the courthouse at nine-thirty the next morning to show cause why the injunction should not be made permanent.

34

□ The courtroom was old, unbeautiful and so chilly that the judge wore his overcoat on the bench. He had a parrot-beak nose. Emory remembered him vaguely as a second-rate lawyer who had sometimes done legal work for Wellington, and suspected that he owed his present prominence to General Fenton's backing. His sympathies were therefore predictable.

Monck was represented by a local attorney whom Conner had recommended, and the publicity man had accompanied him to the appearance.

Despite the hour and the indoor temperature the room was filled, proof of Riverdale's interest in and perplexity at what was transpiring on the hill; the crowd while not openly hostile was not friendly either.

The judge did not conceal his bias. "I find this entire situation inexplicable." He opened his broadside. "I hope you can offer some justification for your deportment, for instigating a strike, supporting a rebellion, diverting students and faculty from the university."

Monck's attorney objected. "The students and faculty struck, Your Honor. Dr. Monck did all he could to arrange a compromise, and was fired for his effort."

"Does he deny that the students resorted to force, are in fact still holding the entire school by force, barring the entry of officers of the law with guns?"

Monck answered for himself. "I do not deny the condition. I do deny that I had anything to do with it."

The judge perched forward, pointing a long index finger. "Do you deny that you ordered General Fenton held a prisoner in his office for twenty-four hours? That, sir, amounts to kidnaping."

Emory Monck bowed his head humbly. It would be a hell of a problem if they charged him with that, but apparently the judge was more concerned with castigating him publicly than involving himself in that kind of a circus, and he passed over it with a bluster of indignation.

"Do you deny that at your direction property belonging to the school was seized and transferred under armed guard, unlawfully, and unlawfully impounded in an unauthorized location?"

Monck looked up, bland. "I understand that the transcripts of the students' records were moved. There is some question in my mind as to the ownership of such records. Does a transcript belong to the school or to the student?"

The judge used his gavel. "They belong to the school, and I order you to return them at once. You are hereby permanently enjoined from removing from the campus anything that can be construed as school property. And I herewith order the rebellious students to return to Wellington University and resume their studies. If this order

258

is not complied with at once I will hold everyone involved in contempt of court."

Monck said quickly, "It will take some time to return the records."

"You have until five o'clock this afternoon. Hearing is dismissed." The man stood up and sought sanctuary from the flash bulbs with a quick withdrawal to his chambers.

Monck stood patiently for ten minutes, Conner beside him, giving a generous interview, extending himself to be friendly and cooperative. Just now a sympathetic press could be very helpful. He let them satisfy themselves, working slowly toward the door, and then suggested that Conner set up a press tour of the base. They all appeared relaxed and pleased when he called a halt at the curb. When they had gone he touched his attorney's arm.

"Can he make the kids go back to Wellington?"

The lawyer's laugh was ribald. "How? Sure, they're legally liable on several counts, using arms to take the campus, detaining Fenton . . . but what's he going to do, put ten thousand young adults in jail? He hasn't got that big a jail."

"Frustrating for him. What about the records?"

"Those you had better take back."

"All right. Thanks. I'll be seeing you."

He beckoned to Conner, walked rapidly around the corner and crossed to the Eatery, the closest place with a phone. He called Ward Perry at the hotel, reported on the hearing and said:

"Get hold of every Xerox machine you can find. Call the dealers for a list of their customers and see what you can borrow from them, and move fast; we've only got until five this afternoon."

He called the base and talked to Eliot.

"As soon as the machines arrive put a gang to copying the transcripts. As soon as a file is finished, truck it back to Wellington."

When he hung up Nicholas was at his elbow, dressed in the rusty black suit that was his off-duty uniform.

"I was in court." The heavy face showed a St. Bernard sadness. "Jesuschrist, Emory, what you trying to do?"

"I'm trying to get a cup of coffee." Monck eased over to the counter.

Nicholas dogged him. "People, they're very upset. I

hear them talk, in here, on the street. They can't believe you move the school. It's not possible."

"They'd better believe it."

The counterman had filled two cups and Conner picked them up, wagging his head toward the booths. Monck changed direction and Nicholas stayed close behind.

"The general is a big man, Emory, and don't you forget it. He'll get you, get you good; you watch what I warn you."

"The general will try." Monck maneuvered into the seat. "But the general has bitten off a lot to chew. Forget it."

The restaurant man hung above them a moment longer, unhappy, not understanding Monck's callous disinterest, then shrugged his heavy shoulders and went away.

Conner said, "Take it easy, he's talking for the town. Riverdale hasn't felt so cut off since the Navy closed its operation."

The reaction annoyed Monck. "They'll get over it when the new jobs begin opening up. I've more to bother about than Riverdale's miff."

"I wouldn't be too cocky. Public opinion can be pretty queer; it doesn't always follow reason. To most of these people there's something holy about Wellington University. The Wellington name is sort of a godhead around here. It started with old Amos, the same kind of mass hypnosis that made the Minoans of Knossos permit Minos to turn himself into a god."

Monck favored him with a sardonic grunt. "A damn name dropper."

"Sorry about that. I just happen to be interested in Bronze Age civilization, and it's plenty applicable. According to Gordon Childe, about the first thing man did after he managed to scrabble out a surplus of food was to create a god image. Then that was transferred to the god's temporal representative, the king, the emperor. Rulers have always had a divine association, and we do the same sort of thing to this day, unconsciously attribute an extra power to our leaders, to the President, for instance."

Monck sounded negligent. "Sure. That's why I want to move to Olympus."

"Be smart. I'm trying to get something across to you. Wellington University represented a temple of learning, close to a sacred symbol to people who never had the opportunity to go to college. And in one swipe you—whether you had to or wanted to doesn't matter—have wrecked the cathedral. That's what they see and they aren't liking it."

"Christ, Al, I'm building a better school."

"Sure, and the situation wasn't your fault, but people aren't remembering that right now. They're thinking about a young wheeler-dealer who moved in and did something they didn't believe could be done; he stole their university. You see how your friend Nicholas feels the effect."

"Oh hell," said Emory. "Let's not borrow trouble, let's get out to the base."

Every time he arrived there was further evidence of progressing work. The litter was gone from the streets; the broken windows were all replaced. But what was more impressive than the physical accomplishments was the eagerness of the labor force. There was an air of excitement like nothing he had seen on any campus before.

He located Martin Strindberg in the Physics warehouse, directing its conversion by the use of temporary partitions into classrooms and laboratories. Strindberg was having the time of his life. He was on the phone talking to a Chicago lab equipment company, tilted back on a kitchen chair behind a door laid on a pair of horses, a commodious if not an elegant desk. When he hung up he stretched luxuriously.

"Hot zing, kid. I think I'm dreaming. That Price Davis is a wonder man. I ask for something and he waves a wand and here it comes. I wish we could keep him as financial vice-president."

This was more pleasant than Conner's talk. Emory grinned at the old man.

"You'd have to fight Gordon Randall hand to hand. Is Price back from Washington yet?"

Strindberg did not know. "When are you moving in the rest of the youngsters?"

"As soon as we get beds. You'll have to ask Perry. How about you?"

"We're here now. Helen's over at the house fussing

about what to put where. But she admitted that she likes the place. It's a lot newer than the old one and it looks out over the golf course. Those Navy folk did all right for themselves."

He had a paper layout of his warehouse spread flat on the door and hammer and saw teams cruised by to refer to it, then hauled back fresh material. Strindberg led Monck on an inspection tour, explaining, dodging through the clutter, all but licking his chops in anticipation.

From there Monck walked on to the administration building. The Xerox machines that Ward was scrounging had begun to arrive and volunteers were pulling transcripts from the files, feeding them through. As soon as one file was reloaded it was hoisted into a truck for the return trip to Wellington. Eliot was supervising and chafing at the waste of time.

"It's damn nonsense," he said. "What's the judge trying to prove? What value can this stuff have to Wellington if the people it concerns are no longer enrolled there?"

"Relax. He's taking orders from Fenton."

"Damn Fenton. He's just trying to make things as hard as he can."

"Sure. But things have been handled in a pretty high-handed manner on our side too. You and I may wind up in jail yet."

"So what?"

"So let's conform to the law as close as we can. The quicker we get everyone off that campus the better it will be. I wish those beds would get here."

"Flying Tiger is on the way with one batch and Ward found another bunch in Grand Rapids. They're trucking them down."

"Good. I want everybody over here by the end of the week. As long as we're holding that property we're vulnerable."

"That reminds me." Cec looked uncertain. "The head coach and graduate manager were in this morning wanting trucks to clear out the fieldhouse. I told them we couldn't move any athletic equipment until I talked to you."

Monck swore to himself. He had not even considered the Athletic Department, had forgotten all about it. This raised another peck of questions. Baseball season was approaching, spring football practice should start any day, and the track and field events. It was more complicated than merely finding new equipment and uniforms. The games already scheduled had been arranged in the name of Wellington University. Would the opponents accept the representatives of the substitute school?

"Where will I find them?"

"On the athletic field, I guess. Coach had all his men out there this morning cutting grass, cleaning out the field-house and repairing the track."

Monck caught a passing truck headed that way. The field was a mile out. As he rode across the base he played with the idea of using the railroad tracks when the school got running, putting in gasoline equipment and special trains for student transportation. Now there was a new idea for schools, as big as they were getting.

At least two hundred men, like a flock of crows in a grain field, dotted the long oval. They had three tractors. Two pulled lawn mowers and the third used its blade to scrape the grass from the track and level it. The coach, graduate manager and the director of athletics were in the fieldhouse, attempting to get it back in shape.

Monck had met them all, but casually; when he came in they stopped the clowning that he surprised them at, looking ridiculously guilty. He laughed at them.

"Go ahead, have fun, stay loose. I'll get more work out of you that way."

The coach asked sheepishly, "Do we go after the stuff back there, Chancellor?"

"Emphatically not. I don't want so much as a jock strap taken from Wellington. Write up what you need and get it to Ward Perry or Price Davis. We'll fill the order as soon as we can."

The coach was a powerful-looking figure. He had been All-America at Alabama and had played three years with the Cleveland Browns before a shoulder separation turned him to coaching. Success had given him confidence without arrogance and Monck knew that he had hesitated before coming to Wellington for the expanded athletic program. He scuffed one foot against the floor with a strange diffidence.

"There's a couple of questions I'd like to ask, Doctor. For one thing, what's the name of the school?"

It struck Monck as enormously funny and his grin was infectious.

"That is an item, isn't it?"

"It would help," the athletic director put in querulously, "if we knew the name so we could put it on the uniforms."

"That wasn't what was really worrying me," the coach said. "I'm more interested in what the future policy is going to be regarding sports. Are we going to continue as we were on the hill, or will they be de-emphasized?"

"To answer the first question, the students held a lunch hour meeting yesterday and voted to call us Jordan University. I thought you'd have heard."

"There's a lot going on. Well, so it's Jordan. That's going to be a gas." The coach began to sing in a fine clean bass. "Let us gather at the River, the beautiful, beautiful River . . . I want to pass over Jordan . . ."

Yes, whatever schools they played would have a picnic with the name.

"Maybe we can beat them to it." Monck joined the laughter. "We could make a fight song out of 'Roll, Jordan, Roll.'"

When they quieted down he came back to the policy question, thinking of old Sam and the way he had adopted the Wellington team.

"I don't think there's any danger of de-emphasis. The men in the Foundation that's backing this school like winners. I think that's as near an answer as I can give you at the moment."

The coach was wearing a long-billed sunbeater like Sam's. He took it off and scratched his scalp with a delicately bent finger.

"That's what I wanted to know. I wasn't thinking entirely of myself. I got a lot of the boys to come to Wellington; most of them are pretty good kids and their future in professional sports rests largely on the showing they make as undergraduates."

Monck understood. You played football because you wanted something, not just for the game.

The coach was still worrying. "De-emphasis doesn't bother me so much as whether the teams who have already signed up to play Wellington will transfer the games over to us."

The athletic director took up the subject. "I don't

know, of course. I'll write letters explaining our position as soon as I can get an office put together. But we may not have too much trouble. We don't belong to a conference, and while we try to follow the Big Ten's rules we won't run into the transfer requirements that might have tripped us up. Also, Doctor, don't forget that football is big business. Wellington was becoming a drawing power last season and all the publicity there's been about the shift-over will make people curious to see what kind of a team we can field."

35

☐ Jordan University. Born on Tuesday, christened on Thursday, anthemed on Friday. Roll, Jordan, roll.

And she was rolling. Ten thousand students at the beginning of Easter vacation, and where were they? What were they doing? Going home? Scattering for a week of Bacchanalia? Protest marching against war? Burning draft cards?

Like hell they were. A dutiful president, Cec Eliot had put the vacation to a vote and been screamed down. Services would be held in the stadium on Easter Day. Until then it was mops and brooms, hammers, saws, wrenches, lumber, paint, pipe, moving, recording, filing, collecting. And elbow grease.

The weather was with them. It rained once at night but the days continued clear. The hot wave moved on north. Spring paused to rest. Crocuses that had opened their cups the day the snow left stood fresh, transfixed. There was a lull in the process of growth. Daffodils spearing out of their bulbs broke through the ground, then slowed their thrust to a standstill. In the woods violets, arbutus, trilium, lilies, marsh marigold gathered in sun to swell their roots, nourished themselves with the water released from the ice, making ready for the concerted, triumphal blossoming predetermined in the precise schedule of their cycle.

Only the men and women of Jordan University were not resting. Emory Monck, driving through the gentle evening toward Wheeling, laughed aloud and sang the song that inevitably belonged. "Roll, Jordan, Roll."

He had thrown the name at Conner off the top of his

head. It sounded like good business. He had not actually expected the kids to buy it, and it did not really matter. Sam's crowd was not egocentric. Any name with a dollar sign stamped on it was good. He had thought the students' choice would be a more lofty sounding word, something sonorous, like Wellington. Why had they chosen Jordan? Cec had said without humor that Al Conner had passed along Emory's suggestion. The Senate had talked it over. They *had* considered Monck University; Emory had felt a touch of disappointment—it could have been of political help. They had debated other names, Cec had said; he hesitated and then quite firmly admitted that the decision had been made on unemotional, commercial grounds. With Sam Jordan's name over the door they thought him less likely to get bored with the project and take his money elsewhere. That, Emory assured him, was a sound and worthy basis for their judgment. The kids were indeed growing up.

There was a midnight conference at the Reid Hotel. They sat around the big table Jordan had moved in for the poker game, Gordon Randall, Harry Hertz, Fred Thomas, George Pappas, Ward Perry, Sam and Emory Monck. Price Davis was speaking. He had returned from Washington less than an hour before.

"Your friend Fenton is making tracks," he told Monck. "He's got a lot of friends in the Defense Department and several of the Senators think highly of him. He's pulling all the strings he can lay his hands on to have the transfer of the base to the Foundation blocked."

"Think he can?" Monck had a picture of the utter choas that would result if they had to move again. Also, he was glad now that he had yielded to sentiment and not mentioned the naming of the school, leaving that for the kids' surprise.

At the far side of the table, his jaws rotating unhurriedly on his habitual wad of gum, Harry Hertz shook his head.

"Not a chance. Dick Garmon has wanted a Jennifer vice-presidency for five years. He knows the only way he's going to get it is to see that our purchase is okayed, and don't forget, he has The Man's ear."

Monck relaxed. If Harry said it was solid, it was. Hertz

had never gone off half-cocked that he knew of. Davis' precise voice agreed.

"I think Harry is right, but there has been a stall. The papers weren't ready to sign as they were supposed to be. They promise them now for the first of the week, but Fenton is no help. He was in Washington today, talking to reporters, talking to anyone who would listen. He's howling that this is a ploy for us to get hold of the base for nothing, that we're using the school as a smoke screen."

Sam shoved his glass across the table for a refill. "What does he think we want with it?"

"He isn't thinking. He acts like he's obsessed. I'd say the smart thing would be to get him out of the picture."

"How?"

They fell silent, each sorting through his experience for an answer, but Price sidetracked them by bringing up another point.

"More important at the moment, we're going to run out of money pretty soon. Emory is spending it like the kids were printing it at the base. Who wants to increase his bite?"

There was no rush of volunteers. Monck looked at Jordan. Jordan was the key, always. If he could pry, say, an extra million out of Sam, the others would fall into line. Now he was truly glad that he had listened to sentiment. He said easily, "Which reminds me, who is the Foundation supporting? What's the name of the school? We'll have to have one."

"I guess we do at that." It was Gordon Randall. "How about Strindberg University? His name is almost on a par with Einstein."

Monck frowned and Harry Hertz spotted it, thought he saw a crack in the other's armor and probed it.

"What's the matter with Monck? He started the business."

Monck silently thanked him for the lead. "Sure, but I couldn't have done it without Sam. I think we ought to call it Jordan."

For the first time since Emory had met the man, Sam Jordan showed embarrassment.

"Hell, I never went past the third grade."

The discovery elated Monck. "What's that got to do with it? Damned few schools are named for scholars. You don't think old Amos Wellington was an educated man, do you? All he knew was how to make steel."

Jordan's eyes glittered under drawn brows. "You're trying to sucker old Sam, boy, now ain't you. You want more money and you figure that if you stick my name on this warmed-over plant that I'll sit down and write you a blank check."

"Come on," Monck bored in. "You never wrote a blank check in your life. But don't tell me you wouldn't like the recognition. How many men do you know who are given that kind of an honor?"

Jordan fussed. "Every dealer in the country would give a horse laugh. They'd say old Sam was getting uppity."

"What would Eli say?"

Sam squinted. Monck knew that he was holding his breath and could not release it. Finally Sam cackled.

"Boy, I'll tell you what I'll do. I'll cut cards with you. I lose, you name the school for me and I'll give the Foundation one million bucks. You lose and you go hunt yourself another patsy."

Monck said, "All right, if you'll make it one five card stud hand, face up."

"Sold."

"And Harry deals."

Harry Hertz was pulling for him more than any man in the room; he was betting on that and the knowledge that, when he chose, Hertz could deal whatever hand you asked for.

Jordan's underlip thrust out and he studied Monck sharply, then studied Hertz. Hertz looked bland as a well-fed baby. The thin old lips twitched, and then Sam nodded.

"Get some new cards, Harry."

Hertz rose, limp and langorous, took an unconscionable time making fresh drinks around, and then fished a pack from the drawer of the stand beside the window. He broke the seal, flipped out the advertisements and jokers, riffled the deck without apparent attention. Then he dealt, dropping the cards neatly before each man.

Jordan got a pair of fat red kings, Monck caught aces. Jordan drew a third king, Monck an eight and then another, the ominous "dead-man's hand" of Western legend. Jordan's last two cards were worthless, and only then did

268

Hertz fill Monck's hand with the final, winning ace. Hertz believed in doing things the hard way.

Monck felt drained. By his sweat he had earned his million. Under his breath he cursed Hertz, but later, when he joined Eli Jordan and Denise Dempsey downstairs in the hotel's dark bar he could laugh again.

The bar and the dining room were still busy. The Reid Hotel was having a boom, but mercifully the celebrity seekers were now content to watch from a distance that allowed Monck a little freedom of movement and privacy. The women had a tiny table in the rear corner, and Eli looked pleased as he stopped before them.

"How'd you break loose from the game?"

"One hand was enough." He sat down and explained. "Sam was tickled pink to have the school named for him, but damned if he'd admit it. He had to hide behind the phony bet."

"You mean it was a cheat?" Dempsey straightened up.

Monck laughed at her. "Sam knew as well as I did that it was a put-up job, that Hertz can deal any cards he wants, any time; but he went along, even pretended he was sore at losing. Damn Hertz anyhow. I had to catch that last ace to beat Sam. I was sweating, afraid Harry would make a mistake. He had me on the hook to the end. He's the worst sadist I know of."

Eli's chuckle was a purr. "A school named for Sam Jordan. . . . Wait until my brother hears that. He'll have a heart attack." She leaned toward Denise. "The two boys don't get along. Sam took General Consolidated away from Hanson, and Hanson has never forgiven him." The way she smiled made it plain that she was not disturbed by the situation.

"So I'm all right," Monck said. "Gordon put Jennifer in for another million; Fred Thomas kicked in and George Pappas gave us half a million. Now if we can just find enough beds . . ."

Eli squirmed along the leather bench. "I'd better go upstairs and listen to Sam crow. You two ought to catch some sleep, you look groggy."

Monck offered a hand to help her up, rose and stood watching until her small figure was lost in the lobby. "There goes a great gal, Dempsey."

"I've always thought so, and I just can't visualize that

marriage. That old pirate is so disgusting."

Monck sat down and motioned for the waitress. "You'll find a lot of agreement on that. There's nothing you can call the buzzard that isn't true. But he's still the most exciting person I'll ever know. Nothing ever stops him. The rougher the challenge the more he revels in it. And he gave Eli something nobody else did, importance as an individual. Her father and then her brother didn't think much of women's ability. They tried to make all her decisions, to keep her in a vacuum. Sam Jordan doesn't play that way. He expects everybody, man, woman and child, to be able to look out for himself, to keep him from taking advantage of them. It's been salvation for Eli. She's the only one who can stay one up on him and they both know it."

The girl wrinkled her nose. "What a way to live, knowing that every minute you have to keep your guard up to protect the gold in your teeth. Thank you, no."

He waited as the drinks arrived, then said quietly, "You'll get used to it. You underestimate your own ability."

"Meaning what?"

"Al Conner was right the other night. You and I should get married."

She looked at him quickly, then lowered her eyes to the glass and twirled it slowly between her hands, drawing damp patterns on the tablecloth with its wet base.

"Just like that, huh?"

He reached his hand across, palm up, wriggling his fingers in invitation. "I'm not very good at getting down on my knees and playing love scenes. You will marry me, won't you? We can have a lot of fun together."

"Emory Monck." She was suddenly explosively angry. "I don't believe you have the least comprehension of love. You haven't a glimmering of what life means to an average human being, a woman especially. All you want is to win. Everything else you take for granted. You can euchre Sam Jordan, you can manipulate people like chessmen. You maneuvered Esther Hollister, you got Al Conner to handle your campaign and you changed Cec Eliot from a campus politician into an image of yourself. But you are not going to pop me into your box of jumping jacks."

270

He wanted her. He wanted Dempsey. He wanted her warmth, her quickness, her brightness, her passion, her funny little tea kettle fierceness. He had not acknowledged how much he wanted her until he had spoken, but it came through him like a hot wind and made his hands shake. He was thoroughly surprised.

"Dempsey," he said. "I don't want you in a box. I want you with me. I'm not offering you a deal."

"Yes you are. You don't even know it; but I know it. You're not human. You're cold and hard and efficient and made out of timing devices all ticking away inside of you. I don't want any part of it. When I find a husband, if I ever do, I want one who's capable of making mistakes and being hurt and letting me in. And I don't want to spend my life Indian wrestling with him and wearing armor and watching my back."

She pushed to her feet; as he started to rise she stopped him.

"No, don't get up. Let me bow out by myself. I'm sorry I teed off on you, but it had to be said, and it's better said here where we can't scream at each other than someplace where we're alone. You're just too damn charming. You get me all steamed up. Good night."

He watched her go. He turned to his glass. He thought bitterly that Eli Jordan was the only woman who made sense. He had not expected this from Dempsey. He had given her credit for more understanding. He signaled the waitress and set out deliberately to get drunk.

36

☐ It was moving day for the Deltas. Cec Eliot had purposely left fraternity row until last, and none of the brothers was at all happy about leaving his house. The Deltas were more regretful than the rest, departing the best quarters on the campus.

There had been a row of some proportion and a number of students had given up both schools and left. More would have except that they would forfeit the semester's credits. It had been a reaction to Monck's edict that there would be no fraternity houses at Jordan University, that the Greek letter men would have to find space in the converted barracks along with the rest.

"It isn't fair," he had said. "You are all in this move together; the house members haven't worked any harder than anyone else, and everybody should have an equal share."

Cec had agreed and stood staunch amidst the tempest. With the weight of the great majority against them the dissidents had calmed down.

Another small flap had revolved around the Delta house. The building belonged to the chapter, but it stood on ground that was an integral part of Wellington. Gabe Glasscock had consulted lawyers on the feasibility of moving it. They discouraged him, however, pointing out that the university could probably claim any structure erected on its land.

So they were stripping the house of everything they considered their personal possessions. Kurt Pfiester was on a ladder above a hedge of upstretched hands, taking down the gaudy chandelier. Wymer Edwards had dismantled the still. He had no idea where he would reassemble it, but there had to be a place in one of the many buildings at the base. He still thought of it as the base even though it had been two weeks since they had named their new school. Not that Wymer disliked Sam Jordan. He approved of all he had learned about the oil man and hoped that at graduation he could find a home in one of General Consolidated's cracking plants. But somehow the name Jordan University did not have the ringing cadence of Wellington.

He carried the copper coil out and stowed it in the seat of the truck for safety; he hoped that the supply of corn sugar would be as readily accessible in the new laboratory as it had been in the old.

Moving vans lined the whole row. The furniture belonged without contest to the brothers and they shuttled in and out with noisy entreaties for care, to lift, to carry, to take it away. But there was so much to move that it was dusk before the last van was filled and rolled out along the curving drive.

The Deltas' final van was the last to go. At the gate the guard that had been maintained for nearly three weeks was forming into a squad, preparing to climb aboard the truck that would haul them the seven miles south to the raw new compound.

The van stopped, blocked by the loading truck, and Cec Eliot, on the tailgate, looking back, noticed the flag at the top of the pole in the landscaped traffic circle. Technically it belonged to Wellington. But who was there left to minister to it? It had been raised and lowered daily, and was it to be abandoned?

He slid from the truck and started forward. The guard took the hint. The banner was properly brought down. A rattle of rifle fire saluted it. It was folded and taken away in the truck.

Far across the shadowed, mellow acres, at the head of faculty row, a single light gleamed. Around the campus the buildings were silent, forlorn and deserted.

Cec Eliot choked. For nearly four years this had been his home, with life pulsing through it, physical activity, intellectual ferment; sometimes potent and seething as a volcano. Now the lights had gone out at Wellington. Only the winking window of the old manse remained in the gathering gloom.

They closed the wrought-iron gate. The truck pulled out. The van followed with a heavy rumbling. Cec began to hum without really knowing that he did. The brothers on the tailgate with him took it up and began to sing. The chorus rose and the roadside rang with the solemn strains of *Wellington We Will Remember*.

Within the old parlor Alice Wellington could not hear the voices, but she had heard the shots and the growl of the departing trucks. She went to the front window, held back the glass curtain and looked into the shadows. Never in her memory had there been no night lights in the buildings, no street lamps along the drives. But tonight there was no one to turn them on.

"Damn him," she said. "Damn him, damn him, damn him. I wish I'd bitten out my tongue before I ever suggested bringing him back here."

She felt lost, deserted, frightened at the emptiness about her and the funereal quiet where there had always been sound. She looked at her father, who was pretending to read the evening paper, and saw an old man. She crossed and sank to her knees beside him, taking his hand.

"How could anyone do this to us?"

The old classics scholar let his paper fall, pressed her fingers gently and lay back against the chair.

"Alice, what's happened to us is not as important as what's happened to the school. I know, you're blaming Emory, and without him there would not have been this drastic situation, but to be honest I don't know what else he could have done. He's right that education is changing, and we have to keep abreast. Those of us who were running the school obviously were not up to snuff. We were already foundering. I wish I could somehow undo the mischief."

She made a silent protest.

"It's the waste that troubles me," he said. "All these buildings not being used when they're needed so badly."

"Isn't the state going to take them?"

"No. The eighteen million dollars in bonds is stopping them, and the other millions it would require to operate. There's always a scramble for public school money; they couldn't hope to get the appropriation for us even if the legislature were in session. I'm afraid that's another of Fenton's errors."

He had never criticized the general before in her hearing. In his mildness he seldom criticized anyone.

"I think it's contemptible how everybody has failed you."

"Never mind." He pressed her hand again. "The thing I regret most is you and Emory. I thought that would be an excellent marriage."

"I did too." She was too unhappy to dissemble. "But it wouldn't have worked. Our values are too wide apart. . . . Let's go away. Let's go to Paris. We can't live in this graveyard."

"I don't know what we're going to do about the property yet."

General Jerome Fenton did not know what they were going to do either. He was having dinner with Don Dundee, Dr. Binford, and Edgar Hyman at the Wheeling Club, nettled by the knowledge that only two blocks down the street Emory Monck and his entourage were probably celebrating at the Reid.

"We've got to do something," Hymen was saying. "We can't simply sit by and let the place fall into ruin."

Fenton felt the criticism in his tone. "What else could we have done?"

274

Binford shrugged his massive shoulders. "The mistake, I think, was in firing Martin."

"The mistake," Fenton corrected him sharply, "was in ever hiring Monck."

"I didn't believe he could do it." Don Dundee sounded dazed. "They're all gone, even the football team."

Hyman grumbled. "You and your damned football team. I still say we'd better have a talk with Monck before it's too late. The general couldn't even block them in Washington."

Fenton said angrily, "That crowd has influence in every corner of the government. But we still have the court order enjoining the students from leaving Wellington."

"They've left. Who do you think could make ten thousand of them come back even if the order was legal, which I doubt." Binford was not a lawyer; he was a doctor with a medical man's strong sense of reality. "I believe we're whipped and had better make the best deal we can."

"I'm not through yet." Fenton was adamant. "These people aren't in as strong a position as you think. I've got a couple of aces up my sleeve. I spent all yesterday talking to lawyers in Washington."

"What aces?" Dundee snapped at the possibility of reprieve.

Fenton smiled at each of them in turn.

"Simple matters they have overlooked in their haste. For one thing, the Educational Assistance Foundation they set up is vulnerable. We are entering a suit in federal court for an accounting of the funds, and entering a charge of misuse. We have the signed developmental research contracts as proof that the money was raised for Wellington."

"You think you can make it stick?" Binford was doubtful. "Even if you win the case they'll stall in the courts until the buildings rot away."

Fenton shook his head. "That's beside the point. We'll ask for an injunction preventing them from plundering the funds until the case is heard. Then we'll see what Emory Monck does, without money."

Hymen's voice was impatient and sour. "Jerome, don't you know who you're playing with? You freeze the Foundation money and make that crowd mad and they'll sit down and write out personal checks. Hasn't it dawned on you that Sam Jordan is as rich as Croesus? Between him

275

and his partner, Donovan, they control the biggest oil pool ever discovered."

Fenton was unimpressed. "I've got another ace. They have to have lights and power to run that place."

Dundee threw his arms wide. "It has its own plant; are you nuts or something?"

Fenton was too pleased with himself to take offense. "It's only a standby arrangement for emergencies, Don. I talked to some Navy people, who told me they had always bought power from the Tri-State Transmission Company." He shook a finger at them. "Now here's where Monck's gang outsmarted themselves. The way the Foundation is chartered it cannot engage in private business. It can hold real estate and lease it to independent firms, but it cannot operate a business itself. Since their so-called school is not incorporated separately, but is directly under the Foundation, it cannot run a power company."

Dundee looked confused. Hyman still doubted. "Surely there isn't any law to keep them from generating power for the school's own use?"

The general was triumphant. "That's not what I mean. Monck has already leased some of his spare buildings to industries that are going to establish experimental units in them. He agreed in the leases to furnish power. My lawyers got hold of one of the contracts. So here we've got them. Since he can't run a company tapping power from Tri-State, he can't deliver unless the local power company runs outside lines in. I'm on the board of directors of that local company. We'll just take our own sweet time processing his requests."

Dundee whistled. "General, I've got to hand it to you at that. You know, I never thought you could take on Emory Monck and beat him at his own game."

Three days later Price Davis was served with papers enjoining the Foundation from expending further funds on Jordan University. He called a war council, more amused than disturbed.

"It won't hold up," he said. "When we put the Foundation together originally we took care to state that the trustees could use the money at their discretion."

Price and Monck and Ward Perry were alone in the new offices in the administration building. For all the fun Jordan, Randall, and the others had had in midwifing the school they had not been able to linger. Too many other interests called for their attention. A few days was all they could spend in Wheeling; then they had gone. Of the three it was Ward Perry who worried.

"But in the meantime, what do we do for dough?"

Price Davis' chuckle was dry as rustling leaves. "We're in luck. The new assessment Emory euchred out of us the other day hasn't been paid into the Foundation and therefore does not come under this court order. There's enough to last us until we blow the order down."

Perry scratched his head slowly. "Maybe someday I'll get used to the way you people play with that kind of money, but it's going to take time." He smiled faintly. "I guess that will take the wind out of the general's sails for a while."

The words brought Monck's thoughts around to Perry and the table of organization. He had insisted that Strindberg take the presidency and argued down the physicist's loud protests.

"We need the prestige of your name, and you know it. We have to be accredited, and they can hardly refuse if you are head of the faculty."

The old man had balked. "I'm a teacher and a research man. I'm not a business administrator."

"I'm not asking you to be. I'll go in as administrative vice-president. Price Davis says he'll handle the financial end until we're straightened out; then he'll bring in one of his young men and train him for the job. It would be silly to ask an educator to run the finances in this day of specialization. We'll make Ward chancellor, and I'll stay until he's ready to handle it alone. You don't have to work at the job, but we need the name Martin Strindberg at the top of the list."

Strindberg had squinted at him, trying to read Monck's mind. "You're still set on going into politics, huh?"

"Of course. Why the question?"

"Well, I don't know . . . All this challenge here, I thought you might have got interested enough to stay around."

Monck had laughed at him. "Don't try to con me again, Martin. Once the school shakes down there won't be enough for me to do to keep busy."

Watching Perry now he debated how soon he could

turn over the reins and step out. Perry said, "Well, if that's squared away, I've got a problem. I'm running into a little trouble with the power company."

Monck thought that had been taken care of. Since the Foundation could not operate a company itself, he had organized a separate corporation with himself, Price and Perry as officers. The Foundation had sold the lines and installations to the corporation, together with the standby plant, the water system, the railroad, and the heating plant.

No money had changed hands. The corporation had issued stock and given it to the Foundation as the price of the utilities. In turn the school and the industrial lessees would pay cash for power and service. The money would return to the Foundation as dividends on the stock. The three of them held ten shares each, the only voting stock in the corporation.

"What's your problem?"

"The Tri-State Transmission people say they can't sell us power until we're licensed by the State Utilities Commission."

"So get a license."

"I applied. I got a letter this morning. They turned us down."

Monck's attention sharpened. "What reason?"

"They say this whole region is serviced by Riverdale Power and Gas, and it is not Commission policy to franchise a new concern in a territory already being adequately served by an existing company. We can ask for a hearing of course, but that will take time and we have three industries moving in as of next week."

Monck whistled tonelessly. It looked like a squeeze of some kind, but he did not think it was too important.

"Quit worrying, I'll take care of it first thing tomorrow."

37

☐ The headquarters of the Riverdale Power and Gas Company was an old brick building below the steel mill, against the river. Originally it had been a small steam generating plant, but this had been abandoned twenty years ago as obsolete; now they bought power from the

Tri-State Transmission line. The company had been started by old Amos to supply his mill and his workmen's houses, but it had long since passed into public control, owned primarily by the local citizens.

The entrance was reached by following a narrow, twisting street, once paved but broken now and going back to mud. Monck dodged what chuckholes he could and parked in front of the two steps, planks worn and cracked and pitted by gravel.

Four elderly clerks bent over desks behind a time-blackened fence partition. The smell of dust, age, decay in the room invited sneezing.

The manager, Hume, was in his late fifties, a little man with an extremely pointed nose. He came to his office door, shook hands and escorted Monck to a straight-backed chair facing an antiquated desk.

"Yes, Dr. Monck, how may we help you?" There was an unctuous drawl in the voice that Monck found distasteful.

Monck sat back, crossing an ankle over his knee, and dropped his hat casually on the floor.

"You know that the Navy base we've taken over has its own power system . . ."

The man inclined his small head, showing the beginning of a bald spot in the sparse hair.

". . . We set it up as a corporation, intending to buy power from the Transmission people. They tell us they can't sell to us unless we're franchised by the State Utilities Board."

"That is correct." Hume's lips parted in what might become a smile of satisfaction.

"The Utility Board says its policy is not to franchise a new company in territory already adequately covered by an existing company, in this case, you."

"I believe that is also true."

"We could ask for a hearing on our application, but should I expect that you would enter a protest?"

"Probably." Hume moved his hands in a brief helpless gesture. "I do not make our policies, Doctor, our directors do."

"All right. We have no real desire to go into the utility business, and we certainly do not want to injure anyone in Riverdale, but we need power. I'll make a deal with you.

I'll turn over to you all of our installations at a reasonable price, and take the payment in power."

Hume placed the tips of his fingers together in a thin steeple, rested his elbows on the edge of the desk and leaned his chin on the sharp point.

"The suggestion has possibilities. It will require board action, and it would take some time to make the necessary connections."

"How long?" Monck knew when he was being traded with; he had expected it.

"Three months, maybe."

"Why so long? You have lines running past the base."

"They aren't heavy enough."

"There's a high voltage line from the Transmission substation the Navy used."

"We couldn't use that. We'd have to run the power through our own station."

"Could I talk to your board of directors?"

"That might be wise. I'd suggest General Fenton. He takes an active position on the board."

Monck sat looking at the sly grin, now seeing the plan clearly. "Forget it." He stood up without warning. "I wouldn't deal with you now if we have to use candles for lights."

Hume rose but made no motion to come from behind his desk, as if he felt the need of its protection.

Boiling as he was, Monck managed a graceful exit, saving his explosion until he walked into Perry's office at the base. Price Davis was there, going over the figures for the new library, and both men listened in deepening silence.

"I'm going to Columbus," Monck finished. He reached for the phone, called the pilot he had borrowed from Jennifer when Hertz sent him the Humming Bird, and told the man to gas and warm the ship.

"What good can you do there?" Perry sounded sepulchral.

Monck said, "I don't know, but I'm not about to sit tied and let Fenton get away with this one."

He called the governor's secretary and asked the man to arrange a meeting for the afternoon with the chairman of the Utilities Commission. Then he drove out to the runway.

Below him the rolling countryside was pastel green, the woods washed with the pink of flowering fruit trees. Tractors scurried across fields, turning the earth. The soft scene did not soften Monck's thoughts. He let the pilot handle the ship and concentrated on what he could say to the Utilities man.

Walter Abbott gave him a friendly and sympathetic reception. He had met Monck on one of Emory's speaking tours and he listened with interest to the short history and the projection for the new school.

"It's a sensible idea, industry right on campus, giving students the business experience and interlocking with their study."

"There will be no industrial participation unless we can get electricity in sufficient quantity to run their laboratories and plants."

"I understand that, but honestly, Dr. Monck, I don't know what the Commission can do to help. It looks like a planned holdup all right, but we've got to follow our precedent, and if the Riverdale people protest your appeal the protest would pretty certainly be honored."

Monck could not believe it. "You mean that you would cut off twelve thousand people from power? That's how many we'll have resident on the base, more as further industry comes in. That's a whole city. . . . That's it!"

The two words burst out with an emphasis that made the Commission chairman start.

"What's what?"

"A town. Our own town. Tell me, Mr. Abbott, what is the Commission's policy on publicly owned utilities?"

"Why, we . . ."

"Supposing I had an incorporated town on the base. Supposing that town wanted to own its own utilities . . . water, power, gas, telephone . . . would we be green-lighted?"

Walter Abbott was not Emory Monck's equal in mental agility. Monck waited. As full comprehension came, Abbott was smiling, rubbing his hands together, kneading a pleasant vision between his palms.

"A town, yes. We have always supported public ownership wherever possible."

Monck reached across the desk for the phone with a cursory "May I?" and called Price Davis collect. The word collect would insure Price's sharp attention.

With the connection made he omitted the amenities.

"I'm with Abbott. He says the Commission will okay a municipal utilities department. Have Ward make up a petition to incorporate a town and get it signed by every resident on the base."

Price Davis said simply, "Yes."

"We'll turn over the swimming pool, Officers' Club, and golf course as a public park."

"Yes."

"We elect a council and mayor. How would you like the office?"

"I would not."

"We'll use Al Conner then. It will serve him right. He's been playing at politics from the other end long enough.

"Now. The council will issue fifty thousand dollars' worth of municipal bonds and trade them to our power corporation for the juice, water and phone systems. And the railroad, we'll probably be the smallest city on record with its own railroad. That will screw Fenton. The Tri-State Transmission people will have to sell us power, we'll tie the phone onto Mother Bell and make a connection for our rails with Penn Central. Then we can charge for everything switched in over our line and we'll pick up forty percent of the freighting we initiate. The income ought to finance the town."

"Yes." Davis' voice was clipped and delighted. "What do we call it, Jordan or Monck?"

"Neither. It will take at least a year to get us on the map. Let's not make it confusing. South Riverdale? No, I don't like the wrong-side-of-the-tracks sound. Let's go like Malibu West. We are Riverdale South."

He rang off. He was feeling extremely good. Abbott was looking at him as if he were watching a theatrical production.

"I've heard about you," he said in a dreamy tone, "but I never saw anything like this. Get your town and department set up and I promise you'll be in business. Just give me the privilege of telling the governor. Sharkey hasn't had this good a laugh in a long while."

38

☐ The faculty and staff of Jordan University and the industrial personnel that was increasing daily, who would be permanent residents, and who already totaled approximately three thousand eligible voters, delivered a majority in favor of incorporating Riverdale South, a community a mile wide and three miles long. They elected a town council, a board of public utilities and Al Conner as mayor.

The students thought it was cute to have their own town but gave little attention to it. Their own affairs amply occupied their minds. Spring football practice was under way. Baseball season had started. The track team was readying for its meet with Pittsburgh. The glee club was rehearsing. Martha Yates's folk singers were preparing for a tour under the new auspices.

Emory Monck believed that Ward Perry could take over the full burden of the chancellorship between the end of the spring term and the beginning of the summer session. The job he had originally agreed to do for Martin Strindberg was about cleaned up, albeit there had been some changes along the way. There was one more item he wanted to take care of before he stepped out and delivered himself into the hands of Al Conner, before he started on the campaign trail.

He had been so busy in the hasty creation of the new town, in transferring the utilities complex to the council, in shepherding the arrangements by which Tri-State Transmission would furnish them with electricity that he had given little or no thought to the impact that Riverdale South was having on old Riverdale.

He came into the Farmers' National Bank in the morning, not anticipating the slightest opposition. Dutton Andrews had been president of the institution ever since Emory could remember, had been a personal friend of Monck's father and was still close with Martin Strindberg.

Andrews did not rise as Emory crossed his office. He sank deeper in his chair, a slight man with fine silky white hair. Monck, in his usual hurry, did not notice his withdrawing manner. He was relaxed and smiling.

"We've got quite a town down at the new school," he said. "It's already big enough to support a community bank. Open a branch for us and we'll give you all the facilities you need for free."

Andrews was not rude, but there was no friendliness in his answer.

"That's generous, but no thank you."

Monck's thoughts, which had been running smoothly ahead, backed up. Was this Fenton again, relentlessly obstructionist?

"No thank you? You're not interested in three thousand customers? For what reason?"

"You just said it. A bank out there would make it just that much more unnecessary for those people to come to town. Business was bad enough before you opened that place."

Monck gaped at him. "What the hell? I'm offering you new business. Growing business. More every day."

Dutton Andrews watched Monck carefully to see if he were acting or if he really did not comprehend. He could not decide. He lifted his white eyebrows, in doubt about attempting a serious explanation, wondering if it would open him to Monck's ridicule.

"Emory, our Chamber of Commerce is up in arms about what you've already done. The bank is owned by more than fifty Riverdale merchants. The board would not even consider your proposition. You are a long way from being the most popular man around here today."

"I'm afraid I still don't get it. What have I done wrong?"

"First you moved the university away. A lot of our business came from the school."

"For Pete sake, I only moved it six miles. Where do you lose?"

"Now you're cutting the throat of the town itself. Don't you realize the effect your incorporation of the base into a separate town is having on everyone who owns property in Riverdale?"

"Oh for God sake, Andrews, come off it. As our industrial pilot program gathers momentum we'll have jobs for everybody down there. With our salaries coming in here, Riverdale will be in better shape than it's been for years." He began to laugh, trying to bring the other man into the joke. "Our incorporating was only a device to get the electric current we need. If the power and gas company had been willing to cooperate I wouldn't have done it."

Dutton Andrews' eyes changed enough to tell Monck that the banker knew all about the power company's opposition and its reason.

"Anyway, Riverdale South is not a town in the sense you mean. We're not in competition."

"You are here asking me for a bank right now. It's only a matter of time until someone puts in a restaurant, a shopping center and the rest."

"Oh no, not on the base, I promise that. We haven't even got the room under our projected development plan."

The banker moved his shoulders with impatience. "There is ground outside the base, ground that can be bought fairly cheap. Riverdale has been running downhill with the rest of this Appalachian country. You can't blame our people for feeling insecure. And the way they see it, you're deliberately ruining them."

Monck wanted to laugh at their short-sighted fear, but he did not. This was hardly funny from his personal point of view.

"Forget the branch," he said, and stood up.

Andrews' voice was warmer with relief. "I'm glad you're taking that attitude. I half expected that when I turned you down you'd bring in someone from outside."

"Apparently I can attract enough trouble without going hunting for it."

Monck left the bank, aware now of people turning to stare at him in accusation. The freeze continued as he swung from Main Street into Wellington Road and went into the Eatery.

Nicholas was not on duty, but sat in a booth, hunched over the Form that lay open on the table. Except for the short-order cook and the dishwasher, the place was deserted. Monck slid into the seat opposite the Greek.

"Don't you know by now that you can't tell a horse from a haystack?"

Nicholas did not look up. He spoke to the paper. "What you trying to do, Emory, kill us all dead?"

You too, Monck thought, and said aloud, "You damn fool, I'm not trying to kill anything. I'm trying to pump some new life into your miserable graveyard."

"Sure. You pump in new life. Look at my place. You swipe my business, everybody's business. You even swipe our name. Riverdale South. What kind of smart-ass crap is that?"

Irritation rode Monck and he said, "You want to blame someone, lay it on Fenton and his ostriches."

He left and drove in disgust back to the base. He found Denise Dempsey in Al Conner's office, the two of them working on publicity releases for the upcoming graduation ceremonies.

"I ran into a beaut downtown." His voice had an edge. "Riverdale's decided that I'm a rat fink. I stole their town."

"I got the same rumble." Conner did not add that he had warned Monck earlier of the likely reaction. "I haven't mentioned it because I couldn't see how to head it off."

Riverdale's change of heart was news to Dempsey. "That sounds pretty childish. Don't they see how big the long-range benefits will be?"

Conner sounded gloomy. "Not right now they don't. Right now Emory couldn't be elected dog catcher in this territory."

Monck was still nettled at the unexpected obtuseness of the voters on whom he had counted. "You want to abandon ship, Al? You quit that easy?"

The jibe ruffled Conner's feathers. "Take a good hard look at the facts, kid. I haven't seen you to tell you, but I had a long phone call from the Senator last night. He's been getting protests from some of the local boys and he doesn't like it. He says that the more popular a man has been the farther he falls when the tide turns. People feel cheated. Starting this town can well have cost you the election; Lightner isn't about to back a potential loser."

Denise Dempsey looked from one to the other. "He can't just pull out and leave Emory stranded. What kind of a man is he?"

"Party first, people later, that's the Senator. And unless Emory does something to knock this antagonism down we aren't going to have any help from the organization."

Dempsey sputtered. Monck put a hand on her shoulder.

"Slow down, Dempsey. It will all blow over before next year somehow. I've been up against worse and come through."

Rather than reassuring her the words sparked a sharp impatience.

"You're always so cocksure of yourself. Can't you ever worry like an ordinary person? You ought to be thinking about how you're going to win those people back, what you're going to do."

"All right. I don't think it's that important, but how about this? I'll make a pitch to the Chamber of Commerce. We'll get up a projection chart for them, hang it on an easel, take a schoolroom pointer, cross the t's and dot the i's and show them how in actuality I am rescuing my old hometown from the horrible fate of its decaying sister cities up and down the river. That ought to grab them, what with the delight people generally take in upstaging each other."

Conner was not buying it. "You're a glib son of a bitch," he said, "but you can't talk yourself out of this one. Jobs or no jobs, salaries or not, Riverdale South is still going to be the rich relation. None of the new people coming in here are going to want to live in Riverdale or do business in the grubby hole. They're going to want new, clean, modern stores close to home, and they're going to get them. You can't stop it. You can't buy up all the land around here. The handwriting is on the wall and you can't charm it away. So pull another rabbit out of your hat."

Monck felt the closeness of the room. He knew that Conner was right but he did not want to admit it. And he did not feel like tackling the problem in this atmosphere.

"I'll think about it. There's an answer somewhere. Right now I need some air. Dempsey, I'll take you to Wheeling for lunch."

She went without argument, concerned and wanting to help. In the car she said, "Do you want to try some brainstorming?"

He was pleased with the girl's attitude and the contrast between it and Conner's acceptance of political defeat. He reached across to pat her knee.

"I want to forget it for now. But Dempsey, it's about time I said thank you for back-stopping me all this while."

Her head bobbed for emphasis. "Well, doggone it, I believe in what you're doing." She flushed. "In spite of the way I bawled you out in Wheeling. I believe you can be elected."

He turned his head to look at her. "Come on and go to Washington with me."

She frowned. "I didn't mean I'm that convinced you could be the husband I want. You're too much like Sam Jordan. I want someone who doesn't scare me so much."

"You going to marry Ward Perry?"

She did not take kindly to the question and did not answer it; he decided that he had better get off the subject for the time being.

"Well, anyway, it's a pretty day. Let's pretend we're sophomores playing hooky. Is it a deal?"

"Deal."

Back in his office two hours later he found a pair of strangers in the waiting room and looked inquiringly at Vivienne Krump as he passed. She followed him into the inner room.

"Misters Hibbs and Jones from Trans-Financial. I didn't know where you were or when you'd be back, but they said they'd driven down from Cleveland and had to talk to you personally."

He was distracted, still thinking about Dempsey and Ward Perry.

"Funny they didn't make an appointment. Any idea what they want?"

"Not the slightest."

"Well, send them in."

Both men were young. Jones, the older, he judged could not be over forty. Both were well dressed. Monck had dealt with enough bankers to know the type.

"Sorry I wasn't here and you had the wait. What can I do for you?"

Jones was the spokesman, unhurried but sure. "In case you're not familiar with us, we are in effect a banker's bank. All banks at one time or another acquire assets that become frozen, that have to be sold, or foreclosed upon."

That did not tell Monck why they were here.

"The banks," Jones continued, "and the underwriters who furnished funds for Wellington's expansion are far from happy about the present situation."

Monck was beginning to see but he waited, always a careful listener.

"Loans of this type are seldom made on a strictly commercial basis. Other factors are involved. Unfortunately, the banking laws do not permit us too much leeway. Unless interest is paid regularly we have little choice but to start action."

Monck said without emphasis, "You know, of course, that I no longer have any connection with that university?"

Jones's smile was bleak. "We are very conscious of it. That's why we are so concerned. What is going to be done with the plant?"

"I have no way of knowing."

Jones raised his brows and tipped his head. "Would you consider moving back onto that campus? Certainly the facilities are more fitting than those here. We looked over the base this morning. You have done a truly remarkable job in an astonishingly short time, but it would take decades to develop buildings and planting to compare with the beauty of the Wellington site."

Monck smiled his agreement. "You don't have to spell that out to me. I was raised over there. But I wonder how much of the story behind our move you know."

"Most of it, I think."

"Then you understand that the trustees would make no concessions to either the faculty or the students, and I have no indication that their thinking has changed in the least."

"There are no Wellington trustees, as of five o'clock last night."

Monck was flabbergasted. "You mean they quit?"

"The Wellington Corporation went out of existence. With its passing went their positions. Don't you know about the reversion clause in the original deed of gift?"

Monck moved his head sideways slowly. "Never heard of it."

Hibbs opened the dispatch case on his lap and brought out a folder. Jones flipped it open, fingered through it.

"Let me read paragraph fourteen of the deed which transferred the land on which the school is built to the Wellington University Corporation.

"It is understood that if at any future date, for any reason whatsoever, the said property shall no longer be employed for educational purposes, said property including all buildings now standing or to be built in the future shall, at the end of one month after the cessation of the agreed educational employment, revert to my legal heirs without

restriction, to do with as they see fit."

"May I see that?" Monck extended his hand and when the banker surrendered the paper he read the clause himself. Finally he returned it, looking up.

"So Amos Junior owns the whole thing."

"Subject to our loans. At the time the school borrowed the money no one thought of the possibility that it might cease to exist, but because this clause in effect constituted a lien Dr. Wellington also signed the covering notes."

"For eighteen million dollars?"

Jones inclined his head. "So we came down to confer with him. He does not want the property. He doesn't know what to do with it and his personal fortune is too depleted to permit him either to assume the loans or to pay them off. In this extremity he suggested that we talk with you."

"He suggested?" This was a day for surprises.

"Of course. We would not have approached you unless the suggestion had come from him." Jones's tone said plainly that he wanted Monck to understand that they were operating in a punctilious, legal fashion. "His words were that if anyone in the world could straighten out the tangle it was Emory Monck."

"Well I'll be damned."

"So we are here in an attempt to work out some solution. Dr. Monck, we could offer you a six-month moratorium if you would agree to move back, form a new corporation and assume payments on the indebtedness . . ."

Monck felt an unbusinesslike elation, but he said, "That's a decision I can't make alone. A lot of people, the students and faculty, worked like the devil to create this school, and they feel it belongs to them. I would want their vote before I could give you a definite answer. I'd also have to have the okay of the men who financed us."

"Of course."

"I think the first thing is for me to go over and talk to Amos. Then I'll talk to the lawyers and see how we stand and what steps would have to be taken. I would not want to revitalize the old Wellington Corporation. I don't want those trustees in my hair again."

Both bankers were quick to agree.

"So give me a few days to see what I can work out. I'll call you."

He walked them to the door and watched until they were clear of the building before he returned to Vivienne's office.

"What was *that* all about?"

He told her and saw her consternation.

"You're not going to do any such thing . . . are you?"

Monck chuckled. "Maybe. Nothing we ever do here will transform this complex of hangars and warehouses into a campus with the charm of the old place."

"Oh God. Not for me. I hate that joint. I feel like I'm living on Mars over there. You go back and you can get another secretary."

He let her fume for a while and then relented. "I'm not going to stay at either place, remember? When Riverdale hears that I'm bringing Wellington back to life you couldn't keep me out of Congress with a rocket."

"Happy the day," she said. "For a minute you had me scared. I don't think much of Washington, but after this joint it's going to look like heaven. Come on, election, let's get moving."

39

☐ The Impala turned in at the unguarded gate and cruised along the empty drive, past the lonely buildings and the silent faculty houses.

The roads were dirty, littered with the stained debris accumulated in the snow and left on the ground after it melted. The trees were leafing out and the perennial spring flowers beginning to bloom, but the lawns were untended and ragged.

Monck parked before the Wellington manse, and noticed that a thin plume of smoke rose from the old chimney although the sun was warm on his bare head. He went up onto the long, shadowed veranda and twisted the bell in the middle of the door panel.

He waited. He had almost concluded that in spite of the smoke there was no one inside, when Alice opened the door.

Surprise straightened her face and lengthened the lines

around her mouth; she was mute for a moment until she recovered enough to say, "Emory."

"Hello, Alice." Monck consciously kept strain out of his voice. "Is your father here? . . . Didn't he tell you I might come to see him?"

"No."

"He isn't here?"

"Yes, he's upstairs in his study."

She stood aside in silent invitation. He went past her and up the wide steps to the balcony hall.

"Emory?"

He stopped and looked down behind him.

"Be easy with him. These last months have not . . . have not . . ." Without finishing the sentence she turned quickly and disappeared into the parlor.

Amos Wellington looked shrunken in the big over-stuffed leather chair that had been his father's. He put his hands on the arms to help himself up when he heard Monck come into the room, but Monck waved him back into the seat. He had obviously been asleep. His baby round face was flushed and his eyes were dull. He moistened his mouth and cleared his throat.

"Must have dozed off."

Emory did not risk asking after his health. He found a perch on the roll top desk.

"I had a visit a little bit ago from a couple of bankers, Trans-Financial people."

"Oh, yes." Amos's eyes were clearing as the sleep receded from his brain. "Nice fellows, Jones especially. I'm afraid they're not very happy."

"I judged that."

Wellington worked his veined hands together. "I told them I didn't know what to do. I didn't want the campus back. What in the world would I do with it? It couldn't be sold for anything except farming, and the buildings would get in the way of that."

Emory found nothing to say, Amos sounded so like a hurt child.

"So I sent them to you. I warned them that I didn't think you would be anxious to do anything, that there were probably hard feelings and that I would not approach you, but if they wanted to it was all right with me. After all, they do have a large interest."

"Large enough." Monck smiled, trying to erase the other's discomfort.

Amos responded with the hint of a mischievous smile, and surprised Monck with his unexpected perspicacity.

"I think they would agree to refinance the loans on very favorable terms. They'd be so grateful to someone who took them over."

That recalled to Monck the first rule of his doctrine. He said bluntly, "What do you want?" emphasizing the *you*.

The older man's eyes popped open. "Me? Want? Why, nothing, except to see the school the way it was."

"Would you turn over the plant to any corporation I put together?"

The white head nodded. "Certainly. I don't know anything about business . . . I never should have been president. I didn't want to be, and I didn't know how to run the school. It always worried me."

Emory Monck made his decision. "All right. I can't say yes for certain until I hear the opinion of the students and faculty and my group, but I'll give it a good pitch.

"It should line up this way. We establish Wellington Incorporated, nonprofit. As trustees I'll pick seven men in whom I have faith. One chair goes to the pro-tempore student body president with a full vote. You choose three people, but not any one of the old trustees—I don't think either the students or the faculty would stand for that . . ."

"But I don't want to choose anybody. I don't know anybody who could think on the same level with your people."

"Okay, let's take three local men. Andrews from the bank. The head of the Chamber of Commerce, whoever he happens to be: make him a revolving member too. And the president of Wellington Steel, what's his name, Udell?"

"Yes, Udell, he's well thought of."

"We need a local sense of participation. Riverdale has the skitters now and we'll have to restore their confidence in the school. You'll be president emeritus, Strindberg president. Ward Perry's going to be a good chancellor and I'll have Price Davis stay as financial officer until the wrinkles are ironed out."

Amos relaxed visibly as Monck talked. "God bless you, Emory. I haven't felt so well in weeks. It's been horrible, simply awful, sitting here night after night without a sound on the campus, with all the lights out. It's like living in a cemetery, and old as I am I'm not ready for that yet."

"It isn't solved yet."

"It will be." The old scholar lifted himself out of the chair. "I never saw you fail at anything so far. Come along, Alice has a bottle hidden somewhere. This calls for a drink."

On the way down the stairs he continued to burble. "I just sit back in awe and watch you play volleyball with whole groups of powerful men, with entire universities, with complete towns. It's totally beyond my comprehension."

Alice sat by the parlor window staring out at the ghosts, a forlorn figure. Her head came around and she looked first at Monck, then at her father to see if Monck had hurt him further.

Amos crossed with a bobbing step, took both her shoulders and kissed her lightly on the forehead. "Alice, Emory's going to bring the school back."

It embarrassed Monck to see her eyes.

"You really are?"

"I'm going to try."

"Oh, Emory."

Emotion brought her to her feet and for an instant Monck was afraid she was going to kiss him, but her father diverted that with a clap of his hands.

"Where's that bourbon you used to keep for Martin? I want to celebrate."

Driving back to the base Monck knew an inner satisfaction. He had outmaneuvered Fenton. Originally he had underestimated the general, and it had been a battle, but now he allowed himself to gloat. It was childish but it was fun.

He went directly to his office and phoned Denise Dempsey, but she was in conference with a group of girls. He left word with her secretary, asking her to come over as soon as she was free. While he had Vivienne on the intercom he said:

"Tell Al Conner I want to see him. Then get hold of Cec Eliot and Strindberg. Have them call a joint meeting

294

of the Student Senate and the faculty committee in the Officers' Club at nine o'clock this evening."

After his discouragement of the morning, Conner listened eagerly to the proposition.

"We're going to wear this damn school out if we keep moving it, but it's good news from your angle. Riverdale is going to breathe easy again and putting local men on the board is great. It will save your political hide." With that settled in his mind he turned to what the change would mean to the school. "Sam Jordan's not going to like having his name taken off this place. . . . What are you going to do with the base, give it back to the government?"

"Not on your life." New visions had been taking form at the back of Monck's mind. "We'll leave the technical schools here. If we open a new road across the top of the bluff it's only three miles or so from here to Wellington. We might even extend our tracks and run a shuttle train between the two campuses. Sure, that's it, that's what we do about Sam. We leave his name on this side, make it the Jordan Technical Institute of Wellington University. We'll continue to lease buildings to industry and they can still employ students part time."

Conner watched with amusement as Monck continued planning.

"When we reorganize I'm going to split the school into a number of small colleges, the way a university was supposed to be in the first place. Wellington's growth rate is going to jump and I don't want to lose the personal touch between students and faculty the way a lot of big places have done.

"See, we can have Liberal Arts, Business Administration, Philosophy, Language, History, and the like on the old campus and put all the science courses over here. Maybe we can buy the hill between for the medical center Binford always dreamed about. And a law school . . ."

Conner's laughter burst like a balloon. "You never stop, do you? You're never going to get away from here."

"Oh yes I am. I'll keep a place on the board, but Ward Perry is perfectly able to carry on the work. With a decent board behind him he'll develop into one hell of an administrator."

The intercom interrupted him and Vivienne announced

that Dempsey was there. She added in reproof that it was nearly eight o'clock and he had had nothing to eat.

"Shoo Dempsey in," he said, "and call the cafeteria; have Emil send over coffee and sandwiches."

Al Conner stood up. "I'll go and call Lightner now. If you need me later, yell, but if you don't, the wife's throwing a dinner party."

"Go ahead. Have fun."

Conner moved toward the door as Dempsey opened it and came through. He grinned at her.

"Wait until you hear. You won't believe it, but hold onto your hat. The school is going home."

The Officers' Club sounded like a clover field in midsummer. Monck heard the hum of speculation as he came up the walk.

Inside, the head of Mathematics was commenting on the unusualness of the short notice, and History asked wryly what was *not* unusual about Jordan University.

They heard Monck out in a breath-taking stillness. He painted the picture in considerable detail, enlarging on what he had said to both Wellington and Conner, working toward making as favorable an impression as he could. In finishing he requested that both faculty and students take a vote of their full memberships the next day.

The first question from the floor was asked by Gabe Glasscock.

"What about the fraternities? Can we go back to the houses?"

"That's up to the brothers, I'd say."

Cec Eliot was on his feet, waiting his turn. "Supposing the vote is not to go back?"

"Then we stay here. Will you people get it through your heads that this is your school? We'll do everything we can to make it as good as possible, but in the final analysis what Wellington becomes is in your hands. What you make it will be passed on to the students who will come after you."

The meeting broke into groups and these scattered shortly to talk among themselves, out of earshot of other factions, to gather with personal friends and spread the word, to consult, debate, conjecture. Jordan University would be in bull session most of the night.

Perry and Strindberg lingered with Monck. Strindberg worked at a snail's pace, packing his pipe, and his voice had more than its usual gruffness.

"I didn't believe this would happen. I didn't see how it could, but you'll never quite realize what it means to me. Leaving the old campus was like going into exile."

There had been few times in their association when Monck had seen Strindberg exhibit real emotion, and this brought home to him what a wrench it had been for the old physicist to turn his back on his familiar haunts. He said:

"Think the kids will vote to go back?"

"Sure." Perry had no doubts. "Most of them hated to leave in the first place. It was the adventure that made the move so unanimous. They like the prestige of Wellington on their diplomas, and in spite of what they say they like the traditions. College even to this generation is a lot more than an educational factory. It represents shared experiences, bands, football heroes, dances, a proud heritage, being a part of an honored house. But beyond that it represents the last of their youth. No matter how quickly anyone wants to grow up he knows that he is living through days that will never come again, and he wants them to be the best."

Monck winked at Strindberg. "He's as bad as Don Dundee."

"There are worse people than Dundee," Perry said. "Don always meant to do the best for the school as he saw it. Fenton was different. With Fenton it was more important to impose his will than to consider the end effect."

"Well," said Monck, "we're rid of him. He's finished. He can't hurt us now."

40

☐ Debate rang through the warehouses and the still unsettled faculty homes. Unlovely as it was, the kids had a proprietary affection for the campus they had created with their own hands. Harold Polly decided to vote aye on the question of return, and switch his major to one of the sciences in order to remain at Jordan. There was testiness among the faculty wives. With a taste of the modern appliances and simplified housekeeping in the houses on the base they were not anxious to return to the old residences of Wellington.

A lengthy ballot was drawn up in a conference between Ward Perry, Cec Eliot, and Martin Strindberg in their official capacities as chancellor and spokesmen for students and faculty, a conference that had taken place after Perry had sought out Emory Monck.

He had entered Monck's office that morning, closed the door and put his back against it. His manner was tentative, searching; he acted like a boxer coming out of his corner to face his opponent.

"Emory, I don't want you to take this wrong, but I've been wondering about something. Am I expected to be chancellor in name only?"

Monck noticed the change of manner, a new hard temper of assertiveness.

"What gave you that idea?"

Perry smiled, but it was a conscious effort. "Well, last night you talked this move over with Al Conner and Eliot and Strindberg. I didn't hear about it until Vivienne called and told me about the meeting. Was I left out deliberately?"

Monck appeared unaccountably pleased. It confused Perry and Monck's words confused him further.

"Come on and sit down. No, it wasn't deliberate. I guess I just took it for granted that you'd go wherever the school chose to be. But I'm glad it happened this way. It sounds to me like you want to take the reins."

"Well, hell," Perry's confusion held a touch of embarrassment. "I don't want to usurp your authority, but . . ."

Monck got up and came around the desk. If Perry would not sit, he did not want to be seated for this conversation. He grinned widely, walking forward with loose, rambling ease.

"This is just what I've been waiting to see, Ward. You don't hand authority to a man; you wait for him to reach for it. That's what I've been doing. I haven't told you because I've been waiting to make sure, waiting for you to reach.

"Here's the deal. I never intended to remain here per-

298

manently. I only came in to straighten out the mess and find the right man to run things. It's straight now, I think, whichever way the vote goes, and you've proved to yourself that you can handle the job probably better than I can. You're more suited temperamentally to deal with faculty and student problems than I ever will be. So now I can step out."

Ward Perry had gone rapidly through a series of emotions, from suspicion that he was undergoing the Monck treatment to unabashed eagerness for power to a moment of floundering at being so unexpectedly cast adrift. He went to the chair as if he really needed to sit down.

"Christ," he said. "That's a slug in the gut. That's out of left field. I never guessed. Emory, there are so many things I don't know."

Monck dropped onto the couch. Now that the breach was made he did not want to imply that he was continuing on a superior level by using the seat behind the desk.

"You know what kind of a school you'd like to see?"

"Of course, but . . ."

"And you understand how to integrate it with industry."

"Well, yes."

"So quit worrying. I'm going to stay on the board, and the other men on it are people you can rely on. You'll have to sell them your program, but they'll understand what you're talking about. And I'll be on deck until the semester break."

Perry began to grin. "Then what are you going to do?"

"Take a vacation, for one thing." He did not add that by fall he wanted to be free to swing into a full schedule and head straight for the spring primary.

A new chancellor was blooming under Monck's eyes. He gave the impression of expanding, relaxing; he let his tense body go slack in the chair and extended his feet in a comfortable stretch.

"Well. Thanks. I can't say I haven't been sweating to get my hands on the wheel. And if you'd told me before I'd probably have pressed and blown the chance.

"So. Here's what I'm thinking. There's more to decide than simply whether to reactivate Wellington. It doesn't sound like sense to me to try to move everything back before the end of the semester. We came over here in a furor. Everybody was mad and willing to pitch in and work like a maniac, but we can't expect that kind of pace if we go back. It's anticlimactic. We've got finals coming up and all the graduation commotion."

Monck nodded without speaking.

"There'll be the questions of who goes back and who stays here, and more immediately where the ceremonies and wind-up activities should be held. I think all of those decisions ought to go on the one ballot. I want to keep this full participation of everybody in major decisions as our trade-mark. What do you think?"

Monck laughed at him. "It's your baby. But I like it, if that makes you any happier."

It made everybody happy. Jordan University voted in unmistakable favor of combining the two campuses. The summer session would be eliminated this year and the time used to refurbish Wellington's buildings while they were still empty, to separate and move the departments. The fall term should open smoothly. Graduation exercises would be held in the Wellington stadium and the parties take place in the more gracious old rooms. Illumination Night, the traditional festivity for which the alumni annually returned, would find the fraternity houses aglow, all buildings lit to the hilt, and both campuses thrown open to visitors for a monumental celebration.

The Engineering Department entered an immediate bid, urging that they be allowed to build the new road as a summer project.

And Ward Perry came to Monck again.

"Something I think I want to talk over with you. Under the new corporation we're writing new faculty contracts."

"Sure."

"I'm thinking about Denise Dempsey. She's still acting dean, you know. We never did get around to confirming her in the dean of women job. I just talked to her about it and she told me she thought it would be better for the school if she did not return next year. I asked her what she meant, and she harked back to Hollister's insinuation about her activities at Columbia. It sounded pretty inconsequential to me, but I couldn't talk her out of it. You want to try?"

That, Monck thought, took another obstacle out of his way. He had other plans for Dempsey, but this was another item and he did not tell Perry. He said:

"I won't pressure her, no. Why don't you let it alone for now?"

He watched Perry leave, unsatisfied. Everything was dropping into place for him with the tidiness of tumblers in a lock. He felt happy with the world and the future.

In her office, Denise Dempsey was far from happy. The *Jordan Daily News* lay on her desk. The masthead of the young paper was crossed through with a strong black X and under it was reinstated the old *Wellington Warrior* banner. Below that a headline in bold block type extended across the page.

GOING HOME

The makeup was gaudy; most of the first sheet given over to an exhaustive report of events leading up to the vote and a detailing of the time table for the move; carry-overs shared pages two, three and four with peripheral stories.

It was a small notice in the lower corner of page one, a report that would probably be skipped by most readers, that had stirred Dempsey's spleen.

It read: *Rathbone to speak on Jordan campus. Pacifist to discuss draft and peace effort.*

She doubled her fists, scanning the story.

The head of the Student Union for Progressive Thought has recently returned from an unauthorized visit to Asia where, he claims, he had illuminating conversations with representatives of Hanoi.

She was furious. Vincent Rathbone coming here? She had seen the effect the man had on other campuses. He would be dynamite, just when the press and television cameras had turned away from Wellington and Jordan, just when the road ahead looked so hopeful.

The common experience of creating the new school with their own labor and vote was giving the students a real sense of unity. She could not let him come. He must not be permitted to stir up the small hard knot of noisy antagonists that seemed to exist in every school, with his senseless agitation for draft card burning.

She tried to think rationally. She did not want to take her fear to Monck. There was the personal matter that she did not want to dredge up.

Ward Perry was chancellor, but he was new in the job and cautious about interfering in student affairs.

It was, she saw, within the province of the students themselves. They had made their rules and it was their job to police them.

She went looking for Cec Eliot. She found him supervising a labor gang laying a concrete walk between the two warehouses that served the Chemistry Department as laboratories and classrooms. She called to him from a distance and he came toward her smiling a welcome.

"Hi, Miss Dempsey. You want me?"

She nodded and beckoned him into the field behind the buildings, out of earshot. She carried the paper under her arm until they were safely alone, and then shook it out, stabbing her finger at the item.

"Cec, that man is a phony. He's a racketeer. He doesn't believe one God damn word he says."

Her vehemence took him by surprise. "Oh?"

"I'm serious. How did he come to be invited here?"

He left off smiling. "Marty's committee. He read about her in the papers and wrote to ask for permission to speak."

"Damn him, he would. He worms onto every campus he can. And everywhere he shows up they have trouble." She was beginning to bounce. "You'll have to bar him from here."

Eliot did not know what to make of the situation. He was fond of the dean and he felt that he owed her a lot, but again, he had authored the regulations concerning speakers and he knew the howl of protest that would be raised if he tried to take summary action. Even the students who were not interested in Rathbone would instinctively join the chorus in defense of the statute. He kicked at a tuft of grass.

"I don't see how I can do it. I doubt that the Senate would go along if I tried, and Marty would fight me every inch of the way. She's enthusiastic over what she's read about the guy. What could I tell them?"

Her words were brittle and quick. "That he is dishonest. His Union for Progressive Thought is a pure racket. They collect a dollar a month from every member. It's supposed to be used on a Washington lobby, but most of it goes into the pockets of Vincent and his little clique. They have

302

hundreds, thousands of members and every time he appears at another school the membership jumps."

He looked at her intently, partly nonplused, partly skeptical. He knew that the organization had been listed as subversive by the Attorney General, but this point did not disturb him too much. He considered himself liberal and while he had no use for Communism he still believed that any man should be allowed to speak his piece; he resented any kind of imposed censorship.

"How do you know that this is true?"

There was no way she could duck the question now, and Dempsey thrust out her chin.

"When I was in college I was secretary of the local chapter for a while. Until I realized what they were doing, what a cynical bunch they are. Vincent is particularly dangerous because he is charming. He's an emotional speaker, with a strong appeal for women."

She stopped to catch her breath, now that it was said, and then rushed on.

"You've read about his tactics, whipping an audience up to a pitch of excitement, urging boys to burn their draft cards as a protest against conscription and Vietnam, making a big show of burning what he says is a copy of his own card to get them started. . . . Have you ever wondered why his own draft board hasn't done anything about him? I'll tell you why. He is not eligible for military service. He's got a slipped disc in his spine.

"So he's not sticking out his own neck, oh no. He's asking other people to take the risk."

"What makes you so sure of this, Miss Dempsey?"

"I've known him for over eight years. Here's another deception. He's past thirty and claiming to be twenty-six. Cec, he is a vicious, ruthless man out to take advantage of the students of this country who hold liberal views. Now will you agree that he must not come here?"

Cec Eliot was convinced. "Yeah. I'll take care of it. I don't see just how right now, but don't worry about it."

Dempsey left him in weak-kneed relief and Eliot, as he usually did when he was confronted with a problem for which he had no solution, consulted Gabe Glasscock. They were of opposing political persuasions but each respected the other's thinking processes.

Gabe listened with gathering indignation. "Where did you get this?"

Eliot saw no reason to bring Dempsey into it. "A reliable source."

"Marty?" Glasscock was suspicious of the evasion.

"Certainly not. She thinks the guy is some kind of a messiah. It's someone I know you trust. How are we going to stop the jerk?"

Glasscock considered, decided to accept Cec's word, and his eyes half closed.

"Maybe we're not."

Eliot did not understand. Glasscock bragged that he was a Bircher.

"You mean you still want him to talk?"

"Yep. If we don't let him, our radical bunch will make him a martyr, and that's what these guys trade on. But supposing we let him make his pitch and then prove him a phony in front of his audience. What happens?"

"How do we prove that?"

Gabe had begun to smile. "We let him make his play, clear up to the point where he calls for the suckers to come up and make their bonfire. We go along, march a crowd up on the stage. We'll get Steve Bates to line up the football men. We grab Rathbone and go through his pockets, find his 4 F card and show it around. He's branded right then, not just here but everywhere else."

"What if he hasn't got it on him?"

"He'd be nuts not to carry it, in case the military decided to make a grab for him."

Cec had some doubt but he could not produce a better alternative. Denise Dempsey too remained uneasy when Eliot assured her that all was under control but would not explain what they had in mind.

Martha Yates had no shadow of doubt. Cec had agreed to say nothing to her on the chance that the redhead might alert her new hero in advance.

She had stayed out of the light of controversy to help bury the campus memory of her brush with sensationalism, but Rathbone's letter had been too much temptation to ignore.

He had written at length, under the letterhead of the Student Union for Progressive Thought. He had, he said, followed her career through the newspapers with interest. Her sleep-in was imaginative. Her arrest proved her sincerity and courage. He complimented the students on their strike and the move to the Navy base, giving her credit for the generalship. He deplored Fenton as representing the worst in school administration and hinted that he knew she alone had prevailed against him. He would consider himself honored if she would organize a day for him at her school.

Yates met him when he arrived. Vincent Rathbone's face had a haunting attractiveness, and he had an easy smile. He was well spoken, mellifluous and resonant. Yates was proud to sit beside him at the luncheon in the cafeteria.

Even Cec Eliot was impressed and began to wonder if Dempsey could be wrong. The man appeared so dedicated, so concerned with the problems of the day. He played down his own part, paid homage to the students for successfully demanding a greater voice in the management of their school, accepted them as his equals. He asked probing questions about the trustees, Monck, even Denise Dempsey. His knowledge of the school, its problems and accomplishments was broad which was flattering, a compliment to them all.

When the lunch meeting broke up, Rathbone singled out Marty and asked her to give him a personal tour of the base and talk about her future plans for it. She took him, riding on cloud nine.

She had borrowed Cec's Olds for the excursion, and when she had showed him everything, told all she could think of, she returned him to the dormitory where he was to spend the night. He did not get out of the car, but sat with his arm draped across the seat back, his fingers playing with her hair.

"Marty," he said, "I want to help. What you're doing is so exciting. We're going to open a Union chapter here next fall, and in the meantime . . . we're going to conduct a conference school this summer, somewhere in New England. There'll be workers from a couple of hundred campuses. We'll hold seminars and discussion groups. Sound interesting?"

It sounded fabulous. She told him so.

"Where is it going to be?"

He was evasive. "It isn't decided yet, but I'll let you

know. It will be a grand summer, honey, the kind you will never forget."

Lost in euphoria, Marty did not know that Denise Dempsey had come up until she spoke. Then she made the introduction proudly.

"We know each other," Dempsey said. "Martha, will you excuse us? I want to talk to Mr. Rathbone."

Marty was reluctant to sacrifice a moment of time with him but she got out of the car without protest.

"I have to go dress anyway."

Indeed she did. Capris and flats and hanging hair were not going to be the last impression of herself that she left with this dazzling personage.

He got out of the car and patted her shoulder, returning her smile with warmth.

"I'll see you later, doll."

Dempsey watched until Martha had gone floating down the street. Something had obviously gone amiss with whatever plan Cec Eliot had had to keep Rathbone away, and so it was up to her. But first there was this new development.

"Vince, you keep your hands off that child."

He looked down from watching the departing girl. "I didn't know I had a jealous wife."

Dempsey came up on her toes. "I am not your wife."

His smile was lazy. "Oh yes. I decided not to get the Mexican divorce. Sometimes a wife comes in handy." The smile widened and he reached to clasp her shoulder in a comradely gesture.

She jerked away, blazing with fury.

"You sent me the papers."

"Sure." He laughed. "They cost me two hundred pesos for an attorney."

"Oh, God damn you." Dempsey could hardly speak, and her mind ran in crazy, broken patterns. "I'll get my own divorce. Now you get off of this campus. Now, now, now."

"How do you think you can make me?" He sounded bored.

"I'll make you. If you try to stay I'll get up on that stage and tell what a liar you are. I'll show those Mexican papers and tell everybody you admit they are fakes."

The hawk face, the deep-set eyes no longer smiled.

Rathbone caught her arm and his fingers bit into it.

"No you won't. You make trouble for me and I'll go to Fenton so fast it will make your head swim. I know how he'd like to nail Monck, and he could do it if he knew that Monck had hired my wife."

Too late she understood what he meant. But she still fought.

"I am not a Communist."

"So what? Everybody believes I am, and it would be a little hard to convince the dear conservatives around here that we could be married if you didn't follow the party line." He was smiling again, certain of himself. "No, darling, you aren't going to open your yap, now or ever."

41

☐ The lunch crowd had spread the word that Rathbone was someone not to be missed. The evening meeting filled the auditorium. Martha Yates was in her glory.

Her hair was piled on her head in the coiffure the girls had arranged for her disastrous Columbus trip and she had borrowed a striking dress from Patti Karger.

When everyone who could had crammed into the hall she rose to introduce her speaker, looking across the audience with supreme satisfaction. The Senate, she knew, had filled the first two rows of seats with a buffer of selected men to seal off the stage in the event of any trouble. She was not surprised to find Cec Eliot, Gabe Glasscock, Steve Bates, and Hal Polly against the aisles that led to the steps at the sides of the stage, and she approved their choice of the burly football squad to guard Rathbone from any chance discourtesy.

Not that she expected them to be needed. There had been no opposition, not even any heckling outside the building, for the student body in general respected the Senate's ruling on freedom of speech.

It had seemed to her that Rathbone had been mildly disappointed at the lack of hostility, but when he moved to the mike he lived up to all her hopes.

He talked about his experiences in the Orient, telling harrowing stories that had never appeared in the American press. There was, he maintained, a stifling censorship and a deliberate warping of the news. He attacked the Vietnam involvement as a CIA war, accused the government of allowing itself to be blinded and deceived, and upbraided the military. He charged that there would be no end to the tragic, senseless killing until the students of the nation rose in protest.

He had the audience with him. Cec Eliot sweated. What if they were wrong? What if Rathbone did not carry a 4 F card? What if they tried and failed to prove he was a phony? He glanced sidewise at Gabe Glasscock's stony face but could not catch his eye.

Rathbone had built up to a climax and his voice thundered through the mike with the call to rise.

"Where are you? Who in this hall will stand up and make our protest heard? Who will swear to take no part in this legalized slaughter of Vietnam's innocent people? Who has the intellectual courage to stop the carnage? Come up here. Burn your draft cards. Let us make a blaze, a beacon to our rising brothers. Let us start a fire to sweep the nation until Washington must see, must listen. Come on. I stand here with you. My card is burned and I am still alive. I burn it again now, a copy but a symbol."

He flipped into view a card he had held palmed. Shouts answered him and half a dozen boys clambered toward the aisles and ran down them waving cards above their heads. Eliot recognized them as members of the far left group that had gravitated around Rathbone earlier in the day; he suspected the man had planted them through the audience as decoys.

He looked down the row of seats, saw Glasscock lean forward.

"Now."

Glasscock rose, flourishing a card, and headed for the stage. Behind him followed Steve Bates and the linemen from the varsity eleven. Eliot went up the steps on his side.

Rathbone was not prepared for so large a response, but then, he thought, this was not the campus of an ordinary American university. These people had already proved their initiative.

He smiled, waving them in toward him and continued to smile until Steve Bates stepped behind him, took hold of his arms, bent them at the elbows and held him pinioned. When he tried to break free Bates lifted him clear of the floor.

Glasscock moved swiftly. He shucked open Rathbone's coat, found the wallet in the inside breast pocket, riffled through it and pulled out the convicting card.

Cec Eliot let out his breath. He had not been sufficiently certain that it would work, that the man would actually carry the thing on him.

The auditorium was struck dumb, not comprehending what was going on. Marty and her committee of welcome ran toward the speaker. They were held back by the half circle of football men around the small group.

Gabe Glasscock stepped up to the mike, exhibiting the card. His voice was level; without excitement, he repeated his words over and over into the quiet that was sustained by the crowd's curiosity.

"Four F. Four F. Four F. Take a look. He didn't burn his card. He didn't have to. He's a liar and a phony. How do you like being taken for suckers?"

The audience came to its feet and found its voice. The cry rose and a surge for the stage began. The buffer guard faced about to repel the advance as if it were the charging line from Michigan State.

Behind the scrimmage Gabe Glasscock shoved wallet and card back into Rathbone's pocket, dancing to avoid kicking legs.

"All right, let's get him out of here. The side door."

Bates carried his prisoner. It was easier that way. Eliot's car was ready at the stage entrance. Bates shoved Rathbone onto the rear seat floor, climbed in and planted his feet on the man's back, holding him prostrate.

Cec drove, gunning the car, racing the crowd that was now spilling from the front of the auditorium. He beat them to the street and outdistanced them, heading for the gate. The mob that howled behind the car might be college boys, but they were no younger, no weaker, no more gentle in this mood than were their brothers overseas, in uniform, engaged in war. No magic change would take place in them between now and the not distant day when many of them would have to survive by violence. They were ready for violence now.

At the highway Eliot stopped. Bates sat as he was until Glasscock had got out and pulled off Rathbone's shoes;

then he hoisted the man to the roadside. Glasscock tossed the shoes into the car.

"Now, you bastard, start walking, and you'd better hurry. I don't know that we can keep that gang inside the fence."

An hour later Cec Eliot and Marty Yates answered the summons to Monck's office. The campus was a regular hornets' nest. Rumors were everywhere. Rathbone had been lynched. He had been thrown into the river with scrap iron tied to his feet. He had been tarred and set afire.

Ward Perry ushered them in. Martha was having trouble with her tears, Cec with trying to console her.

"Nothing happened to him, I'm sorry to say." Cec's savage mood was not yet dissipated. "We drove him down to the highway, took his shoes and headed him toward Riverdale. He's probably safely on his way to Pittsburgh by now."

Perry asked, "Whose idea, the shoes?"

"Gabe's. He saw it once in a Western."

"That's a relief," said Monck, "but I'd like to hear the whole story."

Eliot saw no harm in telling it now. "Miss Dempsey alerted me about the guy. She knew him at Columbia. It's damn lucky she did. Gabe figured out how to use the dope we had to expose him. I didn't know . . . I thought it was risky, but then I saw the way Marty was getting so jazzed over him." He frowned, glancing toward the girl. "She keeps going off like this. I guess the only way to keep her out of trouble is to take some time off and marry her."

Sunk in the corner of the couch, Martha Yates' first reaction was an angry defense of her sense of balance, but the words never reached her tongue. She colored deeply, her eyes wide on Eliot as he walked to her, bent and kissed the top of her red hair. Her pupils rolled back, trying to watch.

"Okay, kid?"

She blinked. Her first nod was barely a movement, but then she nodded with vigor.

"Okay."

Monck had been wondering why Dempsey had not

told him about Rathbone, but forgot it for the moment in the relief of watching the kids. If Martha had been crushed again by another misplacing of her heart it would have been bad. In gratitude that he had not had to field this one he said, "I'm glad for both of you, and I'll tell you what. I'll loan you the plane and pilot. Fly out to Nevada tonight. The trip can be your wedding present."

It was not unmixed generosity. He did not intend to leave Martha Yates time to change her mind. He picked up the phone, located the pilot and told him to warm up the Humming Bird.

The kids used the time to absorb the idea and improve on it. Their thanks were effusive. Then Marty asked hesitantly:

"Could we take Jane Cullen and Steve Bates along for witnesses?"

"Good idea."

He waited while they phoned the other pair. He escorted them out and watched Ward Perry drive them off to collect the witnesses and take them all out to the runway. Then he returned to the office and called Dempsey.

The faculty dormitory manager said she was not in the building, that she had not seen the dean since before dinner. He called her office but got no answer, tried the Officers' Club with no better luck, and at last went looking for her. He felt good, happy about Cec and Martha and the harmless end of the Rathbone affair.

On the flight out, Jane and Steve decided to take advantage of the opportunity rather than wait until the end of the semester, for by June, Jane said, she would be showing. Her Greek god was stronger than the pill.

On their return the two couples moved into Fertile Hall, a section of dormitory blocked off into apartments for married students, and the pace of their living stepped up with Cram Week ahead, examinations and graduation. But a keen disappointment had marred their otherwise joyous return. By the time the plane brought them back to school Emory Monck was gone.

It was not late. Dempsey might be in any of a number of places, but he tried them and could not locate her. He called the girl who acted as her secretary, but all she knew was that when she had left the office for the day the dean had been there. He called the dormitory again to see if she had returned, but the answer was no. He walked to the parking lot beside her building. Her car was gone.

Puzzled now, he went to Conner's office. She could be there. He knew that after the evening's fracas the publicity man would be at his desk, busy with inquiries from the press, but he did not expect Conner's greeting.

"I've been trying to get you." His tone of voice spelled trouble. "That God damn Fenton. I'll kill him, so help me."

"What's he done now?"

"The Pittsburgh *Telegram* phoned me ten minutes ago. Fenton was in the office with Vincent Rathbone."

Monck sat down on the corner of the littered desk. "That should be an interesting combination."

"Yeah. Great. Rathbone is throwing accusations around like confetti. Says we hired a goon squad to manhandle him and that he barely escaped alive."

Monck's lips twisted. "That's not the way the kids tell it."

"There's more. A lot more. He says the attack was made to try to shut him up, to protect you and Dempsey, cover the fact that she is a Communist and that you knew it when you hired her."

Monck was very still, then he said quietly, "I don't believe it."

Conner went on. "Rathbone claims she was secretary of the Student Union for Progressive Thought and that she's his wife. He had a marriage license with him. True or not, the story's on the wire."

Coldness settled through Monck. He felt no emotion. His brain was clear, sharpening. He pulled the phone to him, called the faculty dormitory and asked the manager to see if Denise Dempsey's clothes were in her room. They were not.

He hung up, brought the extra chair to the desk and sat down, relaxing his body. His voice was flat but there was no tension in it.

"I should have got rid of Fenton before."

"Never mind Fenton now. You call Lightner before somebody else does."

Monck looked at Conner, pulling his mind back from

its desire to instantly destroy the general, seeing what Conner meant. All of their months of effort, all their careful planning was in the ash can for sure this time, but Lightner must be warned.

"What's his number?"

The Senator did not sound surprised, nor did he sound upset. He listened and then said:

"I'm glad you caught me before the press did. Now, you'd better get here as soon as you can. I'll get you a room at the Shoreman. Bring Conner with you."

Monck rang off. Conner's eyes asked the question. Monck said:

"He wants us both in Washington."

He lifted the receiver again, intending to call his pilot, and then remembered that he had loaned the plane to the kids. Instead, he called the Pittsburgh airport.

It was quarter to five when they met the Senator in the hotel suite. Every time Monck saw the man he was reminded of a lion. Despite his age Lightner's hair was still thick as a mane; his big body was still erect and there was power and decision in his every move. They went over the story again, and the background of it, until Lightner sighed.

"Didn't it occur to you to investigate the Dempsey woman when Hollister and Fenton first made their charges?"

Conner snorted. Monck said, "You only have to know her to know there's nothing subversive about her."

The Senator was coldly impatient. "It is not a question of personalities. Obviously there are grounds for Rathbone's statements. What does she say?"

"We can't find her. She left the campus before this broke."

"Don't you think that alone makes her suspect?"

"I won't believe any of it until she tells me herself." He spoke angrily. "Furthermore, it does not matter to me, even if it does finish me politically. And obviously, whether it's true or not, the hint of an association with Communism will kill my chances."

Lightner prowled around the room, stopped to stare down the ten stories to the street, then turned and came back.

"I don't agree with that. You have a lot of plus value.

God knows you've had exposure enough, and the party needs new faces, fresh blood. I wouldn't advise running next spring. Wait a while. There'll be another election two years from then. We'll crowd this down, keep building your affirmative image. We can put you over. But for God sake, stay away from that woman completely. And don't get tangled up with Fenton again. Just keep your head and you'll go to Congress all right."

When he had left Conner breathed in deep relief.

"I told you he was shrewd. That's one boy you don't stampede. He just doesn't panic." He stopped, frowning, becoming suddenly aware of the full implication of Lightner's words. "But that leaves you with a hard choice, doesn't it? Which way are you going?"

"With Dempsey."

Conner looked at the brooding face, searching it. "She means more than your dream of having a hand in running the country?"

"Yes."

Abruptly Monck's mouth tightened and he swung away, going to the phone. "Now," he said, "I am going to take care of Fenton."

He put in a call for Geronimo's Spring. There was no delay. Eli answered and summoned Sam.

Monck said, "Where's Larry Donovan at the moment?"

"Probably in bed with his wife." Jordan was in a fine humor. "What's on your mind?"

"He at home? His number is unlisted and I haven't got it with me. What is it?"

Sam gave him the number. "What's going on?"

"Tell you later." Monck hung up and dialed Donovan's apartment.

Donovan answered on the third ring.

"Larry, I need a favor," Monck said.

"Who doesn't?" said Donovan. "I know, you want me to give the Commencement address."

"Hardly. There's a general in Riverdale who's being a nuisance. I want him out of the country. Is your friend Shaban still in New York?"

Donovan sobered at Monck's quiet tone; the usual banter was missing. "Yes. He's still heading the Kyruit delegation at the United Nations. What's my prince got to do with it?"

"From all accounts my man has a pretty fair Service reputation. Will you convince Shaban that his brother needs a military adviser and that Jerome Fenton is his boy?"

"What in hell does the Sultan need with a military adviser? He hasn't fought anyone since the First World War and he's not about to. He's too fat to move."

"I know how fat he is. But he's got his palace guard and it would give him stature with the other sheiks to have an American general at the head of it."

"How do you know Fenton would go for it? He'd be nuts to walk into that sweat box."

"Tell him they're afraid of a Communist takeover in the oil fields."

Donovan laughed. "Act your age."

"Look, Fenton's hipped on Communism. Give him a three-year contract at thirty thousand and let him design his own uniform. I'm in a hurry."

"Who's going to pay the thirty thousand?"

"It wouldn't hurt Arabian Southern. Charge it to good foreign relations."

"Monck," said Larry Donovan, "you've got more crust than Sam Jordan. First you walk out on us overnight, then you put the bite on us for your moth-eaten school and now you want thirty gees a year to exile a tin soldier. What do we get out of it? What's your trade?"

"What do you want?"

Donovan began to sell. "Look, boy, something damned interesting is coming up and we need the right man to run it. I suggested you, but Sam said you were going into politics and couldn't be had."

Part of Monck's mind relished the situation. He was out of politics. Lightner had ordered him to stay away from Dempsey, and this, he knew, was simply not possible. Between the girl and the chance of a career in Washington there was no choice.

"What's the deal?"

Donovan smelled the possibility of success and pressed. "You remember the experiment East Ohio Gas tried back in the forties, compressing natural gas into liquid at extremely low temperatures and shipping it in that form?"

"I remember that one of their tanks burst in Cleveland and they had one hell of a fire."

"I know, I know, but since then a guy named Prince, out of Chicago, has combined with Continental to build special tankers and haul liquid gas from North Africa to England."

"I can read the papers."

"Well, listen, Emory. We're sitting on the world's biggest gas pool in Kyruit. We've been burning it as it escaped from the wells because there was nothing else to do with it. Now Sam's interested in the liquid gas idea. He's contracted for a dozen of the special tankers. Half the countries on earth are hungry for gas, and there are all the rubber, textile and fertilizer people yelling for more and more. We'll build a compressing plant and swamp the market. You want to handle it?"

Suddenly he did. The dream of political power was gone, you paid for what you got in life one way or another, and regrets were futile. He needed a job. He wanted this job. But he must not appear to give in too easily.

"I'll tell you what, Larry." He sounded slightly reluctant. "You take care of Fenton, make me president of Arabian Southern, give me a free hand, let me do the research and build the pilot plant at Wellington . . ."

"You bastard, you're working both sides of the street."

"You're asking me to give up a lot. Take the deal or leave it."

"All right. I'll call Shaban in the morning. When can you be in New York?"

"By noon tomorrow."

When he put the phone down he gave Conner a lopsided grin. "I hope Fenton enjoys parading in a hundred and forty degree temperatures."

Conner was shaking his head. "I hope you never decide to slap me down."

"It wasn't only that. I didn't want to leave him around to keep crawling in Ward Perry's hair. The guy is mad; he'd never quit making trouble."

"You didn't do so bad for yourself either. One minute Fenton has kicked you in the stomach, the next you're on top of the world. Kid, take me with you. That campus is going to be a dull place with you gone."

"Welcome aboard."

Conner grinned, then found a single flaw in the new scheme of things.

316

"Only one angle I don't like. That's Fenton getting thirty thousand a year."

Monck's smile was appreciative. "He'll earn it. Kyruit is a hell hole for a young man. Before he gets out of there he'll wish I'd sent him to Leavenworth.

"You'd better go back to Wellington and stay until after Commencement, break in a replacement. Tell Perry I'll be in touch."

"And where will you be?"

"Looking for Dempsey."

42

□ She was in the gambling room of the Ranchinn at Elko, Nevada. Not Reno, not Vegas, but Elko, so it had taken quite a while to locate her.

In the subdued hubbub she stood apart, at the end of a crap table. She was not gambling, just standing, watching a big man in a wide hat fling the dice across the green felt.

Beneath the glistening lights her pile of teased hair had a dark sheen but the special blaze of life was not in her face. She seemed sealed off from the world around her.

He worked around the rear edge of the crowd at the table, eased in at her side and stood quietly, looking down at her. She took a step away, absently, her attention held by default on the rolling dice.

He put a forefinger under her elbow and said softly, "Hi."

Her head came around and up, then snapped up. A light came into her eyes and almost as quickly it faded and she looked for escape.

He took hold of the elbow, nodded toward the door and led her that way. No one at the table made note of their leaving.

Outside, the traffic on Highway 40 passed with a rhythm of sharp swishing sounds. The spring air, thin at the mile-high altitude, was chilly; he hurried her through the parking lot to his rented car.

In the car she shivered. He turned the ignition key, flipped on the heater.

"I wish you had told me."

She sat looking forward, resignation in the droop of her shoulders.

"How did you find me?"

"Not hard. I called your father."

"I didn't tell him where I was."

"He said you believed you were divorced. Rathbone said you weren't."

She nodded confirmation. "What made you look here, so quickly?"

He smiled at her, turning, resting his arm on the wheel. "Business training. I called an investigator in Reno and his office checked the county courthouses and found that you had filed up here and were registered at the inn. I'd have found you sooner if you'd gone to Reno or Vegas."

She twined her fingers in her lap. "You shouldn't have come at all. It's hard enough as it is."

"I would have helped if you'd asked me. Why didn't you?"

She shook her head, wanting not to answer, wanting not to risk talking at all because her voice was undependable. But she spoke nonetheless.

"In the beginning I guess I was afraid of you. I thought you were something like Rathbone, that all you wanted was to grab things. Then it got more complicated."

"I'm no longer a grabber?"

Again she shook her head. "I know you won't even admit to yourself that you're *not* really out for the main chance, that what you do is for the fun of doing it. But it finally dawned on me that that's your driving force."

"I'll buy that. I said before that we could have fun together."

"Damnit, no. There's still Rathbone."

"Tell me about it. Tell me about him. How did it happen?"

She drew an uneven sigh. "It was all in the letter I left you. On my desk."

"I didn't get any letter. I didn't go to your office. I left the same night you did."

She looked at him for the first time and then dropped her head again.

"Very well. I was raised among adults—gamblers and horse people. When I went to Columbia kids in such numbers were new to me, and I wanted to be a part of

318

them. There was a lot of concern with social consciousness and I agreed with most of it. Rathbone impressed me and I was flattered when he singled me out. I wanted to help him organize his Union, and I was glad to marry him. Then I found out that he and a few others were putting the Union money in their pockets. I faced him with it and he laughed at me. So I left. I was only with him three weeks."

Monck reached for her hands, unwound them from each other and held them.

"Now what is there in that for us to brood over?"

She tried to draw her hands away but he would not release them.

"In the facts, nothing. It's what he told the newspapers. That has already ruined your chance to win anything in this next election. Alone, you can live down the suspicion by next time. With me you never could. That's why I had to leave."

Now he remembered that she did not know of the changes in his plans. The weight of misunderstanding, his fear that there was some personal unwillingness on her part, lifted and he leaned forward, tightening his fingers.

"Then we haven't got a problem. There isn't going to be any politicking. I'm going into oil again."

He should have expected the reaction, but it startled him and made him laugh. Dempsey's back straightened.

"No politics? You're not going to let Fenton and Rathbone run you out?"

Whether she wanted it or not he wrapped his arms around her and kissed her. She fought him, but he only held her closer, held her mouth until her energy was spent. Then he said against her hair:

"I'm not being run out. I came up with a choice. Sure, I could go to Washington, in time. But I found that I wanted something else more. Much more. I want you. I can't have both, so you're it."

She struggled again, to argue, and he sat back, took her shoulders and shook her firmly.

"God, you're hard to convince. Listen to me. I got rid of Fenton. Rathbone is a discredited witness. Certainly I could stay and battle it through. But I don't want it. Here's what I do want, and what we're going to do."

He told her about the presidency of Arabian Southern,

the liquid gas project, the pleasure he would take in creating something new and valuable.

"Our headquarters will be in New York but I'm going to build the pilot plant at Wellington. We won't be there much, only to get it started. Then we'll go to Kyruit. It's a miserable hole on the Persian Gulf, but we'll survive, and we'll get out as soon as the compressing plant is operating. There's a company town, a few wives . . . I'll introduce you to the weirdest Sultan you ever dreamed up, and . . . good God . . ."

"What's the matter, Emory. What is it?"

He put his palms over hers where they cupped his face and began to grin, a little boy who has just betrayed himself ridiculously.

"I really outsmarted myself. Do you know where I sent Fenton? To Kyruit. We'll have the bastard in our hair as long as we're there."

"Oh no. He'll be able to hurt you again?"

"Uh-uh. We'll be top dog. We're Arabian Southern, and the Sultan knows where his money comes from."

Dempsey slid her arms around his neck and kissed him with compassion. When she stopped to breathe she began a low, slow laughter.

"Well, my dear, as my father says, every man has his cross. Job had his boils. I guess Emory Monck has Jerome Fenton. And I'll have to get used to Sam Jordan."